5 DETECTIVES

5 DETECTIVES

Chanler Rao
Brinsley Moore

Worry-Worry Williams
Leavitt Ashley Knight

Miss Fanny Gordon
Edith MacVane

Clara Pryor
Carolyn Wells

The "Gum-Shoe"
Philip Curtiss

Coachwhip Publications
Greenville, Ohio

5 Detectives: Chanler Rao, Worry-Worry Williams, Miss Fanny Gordon, Clara Pryor, The "Gum-Shoe" (Edited by Chad Arment)

The Chanler Rao stories by Brinsley Moore (1910)
The Worry-Worry Williams stories by Leavitt Ashley Knight (1913-1914)
The Miss Gordon stories by Edith MacVane (1913-1914)
"Mystery of the Jade Buddha" by Carolyn Wells (1906)
"The 'Gum-Shoe'" by Philip Curtiss (1921)

ISBN 1-61646-226-4
ISBN-13 978-1-61646-226-0

CoachwhipBooks.com

CONTENTS

CHANLER RAO, CRIMINAL EXPERT

BRINSLEY MOORE

Three Chanler Rao stories were published in *Pearson's Magazine* (US) in 1910. A fourth story, "The Problem of the South Corridor," was scheduled to be published in the January 1911 issue, but didn't appear. A silent movie based on the Chanler Rao stories was issued in 1914.

THE THEFT OF THE DIAMOND RING

I WAS IN MY consulting-room writing letters, when Jenkins announced the visitor.

"A gentleman to see you, sir."

I took the card from the salver and read:

✖ ✖ ✖

32 Ophir Street (Turning out of New Bond Street).

CHANLER RAO.

(Failed B.A., Calcutta, 1889 and 1897.)

Eastern Magic, Hypnotism, Palmistry of the Hand, Crystal Gazing, and all Occult Mysteries.

BRITISH SUBJECT. GOD SAVE THE KING!

✖ ✖ ✖

On the back was written in a neat but curiously difficult handwriting:

"*Requesting the favor of a strictly under the rose consultation.*"

"But it is not my time for seeing patients," I said.

"I told the gentleman so, sir," answered Jenkins; "but he said that was just why he had come now."

I hesitated. I hate to break rules.

"What sort of a person is he?" I asked.

"I should take him to be a native, sir—from his color and the costume," said Jenkins. "Quite a crowd to see him come in, sir. With a little boy, too."

The strange description rather aroused my curiosity.

"Show them in," I said.

A moment later there entered the most dignified figure I have ever seen. A Hindu in the prime of life, tall and strikingly handsome in his picturesque Eastern dress, with lustrous, dark eyes that appeared to be soft and dreamy till he fixed them on you, and then, seemed to read your innermost thoughts. Chanler Rao was certainly a man to make an immediate impression.

He was followed by a small slip of a boy bearing a flower-pot, and one had not to look twice to recognize father and son.

The two advanced with a succession of low *salaams* as Jenkins closed the door behind them.

I motioned my visitors to be seated. But the Hindu, ignoring the invitation, silently directed the boy to set down the flower-pot. Then he unrolled a square of carpet which he carried under his arm, and spread it upon the floor; and there, in my Harley Street consulting-room at five o'clock on that dull November evening, he proceeded without a word to perform the famous Indian mango trick—the whole real thing, from the planting of the little seed in the pot to the production by successive stages of the growing tree!

The unusual nature of the interview for a moment left me speechless. As soon as I recovered from my first astonishment I endeavored to interrupt, and to explain that I did not desire a conjuring entertainment. But the Hindu waved on one side my protests, and, without uttering a word, proceeded with his performance. It was only when at last he could produce for my inspection a little green tree some eighteen inches high, apparently growing healthily in the pot, that he broke the silence.

"Genuine?" he said inquiringly. "The noble physician is convinced that Chanler is what he claims to be—real, true, genuine Indian magic-worker? Only in England one fortnight—not well known yet—but genuine?"

I thought it best to acquiesce at once. Of course, I had my own ideas about the mango trick. I had read the explanations furnished by Eastern travelers—only, unfortunately, such explanations did not quite fit the thing as done by Chanler Rao. So I nodded my satisfaction.

"And you will be secretive?" he asked.

I suppose I looked puzzled, for he explained:

"About my case—you will not tell anyone?"

I assured him that a medical man may be absolutely trusted to observe a professional reticence about any patients who consult him.

"Then," said Chanler, "you may look."

And opening his mouth wide, he pointed with his long finger down his throat.

I drew him to the light and made an examination. The throat was cut in several places and greatly inflamed; low down I thought I could perceive some bright obstacle across the gullet.

"What is it?" I asked.

"The great knife-swallowing mystery," my strange patient answered. "A slight defection in mechanical construction—the little blade lost itself at the inopportune moment; it is there since three this afternoon."

The matter looked serious.

"It will be an awkward operation," I said, "and there ought to be no delay. I should advise your going to the hospital at once. I will call a cab."

But at the mention of the hospital my visitor threw up his hands in protest.

"Ah, no, no!" he exclaimed vehemently. "The publicity—the talk—the explainings! It will be my ruin! People will say: 'Chanler Rao is an altogether humbug.' I would rather die than that."

"Well, at any rate," I said, "you must not try to talk. Come to my surgery, and I will see what can be done."

It was rather a ticklish business. But my patient helped me by his absolute immobility and apparent indifference to the pain; he never flinched or moved a muscle. In ten minutes the tiny blade of a penknife lay upon the table, and Chanler Rao was weeping tears of gratitude. I do not know which surprised me most—the man's extraordinary fortitude, which enabled him to go through the elaborate mango trick with that diabolical little blade sticking in his throat, and then to bear without a flinch the painful operation of its removal, or the feeble collapse at the end, and his childish weeping as he clung to my hand and poured out his thanks.

I was his "noble, glorious preserver"; never would he forget what I had done. His life henceforth was at my service, and, if ever I needed his help, I had but to command, and, though it meant going to the ends of the earth, he would gladly do it. This, and much more of the same exaggerated gratitude, he continued to shower upon me—until at last, for my own relief quite as much as out of consideration for his condition, I bundled him and his dusky little son into a cab, hurriedly gave a few directions about ice and a milk diet, and sent them home.

On returning to my room, I found the flower-pot had been forgotten. A vague desire to try to cultivate a real, live mango tree speedily gave way to my natural curiosity to know how the thing had been done. I pulled the tree out of the pot; then I discovered at once the futility of my original intention. No amount of watering or care would ever have made that plant grow. It had no root.

For four days I saw and heard nothing of my magnificent humbug. On the fifth day the afternoon post brought me a letter from my sister. Cissie, you know, married Gerald Thornton, and they live at Beecham Towers, in Surrey—just half an hour's run down from town. She wrote, as usual, "in great haste." Would I go down to dinner and stay the night? Their house-party included several old friends whom I should be glad to meet. Besides, she wanted to consult me about a most dreadful thing that had happened. Her diamond ring had been stolen—the one Gerald gave her a week before on her birthday; and as there were no signs of burglars or anything of that sort, it was clearly one of the servants, though, of course, they all denied any knowledge of it. Would I please come down and advise.

It happened to be a free evening, so I wired that I would go down by the five o'clock train. Jenkins had packed my bag, and I was waiting for the cab to convey me to the station, when once again Chanler Rao was shown into the room. As before, he approached me with a succession of profound *salaams*, and, though I knew him to be such an awful fraud, I found myself again most powerfully impressed by the noble appearance and splendid dignity of the man. He began once more to pour out his fulsome expressions of undying gratitude, asserting anew his readiness at any time to do all sorts of impossible services for me; then he laid on my table a fee at least four times as large as that which I could have asked for what I had done.

I explained to him that I had to catch a train, and could only spare him a moment; but a rapid examination satisfied me that the throat was healing normally, and, thanks to his magnificent constitution, more rapidly than one might have expected. I thought the cure might be hastened by a mild astringent gargle, and, seizing a sheet of note paper from my table, I hastily scribbled for him a simple prescription. Then, thrusting the paper into his hands, I rushed off to my cab, glad of so good an excuse for escaping a new torrent of thanks.

There was a large party at Beecham Towers, and I did not get an opportunity of a quiet talk with Cissie until the guests had all retired for the night. Then the story she had to tell me was very much what I had expected. The night before, my careless sister had removed the ring from her finger to show it to some of her guests, had placed it on the hall table, and then forgotten all about it.

In the morning, although she came down early to look for it, it had gone. As all the servants would pass through this portion of the hall, both on going to bed and also on coming down next day, suspicion pointed very plainly to one of them as the thief; but, although she had questioned each one of them very closely, they all denied even having seen the ring. She had not yet dared to tell her husband of the loss; he would be so angry about her carelessness. And now please would I advise what ought to be done?

My advice was very clear and simple. First thing in the morning Thornton must be told; he would know best how to deal with the servants, and should question them himself. Then, since the ring was really valuable, if it became clear that the mystery was beyond our powers, we might wire for a detective from town and place the matter in his hands.

On this understanding I went to bed. You may judge of my surprise when, on coming down to breakfast next morning, I found on my plate the following letter, addressed to "Dr. Murray Browne, at Beecham Towers, Surrey."

> Dear Preserver.—
> I can find the stealer of the ring. Am coming down post-haste to Beecham Towers by 2.15 train in the P. M. of the day of this receipt, and all will be settled in an eye-twinkle. Let not anxiety for one instant cloud your noble mind; only in no wise enlighten any interested participator concerning the wherefore of my arrival.
> Your respectful and devoted communicant,
> Chanler Rao.

After breakfast I found Cissie alone in the morning-room, and handed her this extraordinary epistle, at the same time sketching briefly my encounter with the writer. To my surprise, she at once recognized the name.

"Chanler Rao?" she said. "Why, that is the wonderful man Laura Benham was telling me about the other day. You have to send an old glove, date of birth, and a postal order for two-and-six. She did it—just by the way of a joke, you know—and she got back a paper of things about herself that she says are simply marvelous—things that even her most intimate friends couldn't have found out. It was an awfully happy thought of yours to consult him about my ring."

"But I didn't," I said. "That's just the point that is puzzling me so. I only saw him for a moment before I rushed off for my train, and I never even mentioned where I was going, still less anything about you or your ring."

Cissie opened her eyes very wide.

"Then you may depend upon it Laura Benham is right. He's really genuine—a real, true, Eastern seer who *can* do what he professes," she decided.

For my own part, bearing in mind the rootless mango-tree, I had my doubts. Clearly the sensible course would be to telegraph to Chanler Rao not to come, and at the same time wire for a properly qualified detective. But my sister would not hear of this. With a woman's innate inclination to the marvelous, she was now absolutely convinced of Chanler's ability to do almost anything.

"It will be *so* interesting," she said; "and, even if he fails, we can send for the detective afterwards. A few hours' delay can make no difference now. But he won't fail; you can see from his letter that he knows all about it already."

She was so bent on this interesting experiment that all my reasoning was wasted upon her. But from the first I felt rather ashamed of being mixed up in such a mad scheme, and long before afternoon I was heartily regretting my acquiescence.

I was still more impressed with the folly of our proceedings when, at Cissie's request, I went down with the carriage to meet Chanler's train. He alighted from a first-class compartment with his little son and a mass of luggage that suggested he was coming to stay for a month.

"The paraphernalia," he explained—"the apparatus, you know, for my exhibition."

"But, my good man," I began, "you are not going to perform?"

"Of course I am," he replied. "What other reason could you give for my coming? And it is of the very essential of success that till the supreme instant of discovery not a soul should guess what I come to seek. To everybody, please, I am just Chanler Rao, the renowned Hindu wonder-worker, come to entertain your gracious hosts and their noble company with a unique display of our marvelous Eastern magics."

He rolled out the words in what was evidently his best platform manner, and seemed inclined to address some further remarks to the little crowd which had assembled to witness our departure. So I hurried him and his numerous packages into the carriage, and instructed the coachman to drive off. The boy was accommodated with a seat on the box.

"I could not bring the vanishing carpet," Chanler began, as soon as we were seated, "because it is undergoing a necessary reparation. There are also other marvelous wonders which demand a wider interval of preparation than was allowable to the urgency of the case. But," he added, laying a long, brown hand on my arm, "let not my noble preserver be downcast. I have marvels to show that will stop the breathings of spectators and afford speechless satisfaction to all friends."

Then he began to sketch the program of a performance which, as far as I could judge, would occupy several hours. And his descriptions were so elaborate and verbose that we were rapidly approaching the gates of Beecham Towers before I found a chance of directing his thoughts to the real business in hand.

" Now," I said at last, "with regard to the theft—"

"Ah!" he exclaimed; "the theft. Yes. A diamond ring, you say? And stolen by one of the servants? Well, leave it to me, and lo! at the right moment, in a jiffy of time, the culprit shall be caught."

"But the details—the circumstances of the loss," I said; "I had better tell you briefly now while we have opportunity."

Chanler Rao gazed at me dreamily, with a far-off look in his handsome eyes.

"The details?" he murmured. "But—why bother me with those? They will only confuse me. It is quite enough to know that a diamond ring has been stolen, and that one of the servants is the thief. The case is so simple. . . . Besides, I have the performance to arrange for, and it will require all my thoughts."

Then, indeed, my heart sank. I realized at once the Oriental craft of my dark companion. He had used me simply as an agent to work in an engagement at a desirable country house—an engagement which would enlarge his reputation and fill his pocket. His pretence of tracking the thief was manifestly a fraud.

It was in no amiable mood that I arrived at the Towers, and duly presented Chanler Rao and his diminutive son to Cecilia. I felt myself a fool for my share in the silly business; and my chagrin was not lessened when the Hindu, after bowing elaborately and kissing my sister's hand, calmly proposed my dismissal from the room.

"The lady of the house," he said, "will now condescend to take my directions for the performance; after that I must rest to be fit for my great effort."

Then he opened the door, and bowed me out.

Ten minutes later, Cissie joined me in the library. She was jubilant and excited.

"Isn't it lovely?" she said. "He has brought his boxes and things, and is going to do all those wonderful tricks that we read about in Indian books—here, in our own hall! Half an hour to rest—then half an hour alone with his funny little boy in the hall to get things ready. The performance is to begin at five. And as he wants all the servants to be present, I am putting dinner an hour late so that every one of them can come."

"And the discovery of the thief?" I asked.

Cissie started.

"Why—how stupid of me!" she exclaimed. "I had forgotten all about that. I was so interested in his quaint talk and the wonderful tricks he promised that the thing quite slipped out of my head. . . . And I am afraid Chanler Rao must have forgotten it, too."

I turned back to the drawing-room. My dusky friend was already stretched at full length on the sofa, apparently fast asleep; his imp of a son held up a warning finger as I entered.

"But I must speak to him," I was beginning, when Chanler Rao opened his eyes lazily and fixed them upon me in mild rebuke.

"A *séance* here from five to six—packing up—train back to London at 6.45 to be ready for exhibition there. Might you not let me rest in peace?"

"But," I said, "you know, it's all very well, this conjuring business—and it's awfully good of you to take the trouble. But it isn't really what we wanted. You came to discover the thief, you know."

"And have I not said that all will be well? The thief will be discovered in due time, if you will leave it to me. Before fall of night, he shall be in your hands, to do with him as you will. . . . But, stay—you English have much prejudice about the law. Tell your police to be here on the stroke of six—neither before nor after—to arrest the guilty one."

And with that Chanler waved me off with a graceful movement of his hand, and I left the room feeling—as I always did in my dealings with this dignified Eastern—unaccountably young and foolish.

Of course, I had not the smallest intention of sending for the police—my trust in the lazy Chanler Rao as a detective having now reached vanishing point. But here again my better judgment was overruled. The moment I told my sister of the request, she insisted on its being carried out. Her faith in Chanler Rao was still unimpaired; she was certain that he would succeed in what he had undertaken—and, in any case, he must not be able to complain that the failure had been on our part. So, in the end, in spite of my skepticism, I had to undertake to look up the village constable—it would not do to send a servant on that errand; besides, I thought I could myself best invent an excuse that would insure the policeman's presence without pledging ourselves to any occupation for him when he came.

The village is some distance from the Towers; and I had no small difficulty in finding my man when I got there. But I came up with him at last—suspiciously near the Yew Tree Inn—and arranged for him to call round at the Towers at six o'clock precisely.

"We probably shall not really want you, after all," I said, with a view to saving my reputation for sanity; "but, in any case, there will be a little refreshment and a tip for your trouble."

And P. C. Jones, who had doubtless often sampled the Towers beer on former occasions, accepted the mysterious commission without asking any awkward questions.

Chanler Rao was already in possession of the hall when I got back, busy with his preparations. I had hardly time to explain to Cissie the arrangement I had made when little Rao appeared to announce that everything was ready, and that we might assemble at once for the performance.

The hall at Beecham Towers is really a great open lounge. A portion at the far end raised two steps high, with a large folding screen at the back, furnished Chanler with an excellent platform for his purpose. The guests were grouped near the door which leads to the vestibule; the servants occupied a sort of large alcove at the side. By Chanler Rao's special request, as my sister had explained to the housekeeper, the whole of the domestic staff were to witness the entertainment—all were there, from the fat old butler, who looked infinitely more important than Gerald Thornton himself, down to the little page-boy in his first uniform.

Then the performance began.

I suppose that by this date most people have seen Chanler Rao's public exhibitions, and I need not describe his wonders in detail. Of course, we had the great mango trick—only, as Chanler explained, since mangoes did not grow well in our cold English climate, he did it in oak; from an acorn, buried in a pot, by progressive stages he produced in about ten minutes quite a respectable young tree. Then he popped young Rao into the magic basket, and thrust his sword through and through to the accompaniment of such heart-rending shrieks and streams of blood that the old housekeeper, who had a young grandchild of her own, rushed forward to the rescue, and was only checked when Chanler opened the basket and revealed its emptiness.

His grave, handsome features as he sits gazing intently into the crystal ball—his picturesque Eastern costume—his air of being so much older than he looks, the air of inheriting the wisdom of the ages—his rapt earnestness as, in slow deliberation and quaint English, he tries to describe what he sees—his apparent conviction that he is engaged in something tremendously solemn and mysterious—all these combine to throw you off your balance and persuade you to believe, against all reason and commonsense, that the power he claims is real.

I could see this influence acting on others as well as myself. As he sat in the dimly-lighted hall at Beecham Towers and began to see his visions in the crystal globe, I felt at once the spell he was casting on all present; awe is the only word which adequately expresses it.

Chanler began by describing a battle scene, which the army men who were present declared to be an exact and accurate account of the engagement in the South African campaign in which Gerald Thornton himself was wounded.

Then, still gazing into the crystal, he pictured in slow but vivid language the fall of a child over a railway cutting in front of an express train, which the cook declared was just what had happened only a week before to a young sister of hers.

At this point, the butler, who had been strictly brought up amongst a somewhat narrow sect, audibly expressed a doubt whether Christian people ought to get mixed up in doings so manifestly due to evil spirits as "this 'ere cryschal gazin' and fortunetellin'"; but everybody was too much interested to pay any attention to him, and the objection passed unheeded.

A third vision of a young man, who appeared to be forging a will, seemed rather to miss the mark—at least, nobody claimed it, either for himself or any of his relations.

Then, after a pause, Chanler Rao began afresh.

"I look," said he, "and behold a beautiful diamond ring—very priceless, and treasured by its devoted possessor. But lo, while none are beholding, there comes the hand of a thief to steal the ring. . . . The hand bears it off secretly, thinking that none know of the wicked deed. The thief will hide it for a while, hoping by and by to convert it into much wealth. . . . But that is not to be. I look again, and I see another figure. It wears a helmet and a belt—it walks heavily on its heels. It is a noble police—the agent of your mighty English Law. . . . I see him even now approaching—coming to arrest that thief! . . . But stay—why grows the crystal clouded and dull? . . . Ah, I know! It is telling me that the thief is also near. . . . In this village. . . . In this house. . . . In this hall! . . . There is a hand deep down in the crystal to indicate that wicked thief. And it points straight over there—!"

And Chanler Rao's own long finger shot out towards the alcove where the servants were assembled. An indignant murmur of expostulation at once arose from that quarter. But Rao imperiously checked it at once.

"The innocent," said he, "have naught to fear. But let the guilty one tremble—he cannot escape. . . . One chance only will I offer him. Before I go farther, he shall have two minutes as an opportunity for confessing, and restoring that which he has stolen. Then, if he still remains obstinate, I shall have no mercy—I myself shall reveal his guilt."

My sister looked across at me inquiringly. I could only shake my head—it seemed so utterly preposterous to suppose that this charlatan, confident and impressive though he was, could really have discovered anything.

In dead silence we waited for about a minute. Then we heard the great clock in the tower slowly strike six; and as the last stroke died away there came a vigorous peal at the hall-door bell. By Chanler's direction, the small page was despatched to see who it was. After a brief absence he returned with a very white face, followed by the burly form of P. C. Jones.

I should guess that the village constable in his round of rural duties was seldom so astonished as he was now at the strange scene into which he was ushered.

But his astonishment was nothing to that of the now terrified domestics at his appearance. This sudden fulfilment of Rao's vision in the crystal banished the last glimmer of hesitation or doubt; from that moment Chanler had them like children under his control.

He motioned the policeman to stand on one side.

"The time of mercy has expired," he said solemnly. "It now only remains to denounce the thief. The crystal has already revealed to those who can look into its mysteries which of you has done this deed. But I shall not ask you to take my word. I will give you proof—proof positive that shall convince all who behold. Let everyone fix the gaze on me!"

He paused a moment as if to make sure of a general obedience to his direction; then he lifted a metal casket from the table, and took therefrom a number of small, cachet-like objects.

"The Thief Test," he explained, holding one up. "Perfectly harmless." He placed the cachet in his mouth, let it remain for a moment, and then held it up for inspection. "It does not dissolve—in fact, it does not do anything, because I am innocent. No one who is innocent need fear them at all, for they will only reveal how innocent he is. But let the guilty one fear and tremble—for the cachet will infallibly reveal his guilt."

I was watching the domestics carefully during this extraordinary speech, and fancied I could plainly recognize undoubted signs of some sort of mesmeric influence—only there was an alertness and concentrated interest in their attention to Chanler which one does not usually associate with the hypnotic condition. Anyhow, whatever the influence was, it was there. This strange man took in hand that band of a dozen independent English house servants and, without a sign of protest from any one of them, placed a cachet in the mouth of each.

A moment later he was round again, collecting what he had thus distributed; and, as he took each cachet from the mouth of the recipient, he seemed to break the little case open and examine the contents with his fingertip. The whole thing was done so quickly and speedily that one had hardly time to recognize how absurd it was. Only twice did he pause on his round; once opposite the young hall-porter, as if he were not quite sure of his identity; and again, for a longer period, at the last in the row—an anaemic under-housemaid, who was trembling violently and seemed on the verge of hysterics.

"Why are you so frightened?" asked Chanler Rao.

But here my sister intervened.

"Louise has been ill—she only came back from the Convalescent Home this afternoon," she said, "and I think perhaps we have all had quite enough of this rather upsetting performance."

"Let Louise go," said Chanler. "The rest will remain for one moment."

Then he strode across to the tripod, and holding the cachets he had collected in his right hand, he let them drop one by one into the crucible.

One, two, three, four were thus dropped in—and nothing happened. But as number five fell there was a terrific explosion; a great flame shot up from the crucible, followed by a dense cloud of smoke. As it cleared away we saw Chanler Rao pointing an accusing finger at the young hall-porter.

"The fifth cachet reveals the truth. That is the thief of the diamond ring!"

Of course, I expected the man indignantly to deny the accusation—the whole proceeding had so manifestly been a piece of theatrical tomfoolery that it could only end in farce. But, to my astonishment, the young fellow was already on his knees, pale and trembling.

"I never meant to do it," he was calling out with tears. "But I saw it forgotten in the hall, and thought nobody would ever know. . . . The temptation was too strong. . . . But I will restore it—indeed I will. It is quite safe—hidden in the chimney in my bedroom."

P. C. Jones came forward and laid a heavy hand on his shoulder.

"I guess you'd better come and show me," he said.

AT 6.45 CHANLER RAO, with a contented smile on his handsome features and a substantial cheque in his pocket, was seated opposite to me in a reserved compartment of the train back to town.

"I trust my noble preserver is satisfied?" he said, in his lazy Eastern fashion.

"Quite satisfied as to the result," I replied; "but rather puzzled about the process."

"The process?" he said, looking somewhat perplexed. "Ah, you mean the method—the how it was done?"

I nodded.

Chanler looked out of the window dreamily as if considering whether I could be trusted with the secret.

"And yet it is so simple," he said. "It is a method practiced in India for generations past. As thus: Suppose you are great *sahib* over there. One of your many servants has committed a crime. You question them closely with all your skill. But, alas!—no good—servants everywhere, even in my own dear country, are ready liars. They all say 'No!'—with protests most indignant. Then what shall you do? You send for the Magic Man, whom they all fear. He comes and calls for rice. He bids each servant fill his mouth with the rice, held it for a moment, and then spit it out. Now, at a single glance, he can point out the culprit.

"For why? Fear—the fear of the impending detection—has parched the tongue of the guilty one. The other portions of rice when spit out are wet—very wet; but not so that from the mouth of him who is guilty of the crime. His mouthful of rice is almost as dry as when it went in.

"Human nature is much the same all the world over. Only the case to-day had special points to be considered. In the first place, people here do not believe in the Magic Man—to them he is only a conjurer and sleighter-of-hand. I must first of all make them respect and fear. The program, which caused my preserver so much impatience, was all necessary—carefully arranged to impress—to lead on to wonder, conviction, fear, obedience. And I felt much obstacle—especially with the old butler-man of the solid paunch and the religious scruples. He nearly made the hash of it all. But perseverance and the noble policeman brought success. The appearing of the officer of Law, just at the right moment according to the crystal, turned the scale. From that instant I held them in my power.

"A sort of hypnotic influence—?"

But Chanler shook his head.

"No, no; hypnotism is but the silly Western imitation of the real thing. Your hypnotism is too feeble, too dreamy for what I had to do. The influence has no English name—it is not understood here. But it is the power which makes the Eastern Mystery Man—the power to influence people so that they will obey. . . . But even then you must consider. You could not fill English servants' mouths with rice—even under the influence, they would rebel and knock you down.

"I had to prepare means more delicate and fine. The little cachets—they are celluloid, perforated; filled with a special material very drawing—what you call absorbent to moisture. Most accurately do they register which mouth is dry. So is the marvel explained."

"But," I said, at last running in the objection that was in my mind, "surely the test is a very risky one. With nervous people mere excitement and fright will check the flow of saliva quite as effectively as the consciousness of real guilt."

"In the East, never!" said Chanler. "No Hindu is ever afraid unless he has reason to be—why should he? But in the West it is different. What you call your nerves are overstrained, and liable to all sorts of fits and starts. One never knows. And it makes difficulties—it did to-day. There were two dry cachets."

"The pale under-housemaid?" I suggested.

"Yes," said Rao; "Louise. She gave me much alarm, for she furnished the second dry cachet. For a moment I was up the tree, and feared the method had failed; then I bethought me—perchance she is a confederate. It was only the interference of your sister, the lady of the house, that showed me how, since Louise had been away till this very day, she could not be concerned. From that point all was perfectly plain and cock-sure; my man was marked."

"And the explosion," I hinted.

Rao smiled indulgently.

"Ah—that," he said, "was perhaps what you would call a little trick. Yet, again, not without purpose. I do not choose that everyone should know the how; the explosion covered up the method, and put spectators on the wrong scent. And it had a further object. When once your man is seriously disturbed and anxious, with the nerves, as one says, on the stretch and quiver, there is nothing like a sudden bang and flash to throw him altogether off the balance and self-control. And it was so here. You noted—did you not?—that the guilty one was trembling and almost on his knees even before I had time to point him out."

"And yet there is one thing that seems to me quite inexplicable," I said. "How did you get to know of the robbery at all? It was so extraordinary—your writing to me like that, just when we were about to send for a detective."

"My noble physician has the right to learn the whole truth," said Chanler Rao. "He wrote my prescription on the back of his gracious sister's letter."

THE DAVENPORT MYSTERY

I HAD NOT SEEN nor heard much of Chanler Rao for several months.

He had started, with his little son, on a professional tour of the principal provincial cities, and was astonishing the big towns in the North with his unique exposition of Eastern magic.

I saw by the notices in the papers that he was due at the Winter Gardens, Scarborough, for the month of July. Then I lost sight of his movements altogether until the Davenport Mystery threw me once again into his strange company.

The matter began with a little paragraph in a London halfpenny paper:

STRANGE OCCURRENCE ON THE SCOTCH EXPRESS

The friends of a Brixton young lady, Miss Clara Davenport, are seriously concerned at her mysterious disappearance from the Great Northern Scotch express yesterday. Miss Davenport, who has been living for the past three years with her maternal uncle and aunt at Brixton, had arranged to pay a visit to some friends in Scotland, and on Monday morning started on her journey northward by the 10.30 from Kings Cross.

Her uncle, Mr. Arkwright, saw her safely into the train, in which, by Miss Davenport's particular request, a first-class compartment had been reserved for the whole journey. Her Scotch friends were to meet her at Aberdeen; but on the arrival of the express at that station they were surprised to find that, though her labeled luggage was duly put out, the young lady herself was not amongst the passengers alighting, nor could they discover her in the train.

At first they supposed that there had been some change in her plans, or that she had missed her train in London. But on telegraphing to Brixton they learned that she had duly started as arranged; and, in some alarm at her non-arrival, they communicated with the railway authorities and with the police. A disquieting feature of the case is that the outer door of Miss Davenport's reserved compartment, though presumably closed when the express left Montrose, was reported to be wide open when the train steamed into Aberdeen station.

A careful inquiry along the line has been instituted, but up to the time of going to press no signs of the missing young lady have been discovered.

NEXT MORNING the same newspaper was able to furnish fuller particulars. It was perfectly certain that Miss Davenport had duly started from King's Cross; Mr. Arkwright had not only seen her into the train, but had also stood on the platform talking to her till the actual departure of the express. The reservation of a whole compartment for one person naturally excited some attention from the outset, and at various points there appeared to be satisfactory evidence that Miss Davenport continued her journey northward.

On the third day the *Morning Meteor* took up the case, and its enterprising representative interviewed the uncle, Mr. James Arkwright, at Brixton. With the assistance of this somewhat loquacious gentleman, the reporter provided a column of personal gossip which, if it did not greatly elucidate the mystery, certainly gave additional public interest to the affair.

It appeared that Miss Clara Davenport was a lady with a history. Her mother had died during her childhood, and she had been brought up with her two brothers on the ranch which her father owned in Texas. It was a rough, but happy life for the young girl till the death of one brother, who was thrown from his horse and instantly killed; and the disappearance of the other, with everything he could lay hands on, so affected the father that he was stricken with paralysis, and died at the early age of fifty-three. An examination of his affairs showed that, owing to unfortunate speculations and the depredations of his younger son, he was practically bankrupt. Thus Miss Davenport found herself left alone at the age of twenty-one in a rough country, with hardly a five-pound note to call her own.

It was at this stage that she bethought herself of her mother's brother, Mr. Arkwright, in England, and wrote to him an appealing letter, explaining her destitute position and begging his advice and assistance. Mr. Arkwright at once proposed that his niece should come to live with himself and his wife in England, and sent out the necessary money for her passage and other expenses. She arrived at Brixton in October, 1899, and had resided there with her uncle and aunt for the last three years.

The Arkwrights were described as fairly wealthy people, highly respected in Brixton and the neighborhood. It seemed, therefore, a most fortunate and happy arrangement for their young niece. But from the very first, as Mr. Arkwright explained, Miss Davenport appeared uneasy, and discontented with her new surroundings, and often expressed a strong desire to return to Texas. She gave, as a reason for this, her dislike of the stiffness and conventions of English suburban society, which, she declared, were most irksome and galling after the freedom of her outdoor life abroad.

But Mr. Arkwright hinted pretty plainly his own conviction that the real reason of his niece's discontent was an attachment she had formed with an unsatisfactory young man of inferior station out in Texas, with whom she still corresponded in spite of all the efforts of her relatives to break off the connection. It was the restlessness resulting from this state of things that led to the proposal of a visit to some Scotch friends, in the hope that the freer life of an unconventional household in the North might in some degree reconcile Miss Davenport to her surroundings, and distract her thoughts from this mad infatuation.

Mr. Arkwright declared that his niece left London in robust physical health and good spirits; indeed, she seemed unusually elated at the prospect of this Scotch journey. There had been a slight upset earlier in the day, in consequence of his receipt by post of the bill of a London jeweler for a large amount of jewelry supplied to his niece. Miss Davenport denied altogether having had the goods, and seemed greatly disturbed and worried by the mistake; but he had tried to reassure her by promising to call on the firm in question to explain the error, and, long before the journey, she appeared to have recovered from her agitation.

Mr. Arkwright was, therefore, somewhat surprised when, at the station, she insisted on his reserving a whole compartment for her use; but, knowing her occasional whims and fancies, he at once good-naturedly consented to an expenditure which, she declared would add so much to the comfort of her journey, and he was pleased to see his niece go off at last in such good spirits. He refused altogether the suggestion of certain newspapers that suicide might be the solution of her strange disappearance; he was convinced that she must have fallen from the train by accident, and that the more careful search now being carried out along the last stage of the route would confirm his sad conclusions as to her fate.

But, when the most careful investigation produced no such result, people became puzzled, and the calamity began to be talked of as the "Railway Mystery."

The police, baffled in their search of the line, now propounded the theory that Miss Davenport had never made the latter stages of the journey at all. They were convinced that she must have alighted at one of the various stopping-places on the way; that the unfastened door was merely the result of an oversight. In other words, that there had been no disaster, but merely a disappearance.

Moreover, there came to light several little circumstances which strongly tended to confirm the new view.

In the first place, amongst her belongings left by Miss Davenport at Brixton were two recent letters from the young man in Texas, in which he expressed his satisfaction at her resolution to come out to him, and his admiration of some plan which she had suggested for raising the passage-money without anyone knowing her purpose.

Next it appeared that Miss Davenport had been making inquiries, ostensibly for a friend, as to the sailing of vessels and the cost of passage to America.

Finally, it was discovered that only two days before her disappearance she had gone into town alone, and, by the use of her uncle's well-known name, had obtained on approval large quantities of jewelry, to the value of some £500, from firms with whom he was in the habit of dealing. As Mr. Arkwright denied all knowledge of these transactions, and the jewels had disappeared along with the young lady herself, it was presumed that they formed part of the proposed means of raising the money to enable her to join her lover in Texas.

On the strength of these significant discoveries, the police at last took action, and a notice was put out offering a reward of £100 for information as to the missing lady's whereabouts. A full description was given: "Age 24; rather tall—about 5 ft. 8½ in.; figure somewhat slight; very upright and active; complexion ruddy and sunburnt; gray eyes; dark brown hair; rather large hands and feet. When last seen she was wearing a dark gray tailor-made traveling costume with a motor hat, and she carried a small morocco wrist-bag and an umbrella."

Then began the great "Clara Davenport hunt."

Innumerable "Miss Davenports" were discovered daily by all sorts of people in all sorts of unlikely places—only, unfortunately in each case, a very little investigation showed that a mistake had been made.

It happened just then, that my annual autumn holiday was due. As usual, I was going for three weeks' golf at Aulish, a quiet spot near Forfar—so quiet, indeed, that when people ask me what sort of a place it is I have to explain that, strictly speaking, it is not what one would call a "place" at all; it is just a links—and nothing more. There is a big, comfortable hotel, a ground where the younger and richer men play polo, and the finest eighteen-hole golf-course you have ever seen.

"By the way," said Charlie Truscott, as he happened to see me at the station before my train started, "you go through Edinburgh, don't you?"

"Yes—of course I do," I replied.

"Well, then," he said, "there's a fine chance for you to distinguish yourself. This morning's *Meteor* announces that at last the police have definite news of Miss Clara Davenport. It seems that at Edinburgh she really alighted from her train and visited the cloak-room to claim a large handbag which had been sent on two days before—the porter who carried it for her from the cloak-room to her reserved compartment has turned up. There seems to be no doubt about it this time. So if you want some sport you have only to break your journey at Edinburgh, pick up the traces of the lady, and solve the mystery which is puzzling all England. I'll leave you the *Meteor*, and you can read all about it for yourself."

I laughed as we shook hands and parted. Then the matter passed entirely from my thoughts. The truth is that by this time I was getting a bit weary of Miss Davenport and her vagaries; moreover, I can never read with comfort in a railway-train; and on this particular occasion I adopted the best of all methods of shortening a long journey—I went to sleep. And I slept soundly.

I had a dim consciousness at last of our stopping at York, and of somebody being bundled into my compartment with innumerable parcels and packages. Then, as the door was banged, and the train began to move on, I opened my eyes and found, to my astonishment, Chanler Rao and his dusky little son on the seat opposite.

Chanler did not seem in the least surprised at our chance encounter. He was gazing at me in his usual placid fashion, and the moment he saw that I was awake he began to overwhelm me with his elaborate salutations and exaggerated protestations of regard.

"But, Chanler," I said, "what on earth brings you in the Scotch express?"

"It is a little holiday," he replied. "No engagements for the next seven days. So I run away to your bonnie Scotland. And whither? Why, to Aberdeen, to find this so mysterious Miss Davenport!"

I could not help smiling to note how the current English excitement had seized on this child of the East.

But Chanler was perfectly serious.

"Your police are no good," he said, with fine contempt. "Even now, with the whole case put under their very noses, they are on the wrong idea altogether, and will let her escape. So I must go myself."

"But," I said, "I thought the police had at last discovered something in Edinburgh?"

"The police?" said Chanler, still more contemptuously. "*They* discovered it not. They were helpless—all out at sea, as you say—till by anonymous communication I gave them my hints. 'Inquire,' I said, 'at the cloak-room—first at York, then at Newcastle, then at Edinburgh.' And now, with all the facts before them, they bungle it again—not only publishing what ought to be kept quiet as the mouse, but actually missing the whole point of the clue I put in their hands! . . . and yet the case is so simple."

"Simple?" I said doubtfully. Of course, the idea of a Hindu conjuror like Chanler teaching our trained police and detectives how to do their work was preposterous; but I was entertained by his bumptious pretensions.

"Perfectly simple," he replied. "You start with the ascertained facts. The lady is bent on getting to her lover in Texas; but there are several obstacles. I put them under three heads. First, the difficulty of arranging anything under the eyes of the uncle and aunt, who will smell the rat, and will watch her closely. Secondly, the impossibility of getting away from Brixton without her flight being at once discovered and stopped. Thirdly, the difficulty of poverty—the absence of all means of meeting the heavy expense of the voyage out.

"The first and second difficulties are met by this proposed visit to Scotland; there, in the house of these friends, she will be able to make all the plans, map out her arrangements, and, at the right moment, upon some specious pretext—possibly a pretended summons to return to Brixton—she will leave, make her journey to Liverpool, and, hey presto! be half-way to America before the old people in London know anything about it. The third difficulty—the want of means—is solved by her fraud on the jewelers.

"And here, too, the Scotch visit is a help. From Aberdeen—a place where she is not known—she will be able best, with the least suspicion, to turn the jewelry into the money she needs for her journey to America. This, I believe, was clearly Miss Davenport's plan, carefully thought out and arranged for, when she consented so readily to make that Scotch visit."

"Perhaps so," I remarked. "But since it certainly was not carried out, I don't see how it helps you now."

"It helps a good deal," replied Chanler, "because it forces one to ask, why was it not carried out? And I find the answer in that communication from one of the defrauded jewelers which reached Mr. Arkwright on the morning of his niece's contemplated departure. That communication seriously alarmed the young lady, nor would she be at all comforted, I guess, by Mr. Arkwright's promise to call on the jeweler at once; she feels that everything is on the very pinpoint of discovery—that there must be no further delay. And I find the plainest indications that she started on that Scotch journey resolved not to meet those friends at Aberdeen at all, but to disappear on the way."

"But," I objected, "if that were really her purpose, why go traveling on to Edinburgh? Surely some earlier stop—York, for instance, with a direct run to Liverpool—would be her obvious line of escape?"

"Obvious," said Chanler; "but she did not take it. Again, we ask why? And the answer is plain; there is something on the way which she wants to get before she disappears. Hence my idea of inquiry at the cloak-rooms. And this bag, which she claims at Edinburgh, is the solution—very much what I expected."

"Ah," I said, "you think that bag contained the jewelry, which, I suppose, she had sent on for safety two days before?"

"Possibly," Chanler replied; "but I think also that it contained something else that she wanted even more than the jewelry. And she got it. We have the clearest evidence that it was duly conveyed to her place in the train. So, then, beyond Edinburgh, you have Miss Clara Davenport still seated in her reserved compartment being whirled away towards Aberdeen, where her relatives—and possibly the police, warned by telegraph from those London jewelers—are waiting to receive her. Now, don't you see what she is going to do?"

I shook my head.

"Why," said Chanler, "you are as slow as the police—they don't see either. And it is just because they don't, that the whole search is useless—they will never find her. I *know* what she did—with the half of the eye I can see the one thing she would be certain to try. And it is just because I know it, that I go to Aberdeen. Within four days I expect to lay my hand upon this lady and to give everybody a surprise."

At Dundee we parted—he with little Rao to continue his journey to Aberdeen; I to my slower train along the branch line towards Aulish. At the last moment Chanler took down my address.

"I will telegraph to you when I have found the lady," he said.

I found the Links Hotel very full—so full, indeed, that at dinner I could not get my accustomed place near the south window, but had to share a table with a young fellow who was already halfway through his fish when I sat down.

But even here the plague of Miss Clara Davenport pursued me. We had not been talking ten minutes before he put his question:

"And what do you think about the Davenport case?"

I tried to hint that I was suffering from a surfeit of the problem. But in his eagerness he ignored my protest. And, in a way, he even succeeded in interesting me afresh. Like Chanler, he blamed the police for slowness and stupidity; and, like Chanler, he had his own special solution of the problem.

In the smoke-room, later in the evening, I was talking to old Colonel Jephson, and happened to mention my dining-companion's theory.

"Ah, yes—young Maxwell," he said. "Nice, bright young lad, isn't he? Quite a new comer, but he's already the most popular person in the hotel. Makes friends with everybody—and everybody likes him. A capable youngster, too—good shot—fair golf—first-rate billiards—and a horseman. Just the sort of young fellow I like—nothing namby-pamby about him. Got brains, too, and can talk."

I mentioned that I had already been favored with a specimen of his conversational powers.

"What? The Davenport nonsense?" said Colonel Jephson. "Oh, yes—he's full of that. Buttonholes everybody about it—comes down before everybody else to see the latest reports in the papers. Got his own theory about it, too—and, by Jove, you know, I am not at all sure but what he may be right. . . . He's been at me all day about writing to the police about it."

Now, I cannot exactly explain how it happened, but certainly during the next few days, the boy and I got on fairly familiar terms; so much so, that I believe his time was pretty equally divided between a Miss Ruth Clifford and myself. Miss Clifford's widowed mother was the misguided matron who had booked rooms for a month in advance for herself and her daughter, under a mistaken notion that Aulish was a health-resort on the coast. I think this approach to intimacy must have been due to him; for, speaking quite frankly, I cannot say that I really *liked* him. He fascinated me by his pleasant candor, his keenness on all sorts of sports, his open-air freshness and energy. But there was, at the same time, something that repelled—an assurance and maturity of opinion and judgment that seemed to me a little priggish in one so young. It was therefore somewhat of a relief to me when, on the fourth morning of my sojourn, his courting of Miss Clifford reached such a stage of success that he received an invitation to sit at their table, and I was left alone.

But the vacancy was soon to be filled. That very afternoon when a sudden shower had driven everybody in, and the large hall of the hotel was crowded, the 'bus from the station drove up, and the manager came forward to greet a new guest. You may judge of my surprise when the door opened and Chanler Rao was ushered in. He saw me at once, and came up with his ridiculously elaborate salutation.

"Why, Chanler," I exclaimed, "you seem bent on giving me surprises! What on earth brings you to Aulish?"

He looked at me in mild simplicity.

"I have come to learn the golf," he said, in a voice sufficiently raised for everybody to hear. Then he turned to the manager to discuss the question of his rooms. The matter seemed to involve so much consideration that, on his own proposal, an adjournment was made to the bureau. But after a few moments, he emerged with a satisfied look, and I seized the earliest opportunity of taking him to a quiet corner to inquire the meaning of this new move.

"It is all right," said Chanler triumphantly. "I have followed Miss Davenport to this hotel!"

"Why—how do you mean?" I said. Then, with a recollection of his recent interview with the manager I hazarded a guess. "Do you suspect her of hiding here as a servant?"

"No," answered Chanler; "I have just satisfied myself as to that. The host—landlord—what do you call him? tells me that all his staff are engaged from the beginning of the season; none of them is fresh. So she must be among the guests."

Then I could not help laughing outright.

"My poor, dear Chanler," I said," you are altogether on the wrong lines this time. Aulish is a man's resort; hardly any women ever turn up here. It is the last place in the world where a woman could hope to hide herself."

Chanler was entirely unmoved by my assertion.

"But she is here," he said.

Now, you will readily understand that an acquaintance like Chanler Rao is a little bit embarrassing—people never seem to be sure whether you are entertaining an Indian prince or hobnobbing with a vulgar adventurer. However, as I was the only person in the hotel to whom he was at all known, I could not do less than propose that he should occupy the vacancy at my table in the dining-room. But we were no sooner seated than he suggested changing places with me, so that he might get a better view of the room.

"Could you," he said, after a while, "introduce me to the little party at the table in the far comer—the fat old lady with the young daughter to whom that straight-backed gentleman is paying such attention?"

"Certainly," I said, "I will manage it directly after dinner." And I smiled to myself as I imagined how surprised Chanler would be when he found that Miss Clifford was barely five feet in height.

"And what do you think of the Davenport mystery?" Maxwell propounded his usual question when I had presented Chanler.

"The—what?" inquired Chanler, with a countenance of bland ignorance.

"The Davenport mystery—the disappearance of Miss Clara Davenport," said Maxwell. "Ah, I see; of course, you don't read the English papers. But it is really the most extraordinary business. I'll tell you all about it. . . ."

And then Chanler had to sit and listen to the whole story—especially to young Maxwell's idea of the solution. He gave a polite, but not very marked attention—indeed, except for an occasional glance at the speaker, his gaze was fixed on Miss Clifford as if he were rather puzzled by her manifest interest in the young man's conversation. It was only at the end of Maxwell's long recital that he turned to him with a look of undisguised admiration.

"You have thought out the whole thing most cleverly. I shall certainly look out for that young lady myself when I go to Liverpool," he said, with childlike simplicity.

Then the conversation drifted to other topics.

"Well," I said, as we parted for the night at his bedroom door, "and what do you think now?"

"I think that your young friend Mr.—Maxwell, is it?—is a most ingenious and clever person," he said.

"Yes, yes," I answered; "but I don't mean that. What do you think about the young lady?"

Chanler looked at me for a moment, as if he thought my curiosity a little stupid. Then he smiled.

"I shall be better able to tell you that when I have played the golf," he said.

And with this enigmatical utterance he went off to bed.

But in the morning the golf seemed doubtful after all. The day opened dark and unpromising, and after breakfast a sharp shower kept Chanler indoors. He has a horror of wet grass; and it was nearly eleven before Maxwell could persuade him that it was fit for play.

Now I have seen many curious things on a golf-course; but I fancy the spectacle that morning of Chanler Rao, in what Jenkins always speaks of as "full native costoom," vainly endeavoring to master the mysteries of the game, must be set at the head of my list. He could make nothing of it at all; and he exhibited a surprising irritation at his own failures—and still more, as it seemed to me, at the ease and skill with which Maxwell played. At length, he threw down his driver in disgust.

"I could do it better with my hands," he said. And picking up a golf ball, he made a fine throw—sending it spinning overhead into some distant bushes.

"Can you beat that?" he asked, turning with a smile to young Maxwell. But his smile died away when he saw the readiness with which Maxwell accepted the challenge, and threw another ball in fine style in the same direction.

It was really a magnificent throw; and I was not surprised when a caddie came running back to announce that Maxwell's ball had gone some five yards beyond Chanler's. But I was astonished when I noticed how disappointed Rao appeared to be, and the almost childish depression that settled upon him after his defeat.

Then, as we left the links, he gave me a new surprise.

"I am thinking," he said, "of buying Colonel Jephson's pony for my little son. Will you come round to the stables to look at him?"

And as Maxwell readily consented, I could but follow, though what on earth little Rao could do with a polo pony passed my powers of comprehension. I was still more puzzled when, at the stables, Chanler himself assisted the groom to saddle the pony, and then suggested that Maxwell should mount him.

"I want to be sure that he is quiet before I purchase him," Rao explained.

Maxwell rather drew back. "Colonel Jephson might not like it," he said.

"But I have the colonel's permission," said Chanler. "I told him I should ask you, and he said: 'By all means'."

The groom confirming this, Maxwell at length consented. He sprang to the saddle with the ready ease of an experienced rider. But no sooner was he mounted than that abominable pony began every equine trickery you can imagine. He plunged, and kicked, and reared, and buck-jumped; then he bolted for a hundred yards or more; then he stopped dead, only to begin the whole performance over again.

Never have I seen a brute more determined to unseat its rider; I marveled that Colonel Jephson could have boasted of its quietness and good behavior. But Maxwell certainly managed it beautifully. He sat unmoved, with all the skill of a seasoned horseman. Nothing that the animal could do seemed to disturb him in the least. And he did not give in until at last he got the pony under perfect control, and trotted it quietly round the paddock.

It was a splendid piece of horsemanship, and set me wondering whether there was anything this dandified youth could not do.

But Chanler shook his head.

"The pony," he said, "would be much too rough for little Rao."

And the disappointment seemed perceptibly to increase his growing discontent.

That afternoon I got my first suspicion that this Davenport business was turning the poor fellow's brain. But I had no time to dwell on the point, for just at that moment the manager came up with a request. Mr. Maxwell and some other guests had been telling him of Chanler's wonderful performances in London and elsewhere; and, with many apologies for the liberty he was taking, he ventured to ask whether Rao would help him to meet the problem of a wet afternoon by entertaining the guests with Eastern magic?

At first Chanler absolutely refused; he had no apparatus—it was a holiday—he had much else to think of. Then just as suddenly he changed his mind, and became quite keen on the project. And the result was that for the next half hour waiters were busy arranging seats in the drawing-room, and Chanler was engaged in collecting a most curious mixture of everyday articles as substitutes for his regular paraphernalia.

The first trick was an old one. It was the illusion of the egg, which in Chanler's hands changes into almost anything the audience may choose. As usual, it finished up by turning into a live mouse in a mousetrap. But on this occasion, by some carelessness or mischance, Chanler opened the door of the trap and let the mouse loose.

The five ladies of our company, who occupied front seats, screamed and gathered up their skirts as the little creature ran towards them. But Maxwell, who was sitting near Miss Clifford, stooped down at once and cleverly caught the mouse in his hand and restored it to the trap. Chanler was profuse in his apologies for the mishap. I judged from his face that he fully realized that this was not a very happy beginning.

The next item in the program was new to me. Rao had borrowed my razor and strop. He now took up the razor and, explaining that he required the keenest possible edge, requested young Maxwell to strop it. I am rather particular about my razors, and was about to offer to do this myself, when Chanler restrained me by a significant glance; but the moment Maxwell took it in hand and began in quite a professional manner to strop from heel to tip, turning the blade carefully each time on the back, I saw that he could be trusted safely.

Even Chanler himself, who was carefully watching the operation, was satisfied that the blade was perfectly sharpened. Then, with apparently nothing in his hand but my highly-tempered razor, he chopped an ordinary kitchen poker into four pieces and handed the pieces round, together with the undamaged razor, for our inspection.

The third trick was with Colonel Jephson's hat. You know how Chanler varies his hat trick. This time it was fruit. A monster melon, three fine pines, grapes, bananas, peaches, and plums—in a few moments, out of that wonderful hat fruit sufficient to supply a large banquet had been piled on the table. Then came Rao's usual little joke—gigantic struggles with the hat, resulting in the production of a very small apple. He held it up in triumph.

"I should like the audience to know that this is really genuine. Perhaps somebody will kindly catch it and hand it round." And, as he spoke, Chanler pitched the apple across towards where Maxwell was sitting. It seemed to be thrown unnecessarily high and fell awkwardly; but Maxwell was ready, and caught it easily. Chanler beamed across upon him in genuine delight.

"Very cleverly caught, *Miss Clara Davenport*," he cried out with clear emphasis.

"AND YOU ARE STILL puzzled?" said Chanler an hour later, as we sat in the smoke-room. The examination of "Mr. Maxwell's" trunks had revealed such damning evidence in the shape of a lady's gray traveling-costume and a quantity of feminine jewelry, that further doubt was impossible, and Miss Davenport was safely in custody. But I was yet in the dark as to how Chanler got his proof.

"Well, go back to where we left the problem when we last discussed it," said Rao. "We left Miss Clara Davenport alone in a first-class compartment between Edinburgh and Aberdeen, driven by the necessity of obtaining her bag at Edinburgh to postpone till the last stage of her journey her real plan of escape. You failed altogether to guess what she would do next.

"But, really, the thing had the plainness of a pikestaff. Her friends at Aberdeen—and, as she fears, the police, too—will be looking for a woman; she will obviously try to escape as a man. And the transformation had already been arranged for. The bag she claimed at Edinburgh contained the necessary clothing. The reserved compartment was insisted on to provide a private dressing-room. The long run between Montrose and Aberdeen will give her the opportunity of changing, and also of cutting off her hair. So she actually arrives at Aberdeen, and passes, with the coolness of the cucumber, under the very noses of her friends and the officials.

"The very audacity of this step—her boldness in going to hide in the very place where people were expecting her—was almost enough to have taken the cakes. No one would dream that she would choose to go there. But the whole scheme is ruined by one never-to-be-got-over mistake. That little trick of unlocking the carriage door—originally, I should guess, an impulsive feminine device to divert the search from Aberdeen itself—had consequences the lady had not foreseen.

"It is not so easy as you would suppose for a stranger, in an eye-twinkle, to turn into money a quantity of new jewelry without provoking awkward inquiries; it requires care, and involves delay. And in the meantime that open railway-door, and its suggestion of a terrible accident, has struck your public's sympathy in a way that a mere disappearance could never have done. In three days the eyes of all England are fixed on the problem. Clearly, till this excitement has abated, she will not have a ghost's chance to get off at any seaport. For the present, then, she will try to hide somewhere—to keep under the rose—till the search is relaxed. And she will, of course, do it still disguised as a young man.

"Now, just because I was sure as the cock that she would adopt this method, I was enabled, with but small difficulty, to pick up the thread where the police missed it, and to trace the lady on here. It was a little startling to find her in a man's sporting center; but that is only of the piece with her boldness in talking to everybody about the case, and in carrying out her assumed character so far as actually to make love to that poor little Miss Clifford—a boldness which by its very audacity was the secret of her success. It was this that made it so difficult to turn one's suspicions into proof.

"The golf did not help me; for in style of play, measure of success, and even in language on occasional failure, the lady was as thoroughly masculine as anybody on the course. I challenged her to throw, because a woman's throwing is nearly always unmistakable; but she did it in a manner only to be explained by the fact that from her earliest years she had lived a tom-boy life with her brothers out in Texas. And she sat the polo pony—in spite of a little harmless irritant which I had inserted under the saddle—she sat the restive animal with a *knee-grip* that I never expected to see in a woman.

"She was equally successful in facing the two searching tests which I planned in our little entertainment. The mouse I let loose did not startle her into the slightest fear. And she stropped that razor in a fashion that was a lesson to many a man. It was only when the sudden idea occurred to me of throwing the apple across the room to her that she gave the show away. Instead of bringing her legs together, as a man, when sitting, instinctively does in taking a difficult catch, she opened her knees wide apart *to make a lap*—and I knew in a moment that she was feminine gender!"

THE AUTOMATON DETECTIVE

IT WAS MY SISTER who was responsible for Chanler Rao's engagement at Highcliff Moor School.

She burst into my consulting room one morning in July in her usual breathless fashion. "Rex has won his scholarship," she exclaimed. "Isn't it splendid? Dr. Searson says he has done awfully well, and he is very pleased about it. I felt I must run up to town at once and tell you."

Rex is my nephew and godson. I duly expressed my gratification at his success. He is a nice, bright lad who is going to make his mark.

"He will go up to Cambridge in October," continued Rex's mother, with becoming pride in the growing importance of her first-born. "It makes me feel quite old to think that I shall soon have a son at college; it seems only the other day the child was in the nursery. . . . But what I really came about is this: Speech Day is on the 27th. The school has done remarkably well in all sorts of ways—sports, scholarships and distinctions of every kind; Dr. Searson says it is quite a record year, and he is very keen on securing a big gathering of parents and friends on the 27th. And as it is Rex's last term, and he will be one of the heroes of the day, the boy is particularly anxious that as his only uncle and godfather you should be present. Now, will you promise to run down to us for the week-end, and I will motor you over to Highcliff Moor?"

I looked through my engagement book and found there was nothing to keep me in town. Moreover—although Speech Day festivities did not greatly attract me—after a long, unbroken spell of work in the sultry London summer, the prospect of a few days' blow on the Surrey hills was a temptation I could not resist. I nodded my acquiescence in Cecilia's proposal.

"Well, then," said my sister, "that settles request number one. Now I come to the second favor I want to ask. You see, this will be rather Rex's show, and I should like to mark it specially in some way. There is to be an Old Boys' cricket match in the afternoon; tea at 5; the regular Speech Day business from 5.30 to 7. And then I thought if we could only get our friend Chanler Rao to come down and give an exhibition, it would be something quite fresh and just what the boys would enjoy. I proposed it to Dr. Searson and promised to bear all the expenses, and he thought it a most happy idea for concluding the day, and was very grateful for the offer. And now I want you to prevail upon Mr. Chanler to come."

I mentioned that Rao's fee for these private engagements out of town was a very high one.

"I don't mind that at all," my sister replied. "You see, one's eldest son does not take a big scholarship every day, and one can afford to be a bit extravagant on such an occasion. Besides, you know, it is just the sort of thing that the boys will appreciate, and it will turn that rather tiresome and dull Speech Day program into something really interesting. So please do send off a messenger to Chanler Rao at once, and let me wait here for his reply."

So I wrote a hurried note and despatched Jenkins with it to Chanler's rooms in Ophir Street. Then I turned Cissie into the drawing-room, so that I might resume my interviews with patients.

My sister's visit had rather upset my time-table and caused a temporary block in the waiting-room; I was kept busily employed for the next hour. But as the clock struck twelve my messenger returned with Chanler's reply. He wrote that he was already booked for the 27th, but would at once cancel his engagement so as to be free to accede to my request—the slightest wish of his noble preserver being equivalent in his eyes to a royal command. I might therefore count on his appearance without fail at Highcliff Moor on the date named. So I was enabled to put my sister in a cab and send her back to Surrey thoroughly satisfied at having achieved successfully the double purpose of her journey.

Highcliff Moor is a big private school, modeled on public lines—one of the best in the south of England. It is situated on the Surrey hills, about ten miles from my brother-in-law's house—the same railway-station serving for both.

It was therefore arranged that Chanler Rao should come down by the first train after lunch, and that my sister and I should motor round by the station, pick him up there, and take him on with us to the school. I explained all this to Rao before I left town, and particularly impressed upon him the desirability of limiting his apparatus as much as possible, as the motor-car accommodation was necessarily restricted.

He appeared quite to understand this, and, indeed, himself remarked that, as the entertainment was to be brief and the audience so largely juvenile, elaborate paraphernalia would not be needed. You may guess, then, at my annoyance, when, on the day appointed, we arrived at the station to find Chanler and his little son surrounded by innumerable packages, including a large wooden case some five feet in height.

"It is the new automaton," said Chanler, beaming upon us complacently. "Only completed yesterday; but now in perfect order. He will write you the answers to any questions, from dates on coins to superior mathematics. And all inexplicable and marvelous beyond explanation. Khokan will be the rage and wonder of all London when they see him. And in my desire to honor my noble physician, I have determined that his first showing shall be at your private *séance* to-day."

"Oh, how delightful!" exclaimed my sister. "And just the very thing to interest those dear boys. You could not have hit on anything better."

Nor was her enthusiasm at all damped when I pointed out the impossibility of conveying the bulky chest on the motor.

"Why," she said, "that difficulty is soon overcome. We can easily get a cart to convey the luggage, and it can follow us on to Highcliff Moor—the things will not be required till evening."

A brief consultation with the stationmaster resulted in the production of a lorry for the packages, and little Rao was left behind to journey with the goods and see that everything was safely conveyed.

It was only after minute directions on this point and a careful examination of the precious automaton to see that it was duly protected from the possibility of damage, that Chanler at length consented to enter the motor, and we were whirled away to Highcliff Moor School.

Most of the guests had already assembled, and were gone down to the cricket ground. But Rex was anxiously awaiting our arrival, and darted out to greet us.

"You had better come over to the cricket at once," he said. "Mrs. Searson is down there. The Doctor is engaged at present. There's an awful row on—the whole of the Fifth Form summoned to his study; and a jolly long jaw he must be giving them—they have been shut up with him for nearly an hour."

Just as he spoke, Dr. Searson himself came hurrying from the house. He is a bustling, active little man—very popular with the boys, and an excellent schoolmaster, but one of the most excitable and impulsive individuals I know. He was flushed and agitated, and could hardly pause to greet us before he began to give expression to his disturbed state of mind.

"Dear me! Dear me!" he exclaimed. "The most unpleasant thing that has happened during the whole of my twenty-five years here! And to occur to-day, of all days in the year, when I was most anxious that everything should pass off quietly and pleasantly. It is really most provoking!"

My sister inquired sympathetically the cause of his annoyance.

"Why, to tell you the truth," replied Dr. Searson, "it is a most unpleasant business; a case of theft—common and paltry theft. And by one of our own bigger boys, too. Unfortunately, it is not the first time that it has occurred. Twice lately, boys in the Fifth Form have complained that money and articles have disappeared from their pockets; but on each of the former occasions the evidence was so confused and uncertain that I concluded the youngsters had been mistaken or had themselves lost what was missing. This time, however, there is no room for doubt.

"The whole of the Fifth went down to Shepherd's Bend to bathe this morning, under the charge of a junior master. The boys leave their clothes, while bathing, in the dressing-shed which we have erected there for their use.

"But on returning from the river, young Stewart at once complained that someone had been interfering with his clothes. To-day is his birthday, and he had received several presents from home—a gold mounted fountain pen, a valuable sportsman's pocket-knife, and £3 in cash.

"There is no doubt that these things were left in his pockets, for only two minutes before undressing he had shown the knife and pen to the master and had asked him if he could give him change for one of the sovereigns. It is equally clear that during the bathing no stranger entered the shed; for Roberts, the master in question, was standing outside near the door the whole time that the boys were in the water. But no sooner were the lads back in the shed than young Stewart discovered that money, pen, and knife were gone—manifestly stolen by one of the boys of the party."

"And what did Mr. Roberts do?" asked Cecilia.

"Do!" cried Dr. Searson indignantly. "Why, he bungled the matter right away by proposing to search the whole company at once—a proposal hotly resented by everyone. And then when he got back here he let the boys loose while he came to report to me—giving the culprit just the opportunity he required to hide his spoils. It is really astounding how incredibly stupid some people can be! . . . And now, of course, the investigation is quite hopeless. I have been lecturing the whole form for the last half-hour without the slightest result.

"Every boy stoutly denies having touched the things—most of them with great indignation, and all of them with protestations of innocence which suggest that the thief, whoever he may he, is no novice at this work of deception.

"Of course, it is almost inconceivable that in a crowded shed any one boy could have done this unnoticed by all his fellows; but even that consideration is no real help, for as you are probably aware the schoolboy code of honor does not allow anyone to tell tales. So that I have been reduced to the necessity of punishing the whole class by detention, and excluding them entirely from today's proceedings, unless the culprit confesses."

I suppose everybody has noticed how people who live their lives within the narrow limits of any institution—a workhouse, a hospital, or a school—are given to exaggerate every incident of their little world, and to treat the most trivial occurrences as if they were matters of momentous importance.

Dr. Searson was an admirable illustration of this tendency. As he faced us on the garden path and related his worry, the concern and consternation written on his face could not have been greater had he been announcing the robbery of the Crown jewels or a complete burglary of the Bank of England. His exaggerated dismay was so comical that my sister and I could hardly keep a straight face.

Chanler Rao was the only one of our party who took the matter quite seriously. He had been listening with deepest interest to this incident of English school life. Now he remarked gravely:

"But this—surely, it is not the true solution—to punish all for the sake of one?"

Dr. Searson turned to him quickly.

"Ah, my dear sir," he said, with the Englishman's ill-concealed contempt for a foreigner's limited knowledge, "you do not see the momentous importance of the question. In our English schools, discipline is a matter of the very first moment; a serious misdemeanor like this—theft of the most disgraceful and abominable character—could not possibly be passed over. Besides, in a conspiracy of silence such as we find here, what else can one do?"

"I do not know anything of school discipline," said Chanler, in his quiet, leisurely fashion, "but I thought I did know something of the English sense of justice. And it cannot be just to punish the many when only one is to blame—especially when it is so easy to discover the real offender."

"Easy!" said Dr. Searson, shrugging his shoulders with a smile. "You should have been in my study with those boys for the last half-hour. You would have realized then that of all created beings on the face of the earth the English schoolboy is the most obstinate when once he has made up his mind to tell you nothing."

"But," insisted Chanler, "the thing is really so simple. I could find you the guilty one in ten minutes."

Dr. Searson gazed at him with polite incredulity. He was beginning to enlarge still further on the peculiar difficulties of dealing with boy-nature, when the arrival of a fresh group of guests demanded his attention, and with an apology he hurried off to greet them.

Rex led us down towards the cricket ground. But all the way, Chanler was greatly exercised by this instance of what he stigmatized as injustice and the abuse of authority.

"It is worthy of savagery," he exclaimed, "to chastise the whole tribe for the crime of one. And all to save a little trouble; for it is so easy to find out the truth if you really want to know it. I never thought to find in an English school such abominable, callous injustice!"

His indignation was so pronounced and voluble that I found it almost as comical as Dr. Searson's own exaggerated concern.

"Here," continued Rao, "is the simplest of all possible problems: a thief to be selected out of a very limited number of individuals—fifteen, I think Dr. Searson said. The time, place, and manner of the robbery are all known—the articles are well-defined and easily recognizable. And the culprit is a mere youth—a lad who, even if, as our excitable pedagogue hints, he has been guilty of similar small pilferings on former occasions, can hardly yet be really sufficiently expert in deception to hide his wrongdoing effectively.

"And yet this learned Doctor of Laws, who is supposed to be sufficiently clever to be entrusted with the training of your boys, is so absolutely blind that he can only confess his helplessness and lock up the whole form. Bah! he is not fit for his work, this Doctor of yours!"

Chanler's criticism of our host was growing so uncomplimentary that my sister feared lest people round about might overhear it—particularly as the appearance of our Hindu friend in his gorgeous native costume was attracting everybody's notice, She therefore endeavored to change the subject by an attempt to interest him in the game we were watching.

To some extent she succeeded in her effort. Chanler had never witnessed a cricket match before, and he plied her with innumerable questions. Whether her explanations of the intricacies of the game were altogether clear to his mind is somewhat doubtful—his chief admiration being expressed for the skill with which the bowler managed to hit the moving bat almost every time, with an utter inability to understand why anybody ever got out.

But I could see that, all through, his attention was divided. Again and again, he returned to the subject of Dr. Searson's stupidity and injustice. And, as I moved away to greet some friends whom I recognized on the other side of the ground, I heard him declare emphatically:

"I shall not perform to-night unless those poor boys are allowed to be present."

I need not describe in detail the events of the day. It passed off much as such Speech Days do. The cricket match ended as usual in a big victory for the school; the Old Boys, summoned from office and counting-house and law-court, were hopelessly defeated by these youngsters who still enjoyed the advantage of daily play and constant practice together. The tea which followed on the lawn was the usual scramble, in which one had either to starve or else to run the risks to a middle-aged digestion involved in the consumption of any rich cakes within one's reach.

Then we all adjourned to the big schoolroom to hear the headmaster's report, and to listen to the "exercises" of the boys—a scene from a Greek play, which I am certain none of the visitors understood in the least; a French dialogue, with the usual English school accent; and a declamation in Latin, which the fashionable pronunciation now in vogue rendered an absolutely new and incomprehensible language to us old stagers.

It was during the Greek play that my sister called my attention to the fact that the boys of the Fifth Form were present after all. I had noticed at tea that Cissie was in confidential communication with Dr. Searson, and I had sufficient belief in my sister's powers of persuasion to guess that if she took the matter in hand, the Doctor's somewhat hasty decree would probably be revised. Her whispered communication now proved that my anticipation had been justified.

"I persuaded Dr. Searson to let them come—it seemed such a shame to exclude the whole lot like that. But he is a very obstinate man, and for quite a long time he absolutely refused to go back on his decision. It was only when I enlisted the services of Mrs. Searson, and made the question a matter of personal favor to myself, that between us we at last persuaded him to relent."

Here a bald-headed old Colonel in front of us, who pretended that he was following the Greek, turned round in silent rebuke of Cecilia's distracting chatter, and she had to hold her peace. But it was not long before she again found an opportunity to whisper:

"And isn't it interesting? Chanler Rao has promised to solve the mystery of those things that were stolen; he declares that before he leaves the platform to-night he will hand over the guilty boy to the headmaster. I am dying to see how he can possibly do it."

For myself, I was seriously disturbed by my sister's communication. I thought from the first that Searson was a little indiscreet in making known at all the unfortunate occurrence; a wiser and calmer man would have dealt with the difficulty privately without troubling any of his guests with an incident that was certainly not altogether to the credit of his school—though that, of course, was his own business. But it was a very different matter for Chanler Rao, in his capacity of public entertainer, to deal with the affair on the platform.

I knew quite enough of our Indian friend's love of dramatic effect, and of the sensational methods he was so fond of employing, to dread his handling of so delicate a problem; and I was altogether doubtful of his discretion or his realization of the risk he ran of causing grave annoyance to both Dr. Searson and the parents of the boys. As far as I could gather, the Doctor had not mentioned the theft to anyone in the room, except to our own party;

and it would be a gross breach of confidence if Chanler should thus make public a scandal to the injury of the school. And as we were entirely responsible for Chanler Rao's introduction on this occasion, I felt it my duty at once to stop this proposed investigation.

An interval in the program gave me my opportunity, and I hurried out to the classroom where Chanler and his little son were engaged in their preparations for the coming entertainment.

For some moments, my tapping at the door was disregarded, and when at length Chanler did appear, he seemed somewhat inclined to resent the interruption. He had already assumed his most professional manner and bearing.

"Why this interference with my preparations?" he asked protestingly. "Do you not realize that every moment is now needed if I am to be ready at seven?"

I rather resented the rapidity with which my dusky friend could pass from an obsequiousness which often sickened me to a lordly superiority which in anyone else would have been positively rude. In no very amiable mood I explained my anxiety about his intention, and requested that all attempts to deal with the unpleasant incident of the bathing party might be excluded from his program.

Chanler listened with blank surprise.

"But why?" he asked, gazing at me in astonishment. "One would think you knew the thief and wanted to screen him. Surely, for the sake of all concerned, it is most desirable that he should be discovered?"

I endeavored to make clear the precise point of my objection, and to explain the risk of giving offense to Dr. Searson and casting a reflection on the good name of his school if this unfortunate occurrence were made public. But Chanler cut me short at once.

"Of course, I understand all that," he said. "It would be most undesirable for everybody to know about it. And I have arranged for the whole thing to be done quietly. The culprit will be discovered in the ordinary course of my performance and handed over to the Doctor—and nobody will really know what he has done, except the persons to whom our friend himself chooses to reveal the facts. You need not worry at all. I shall lay my hand upon the thief in such a way that only those who already know the story could possibly guess what I am doing. Let your mind be perfectly at ease on that point."

And with that I had to be content—though, I must confess, I went back to my place in the great schoolroom with a mind far from easy, and heartily wishing that this obstinate Hindu, with his fatal propensity for detective investigation, were safely back in London. My only consolation lay in the hopelessness of the task he had set himself.

It seemed absolutely incredible that a problem which had baffled the experience of the headmaster himself could really be solved at all by this Eastern charlatan; and I trusted to an early realization of his failure, rather than to his discretion, to preserve us from the unpleasantness threatened by his determination.

As I rejoined my sister, Dr. Searson was making his final speech. He explained that in the ordinary course of things they would now have completed their usual Speech Day program, but that, owing to the kindness of Colonel and Mrs. Thornton, there was on this occasion an additional entertainment provided in the shape of Chanler Rao's exhibition of real Eastern magic.

A burst of cheering from the boys at the announcement caused my sister some embarrassment, and effectually checked the Doctor's tendency to embark on a scholastic disquisition on the antiquity and development of Indian magic.

He contented himself instead with a brief acknowledgment that he had himself witnessed Chanler's performances in London, and was convinced of the genuineness of his claim and the cleverness of his legerdemain. He was sure that the present company would find the exposition most interesting in itself—and even valuable from an educational point of view as an authentic example of the magic practiced from early time by this ancient people, who formed so important a part of our great Empire.

Then the stage was cleared for Chanler's performance, while the audience settled themselves down with a genuine expectation of being entertained—very different from the polite pretense of being interested which had characterized their reception of the earlier portions of the program.

Now I must confess that from the moment of Chanler's appearance on the platform, a great deal of my anxiety vanished at once. Our Hindu friend, as I have already hinted, was rather an embarrassing acquaintance in private life—you were never quite sure what he might be doing next, or how far his imperfect familiarity with Western civilization might land him (and you) in a difficulty. But on the stage, Chanler was thoroughly at home at once and seemed instinctively to know the right thing to do.

With quiet dignity, he introduced himself as a humble citizen of the British Empire, and paid a graceful little tribute to the beneficent rule of the great King-Emperor under whose sway East and West were linked in the enjoyment of justice and liberty.

Then he won the hearts of the parents by expressing his unbounded admiration of British boyhood—especially of the fine body of "young and noble collegians" whom he saw before him. And he captivated the boys themselves by a half-comical commiseration of the scholastic burdens they had to bear, and raised a ripple of laughter by confessing that he knew all about it through his repeated failures to satisfy the Calcutta examiners for his degree.

All this was said with that curious mixture of dignity and humility which would be absurd in a European, but which seemed so exactly to fit in with the character and personality of this gorgeous representative of a distant land.

Then, with a pleasant expression of his delight in relieving their strenuous studies of modern learning with an exhibition of the ancient wonders and wisdom of the East, he began his performance.

Here, again, I could not but recognize that Chanler had exactly gauged what was required of him. The tricks were chosen with a special appropriateness to the audience he had come to entertain. Of course, there was the wonderful growth of the mango tree, and the basket in which little Rao is apparently pierced again and again with a sword—no exhibition of real Indian magic could be complete without these much-discussed marvels.

But the other items—the egg on the side-table which persistently refused to remain an egg and hatched into a crowing bantam cock whenever Chanler's back was turned, the huge cane which changed into a gorgeous bouquet of hot-house flowers the moment our Hindu attempted to chastise his little son with it, the white mice which Chanler produced from the pockets of boys all over the room—these were wonders specially devised for the occasion, and produced roars of laughter from his appreciative audience. Then we had the magic stewpot in which two pigeons, plucked and trussed, were placed to cook over a. spirit lamp, with the result that a. few minutes later, when the lid of the pot was raised, two live birds flew out and fluttered round the room.

Then followed the wonderful bottle which appeared to pour forth whatever liquid the audience might choose; the daring trick in which little Rao apparently catches in his teeth the bullet from the revolver fired by his father; and the startling thought-reading and "second-sight" experiments which seemed too puzzling for applause, and left the onlookers speechless with amazement.

Then the stage was cleared for the great feature of the evening—the production of Chanler Rao's new automaton, Khokan.

Now, I can tell you nothing of the secret of this marvelous mechanical figure, which afterwards drew all London and made Chanler famous. Even to this day, I believe, no one has really solved the mystery.

Of course, as Rao was careful to explain, there may be quite sufficient mechanism inside the figure to account entirely for the movements by which Khokan is enabled to write down his revelations. The puzzle is as to the directing intelligence which guides his answers. Chanler himself never approaches the automaton at all during the performance, except to wind up the machinery and to renew, from time to time, the paper on which Khokan writes his replies to questions.

The figure—an almost life-size representation of an Indian *fakir*—rests upon a transparent glass cylinder which apparently excludes all possibility of outside influence. And yet, when once Khokan has been placed in position with the pencil in hand and the paper on the sloping board in from of him, there seems to be hardly any question or problem to which he will not furnish a ready answer.

On this occasion Chanler began by requesting the assistance of a "committee of vigilance." By objecting to the sixth Form as too old, and the Fourth as too young, be secured the services of the boys of the Fifth Form whom he seated on a semicircle of chairs round the automaton on the platform. Then, opening a sort of door in the back of the figure, he showed them the mass of complicated machinery which moved the hand, at the same time demonstrating the impossibility that any live person could be hidden in so small a space. The door was then locked, the automaton duly wound up, and the writing began.

In deference, I suppose, to the place and occasion, the first questions answered were of the nature of mathematical problems. Khokan extracted the square root and cube root of a series of preposterous numbers. Then he wrote out the value of pi to fifty places of decimals. Then he added up four long columns of figures written out by the boys themselves. These papers were duly handed to Dr. Searson, who after a brief examination, declared, amidst deafening applause from the spectators, that the results were all perfectly correct.

Then we passed to more general experiments. Khokan was invited to give details of various articles handed to Chanler—the number of a boy's watch, the dates of various coins, the postmarks on the envelopes of letters. All these were furnished written in a somewhat jerky and angular handwriting, but with absolute accuracy.

Then the boys on the platform were directed to join hands, one of them grasping the disengaged left hand of the automaton, while Chanler requested the figure to write down the names of some articles of which any two boys might happen to be thinking simultaneously.

There was a slight pause after the question. Then Khokan's pencil was seen to be moving rapidly. A moment later Chanler took the paper and read out what was written.

"A gold-mounted fountain-pen. A valuable pocket-knife. Three sovereigns in gold. These articles lie hidden. Khokan can find them."

A movement of surprise was manifest amongst the lads on the platform as the missing articles were thus enumerated. For a moment Rao himself appeared to be puzzled by what he had read. Then he called his son to help, and between them they wheeled off Khokan into the adjoining classroom. Little Rao came back to his place at once. After a brief absence, Chanler also returned to the stage, and addressed the audience.

"I find," he said, "that Khokan believes that these articles—a gold-mounted fountain-pen, a sportsman's pocket-knife, and three sovereigns—have been put away somewhere carefully; that only one person on the platform is aware of the exact place in which they lie, and that the secret is unknown to everybody else. But Khokan is certain that he can discover the one person who alone knows where these articles are deposited. Is it your wish that the experiment should be made?"

Of course, there was an immediate shout of "Yes," from the boys in the audience, followed by loud applause.

"Then," said Chanler, "what I shall ask is this: Each of you boys on the platform will go in turn alone into the classroom. Each on entering will shut the door behind him, and will be alone with Khokan. Then you will take the right hand of the automaton in yours, just as if you were shaking hands, while you count ten.

"In the case of all who do not know, nothing will happen—they will just come back to their seats. But in the case of the one person who does know where these articles are the matter will be very different—the touch of Khokan will set an indelible mark upon him that I shall recognize at once.

"Of course, the success of the experiment entirely depends upon each one of you carrying out these directions faithfully. You will each be quite alone with the automaton—nobody will be there to see you—and I can only trust to your honor to carry out what I have described. Anyone who is afraid to do this had better say so and withdraw."

Of course, when the matter was so put, nobody did withdraw. For the most part, indeed, the boys concerned seemed to enjoy the fun. One by one they entered the classroom; one by one they came back to their seats. In ten minutes we had before us a row of some fifteen boys all intently gazing at their own hands, and manifestly discovering nothing.

It was, however, very different when Chanler came round to investigate for himself. He bent low over each boy's right hand as it was extended towards him, and the audience waited eagerly for the result.

One, two, three, four, five, six boys successfully passed under his scrutiny, and smiled as he shook his head. At the seventh hand, he paused for a moment and looked up into the owner's face, saying something in a low voice which was inaudible to us in the room.

The lad appeared confused and turned pale; then, after a hurried glance round, he nodded his head. Chanler Rao at once turned to where the headmaster was seated.

"Dr. Searson," he said aloud, "our young friend thinks he would rather explain our little mystery to you privately. Perhaps you will see him in your study alone."

The audience seemed a little perplexed and disappointed at this somewhat indefinite and doubtful outcome of the experiment, and it required all Chanler's skill to divert their attention to his concluding tricks. But as we filed out of the schoolroom and met Dr. Searson coming from his study, I learnt from him that the automaton had been entirely successful; the purloiner of the birthday gifts was discovered.

"THE AUTOMATON?" said Chanler Rao, when I had sufficiently expressed my wonder and curiosity. "Why, surely you must see for yourself that a clockwork thing like that could discover nothing. Khokan is but the outward means adopted to cover my methods. It was *I* who found out that miserable, dishonest youngster."

"But I don't see," I said, still entirely in the dark. "How could you possibly know?"

Chanler gazed at me with a sort of kindly pity.

"Consider," said he, "the working of a guilty mind. The innocent lad rather enjoys the fun of being sent into that room to shake hands with an automaton. 'Hullo! here's his silly old doll that is going to tell tales. Well, here goes—he won't get much out of me!' . . . But the guilty? 'No,' he says to himself. 'Of course, it's all rot—simply nonsense to suppose that a thing like that could tell anything at all. But still—it's as well to be on the safe side; you never know what these *fakirs* are really up to. And as I am quite alone, and the old buffer will never be any the wiser, I think I'll just keep my hands off his diabolical automaton altogether.'"

"But—" I was beginning.

"Stay a moment," said Rao. "You know the perfume of the orphil root? No? Ah, well, to your Western nose I daresay the odor would be hardly perceptible. But to the child of the East, the least atom is pungent and unmistakable. The hands of Khokan were smeared over with orphil. Consequently, when I came to do my little bit of palmistry, I was able in a moment to distinguish by the absence of the perfume the hand which had not dared to touch my detective automaton. I gave the owner the choice between immediate public exposure and a private interview with the Doctor—and, as you saw, he at once chose the latter."

THE ADVENTURES OF WORRY-WORRY WILLIAMS

LEAVITT ASHLEY KNIGHT

These three Worry-Worry Williams stories were published in *Everybody's Magazine* in 1913 and 1914. One could possibly argue that Worry-Worry Williams was the first OCD detective. . . .

THE FIRST ADVENTURE

I WAS BORN on the wrong planet.

Everybody on this dismal lump of dirt is built on a different pattern from mine. During the past year I've held sixteen jobs. All my bosses say the same thing: I ought to be in a padded cell; my mind wanders; I lack a sense of responsibility; I loaf; I dawdle over idiotic trifles; I make mountains of mole-hills.

Well, maybe they're right. I'm a misfit.

Mackintosh & Lowser, engineers' supplies, kicked me out last summer because I fell behind a week in posting their ledger. But I couldn't help it. Their previous bookkeepers had always written Fwd, instead of F'w'd, in carrying an account forward to the next page; so I had to go through all the books for the last fifteen years and insert the apostrophes. I couldn't allow such a mistake to stand, could I? When old Mackintosh discovered my correction, though, he screeched like a tugboat in a fog and threw a paper-weight at my head.

I've never been back to collect my wages from him.

Next I found a quiet post as assistant paymaster for Higginson & Digo, contractors. Four hundred of their Italians were filling in a swamp back of Jersey City, and it was my duty to keep a record of their names, addresses, time lost, and overtime. Well, one day a new shovel-artist on the pay-roll told me that he lived at 1189 Bleecker Street, Manhattan. I was sure that there was no such number, so I investigated. While I was doing this, the next day, the Italian left us and never came back—not even for his pay. That made it very difficult for me to learn his place of residence. Not a janitor in all Bleecker Street could identify the man. (It took me three whole days to consult them all.) I sought out the Italian consul, but he couldn't help me. I went to Ellis Island to scrutinize the records of all Italians who had passed through the immigration office. And I had checked off about nineteen thousand entries when Higginson & Digo's superintendent lost his temper because I hadn't found time to make up the pay-roll for the week.

Some of the laborers were quite peevish, too, because the firm wouldn't pay them off until the pay-roll had been made up and checked off properly. And one of them hit me with the back of his shovel while I was running away.

Next, the famous criminal lawyer, Morris B. Heiter, gave me twelve dollars a week for managing an elaborate card index, wherein he filed complete records of his clients and those who might be clients some day. That was the jolliest sinecure ever! Oily old Heiter slapped me on the back every day and vowed that I was a prize cataloguer. And he was right, I don't mind saying. I introduced three hundred special classifications into that index and put in cross-references for all of them. At any hour of day or night Heiter could turn to my index and find how many times Grubinsky had been acquitted of loft-looting, when Sooty Sue had served her last term on the Island for "jostling" on the cross-town cars, or how many pawnbrokers were hiding collapsible jimmies in their safes for Heiter's old customers.

Heiter was the only man in the world after my own heart. He was conscientious about little things. He knew that they were more important than big trifles. And he could not drop any subject of inquiry until he had discovered all that there was to be known about it. He was almost a genuine scientist—almost, I say. In only one trait was he lacking. He was not quite impersonal enough.

For instance: When he found that I had catalogued all the articles which his clients had been acquitted of stealing, he grew very cross. The next day he looked up the cards on One-Thumb Louie, the big jewel thief whom he had thrice delivered from Sing Sing, and discovered that I had written on it: "Color, weight, and cutting of ruby which Louie was accused of stealing on April 15, 1904, are identical with those of the stone in the scarf-pin which Mr. Heiter wears to church." At that my boss hopped up and down, swore, then suddenly hushed himself—and discharged me.

"Mr. Worry-Worry Williams," he said with a greenish grin, "you take little things too seriously. You'd better quit bothering over trifles. The strong-arm man will get you if you don't look out. Now beat it! And if I hear that you're chattering about what you've learned in this office, I'll—"

But I didn't stop to hear the threat out. I knew Heiter's ways.

Well, this is enough to show you that I'm out of touch with the times. Heiter was right; I do take little things too seriously. They excite my curiosity, and it will not give me peace until it has been appeased. It is an insatiable demon.

"You're going to starve to death, young fellow!" is what the man prophesied who discharged me from my sixteenth job last week. "The world hasn't any place for your kind of rattle-brain."

So I thought, too, as I shambled out of his office, bearing in my pay-envelope the only eight dollars I possessed. But you never can tell. There is a market even for misfits, as any tailor will tell you.

Three days ago, I was looking over the stern of the Hoboken ferry, wondering how it would feel to go down for the third time, and how I would look when the police-boat found me a month later under some reeking dock. Only three days ago! And here I sit, in my cozy new bachelor apartment off Gramercy Park, sipping ginger ale as I write my adventures with a gold-mounted fountain pen, and wondering between the lines whether I'll dine on Fifth Avenue or on Broadway.

And all the while, in a little mahogany desk near my study window, there lies a fresh bank-book; the few ink marks on its first page will rid me of care for five years. Me, Worry-Worry Williams, Champion Misfit!

THE WATERS of the upper bay sparkled and fluttered as I watched them on that eventful morning three days ago. All the passengers on the ferry hung along the rail, sniffing the warm spring air and wondering aloud how soon swimming would be salubrious at Coney Island; or rather, to speak precisely, all were doing so except myself and one other. I was staring dismally across the world, figuring how my lonely eight dollars might keep me alive until I found my seventeenth job. Between my gloomy computations I compiled statistics about my fellow voyagers.

That's an old habit of mine, you know. I've a cigar-box full of such records. I can tell you how many blondes rode on the New Rochelle local leaving Grand Central Station at 5:23 P. M., March 19, 1910. I am accurately posted on the gross percentage of young ladies under sixteen and over forty who chew gum on the northbound subway between Brooklyn Bridge and Fourteenth Street about nine o'clock in the morning (Sundays excepted). There's some mighty fine sociology buried underneath those figures!

Did you know, for instance, that all the girls who chew out loud wear hand-made lace collars? And that eighty-nine per cent. of those who wear hand-made lace collars pin newspapers under their skirts to make a noise like real silk petticoats? And do you know how to discover this scientifically; that is, without being arrested for disturbing the peace or the skirts? It is very simple. You simply . . . *

The only other passenger who was unstirred by the light and the merriment of the waters was a tall man. As he leaned restlessly against a stanchion, with his longish, dark head adroop and his nervous fingers tugging at his pointed chin, the morning sun shone slantingly across his cheeks and showed them grooved with the deep wrinkles that only Black Care chisels. (There are only nine species of wrinkles. Some day I hope to write a treatise on them.)

There was nothing unusual about his dress (a $27.50 Peters & Hicks blue serge, and all the rest in tune with it). Nor was there a hint of strangeness in his haircut; nor in his stride when, a

* Editor's Note.—In order to make space for other articles in this issue, the Editors have been compelled to cut out the next fifteen pages of Mr. Williams's MS., all of which deal with vital statistics. We shall turn the same over to the Bureau of Municipal Research.

moment later, he moved back and forth across the deck, his hands clasped behind him and his coat flung open. A most ordinary man indeed, I concluded; probably a poor devil like myself and a million others, out of work, out of cash, out of courage, and out of temper with himself and the world.

But all of a sudden the fellow did the most extraordinary thing, upset all my estimates, and set the wheels of adventure spinning.

Barely six feet from me he halted, scratched his head, pulled forth a memorandum-book from one vest pocket and a pencil from another, and started jotting something down. The pencil point broke. He sharpened it. Again it snapped in writing the very first word. A second time he sharpened it, now peevishly. Once more the graphite crumbled, and it continued to do so until it had been whittled down to an unusable butt. The man threw this overboard and fumbled through his vest pockets. In these, as his coat was flung wide open, I distinctly perceived two more pencils, both neatly sharpened. The man's fingers closed upon one of them and pulled it forth. But the instant he set eyes upon it, he mumbled in vexation and thrust it back. Likewise with the second one.

Then he turned to a bystander, borrowed a pencil, jotted down his memorandum, and sauntered off with a sigh of relief.

"What the deuce!" I exclaimed. "Why?"

Why indeed? Wasn't that the most irrational act you ever heard of? Was he a miser in the matter of pencils? No, for he whittled the bad pencil too prodigally; a miser would have gently hacked off half an inch, letting the shortest possible nub of graphite protrude.

Well, perhaps the two pencils were architect's tracing graphite; that kind would not make a legible mark on ordinary paper. I rubbed my hands with joy over this theory—but only for a few seconds. Then it collapsed. My eleventh job had been in an architect's office, where I had bought the draughting supplies. And I had there learned to classify all makes and varieties of pencils. Only too well did I know the six and only six styles of extra-hards; and the pair in the queer stranger's pocket were none of them. His were common, cheap, red-painted things, with erasers attached. (Extra-hards never carry erasers.)

Yes! Only miserable, one-cent school pencils!

How the accursed puzzle worried me! Just as surely as the Lord made me Worry-Worry Williams, I *had* to solve it. I would ask the stranger to explain—

At that moment the boat bumped into her dock, the passengers crowded forward, the iron gates shot up, and the human stream squirted down the pier, hiding somewhere in its midst my man. Off I dashed, forgetting jobs and poverty, in search of him.

Where the long, dim passageways of the ferry station debouch into the clamorous expanses of West Street, the crowd divided; one-half trickling into Vesey Street, while the other half spattered a little northward toward Barclay Street. Trembling in fear of defeat, I sprinted at random in the latter direction until I had overtaken the first man off the boat. But neither he nor any of those in his wake was the mysterious one.

Into a cross street I shot and, a hundred yards northward, came upon the other current of travelers. A shrill squeak of joy escaped me. Not very far beyond, my quarry was sauntering across the street, arm in arm with a stout old gentleman who shuffled along feebly and with a slight limp.

I made a move to cross the street too; but a thick tumult of trucks barred my way for a full minute. When I finally pierced the line, my mysterious stranger had reached the corner of Church Street. Somewhat indistinctly I saw him leaning against a pillar of the elevated railway, comparing notes with his companion. From that distance it seemed as though the pair exchanged papers and scribbled something on the documents. That done, they shook hands; my quarry hurried southward, and the lame old gentleman disappeared around the corner toward the north.

I ran like a thief, ducking between porters, swerving from the uncertain paths of baboon-armed draymen who sweated and cursed under great boxes of chinaware and cut glass which the cellars of the neighborhood were spewing up.

As I neared the corner, some other men and a pack of boys began to run; whereat I laughed breathlessly, for I took it to be a case of Social Imitation, a phenomenon of the city concerning which I have compiled many fascinating statistics.

People are worse than sheep. If you crane your neck skyward on Broadway during the rush hour, everybody will be doing the same within two minutes. And as for . . . *

Just beyond the street corner, in front of a dirty little fruit and hand-out-lunch stand, the crowd of runners had focused and come to a halt. A patrolman was pushing them back, while he yelled to somebody: "'Phone fer an ambulance, an' fast too!" Then a rift opened through the sudden press of humanity, and I saw a dusty, black heap on the pavement; a shapeless and still heap.

It was the lame man! His upturned face stared with sightless eyes, and his cheeks shone with a preternatural, deep cherry flush.

"Apoplexy!" muttered the patrolman. "I've seen 'em before. Once in Park Row last spring—"

"He wasn't three feet from me," the fruit-stand man explained to his greedy audience, "and makin' as if to pull out a dime fer his oranges—he allus buys two every mornin'—w'en he jist crumpled t'gether like a piece o' wet paper—"

"My Lord!" a big, powerful man gasped, as he thrust himself to the fore, "it's Mr. Bannack! The wholesale-crockery man over in Park Place! How the devil did he drop off like this?"

He started to spin an incoherent biography of the poor dead gentleman, but I fled. I had to catch my man, you know, and ask him about his pencils. Cursing myself for allowing a trifling street incident to interfere with serious work, I scurried southward. But in vain: the thick tangles and ravelings of traffic had swept the stranger out of sight.

"You'll not beat me!" I cried and shook a fist at the streaming multitudes; "I'll find him yet! I'll ask at the late Mr. Bannack's crockery-store! Somebody there will know him!"

How I raced back to the scene of sudden death! I must find the big man, pump him, have him guide me to the crockery-store.

Didn't I tell you at the outset that the whole world was against me? Well, if you wish more proof, here it is! When I reached the fruit-stand, the ambulance had left with its still burden, and the crowd had melted away. I tell you, my knees went weak at the sight

* Sixteen pages of MS. here omitted.—The Editors.

of that empty street! People and even things inanimate were leagued in a dumb conspiracy to thwart my innocent desires.

Rage seized me, violent rage; I shook my fist at the dusty spot beside the curbing where the old gentleman had fallen, and raved at him for having deflected me from my search. And as I raved my eye shifted ever so slightly from the faint, misshapen stamp of perished humanity on the thick, loose filth of the cobble-stones; and there—snug against the curb—lay a pencil.

A common, cheap, red-painted pencil with an attached eraser. A pencil exactly like those which the dead man's last companion on earth had carried and had not used!

With a yell that made the fruit-vender hop, I lunged at the blessed find, seized it, and fled like a trailed thief. My prize was either one of the original pair or else out of the same factory. The worried stranger with the furrowed cheeks might have lent it when he passed over some papers. Or perhaps the crockery-dealer and his vanished friend bought their office supplies at the same place. But no! This couldn't be; for the man on the ferry wasn't the sort that had an office. He behaved like a poor clerk out of work, and he dressed the part. I scratched my chin. "This," I mused, "must be figured out from the beginning!"

I stepped into a stationery shop, bought six pads of cheap paper, and went over to the cool quiet of St. Paul's churchyard. There, on a cool stone in the blue shadow of the rear entry, I sat down, braced a pad on my knees, and started to compute, by a new logical method, the exasperating puzzle. I sharpened the dead man's pencil, put it to the paper—

And it made a mark exceedingly faint and undecipherable. It was the mark of an HHHHHH! And yet it was a common one-cent school pencil with a cheap, grimy eraser attached!*

* Mr. Williams sent us the six pads of paper covered with his computations and requested us to insert the same at this point in the narrative. Unfortunately, though, the mathematicians whom we have consulted report that only nine experts in the country understand Mr. Williams's symbols and equations. So it seems wise to omit the entire argument, except a brief summary of its conclusion.— The Editors.

So, you see, all the symbolic equations yield a zero member; and this, of course, indicates that there is no rational hypothesis to explain why a man who, as I have proved, is not a draughtsman, should carry in his vest pocket two useless pencils nicely sharpened. We must therefore accept one of the two possible irrational hypotheses: (1) The man was insane, or else (2) the pencils were placed in his pocket by some accident.

Similarly are we forced to a non-rational, residual hypothesis to explain how a one-cent shoddy school pencil comes to have the expensive graphite of an architect's tracing-pencil. We must infer that some accident happened in the factory. Presumably a green apprentice dumped a tray of HHHHHH leads into the wrong machine.

The church clock was dinning four in the afternoon when I came back to the wretched world of Worry-Worry Williams, the worthless bookkeeper with $7.70 and no job. I had been squatting on the cold stone and an empty stomach five hours and twenty-eight minutes! And yet I bubbled over with joy. My work was done, crowned with success.

A newsboy passed, short-cutting through the churchyard. I bought an evening paper to peruse the "Help Wanted, Bookkeepers, Stenographers, etc.," column; and I gave the youngster a dime, with never a pang. I felt very good, you know; and then, too, the sheet was worth ten cents. For half of the first page was occupied by the late Mr. Otto Bannack, the wholesale-crockery dealer.

Mr. Bannack had been poisoned!

The District Attorney had offered a reward of two thousand dollars for the arrest of the unknown murderers. The dead man's brother had put up three thousand dollars. A famous detective had already been retained. The Central Office men were laying plans. And—there was in sight not the faintest clue, not a wisp of evidence! Said the paper:

> It was at first supposed that Mr. Bannack had been stricken with apoplexy. But not a trace of this affliction was discernible at the inquest. Dr. Murley, the

> ambulance surgeon, declared that the peculiar congestion at the surface of the body would ordinarily indicate that Mr. Bannack had inhaled the fumes of hydrocyanic acid. "But this theory does not fit the present case," he added emphatically. "For Mr. Bannack was in the open air. There could not have been gas enough at large to hurt anybody, even supposing that it had been leaking badly in the vicinity. In the next place, it couldn't have been leaking; for nobody was making it thereabouts. And finally, the poison kills instantly; so that, if he had inhaled it, he must have done so on the very spot where he dropped. In that case, though, half a dozen passers-by would have been killed too, for that number were walking within a few paces of him."

The paper also said that the suicide theory must be dismissed. Mr. Bannack was a deeply religious man, perpetually jolly, in good health, prosperous, and on the eve of great good fortune. A patent glazing process which he had lately perfected had just been purchased by one of the great French potteries. Had he lived only a week longer, Mr. Bannack would have received three hundred thousand dollars for his secret formulas.

"Well," I reminded myself, "having proved that the pencil was extra hard, Mr. Worry-Worry must now hustle after a job. Man can not live on mysteries alone!" So I picked up the paper and turned to the "Help Wanted" columns. Four or five advertisements I checked with my new hybrid pencil by dint of flattening the newspaper against a flagstone and pressing the graphite hard.

Then of a sudden I stopped and gnashed my teeth. I had proved that the stranger either was crazy or else had put the HHHHHH pencils in his pocket by accident; *but I had not proved which of these alternatives was true!* Bungler! Fool! Rattle-brain that I was, to cover six pads of paper with computations and at last to leave the task unfinished!

I flung the newspaper down and dashed out of the mute churchyard into the swirl and roar of Broadway's evening rush hour. Before me swam, like a mocking specter, the image of the stranger with the seared cheeks. Him I must find and ask—courteously, of course—whether he was a lunatic or accidentally in possession of HHHHHH pencils.

Old Mrs. Bannack could not recognize the stranger from my description of him. Mr. Henry Bannack, the dead man's younger brother who had offered the reward, insisted that no such man had ever entered the crockery store.

"Well, then," I pressed on, "with whom did the mur—er—the deceased have business dealings recently?"

"Only with Limongi Frères, the Paris pottery firm—" Mr. Henry stopped sharply and eyed me narrowly. "I suppose you have some authority to pursue these very personal inquiries? From the District Attorney?"

"No!" I explained promptly. "Fact is, I'm not interested in the tragedy which has descended upon your family. I'm trying to find out why the stranger was carrying two pencils that he couldn't use—"

The Bannacks tightened their lips and turned me out of doors—quite rudely, too. So there I stood, in the thickening dusk before their tall and gloomy mansion, with only one slender clue. Limongi Frères! There was one chance in ten thousand that the man with the mongrel pencil could be found at that company's office. If that hint failed me—

On my way back to my Hoboken boarding-house I bought every extra edition of every evening paper; and I studied all the twenty-nine special reports, interviews, and editorials about the murder. A preposterous smother of hysteria and nonsense they were! To think that sane men and women could lash themselves and the public into such a frenzy over an ordinary murder of a mere respectable citizen! The case was too simple even to excite the intellect of a ten-year-old. Even the police could handle it unaided.

If Mr. Bannack was murdered, somebody had a motive for committing the act. This motive would be discovered by an inspection of Mr. Bannack's personal and business relations. And it was inevitable that, within a few days, a chemist would detect the poison. The rest of the problem would take care of itself: merely eliminate from your reckoning those persons who might have done the black deed but can prove that they did not. One person will be unable to do this, and he or she will be the guilty party.

How petty and fruitless it all was beside my intricate and unique problem!

LIMONGI FRÈRES' OFFICES filled the thirty-second floor of the Cottonworth Tower. Eight glorious, wind-swept, sun-flooded rooms there were, and in the fairest of them, on the following morning, Mr. James Lamonte, the firm's American manager, was listening intently to my description of the man with the pencils.

"You are a detective on the Bannack murder case, I take it." Mr. Lamonte bowed ever so slightly.

"Of course!" I replied glibly, and therewith I lied whitely. I was taking no chances on being thrown off this, my last clue.

"I know no such man," the manager shook his head. "But I haven't been in New York long. You'd better ask the rest of our office staff."

From man to man he passed me, and each shook his head. There was no acquaintance of theirs with a longish dark head, nervous fingers, pointed chin, and deeply grooved cheeks.

"The shipping clerk over at the Belgian Peachblow Vase Company looks a little like that," somebody said. "But his chin isn't very pointed—"

A door swung behind us, *and in walked my man!*

"I'm from the Belgian Peachblow Vase Company," he addressed the manager. "The last consignment of enamel plate we received from you did not tally with the invoice. I'd like to adjust—"

"Excuse me a moment!" I cried. "These mere business matters can wait. I have an important question, Mr.—er—"

"Murray." The shipping clerk scowled swiftly at me. "And I'm in a hurry."

"Mr. Murray, I shall detain you only an instant. Pray explain this!" And I held out the mysterious pencil. Never shall I forget the flicker of emotions that made hideous the clerk's ill-favored features. More swiftly than the shifting of light on moving waters his hue changed from ashen gray to the bilious green of sick terror. He took the pencil, as though hypnotized, and fixed his gaze upon it.

"You had two of them on the ferry-boat yesterday," I continued. "This is the one which Mr. Bannack was carrying when he died. You lent it to him as you walked up from the pier with him. It is a very peculiar pencil. There is none like it made in any factory. I have been examining it—"

"Damn, you!" Murray shrieked. "Devil from hell! You have been living in my brain like a worm! Only a worm in my brain could have found my scheme. I have never breathed it even to myself. I have carried it out, step by step, in my own room behind locked doors. I have hidden my connections with Bannack and his great secret. And now, after I have won the prize that would make me rich, comes this imp of Satan, traps me like a rat. . . . Ha? . . . I'll never see jail! . . ." A hideous shriek escaped him.

And, as Mr. Lamonte rushed to the telephone for the police, Murray thrust the pencil point into his mouth, bit off the lead, and swallowed it, laughing horribly and making loathsome faces at us.

When the two patrolmen arrived, Murray lay dead. Pretty soon we had a chemist at work on the pencil; and before the newsboys were crying the red-ink Murder Extra in the streets below, we had torn the veils from the double mystery. We split the pencil open and found it not graphite, but *a stick of potassium cyanide crystals* prepared in some unknown manner so that they would dissolve with amazing rapidity in water that was faintly alkaline.

"It is all clear now," observed Mr. Lamonte. "Murray sought Mr. Bannack's secret formula, for which Limongi Frères had offered three hundred thousand dollars. Somehow he stole it; but in so doing had to kill Mr. Bannack. Like most other people, the crockery man would make a hard lead-pencil write legibly by sticking it into his mouth and wetting it slightly. So the diabolical Murray contrived his strange instrument of death. Saliva is faintly alkaline. Mr. Bannack touched the pencil to his lips. That's all!"

And so it proved. We searched Murray's small flat in Newark that very afternoon and in a writing-desk found letters that laid bare the thief's trick. He had posed as the discoverer of a glazing formula—which he did most successfully, because he was a chemist of rare attainments—and he had been urging Mr. Bannack to combine with him and float a huge new pottery corporation. The innocent, good-natured Mr. Bannack had been deceived by the man's technical wisdom and by his connection with the Belgian Peachblow Vase Company. As men of honor, they had exchanged copies of their formulas—and the rest you can guess.

So HERE I LOUNGE, in my cozy new apartment off Gramercy Park, sipping ginger ale and writing my adventures with a gold-mounted fountain pen. My picture has been in all the newspapers, over the title "The Wizard Sleuth." I have collected the five thousand dollars reward. And two detective agencies have given me one thousand dollars each for the privilege of consulting me during the ensuing year.

I shall now write that essay on the nine species of face wrinkles. If you have any interesting facts on this subject, please send them in at once.

THE GREAT PTARMIGAN MYSTERY

AH, BUT LIFE was worth living after the Bannack murder! Not that the old crockery merchant had been a menace to humanity. He was a nice old fellow; all the newspapers said so in their editorials on the day when that scoundrel shipping-clerk of the Belgian Peachblow Vase Company killed Mr. Bannack with a poisoned pencil and was trapped by one Worry-Worry Williams, Wizard Sleuth, to wit, myself and yours truly. No, Mr. Bannack was an estimable citizen. But one man's poison is another man's meat. That cyanide pencil was certainly meat for me! It brought five thousand dollars in rewards and two thousand more as retainers from two detective agencies. It gave me a cozy bachelor suite off Gramercy Park—

And, above all else, my Opportunity!

My Opportunity to write my *magnum opus*, my monumental treatise on the Nine Species of Face Wrinkles. (By the way, it is not too late for you to send in your photo and other interesting facts about wrinkles. The book has been delayed by many strange adventures, one of which I am about to recount. Please typewrite all information except your photo.)

For the first time in my harried career, I owned a desk wide enough to hold both my elbows and my spread-out annotations; and a closet shelf broad enough to bear a gallon jug of ink and fifty pounds of scratch paper; and a floor huge enough to display all my newspaper clippings and photographs of the ear wrinkles of murderers, the chin creases of aldermen, etc., etc. And, above all else, I owned my days and nights! No more bookkeeping! No more adding of wages and filling out of time charts! No more high stools and overheated offices and rasping chief clerks and gulped sandwiches! Yes, life was at last worth living, my friends!

A whole week I loafed. Then, one cool evening, after a plump broiler and a wee, squat bottle of French heart-restorer at Hilary's Café, I drifted home and cleared the decks for action. I shoved my study-table into my bedroom and stacked upon it all my study chairs. Next, I rolled up the pink rug and set myself to chalking numbers on the floor boards, when . . .

(Perhaps I ought to explain to the unscientific reader that floor boards are most useful for filing large masses of documents which you may wish to compare at a glance. You simply number the boards from left to right, and on each board group the documents of some one topic. In case you are suddenly called away, spread the rug over the papers; and there they are, all safe and out of the way. In renting a room, by the way, beware of four-inch boards! They are too narrow. Choose a room with six-inch flooring.)

Well, I was chalking the numbers, when an impatient rap sounded at the hall door; and at my "Come in!" there entered the long, lean Sam Milligan, head of the Milligan Detective Agency, the very Milligan who had paid me a thousand dollars for the privilege of consulting me on mystery cases for one year.

"We need you quick, Mr. Williams!" Milligan clutched my hand, as if it were a plank and he a drowning man. "It's a wretched little job—I'm ashamed to ask you to handle it—almost like asking Elihu Root to defend a chicken thief. But all my men are out on other important cases—and the lady is in a hurry—and so too is the thief, I guess.

"A swell dame up-town—name's Mrs. Elfenstein—wants her rug back. It's a nifty bunch of wool that she brought from Turkestan. Experts say it is worth a thousand bones. Some guy walked off with it last week, and the police have fallen down on the job as usual. Lady suspects a gink who used to work for her. Gink swiped some of her brandied peaches, she fired him, he went off threatening trouble. There you are! Rotten little rumpus, eh? I'd give it to a ten-dollar scrub, if I had one."

"Really!" I protested, as I arose stiffly from the floor. "You can not expect *me* to squander my precious time on petty thievery—"

"I don't expect you to!" Milligan paled. "I only thought that maybe you'd help me out in a pinch, just for once."

"Wait until I've finished this book on Wrinkles!" I insisted. "I'll not be disturbed by *anything* while it is on my mind. Come back in six months!"

"Six—six months?" Milligan gasped, and trembled a little. "How about that little retainer, then? Where do I come out? I guess we'll call our agreement off. Give me back the thousand dollars and—"

"Hm. I'll look into Mrs. Elfenstein's trouble to-morrow," I promised quickly. "Now for the facts!"

Milligan grinned, then talked. And thus was I launched upon my long and adventurous way toward startling discoveries about a mysterious bird, and things and people stranger yet.

Mrs. Elfenstein described rug and rug thief minutely. Milligan learned that a man fitting her description had lately been engaged as a waiter at Porter's, which, as you probably do not know, is Fashion's dearest, most secluded restaurant. Armed with this meager information and my wits, I sallied forth, late the next morning, and sought the place.

A narrow, old-fashioned dwelling it was, scantily hidden behind tubbed trees and potted flowers. Its hushed entry was not allowed to scream its name and fame to the vulgar streets. Its French windows were all tightly sealed, to exclude the city's dusty heat and to retain the refrigerated air, pumped up from the basement, and the chill of the waiters' perfect manners. On that sweltering day of late summer it was a cavern in a desert; a place of pleasant darkness in the midst of a burning desolation. Blessed he who knew its entrances, and blessed I who found one of them and passed in through a crystalled corridor to a great hall almost empty of guests.

Luck followed me. I straightway spied my man: his parallelogram of a face, his matted-moss hair, his hueless cheeks and frozen mouth, all precisely as Mrs. Elfenstein had described. (Oddly enough, he had no face wrinkles.) Luck chased me. The fellow's table was guestless (there is a waiter for each table at Porter's), and I sat down at it.

"Patrick O'Mara, I believe?" said I slyly, as he stood at attention.

"Sir?" The man's lips stirred not at all.

I repeated myself.

"No, sir. Felix Rotisse."

"That's queer!" My face shriveled in a pucker of perplexity. "You are the picture of Patrick O Mara, as Mrs. Elfenstein described him."

"Mrs. Elfenstein, sir?" Still no movement in that masklike visage.

"The lady whose rug you stole," I explained. "The lady you have been working for, you know."

"Beg pardon, sir! But I have never heard of Mrs. Elfenstein. Will you kindly give me your order, sir? You will do well to get it in before the luncheon rush begins."

The man's pencil was poised over the order slip. I don't know what I ordered; I was much bewildered by the amazing and embarrassing resemblance between Patrick O'Mara and Felix Rotisse.

I figured over it a long time after my waiter had left for the kitchen, but all in vain. And, as for my finding the rug thief, it was clear that I must begin all over again; for I had no clues. Frankly, I was glad. I was now free, you see, to dismiss the whole petty and odious business of rug thievery from my mind and spend my luncheon hour profitably, in cataloguing the wrinkles on the faces of the diners, who were now drifting in streamily.

I had collected thirty-nine fascinating types (including one very rare specimen of the compound upper nasal fold, Type B), when the head waiter stepped up to me and inquired whether I had been served. I looked at my watch. I had been sitting there over an hour!

"Beg pardon, sir!" the head waiter bowed, as if he expected me to smite off his head with a scimitar. "I'll look into it at once." And off he scurried toward the kitchen.

Pretty soon he marched back, quite pale and broken of speech. Grave concern deepened his diplomatic dimples. He called a waiter from a neighboring table. "Kindly repeat your order to this man," said the head waiter. "We're very sorry there's been a delay."

"Where's my waiter?" I asked.

"Gone!" moaned the head waiter, wringing his hands. "It's incomprehensible, sir! He fled through the rear kitchen door, they say. During luncheon hour, too. From Porter's!"

"Aha!" I clapped my hands joyfully. "Now I have evidence! He must be the rug thief!" And then I explained. "And now," I concluded, "tell me all that you know about the fellow. Porter's takes on no waiter without his pedigree, bank rating, and letters of credit—"

"We know only that Alphonse, our chef, recommended him," sighed the head waiter, in confusion. "We trusted Alphonse absolutely"

"Then I must see Alphonse at once!" I cried excitedly, and sprang from my seat.

"Show him down to the kitchen!" the head waiter commanded the lesser.

The lesser guided me softly down an interminable and writhing hall full of shuffling forms, clattering dishes, and hot fragrances until we finally burst through green swinging doors into the peppery presence of Alphonse, Commander of the Kitchen.

Alphonse did not notice our advent. Alphonse was brandishing a skillet at two white-aproned colleagues, and the colleagues were waving greasy fists at the Potentate of Pots and Pans. The belligerents hopped about on opposite sides of a butcher's block, whereon reposed the carcass of a bird, sans life, sans feathers.

"Fools of hash-mongers!" Alphonse was yelling, as he pointed toward the bird. "It is what it is named to be. South African ptarmigan. Little you know of fine cookeries! You who have fried onions in cheap two-dollar tables d'hôte along Broadway! Bah!"

"That's a runt quail. I shot a thousand of 'em up state, when I was a kid," roared back one colleague scornfully. "The label on the leg is a fake. And the gink who pays ten dollars for that quail smeared up with your gravies, Alphy, is a North American sucker—"

"Infamous vassal and lunatic!" Alphonse howled. "To suggest that Keena & Kelly must descend to the kind of common lies and fraud that you and your kind practice—"

Zzz! Out flew the colleague's fist and made a nice little *purée* of the chef's lower lip. Swish! Alphonse's skillet sailed across the table and caught the adversary's ear.

"Gentlemen!" I sprang upon the table between them. "Be intelligent! Settle the question logically! If it is hard, allow me to assist you—"

"Get your dirty feet off that chopping-block!" snapped Alphonse, in an instant transformed to a chef again.

"Not until you tell me what this unseemly argument is about!" I retorted.

"Read that tag on the quail's leg, and you'll find out," cried Alphonse's adversaries in duet.

I picked up the carcass. Wired to one of its legs was a linen tag reading thus: "Keena & Kelly, — Greenwich St. Private Importation. South African Ptarmigan."

"Keena & Kelly are swell fish-and-game dealers—wholesale people." Alphonse explained hurriedly. "The most honorable of all honorable—"

"Very honorable!" sneered an adversary. "They stick this tag on a fifty-cent quail, and Porter's sticks somebody ten dollars for the rare South African ptarmigan, whatever that is."

"Is this the only point at issue?" I raised my brows in amazement. "Alphonse says the bird is a South African ptarmigan, and you say it is common quail?"

"Precisely!" exclaimed Alphonse.

"Dear me! What a silly trifle to fight over!" I scolded the trio. "It can be settled in the simplest manner—"

"How?" three voices asked.

"By the Inward Manifests!" I shouted triumphantly.

"Eh?" (There were three of them again.)

"Inward Manifests are the records of goods brought into this country. They are on file at the customs office. They record the names of the shippers, the goods shipped, the port of shipment, and the consignees. Let us run down to the Battery, and see whether Keena & Kelly have imported any South African ptarmigan. If they have, we shall then cable to the shipper in South Africa, and secure from him a minute description of the bird. Then we—"

"Hey you, Alphonse!" somebody roared down the long hall that led to the dining-rooms. "There's a gent yelling for his *filet mignon*. Get it quick! The head waiter is takin' down a complaint from him—"

At that sound, Alphonse grabbed a carving-knife and vanished into a huge ice-box. His two adversaries fell to toasting cheese crackers over a tiny gas stove, and heeded me not at all, although I thrice importuned them to come along to the custom-house in a taxi at my expense.

"Oh, well!" I called out to them, as I moved off, "I shall go alone then. The question interests me. Besides, I'd like to show you how intelligent people settle disputes. See you later."

Forth I sauntered into the street, and a cab was soon rushing me to the customhouse at the lower end of the island.

And then things began to happen!

I shall not stop to narrate my struggles with the brainless hirelings of a timorous government that suspects every citizen who asks to inspect its archives. I wasted a whole afternoon fighting my way to the Inward Manifests; fighting past clerks who declared pompously that the records were not open to the public, past other clerks who insisted that I must present a certificate of reasonable doubt from the Secretary of the Treasury; and other clerks with other obstacles, theories, and asininities. At last, by sheer good chance, the editor of a financial newspaper who knew me by reputation dropped in, and vouched for me.

AH! THOSE WERE HAPPY hours that I spent poring over the Inward Manifests! I fingered the nerves of life. Man's appetites, his whims, his dreams, all bared themselves before me in that big, quiet room above the lazy benches of Battery Park. Never did philosopher peer deeper into the bottomless wellsprings of human nature than did I, as I scanned innumerable items like these:

June 19, 1911. *S. S. Paterland* from Marseilles.
Bergen, Snell & Co. 22 casks Munich sauerkraut.
Bluckheimer Co. 4 cases ipecac.
Angier & Aswell. 10 barrels medicated prunes.
Madame Desmere Corporation. 85 kegs Persian

beauty ointment.
Bingo & Bingo. 2 hogsheads Jordan water.
Empire Furniture Store. 40 rolls Navajo rugs.

And so on, goods without end. Goods that poured out upon the tumultuous stretches of West Street, where the kickshaws and condiments of the continents are spilled shiploadwise, from dawn to midnight, every day of the year, into the maw of a people whose incessant and manifold hungers make a white shark seem like a dyspeptic valetudinarian.

Those were the oracles, those Inward Manifests! They betrayed all the secrets of the heart, the lusts of flesh and spirit, the high hopes of statesmen, the black wiles of international swindlers, the world-plots of governments, the misery of mining-towns, the ignorance of fools, superstitions, madnesses. How so? Why! They revealed, item by item, all the things that men and women use in all the adventures and exigencies of their day-to-day existence.

Spread out before me, in name and imagination, were all the stuffs that people consume, employ, and subdue to the diverse machinations of their unpredictable wills. Would you learn of real life? Give your Shakespeare to the hired girl and turn you to the Inward Manifests. Would you understand people? Forsake the slum, Chinatown, Lenox, Monte Carlo, and Wall Street, and speed to West Street, where the goods of the Inward Manifests are outwardly manifest at all hours. There, on the docks, beneath the mile-long sheds strewn half a city's length along the riverside, you may look upon the silks of Pride, the cotton shirts of Misery, the nostrums of Agony, the giant mahogany logs that imperious Art has summoned from the steaming jungles of the southland, the hair of Chinese women that Vanity has shorn, to hide the baldness of some fading Beauty, the . . .*

* This sentence in Mr. Williams's manuscript contains 732 words, of which 121 are capitalized. The Typographical Union refuses to handle it.—Editor of *Everybody's*.

On my first day of research I studied through all the Inward Manifests of the current week. This was something of a task, for each day's list contained about 550 items, and the August sun burned cruelly, and the archive clerk was peevish at my mussing up his papers. But, in the end, I was still more peevish than he; for on the ships of recent arrival I had found not a single South African ptarmigan.

"You darned fool!" sneered the clerk when I told him this. "Those fancy game birds are kept in cold storage a year or more. That ptarmigan may have been imported on a cake of ice last Christmas!"

"Well," I sighed, "then I must go back and back and back until I find the event."

And back I went, and back some more, every day for the next nineteen. I took temporary lodgings in a seamen's lodging house opposite the custom-house. I went to work with the clerks, and I quit with them. Some day I shall tell you about the strange cargoes I stumbled upon during this prodigious exploring expedition; about the five casks of madmen's brains consigned to a clinic; about the Norwegian sailing vessel that had been chartered by a Ladies' Aid Society in Uruguay, to rush relief supplies to the flood victims in all towns that had gone wet on election day, etc., etc. But let us stick to our bird.

Nineteen days I clung to its trail, and on the evening of the last one I had reached the Inward Manifests of August 30, 1906. This date was precisely five years old. But still no South African ptarmigan! Therefore Keena & Kelly either had sold Porter's a bird that was not a South African ptarmigan, or else they had sold a genuine South African ptarmigan more than five years deceased, or else, finally, they had smuggled in the genuine ptarmigan.

The second of these possibilities was the easiest to investigate. So I turned to it first. I sought out America's most renowned cold-storage expert.

"Tell me," I begged him, "will meat remain toothsome after five years of freezing?"

"It depends upon the meat," said he. "Now, prime Argentine beef—"

"Never mind that! How about South African ptarmigan?"

Narrowly the great man scrutinized me, then snorted disgustedly. "Run along, Little Smarty, and spring your joke on somebody else."

"What?" I shouted, all at sea.

"Come! Come!" the expert grinned. "Did you think you could josh me? Why, sonny! I know every living thing that's edible—"

"Isn't South African ptarmigan edible?" I gasped.

"No. Because it does not exist. Ptarmigans live only in the northern hemisphere. See any encyclopedia. Good day!"

Somehow I managed to stumble out of the office and over to a dock hard by, where I flung myself upon a great case of Swiss doilies, like a fagged stevedore. Those last terrible words of the expert went droning, droning, droning through my sunken head, stinging my tormented spirit, and exhausting me by stirring up a horde of flitting and futile conjectures about that mysterious tag on the leg of the bird in Porter's kitchen. There I lay—how many hours I know not—until a watchman of the piers thumped my hot soles with his cruel stick and ordered me thence.

As I shambled to my lodgings in a daze, my problem began to clear. The South African ptarmigan at Porter's wasn't one. Whence then the tag, and why? Were Keena & Kelly themselves deceived? Or were they deceivers? Was the tag a jest? Or did some earnest lurk behind its humbug? Now, Alphonse was either duped by Keena & Kelly or else he feigned wonderfully to be. But, if he feigned, he would not come to blows over the bird; that would be both painful and purposeless. Therefore he sincerely believed the tag. Thus the leading question became this:

Did Keena & Kelly write the tag and affix it to the bird, or did some irresponsible person do it? And, if Keena & Kelly did it, why did they?

From this simple and brief line of reasoning you will readily note what my next move must have been. I had to visit the fish-and-game dealers and discover whether they were selling birds as

South African ptarmigan. And that is what I did, in a great hurry, too.

The roofed sidewalks and cobbled streets of the vast wholesale district slumbered in the midst of its thousand perfumes; for the hour was midafternoon, and the day's bartering is over at noon. Only bookkeepers were scribbling in their dark cubbyholes, an occasional expressman dropped a crate of melons or chickens, and here and there a scavenger—boy, dog, or cat—was nosing through barrels of refuse at the curb. Keena & Kelly's was a solitude in a solitude. Its dingy, narrow front was adorned not even with the customary empty crates. Beneath its sidewalk roof loitered no scavenger. And within was neither clerk nor scribe. I walked through to the rear, and encountered not a soul.

In a squalid court that I glimpsed through the half-open back door a hulking roustabout dozed, pipe in mouth and back against a stack of shattered strawberry boxes.

"I wish to buy a South African ptarmigan," I spoke up briskly.

The fellow stirred heavily, opened a red eye, and mumbled: "Boss is out. May be back in 'n hour er so."

I sat on a kippered-herring keg and waited. In a few minutes it occurred to me that there might be some "South African ptarmigan" or tags with that inscription lying about. So I nosed about softly, incidentally making note of the peculiar shipping marks on the many foreign boxes, which I hope some day to investigate scientifically. I made the rounds of the place fruitlessly, until I came to the small square next to the firm's solitary desk.

This square was hedged about with a wooden rail, and within it there were huddled, close beside the desk, five small, extra heavy barrels. Their tops were tight, all save one. This I lifted, and by George! there were three or four dozen unplucked birds, each bearing a leg tag and the baffling words, "South African ptarmigan!"

"It is now clear," I announced to the four walls, "that Keena & Kelly are officially responsible for the deceit. Next we must determine whether they are perpetrating it as a jest on somebody or for profit. Now, it is not a good joke merely to ticket a fowl with the name of an imaginary bird. The point lies elsewhere: in the particular name, or in the gullibility of the person on whom the joke is played. On the other hand, it might be a passable joke to palm off a bird of repellent flavor under the guise of a rare succulence. These may be April-fool birds. They may taste like kerosene. Let us see!"

With that I seized the top bird and made off with it, this time to my Gramercy Park quarters, where I promptly installed one of those pretty electric broilers with which flat dwellers do electric light-housekeeping.

My investigations were sadly interrupted for a while by that confounded Milligan—the chap that runs a detective agency, you recall. He had been telephoning twice every day for the past fortnight, so the hall-boy said. And I had not been home half an hour before he stormed in upon me, very red of face and temper, and demanded, almost rudely, whether I had found Mrs. Elfenstein's rug; and if not, why not.

"My good man," I smiled down upon him as gently as I could, "Mrs. Elfenstein must wait. I have something infinitely more important to accomplish than the finding of a thousand-dollar patch of bright wool."

"So you're letting that book on face wrinkles cheat me of my right to consult you, eh?" Milligan went ugly.

"I had quite forgotten that, by George!" I laughed. "I am now pursuing a less comprehensive but more mystifying problem." And I briefly sketched it.

"Allow me to say," sneered Milligan, as he snatched up his hat and backed toward the door, "that you are a gloriously damn fool. Your skull is full of spoiled custard—"

"That sounds like the good old times!" I chuckled, unoffended. "Seventeen employers of mine have expressed that very thought, variously phrased. All they mean, though, is that I am not like them. Good day! Maybe next week I'll find that rug for you."

"You'll return my thousand-dollar fee!" yelled Milligan, as he vanished down the stairs. "I'm going to see my attorney."

Quite distressing, wasn't it? With a sigh I set up my electric broiler, tied a newspaper about my waist, rolled up my sleeves, and fell to dressing the alleged South African ptarmigan.

The feathers came out stubbornly, tearing the tender skin as they came. Then I drove in a knife and slit the crop. It was a very full crop, and packed with small, hard pebbles which clinked faintly as I shook them out upon my table.

"Rather coarse grit for so small a bird to eat!" I mused, as I fingered the pebbles and rubbed the slime off them. And I recalled that even large hens, which devour many particles of earth and stone, seldom swallow a geological morsel larger than a pea. But this alleged ptarmigan was scarcely half the size of a common hen, and the eight pebbles were each as large as a Lima bean!

"Evidently," I inferred—and slapped my knee with a new joy—"Keena & Kelly have discovered a new species of bird, one that lives on stones. Perhaps Burbank has invented it, or—"

My breath stopped, and a cruel pain quivered through me, as every muscle of my body stiffened in a rigor of insane amazement. My right palm burned. The pebbles in it, the eight pebbles each as large as a Lima bean, the pebbles now cleansed by my aimless rubbing, twinkled maliciously at me with the unmistakable blue and white fire of flawless diamonds!

How long I stood over the beauties, bewitched by their flickering seductions, I do not know. But at last the spell was broken—I think, by the mere honking of an automobile down in the street. My paper apron still fast about me, and my dressing-knife in my rigid fist, I leaped downstairs, into a taxicab, and off to Keena & Kelly's. As the car dashed wildly across the island, I settled down to business. Out came my ever-ready pencil and scratch paper; and I, with my new logical method, drove headlong into the blindest, most brain-racking puzzle that I had yet encountered. Must I word it for you? Well, then:

What is there in the flavor of a diamond that would tempt an alleged ptarmigan to devour the stone? And where could a bird with a diamond appetite pick up eight perfectly cut jewels that were worth fully a thousand dollars apiece?

Dusk was blurring the signs of Greenwich Street, and the feverish ebb tide of commuters was running fast past the closed stores of the wholesale district. I feared that I was too late. But no! A light was burning in the rear of Keena & Kelly's, and, silhouetted against its sickly yellow, a thickset man was shaking his fist at the roustabout whom I had seen there earlier in the day.

The door was locked. I rattled at the knob impatiently. The thickset man wheeled, scowled savagely at me, then pressed an ill-favored visage against the dusty pane and growled: "What d'ye want?"

"Information," I answered. "Are you the proprietor?"

"Yes. Who are you?" He was studying me closely, with a glance now and then at my chauffeur, whom I had bidden to await me.

"Let me in, and I'll tell you."

He opened, a little hesitant, and stood athwart my path. "Well—" he grew suddenly diplomatic—"whom have I the honor of addressing?"

"My name is Williams," I said. "I am the consulting detective for the Milligan Agency, among others. But," I added quickly, "I do not come here in that capacity—"

"Milligan Agency, eh?" The thick-set man stiffened strangely. "But not here representing it—"

"No," I went on, removing my paper apron as I spoke, "I come privately—"

"And for what, please?"

"I am very curious about the South African ptarmigan you carry in stock. It—"

"What's the joke?" The man grinned unnaturally. "We haven't any such bird. I never even heard of—"

"So it would appear from the Inward Manifests at the customhouse!" I retorted, not a little perplexed at this unexpected turn of events. "You never imported any such ptarmigan under its own name—"

Then the man's mouth fell open and he stammered: "What do you know about that, heh?"

"I have just spent nineteen days studying your importations," I replied. "Also, I happen to know that you have five barrels of South African ptarmigan beside your desk. And the bird is fond of eating six-carat diamonds. This is a most unusual diet. No standard reference work on zoology alludes to it—"

"Get out of here!" the man snapped his fingers at the roustabout, and the roustabout shuffled forth into the deepening twilight. "Now, young man—" he trembled a little—"we must come to terms. You've trapped me, all right! I knew there was trouble ahead when I found a bird gone from that open barrel this afternoon. Another two hours, and I'd have had all the sparklers out of the way. But you've beaten me, sonny. I'm a good sport. I put up my hands. And I'll put up something better yet, if you will trot off home right away and not come back here until to-morrow morning. Look!"

Before I could utter a sound, he glided to his desk, jerked forth a little drawer, and dumped from it into my hands a scant score of four-carat sparklers! "Now beat it!" he whispered wheedlingly, and edged me toward the street. "Come back to-morrow, at any hour, I'll have everything fixed so as to put you straight—"

"You mean it?" I demanded anxiously. "You will really put me straight, if I come in the morning?"

"Straight as a die," he promised warmly. "Milligan will never catch on. I'll leave a few birds with small sparklers—"

"This is not Milligan's affair!" I corrected him. "It is yours and mine. Nobody else is in on it. The custom-house people know about it, of course. But it's not their hunt. Both the work and, I hope, the reward are mine alone—"

"You're a trump!" declared the fish-and-game man heartily, and he thumped me on the back. "Now, remember! To-morrow morning! And bring along Milligan and the customs crowd, if you like. I'll have everything ready for them—and for you."

We shook hands on that. And the next minute I was standing in Greenwich Street under a sputtering lamp, foolishly pawing over a heaping handful of diamonds. How much were they worth? And why had the man given them to me? Was it a business practice? Or what? The task exceeded my overtapped powers of thought. I needed help. So I rode up to the Public Library and spent the rest of the early evening studying standard works on Commission Agents and the Customs of Trade.

Some customs of trade are very peculiar. Grocers call a pint box a quart box. Butchers weigh in the bones and fat trimmings, charge them to the customer, and then take them out and sell them over again to the bone man. Attorneys accept retainer fees for doing nothing. . . .* But nowhere did I find that fish-and-game merchants have the habit of giving twenty-five thousand dollars' worth of jewelry to strangers who ask questions about ornithology. As I reflected, the practice came to seem highly improbable; so improbable and fantastic, indeed, that I began to doubt that the stones were diamonds and that the thick-set man was a fish-and-game dealer, and that—

"To the pawnbroker's!" I shouted—right out in the big reading-room. And before the indignant guardian of the silences could eject me for paralyzing the bookworms, I had fled once more into the night. And I stopped not until I had flung myself against the counter of a famous Rialto Uncle.

"It's of the first water," Uncle declared over a specimen. "I'll advance you nine hundred on it any day—"

"Then I am rich!" I shrieked my joy. "Rich! I have twenty-two more like that one!"

"Where did you get 'em, son?"

I turned. A tall, sharp-eyed man had come forward from the rear of the shop and put the question with a tone of quiet authority.

"Some I got from a little bird, and the others from a man," I began. Then I went on to explain. But the more I said, the more queerly the pawnbroker scanned me, and the more closely the tall man edged up against me.

"That'll do!" the tall man broke in rudely, after a minute. "You come along with me and tell that wild story at headquarters after you've sobered up—"

"Go along and don't make a row!" urged the pawnbroker. "He's a plain-clothes man."

I bowed ironically to the pair and drew forth my visiting-cards. "I suggest that you come with me to Greenwich Street," I advised the plain-clothes man. "At eight in the morning—"

"No," whistled the tall man, as he read my card, "I'll go with you now. I can't bear to lose sight of your sweet face overnight!

* Eighty-five illustrations of trade customs here omitted.—Editor.

You may be Williams, and you may not," he grinned sardonically. "We'll pick up a couple of officers down-town. Come along!"

THIS IS HOW I returned, at ten o'clock that very evening, to Keena & Kelly's, with four detectives in my wake. They forced the door, flashed their pocket lights . . .

The floor was bestrewn with slashed birds, and in the midst of the smeary mess crouched my friend, the thick-set man, and a beautiful woman; between them a small valise, and in the valise a full quart of precious stones!

"You welcher!" snarled the thick-set man, and, with a lightning-like flash of his arm, he drew a revolver and fired. Something burned in the thick of my thigh, and I fell. Then the tall detective shot, and the thick-set man pitched forward and lay very still upon a mess of disemboweled game birds.

"Gentlemen," I stammered unsteadily, "upon further reflection I am convinced that this—"

Then I collapsed in a dead faint.

THE NEXT MORNING, on my cool cot in the hospital, I read in the newspapers that Williams, the Wizard Sleuth, had unearthed the most gigantic smuggling conspiracy that had ever baffled the Secret Service. Like all highly successful schemes, Keena & Kelly's was incredibly simple. The fish-and-game business was a diabolically clever piece of smuggling machinery.

Kelly would go to London twice a year and ostentatiously buy a few hundred brace of Scotch grouse. His sister would secretly pick up half a million dollars' worth of sparklers in Amsterdam and Paris, and bring them to Keena & Kelly's shipping-office in East London. The stones would be stuffed into the crops of a few score birds, the birds would be tagged "South African ptarmigan" (South Africa being the home of diamonds, you know), and then scattered through half a hundred barrels of innocent and common grouse. Keena, the thick-set man, would receive the shipments at New York and make a great show of selling to the fanciest hotel trade.

In five years, said one newspaper, the smugglers must have brought in five or six million dollars' worth of diamonds.

Mr. Williams, said another journal, had seized half a million dollars' worth last night; and half of this sum would go to him as a reward for his services.

A third daily, in a leading editorial, demanded that Mr. Williams be placed at the head of the Secret Service.

All three papers ran a huge advertisement of the Milligan Detective Agency with an alleged picture of myself, bearing the legend: "Consulting Expert of Our Firm."

"This is discouraging!" I sighed to the nurse, as she placed beside my bed an enormous bouquet of roses and forget-me-nots from the Milligan Agency. "They parade all the sordid details about the value of the diamonds and the size of my reward. But not a word about my new logical method in all of it. Not a hint about my synthetic analysis of complex propositions."

I have engaged a private secretary to help me hurry along my *magnum opus* on the Nine Species of Face Wrinkles. He is up-town to-day, seeking a small apartment with eight-inch floor boards.

A strange lady by the name of Mrs. Elfenstein has been trying to see me. But the hospital doctors will not admit her.

BALTIMORE LUNCH AND HARTFORD LUNCH

THIS WILL INTRODUCE to you my very good friend Leander Seethal, a most remarkable citizen of the world.

Leander is going to lodge with me hereafter; I've rented the adjoining suite for him and guaranteed payment. This last the superintendent insisted upon, because he didn't like Leander's looks and turned up his nose at the references. All of which bears witness to the superintendent's utterly sordid and mammonish point of view. Like most other people on this benighted continent, he can not appreciate Leander.

But that's the way it goes with all really great men. And Leander—let me say it emphatically—is a great man. He irritates me beyond measure—but he is a genius. True, he is earning only seven dollars a week in a newspaper office, and that, too, at the age of fifty-seven. But what of it? The world's greatest minds have fared worse at the cashier's desk. Take Rubinsk, for instance: when he demonstrated the short form of the general solution of the quadratic, his uncle's valet was paying his board. And Hermanos, too, who first formulated the twelfth theorem of probabilities. . . . *

It was a bitter night when Leander first drifted in upon me. I was toiling furiously over a petty case that Sam Milligan, head of the Milligan Detective Agency, had turned over to me. I was

*The twenty-two geniuses here cited by the author are not mentioned in any standard encyclopedia. We shall print Mr. Williams's remarks about them as soon as we have verified his facts.—Editors.

growing weary of Milligan and his trifling problems. They were all unworthy of an intellectual man's attention. But I had to handle them, for I had accepted a retainer from Sam which bound me in his service for a year. So there I was, frittering the night away over the mysterious disappearance of three boxes of Swiss hatpins that had been stolen from a Broadway loft.

That afternoon I had collected data. I had read up on Switzerland, hatpins (by the way, some wonderful hatpins have recently been brought to light by archeologists excavating in Crete), the influence of Switzerland on hatpins, and of hatpins on Switzerland (information on this topic is very scant), lofts, their architecture, their accessibility, etc., etc. But not a clue could I find to the thief.

The clocks of the town clanged eleven. I cursed Milligan and hatpins. The December wind sneered icily past my windows—and then there filtered in through my door a faint but sharp sound, a sound like the desperate gnawing of a hungry mouse against old oak too hard for little fangs. A moment I hesitated, then flung open the door.

There gleamed a bony finger, scratching on the doorframe. And behind the finger stood a little man with a back like a bow, and a long, thin cane upright before him, like a bowstring. On his vast and bulging head was perched a straw hat of ancient form and texture. Then I knew why the wind had been sneering! The hat squatted on a magnificent nest of creamy-yellow-white hair, so dense that the gales had left it unruffled. And an unruffled face shone from below it; a kind, calm face, but a very strange face. It was a living query, an interrogation-mark of flesh and bones. The ink-drop eyes were two Why's. They squinted inquisitively and—glory be!—they made four marvelous wrinkles—transverse, double-groove, sub-contractile—the very sort which I had not yet secured for my great book on "The Nine Species of Face Wrinkles." (Publishers to be announced later.)

"Hurrah!" I shouted, and dragged my visitor in by his sleeve.

"Mr. Williams?" the man asked with something like a squeak of joy over his reception.

I nodded.

"You will help me, sir? It is very urgent. A serious business for me. I come to you as a last resort. I would not disturb such a busy man were it not—almost a matter of life and death to me. If I fail, I starve."

"Pray explain, while I photograph those wrinkles!" I begged, and fell to searching my bureau drawer for a flash-light powder. "Who are you, and why?"

"Seethal. Leander Seethal. I am an editor—" his ink-drop eyes flashed proudly at that last word—"but I shall not be one to-morrow, unless you can answer the question that has brought me here."

"And that question is?" I stopped my search and looked eagerly at him.

"It is this." The old gentleman's voice quavered ever so little. "What is the difference between a Hartford Lunch and a Baltimore Lunch?"

We gazed at each other in stiff silence for a full minute, while the winter storm outside hissed as the gallery does at bad actors.

"Now there's a real problem!" I finally crooned. And, as if to prove it, I shoved all my papers *in re* Sam Milligan and the stolen Swiss hatpins into my waste-basket.

"Painfully real!" spoke up Leander Seethal bitterly, and thumped his thin cane. "Four days I've tramped streets trying to solve it. See!" He held up a foot, and I beheld a blue sock peering through a great hole in the sole. "And this is my last night of grace."

"What do you mean?" I cried, now thoroughly aroused over the mystery behind his words. "Why must you learn the difference between a Hartford Lunch and a Baltimore Lunch?"

"Because I am getting old and out of date, and the young men press me hard. And my friends of old are dead." He wagged his noble head in melancholy rhythm.

"You explain one mystery with a greater one!" I complained. "Doubtless my new logical formulas would reveal the connection between your two last remarks in an hour or two. But I prefer to have you tell me. I'm a little tired of figuring to-night."

"It's all very simple." Leander dropped into a chair and set his head atop his cane. "I run the Asked-and-Answered column of the

New York *Era*. Letters from our readers, you know. They want to know whether Greenland is colder than Iceland; how many yards of silk are needed for a wedding-dress; why some fleas are brown and others white; on what date people first stood up in New York theatres and yelled when the orchestra played 'Dixie;' why a coin never falls on its edge when you toss it in the air; how many—"

"Enough!" I shrieked. "On with your tale, quick!—or I shall discuss that matter of the coin—"

"Twenty-eight years I've been at it," the old gentleman mused. "And I know more facts than any other man in New York. But of what avail is knowledge in a world where men fight one another like tigers for a greasy dollar bill? I mastered the piano and the Italian language, just to make clear to some of the *Era's* musical readers what *tempo rubato* is. I spent all my savings of fifteen years on a trip to British Guiana, to discover whether there are hurricanes there—"

"That was foolish," I put in chidingly. "Anybody ought to know that there are hurricanes all around the West Indies—"

"Perhaps!" Leander sighed, and eyed me sorrowfully, as a converted heathen might contemplate a discarded idol. "But there are no hurricanes in British Guiana . . ."*

"But what did all these efforts and achievements avail me?" Leander went on. "Here I am, the most experienced Asked-and-Answered artist in America. And the *Era* pays me seven dollars a week, while—" his lips trembled—"the city editor and two young cubs are conspiring to snatch even this pittance from me—and—turn me out on the street.

"They say I'm an old fogy," he went on. "But the trouble is that the editor wants my place for his nephew, a good-for-nothing loafer who has been kicked off four papers. The pair of them are inventing excuses to oust me. The nephew has been writing to the editor-in-chief under an assumed name, saying that I have bungled my

* We regret the necessity of omitting Mr. Seethal's interesting lecture on the meteorology of the north coast of South America. It does not seem to bear upon the wider question of the difference between Hartford and Baltimore Lunches.—Editors.

answers to a lot of queries. But I proved him a liar. And now what? The fellow takes to sending in questions to my column—questions that man has never asked before—questions that man may never answer. I see the whole scheme! I shall fail once, twice, three times! Then complaints will begin pouring into the chief, and the city editor will discharge me."

"And this question about Hartford and Baltimore lunches," I asked, "is flunk number three?"

"Right!" Leander bowed in humiliation. "And this afternoon the city editor told me savagely that I'd have to brace up! Said people were getting tired of my blunders, and so on. Well!" He shrugged his thin shoulders and laughed with a raw rattle deep in his skinny neck. "It's foolish of me to appeal to you. You may answer my question about the Lunches, but that will only put off my enemies' victory a day or two. Curse them!"

"Tut! Tut!" I shook a finger at the angry old fellow as I paced the floor excitedly. "Look at the matter impersonally!"

"When I am about to be thrust out of the office into a December blizzard? Ha!"

"I refer to the Hartford and Baltimore lunches!" I corrected him coolly. "Let us investigate them without passion." I popped my hat on, took Leander's arm; and, before he could question me, we were on the deserted street, leaning against the wind that rasped our skins like the lick of a wolf's tongue.

"Where? What are you doing?" Leander panted, as he drew his threadbare coat-collar up about his neck and tucked in his long hair, for extra warmth.

"To investigate Hartford and Baltimore lunches," I informed him. "We shall begin with the one two blocks east of here."

"It's no use!" Leander mumbled dully, as we pushed along past black houses and shuttered shops. "I've studied them all, from kitchen to cashier, from soup to demitasse, from griddle in the front window to garbage-pail at the back door. And I tell you, Mr. Williams, they're exactly alike!"

"Aha!" I rubbed my hands. "Glorious! Glorious! Now we have a real problem!"

"You doom me, sir!" moaned Leander. "I had hoped you would assure me that my enemies had concocted a false problem. But if it is genuine, then we are undone! I tell you I've looked into everything—"

"My dear sir—" I spoke as kindly as I could to the simpleminded unfortunate—"you may have looked into everything. But probably you have not seen through everything! You are by profession a man-of-all-lore. You are a fact collector. But you are not a logician! No offense meant! You're not a whit worse off than ninety million other citizens! Now it stands to reason that two national institutions could not grow up under different names unless they really were different at some point—"

"I don't see that!" Leander whimpered, as a mighty blast from around a corner smote us. "Maybe it's because I'm so cold—and I—I haven't eaten all day!"

"Dear me!" I looked at him in the same way that he had eyed me when I said there were hurricanes in British Guiana. "You are not only illogical, but misinformed. Clear thinking is hindered by a full stomach. A full stomach draws blood from the brain, inhibits the functioning of the higher nerve-centers—"

"What'll I do when they fire me?" Leander continued his wholly irrelevant personal interjections. "What'll I eat?"

"It is true," I said firmly, "that two names are sometimes given to one and the same thing. Hence synonyms. But the conditions of this happening are distinct and peculiar. In the first place, one name is classical and the other colloquial. Thus, 'conservative' and 'standpatter.' In the second place, one name may be used in one year and the other in the next—"

"Here! Here!" Leander clutched me and brought us both to a standstill before a Baltimore Lunch. "You look around while I get a bite to eat. Would you mind loaning me a quarter?"

"Not in the least, after we have inspected the place," I said good-naturedly—though, to tell the truth, I was rather disgusted at the man's greediness. "Let us begin with the interior arrangement."

In we went, Leander slinking hungrily at my heels. A crowd of night-hawks—taxicab chauffeurs all of them—were warming their fingers in the steam of their coffee and thawing their wits noisily over some discarded comic supplements of a long-forgotten Sunday. Leander glued his eyes upon their thick, hot cups, and I heard him murmur: "There is no justice in the world!" With a snort of contempt for his weakness I turned to my task.

Griddle in front window; two rows of armchairs along right-hand wall; blue and white tile floor; counter of ready-to-eat pastry and other desserts on left of cashier's desk; and on the right of it a cigar-stand bearing a huge bowl of toothpicks; at the rear—

But why report the rest? For my beautifully logical diagram came to naught. Leander ruined it. In the midst of my mapping, he stalked gloomily up to the night-hawks and asked in a voice as raw as the wind outdoors:

"What is the difference between a Hartford Lunch and a Baltimore Lunch?"

"Search me, pard!" one of the crowd replied soberly. But the rest of the pack whooped. That whoop exploded Mr. Asked-and-Answered.

"A fine bunch of night-hawks you are!" he raged, and brandished a pitiful, blue-veined fist at one of them. "You think you know the town! You brag of being able to drive to any place blindfold in a fog. You pretend to know what goes on behind every door. And you don't know the difference between a Hartford and a Baltimore Lunch! Hoo! Hoo! Fakers! Bluffers! And you stuff your bellies and doze in the warmth, while I starve and am persecuted! Oh! What a hell-hole the world is!"

"Sic 'em, Bug!" yelled one chauffeur gleefully. But the man Leander addressed hauled out a half-dollar and tossed it toward Leander, muttering, "You poor devil! Sit down and have something on me."

For an answer Leander flung the coin into his would-be benefactor's coffee and snarled hideously: "Me a bread-liner? Taking charity from a tip-taker? Not while the world lasts!"

Somebody lunged at Leander, but the rebuffed philanthropist sprang up and blocked the attack. "Aw, leave the poor dippy alone! He ain't responsible!"

Then I grabbed Leander and made off with him toward the street and the storm. Passing the cashier's desk, I halted. "Sir," I addressed the occupant, a flabby youth and slumbrous, "what is the difference between a Hartford Lunch and a Baltimore Lunch?"

"Search me!" he said with much earnestness—and even with worry, I fancied. "Good night!"

We plunged into the gale and stumbled onward, I hugging Leander's shaking arm, and Leander chattering half articulately. The night was ominous and horrible. Up and down the great thoroughfares sparkled a thousand dazzling street-lamps upon no living creature save Leander and myself.

"My dear fellow," I managed to say after a while, "I was right! You are not a reasoning soul. We enter a lunch-room to discover its characteristics, and you fall to quarreling with a stranger over his manners! Really, you discourage me! If you want me to answer your question you *must* be scientific and sensible!"

Leander said not a word. We marched on. It began to snow. Midnight sounded from the towers. A Hartford Lunch beckoned us from across the desolate pavement.

We entered. Two shivering women and a sleepy messenger-boy were huddled in armchairs, taking microscopical sips of boiling cocoa and pecking at some sandwiches. Plainly they were deferring the hour when they must pay their checks and stagger forth into the merciless night.

"Well! Well!" I chuckled, glancing swiftly around, "I am beginning to see! That Baltimore Lunch, Mr. Seethal, had its bowl of toothpicks on the cigar-stand at the right of the cashier's desk. But this Hartford Lunch puts the bowl on a special table opposite the desk. Another point! I observe that the pies and puddings here are thickly sprinkled with nutmeg. Hartford is the capital of Connecticut, the state of the wooden nutmeg. Let us gather up some of the material. If it is wood, then—"

A clatter of crockery checked my speech. Leander had snatched a bowl of custard from the counter; but his benumbed fingers failed him, and the bowl smashed on the hard oak floor. (Please note that the Baltimore Lunch had a tile floor!)

"Mr. Seethal!" I stamped my foot. "If you persist in making a beast of yourself, I shall drop your case, fascinating as it is."

"Hey you!" shouted the cashier. "Cough up fifteen cents for that spill! *If* you've got the price!" Then to me: "Another darned bench bum from Union Square! That's the seventh one to-night!"

"I shall pay the damages, young man!" I fished up some small change. "And I will add a dollar to them, if you will answer one question. What is the difference between a Hartford Lunch and a Baltimore Lunch?" And, to prove my good faith, I planked down my dollar.

One long minute the cashier contemplated me uncertainly. Then dolefully he thrust back the dollar, shook his sleek head, and said: "Search me!"

"That's what they said all day yesterday!" Leander piped, and, from behind me, he leered wickedly at the cashier. "Search me! Search me! Search me! You'd think they were a pack of crooks who had passed along their stolen goods before the bulls pinched them! Well, they are all worse than crooks! They are fools! Fools! Work in Hartford Lunches and don't know why a Hartford Lunch isn't a Baltimore Lunch! Did you ever hear of a sailor that didn't know the difference between a boat and a woodshed, eh? Why! you—"

"Beat it, old Booze, or I'll call a cop!" raged the cashier.

I dragged Leander once more into the night. I stood him up against a barber-pole and spoke coldly. "I am going to solve this problem of yours, Mr. Seethal! It is obviously worthy of my acumen and my dollar-a-minute time. But I want you to understand, Mr. Seethal, that I am no longer engaged in the task on your account. I am doing it out of a pure, scientific passion for Truth. I have lost all respect for you. You suffer from a loathsome disease—"

"I'm only hungry!" sniveled Leander.

"Again you miss my point, sir, and thus confirm it! I do not object to your getting hungry. That is an affliction that, sooner or later, overtakes all men. But I do abominate that canker of the mind which has smitten you. Mr. Seethal, you are utterly, chronically, congenitally irrational! You drag me from my warm room into the December storm, for the sake of settling a definite question of Fact.

Logically, you ought to have assisted me in establishing the Fact. But what do you do? Insult people! Brawl! Smash dishes! Bah! And you call yourself the best-informed man in America! Once more, bah! You are not even informed about yourself! And, as Socrates said, knowledge begins at home."

"There's another lunch-room! See! On the corner!" Leander's eyes bulged, and he tittered like a maniac. "This time I shall eat! If I drop the dish I shall lick it up off the floor!"

"This time you shall eat!" I promised. "Then perhaps you will listen to reason, after a fashion. Come!"

There was but one customer in this Baltimore Lunch, and he was about to leave as we entered. Leander, I regret to say, was mumbling and shuffling scandalously. The one diner eyed the medieval straw hat on Leander's shock of hair. He studied the shiny spots on Leander's second-hand frock coat. He counted the missing buttons on Leander's greasy vest. Then, shaking his head, he thrust a dollar into the frozen fingers of the man who knew that there are no hurricanes in British Guiana.

Leander stared emptily at the bill for an instant. Then he giggled into the man's face: "No good! Your money's no good! I don't take that kind! No, sir! The last fellow that tried to shove it on me got it back in his coffee! Hee! Hee!"

"Pf!" The man wheeled angrily and stalked out. Then Leander, still giggling, dropped his wobbly elbows upon the cashier's desk, and addressed these rambling words to the cashier, whose cheeks had suddenly turned gray:

"Well! I suppose you'll say: 'Search me!' too, eh? That's what the whole crowd says! Search me! Search me! Like any crook that's got away with the goods! Only they're all worse than crooks! Every one of 'em! Heh! Want us to search you, eh? All right! All right! Give 'em third degree!"

Suddenly the cashier gave a deep groan. And, before my unbelieving eyes, the young man sank back in his chair and covered his face with two shaking hands. Now that was odd, wasn't it? I resolved to investigate the young man—very cautiously. I would say little, but hint much and vaguely.

Leander raced toward the pie counter, stumbled, fell, and lay very still. A chair that he had struck toppled over with a rattle. The noise seemed to pull the cashier together. He took his hands away from his face and looked at me, with a very poor imitation of effrontery.

"Who the devil are you?" he demanded in a hollow voice.

"My name is Williams!" I said evenly. "Here is my business card. You may have heard of me. I'm the man who trapped the diamond smugglers last summer. Remember?"

"What—what do you want here?" The words were scarcely audible.

"I have been engaged by a newspaper editor to investigate a very peculiar case."

I spoke with deep intensity and fixed my eyes upon the young man's. "Let us avoid personalities. Let us put the matter in the form of a generalization. Let's talk about things—plain things. There are, in many parts of this town, two things so very much alike that the ordinary man can detect no difference between them. They differ outwardly in their lettering. And some shrewd people suspect that they must differ even more. So I am here, sir, to lay hold of—"

I never finished. Like a bullet from a gun, the cashier leaped from his stool and shot into the darkness and the killing wind of the winter midnight. I heard the patter of his flying feet die away in the unrelenting roar of the blasts.

Then I stepped behind his desk, seized the telephone, and called up the nearest police station. Another minute, and a hundred patrolmen were spreading their invisible net for the fugitive, and two detectives were speeding to me.

I hung up the telephone and was about to move toward Leander, when I noticed a deep drawer below the desk. It stood open; not wide open, but far enough so that I clearly glimpsed into it. There lay, stack upon stack, great thick packages of brand-new one-dollar bills!

"Leander!" I called out sharply.

Leander was sitting up now, rubbing his skull, while a lunch-counter attendant was trying to tug him to his feet. "Well?" said Leander.

"How many dollar bills would it take to fill one cubic foot?"

"A dollar bill," spoke up Leander, like a phonograph, "is seven and a half inches long and three and one-eighth wide. Its area is therefore twenty-three and seven-sixteenths square inches. Old bills are thicker than new bills. If the correspondent will kindly state whether he wishes—to—to know about new bills or old ones, we shall be glad—glad—to— In the issue of August 23, 1901, the *Era* stated—"

Leander's head dropped on his breast. The attendant looked at me, much frightened.

"Leander!" I spoke sharply. "How many quick lunches would this place have to sell in order to take in fifty thousand dollars a day?"

"Two hundred thousand a day!" The human phonograph encyclopedia shot back. "The average quick-lunch ticket is twenty cents for breakfast, thirty cents for dinner, and—twenty-five hurricanes on the coast of British Guiana—"

Then two detectives stormed in, in their wake an excited cub reporter.

"What's up, Mr. Williams?" they demanded obsequiously. "What big game have you trapped this time?"

"One minute!" I hurried over to poor old Asked-and-Answered. "Here's the real detective! We must fix him up first. He has been disguising himself as a starving man, and it has gotten on his nerves. Waiter, bring a big wash-dish from the kitchen! And fill it half full of something hot—hot water, hot milk, hot coffee!"

The waiter did so. Then I ripped off Leander's thin, punctured shoes and his wan blue socks, and stuck his chilled feet into the dish of coffee. In a minute Leander braced up and yelled a little; and then we poked some hot mince-pie into him, and a few other counter-irritants. While Leander munched and the detectives fidgeted and the cub reporter scribbled, I unlimbered my faithful pencil and computed all over the top of a marble table. Swiftly the giant searchlight of my Logic lighted up the mystery of the fugitive and the drawerful of bills. Leander was gulping his last morsel when there arose a great tumult before the restaurant, and in scuffled a fat patrolman dragging our runaway cashier.

"Aha!" I shrilled. "My pretty boy! Just step behind the desk and show the gentlemen your choice assortment of green goods! Spread them out!"

"You've got me!" snarled the cashier, and showed his teeth at me. "I had 'em all fooled! They couldn't spot me! The whole Secret Service fell down on the job—and now you, ha! If that ain't rotten luck! Say, how did you get wise?"

"Whew!" whistled the two detectives, and into the drawer they dived, bringing up the big, crisp bundles. "Why! This is the famous counterfeit that's stumped the Treasury Department for five years! There's a five-thousand-dollar reward out for the capture of the guy who shoves them! Mr. Williams! Congratulations!"

"You're mistaken!" I raised a protesting hand. "It was my friend, Mr. Seethal—" I waved toward Leander—"who came here to search the cashier. I came on another mission—" I hesitated—"and, I may add, a much more difficult one!"

"What could that be?" cried the cub reporter in an anguish of curiosity.

"My boy!" I smiled. "What is the difference between a Baltimore Lunch and a Hartford Lunch?"

"Search me!" said the cub. "And quit your kidding!"

"Gentlemen?" I turned inquiringly to the officers.

"Search me!" each of them echoed.

"Some day I may have the pleasure!" I bowed. "In the meantime, Leander—" I hauled my now drowsy companion to his feet—"let's be jogging along. Call a taxi, sonny! We're tired, and we've got to get up early to-morrow. Leander has to collect his five thousand, y'know."

Leander slept all the way home. He lacks real intelligence, Leander does. He never mentioned Baltimore and Hartford Lunches after he got his hands on that reward. I despise such an intellect. But I find him very useful around the premises. In fact, I must admit that he is a great man. He has an amazing fund of disintegrated information on which I can instantly draw. His mind is perfectly indexed, which is more than you can say of any standard reference book. In fact, the defects of even the best index in the best edited encyclopedia are appalling. I have found, for instance, ...

What Mr. Williams found will be printed in the next report of the Annual Convention of Librarians and Compilers.—Editors.

THE STRANGE CAREER OF MISS GORDON

Edith MacVane

The first four Fanny Gordon stories were published in *McClure's Magazine* in 1913 and 1914. The fifth story was published a few months later as a "Story of the Month." It seems a shame that no further stories appear to have been published, as these stories show far more care in plot and character development than the average series.

THE ZIBELLINE COAT

I

Out of the elegant Parisian crowd swarming through the hall of the Ritz at the hour of déjeuner, two men suddenly detached themselves to Fanny Gordon's eye. One, a very sallow and cynical-eyed young man, was conspicuous for his red fez and much befrogged uniform. The other, whose blue eyes glittered with an evident excitement, wore a fur-lined coat of noticeable richness. As the two passed by Fanny on their way to the *vestiaire*, the Turkish officer tossed a newspaper into the hand of his Parisian companion.

"There, monsieur," he cried gaily, "do me the favor to read the correspondence from Constantinople, and I think you will be convinced!"

"After déjeuner, Pasha!" begged the Frenchman, with a little deprecating smile, as he stuffed the newspaper into the pocket of his fur-lined coat.

The next moment they had both left their outer garments in the cloak-room, pocketed the checks, and mingled with the drifting crowd that with one accord were moving toward the hotel's restaurant.

Though hungry with the unspoiled appetite of twenty-four years, Fanny dared not follow them. That very morning, after a brief but violent scene, she had separated from Mrs. de Morgan, the young widow who had brought her, a fatherless girl, to Europe. The sources of her beautiful chaperon's facile wealth, the part which the young girl herself was perhaps to play in the proposed motor trip to Monte Carlo—Fanny shivered yet as she thought of the perils that her sharp eyes and quick logic had enabled her to discover in time. As a result, however, the sumptuous touring-car with its merry crew had departed for Mediterranean shores without her. And here stood Fanny Gordon alone in Paris, pink-cheeked and pretty in her blue Paquin suit and dashing furs of black fox, with thirty-five francs in her purse and not a soul in the world to whom she could cable for the price of a ticket home. As she faced this grim fact and its meaning, she turned suddenly sick, like an airman whose machine snaps beneath him in mid-flight.

Suddenly, and for the second time, her eye was attracted by a passing stranger—this time, however, with a warm and inexplicable thrill.

"There goes a man I'd like to know!"

As Fanny by chance had placed herself near the cloak-room, the newcomer perforce passed close by her. As he gave his silk hat and fur-lined coat to the attendant, his eyes met Fanny's for an instant. She noticed the bright blue of the irides, the haughty curve of the Roman nose between them; then, with a little thrill of girlish vexation, their utter and complete obliviousness to her own charming presence. Enraged at her momentary weakness, she turned her back; and when next she glanced toward the cloak-room, the stranger was gone.

Suddenly there came to her mind the thought of her own fur-lined motor-coat, a present from Mrs. de Morgan, which had been left here in the cloak-room at tea-time the day before. She opened her purse. Yes, the check was still there. Should she claim the coat, drive with it to the mont de piété, and see if by pawning it she could obtain the price of a few days' board at some cheap pension?

With this thought in her mind, she turned toward the cloak-room. At that moment the young man with the Roman nose strolled past her once more, carrying a cocktail glass in his hand. With an air of supreme indifference, his clear blue eyes glanced about him as if he had come back from the restaurant to look for some one and that some one were not worth the seeking.

At the entrance of the cloak-room he suddenly stumbled, and the cocktail glass fell crashing to the floor. The attendant sprang forward to mend the damage. Quick as thought, the stranger stepped up to his overcoat, removed the check pinned upon it, and fastened it to the zibelline-lined coat worn by the gentleman who had entered with the Turk. The numbered slip belonging to this last he replaced upon the sleeve of his own garment, took a silk handkerchief from the pocket, blew his nose loudly, tossed a franc to the kneeling attendant, and strolled back toward the restaurant. The whole business had been performed with such assurance and with so admirable a sleight-of-hand that for an instant Fanny hardly realized the significance of what she had seen.

She thrilled with a sudden odd emotion. "He is stealing that fur coat! Why? His own is just as handsome!"

In the midst of her own enforced idleness, curiosity suddenly flamed high. She mused with intensity: "Why does he want that other man's coat? Why?"

Suddenly, with an odd little shock, she realized that if she chose to gratify her curiosity she need be afraid of no risks, because her situation could not possibly be worse than it was at present. Hers was the immunity of the desperate. And, besides, the reward—the cash reward to be gained by returning the coat to the rightful owner! Quick as a flash, she jumped to her feet and strolled to the door of the coat-room, now empty of all but its attendant.

"That's a game two can play at!" she said to herself excitedly.

A glance sufficed to identify her own brown motor-coat, hanging on its peg where it had been placed the night before. With a swift impulse, she raised her hand to her neck. She stumbled. The next moment a dainty pendant of turquoise and diamonds, the sole heirloom in her possession, flew out and lodged behind the steam radiator by the wall. Fanny uttered a muffled scream.

"Oh, please!" she begged the attendant. "My *pendent!* It's gone behind the radiator."

The obliging garçon, warmed by the remembrance of Mrs. de Morgan's lavish tips, went down on his stomach and poked through the pipes with the point of a long pencil. Quick as winking, Fanny detached the green numbered tag from her own motor-coat, pinned it to the sleeve of the zibelline overcoat whose number had already once been changed, attached the latter number to her own coat, and turned to thank the purple-faced and dusty attendant, who scrambled to his feet with her pendant in his hand.

With careless generosity she put a five-franc piece in his hand and presented him with the numbered check which she drew from her silver bag. "My coat, please!"

Her heart beat quickly and painfully. She felt herself launched in mid-adventure. The next moment the garçon had placed on her arm the coat that bore her number, and whose luxurious zibelline lining cuddled with the warmth of a kitten against her side.

She turned toward the lift. Then, down the length of the arched corridor that led to the dining-room, she caught a glimpse of the young man with the Roman nose, whom it was now her chief purpose to avoid. No; her room would be the worst possible place. Who could tell how soon she would be interrupted and the mistaken check rectified? Following the reckless impulse of adventure that had seized her, the excited girl dashed to the door of the hotel and out into the frosty March air.

"Call me a taxi quickly!" she said imperiously to the uniformed attendant at the-door.

The next instant she was installed in a throbbing red motor. "Drive me to the Bois!" she said. "And, chauffeur, listen! I have been much annoyed by a man that is following me. If he attempts to follow the automobile, you are not to let him catch us. There will be a good *pourboire* at the end. Do you understand?"

The chauffeur nodded, and the machine started violently ahead across the Place Vendôme and whirled out into the Rue Boétie. Hurriedly Fanny turned the zibelline coat between her hands. If she could find a clue to the owner's name and address, she might order the chauffeur to drive directly there, and avoid the scene that would be inevitable at the hotel.

There were pockets inside and out. A pair of fur motor gloves and goggles, a white silk handkerchief with the embroidered initial B, a last night's theater-program, a bottle of violet perfume in a dainty satin case, tied up as for a present to a lady—these were all she found, except the copy of the *Matin* still sticking from the outer pocket. With a sudden thought, she opened the paper and searched its columns. Marked passages there were none, but a letter whirled to her feet. She snatched it. Her finger touched the wax that sealed it; but on the other side, to her intense disappointment, her eye beheld no address whatever. So far as its outside went, the envelope in her hand was entirely blank.

Should she break the seal? Should she return to the Ritz and seek the Turk and his companion? At that moment a siren screamed almost in her ears. Turning, she saw a large black car coming, and through its crystal screen beheld the bright blue eyes of the Roman-nosed young man streaming straight into hers.

Her heart leaped. But her chauffeur, noting the pursuer, had crossed the Étoile into the Avenue du Bois at full speed. At this hour of déjeuner the Bois de Boulogne was almost empty, and the two machines thundered along at racing speed. Fanny's first thought was to take the letter which instinct warned her was the moving power of the whole affair, and secrete it closely inside the front of her blouse. Her second was to turn the fur coat inside out and slip it on. The superb zibelline lining, thus exposed to the air, had every appearance of a lady's winter coat. Then, leaning back in her corner, she enjoyed the chase.

But her triumph was brief. The taxi-cab with the advantage which pursued must have over pursuer, held its own with the beautiful high-speeded machine behind it. But suddenly the chauffeur of the stranger, leaning across his master, bellowed to Fanny's driver in an argot whose syllables her keen ears could catch but could not translate. Its import, however, she was forced to understand a few moments later, when her taxi, whirling for the third time about the lake, skidded, trembled, and came to a full stop.

Swallowing her sudden terror, she drew the fur coat about her and gazed out over the gray waters of the little lake. A voice, deep but of singularly agreeable quality, struck on her ear:

"Madame! I make you all my excuses, but I think that by mistake you took my driving coat, just now, at the Ritz."

With an air of languid surprise, Fanny turned. The face that she met struck her anew by its haughty and regular lineaments, which just now were bent on her with some severity, as on a naughty child. She answered briefly:

"Monsieur, it is you that are mistaken. I did not take your coat."

"But, madame," cried the stranger excitedly, "I beg your pardon, but that is my coat you are wearing at this instant! And, as you see, I have none."

In fact, he stood straight and supple in his dark gray suit, unsheltered from the keen March wind. But Fanny was obdurate. She even smiled slightly.

"Monsieur," she answered courteously, "it is always possible—the boy at the Ritz may have given me the wrong coat. If this is yours, describe to me the contents of the pockets and you shall have it immediately."

"Certainly," he replied promptly, "a pair of gloves. A handkerchief—"

"What initial?" interrupted Fanny.

"B!" he replied, and his eyes defied hers. Then he added quickly:

"A newspaper. A—a paper—"

"But these articles you enumerate, monsieur," returned Fanny smoothly, "are such as are commonly found in overcoat pockets. And as for the initial, of course. But this paper you speak of, we have there something more precise. Describe it, please!"

He swallowed his obviously growing rage. "A—a letter!"

She nodded. "Yes—directed to whom?"

"Mademoiselle—my concierge handed it to me as I left my house this morning, and—*mafoi!* I had not yet had time even to glance at it!"

"But, monsieur, it must have been directed to you, or your concierge would not have handed it to you!"

In the handsome face before her the lines of pride wavered and broke. The blue eyes, crinkling up into sudden disarming laughter, seemed for the first time to take cognizance of the girlish beauty before them. He glanced sideways to make sure that the drivers were out of hearing of them.

"Ah, Mademoiselle Sherlock Holmes! I own you have the better of me there. I throw myself on your mercy. I confess, the coat is not mine—any more than it is yours!"

Fanny bridled. "But *I* am taking it back to its owner, monsieur!" she retorted briefly.

The stranger's eyes surveyed her with sudden gravity. He stepped toward her.

"Mademoiselle, time presses. Every moment is of value. That coat, as you see, has two sides—broadcloth and fur. It has also two sides that you do not see: danger and riches. Take it back to Bazin, as you say, and you walk into the jaws of the first. Listen to me and—mademoiselle, mademoiselle, won't you trust me?"

"So Bazin is the name of the coat's owner, is it?" she said slowly, as fragments of gossip heard in Mrs. de Morgan's salon drifted back to her memory. "Bazin, the great financier?"

Excitement at the possibilities awakened by this famous name ran and quivered in her voice. The stranger glared at her.

"Ah, the magic of a name! And yet, mademoiselle, perhaps my name also may have its magic. But, if I present myself, what right have I to expect your belief? The one recommendation I have to you is that you have seen me steal! And yet, it is vitally important that you should trust me." He glanced about impatiently at the lonely trees. "If we were in the city, anybody could tell you who I am." He raised his voice to address his chauffeur. "Barbe, which is the nearest of the Bois' restaurants?"

"Monsieur, I should say—Amenonville."

"Then drive us there. Mademoiselle, will you do me the honor to accompany me?"

Fanny hesitated and her color rose.

The stranger laughed. "Mademoiselle, please observe that if I were a man capable of violence I might long ago have used it in this solitary spot. On my word of honor as a gentleman, you can trust me! Do me the favor to step into my auto, and we will go to Amenonville."

II

IN SPITE OF THE intensity of his voice, its accents invited confidence. She stepped into the tonneau, while the stranger paid her taximeter and flung himself into his place beside the chauffeur. Precisely sixty seconds later he had helped her from the car and was conducting her into the palm-lined hall of the Bois' smartest restaurant. At the desk sat a stout, arrogant man arranging gold coins in symmetrical piles. Fanny's escort strode toward him.

"Monsieur, a favor! Will you kindly tell this young lady who I am? It is a bet."

The stout man slid from his seat, knocking his golden piles into unheeded confusion. Arrogance became supple humility as, bringing his heels together, he bowed and murmured:

"Monsieur le Vicomte! Too much honor! But who is there in Paris that does not know Monsieur le Vicomte Raoul de Chatellerault?"

Fanny started. The Vicomte de Chatellerault was one of the two most celebrated young men in Paris, its most famous duelist, its most dashing horseman, its most exquisite art connoisseur; the brother of the beautiful Duchesse d'Ubzac, gleams of whose aristocratic splendor had penetrated even the tawdry Bohemian circle into which Fanny's late chaperon had presented her.

"And now, if Monsieur le Vicomte will conduct Madame to the dining-room, I will engage to find him a table—"

Fanny hesitated, but her healthy young appetite betrayed her. The next moment she was seating herself at a little flower-trimmed table in an angle of the crowded restaurant. With a courteous gesture, her escort lifted the fur coat from her shoulders, and she saw his hands run like water from one pocket to another. Then he plucked out the copy of the *Matin* and glanced with furious haste through its columns. His brow contracted—the paper rattled in his hand.

"There was something else!" he declared fiercely. "An inclosure—a letter—"

"If there was a letter," returned Fanny sweetly, as she applied herself to the hors d'oeuvres, "I can assure you, it was not directed to the Vicomte de Chatellerault!"

Her host shot her a quick, savage glance. Then he plucked at his watch. "Half past twelve!" he said hurriedly. "At half past one Bazin will be back in the *vestiaire* looking for his coat—certainly no sooner, as he is one of the most celebrated gourmets in Paris and had ordered a famous déjeuner for himself and the Pasha. But at half past one—Mademoiselle, the case is one of life and death, or near it. Instead of being my enemy, can I induce you to act as my ally?"

In his handsome face was all the charm of pride when it unbends to plead. Impulse, which had set Fanny to balking his schemes, now urged her to go over to his side. The waiter placed a plate of soup before her. She hesitated.

"Mademoiselle," said the Vicomte, in measured tones, "there is a reward of a hundred thousand francs to be earned before nightfall. Do you wish a share in it?"

Fanny started. A hundred thousand francs! She nodded, her dark eyes glowing. Her host surveyed her keenly.

"I had meant," he said, "to act alone. But fate has interfered. Without you I can do nothing. But with your help—if I may judge from the wit and audacity you have displayed—I can do that which I might not accomplish alone. And, in any case, I have no choice but to ask your aid. Will you give me your word of honor to serve me loyally? I need not say I give the same pledge to you. I only add, the adventure is one that may involve some risk of life."

At the intense earnestness of his tone a little shiver ran down Fanny's spine. Risk of life! But, after all, what was her life? And, left alone, where were her means to preserve it?

"Yes," she answered.

Like gimlets of light, her host's bright eyes bored into her soul. "Your name, mademoiselle?"

She told him. He drew a long breath and touched her hand across the table in token of their alliance. "Mademoiselle, in trusting you with this secret I am trusting you with my life. But you have eaten of my salt, and your eyes are not eyes that could betray. Listen! This winter I have had heavy losses on the Bourse. And, so, like many others of my *monde*, I occasionally act in the employment of the Secret Service. At this moment"—he lowered his voice and spoke with intense rapidity—"I serve Bulgaria, who wants me to procure for her a copy of the new secret treaty between

Vienna and Constantinople. In this treaty, we have reason to believe, Austria agrees to supply Turkey with munitions of war, for the war she is now waging against the Balkan Allies. Turkey, on her side, grants Austria an exclusive concession for the new Teheran railway. If Bazin gets a sight of that treaty he may make millions by buying up all the land on the right of way, as well as subscribing to the capital stock. It is his last chance—I happen to know that if he does not succeed in pulling off this *coup* he is a ruined man. A desperate man, and dangerous! So, with all the money he can raise, he has bribed Irman Pasha to obtain him a sight of the treaty.

"This very morning the treaty was signed and sealed by the high contracting parties, the special envoys of Vienna and of Constantinople. And, according to secret information received at headquarters, the Turkish envoy drives directly after to the Ministry of War, where from two o'clock to five he is to be closeted with members of the French Cabinet. As for the treaty, he leaves it behind in his rooms at the Turkish embassy, under the care of his beloved nephew, Irman Pasha—while Irman profits by his absence by arranging with Bazin that in these three hours, Bazin shall slip into the embassy and with his own eyes read the treaty. And that newspaper that Irman tossed to Bazin, I have every reason to believe, holds the passwords and the keys."

Fanny glanced at him shrewdly. "And, if you obtain them, you can enter the Envoy's apartments instead of Bazin?"

He nodded excitedly. "And obtain the information for the Balkan Allies! So that they can know when and where to seize the Austrian importations of munitions of war into Turkey. In return for this intelligence, the government at Sofia will pay me a hundred thousand francs."

Suddenly, as the waiter stooped to place a blazing chafing-dish of oysters on the table, the Vicomte snatched again at his watch.

"Ten minutes gone! Mademoiselle, decide quickly, or *tonnerre de Dieu!* I have betrayed my own secret uselessly, and neither of us shall touch a centime of the hundred thousand francs!"

For answer, Fanny drew the envelope from her bosom and handed it to him. He opened it and eagerly drew out the sheet from within. Then his jaw fell and his face withered as at the moment of death. An instant later, regaining his self-control, he passed the sheet back to her. A little bunch of keys dropped clinking on the table, but the paper itself was blank.

"Euchred!" said the Vicomte bitterly. "Here are the keys, but the directions for entering—of course, the Pasha gives them to Bazin by word of mouth. Why should he run the risk of writing them down, when they eat déjeuner together?"

Suddenly Fanny uttered a little incoherent noise. The paper in her hand, on its upper corner, was suddenly covered with characters of pale brown.

"Why, it's not blank!" she puzzled. "*Dire an concierge deuxième étage.*" She glanced up excitedly. "I have it! The flame of the chafing-dish! It's written in sympathetic ink!"

With a courteous "Pardon, mademoiselle," the Vicomte took the sheet of paper from her hand, held it cautiously to the blazing alcohol flame, and studied its contents. When he glanced up again, his face was flushed a light red and his eyes shone.

"You are right," he said. "Here are the full directions for entering the envoy's apartment and finding the document. Every moment is precious. Come! Come!"

Fanny's excitement matched his, but it was born of a new thought. "Not yet!" she said breathlessly, as she turned to the approaching waiter. "Garçon, quickly! Bring me writing materials—plain paper. And, garçon, bring me a sliced lemon!"

"Mademoiselle, you are mad!"

"Vicomte, one moment. It is not yet two o'clock, and we must make our preparations while we have the means!"

With a determined gesture, Fanny's host called for the *addition* and for his fur motor coat. In the instant of waiting, the obedient garçon had filled Fanny's order.

"Lemon—for the oysters, madam?"

"Yes—put it down."

Hastily she squeezed the lemon into the bottom of an empty glass, dipped her pen into the juice, and wrote. Then from her watch chain she detached a couple of small trunk-keys, slipped them into the envelope with her letter, sealed the flap, and rose to her feet.

"That copy of the *Matin*? Here it is under the table."

"Mademoiselle, haste, haste! Are you mad?"

With an impatient step, the Vicomte strode from the restaurant and out to the waiting automobile. Fanny, folding her newly written letter into the crumpled copy of the *Matin*, followed him.

"Chauffeur, to No. 301 Rue Faubourg Saint Honoré!"

Fanny jumped into the automobile. "No. Chauffeur, to the Ritz!" Then, turning to her frowning companion, she smiled with girlish sweetness into his face.

"Don't you see, Vicomte? If Bazin is really such a dangerous man, then we must dispose of him before you go to risk your life at the Turkish embassy! See this letter I have prepared for him, which looks just like that of the Pasha, except that, when Bazin holds it to the blaze, he will read: 'Come to Stamboul!' There, I've folded it inside the *Matin*. Let me put it into the pocket of the zibelline coat, just as it was before. And here are the other articles—his gloves, his bottle of violet perfume—"

In spite of his preoccupation, the Vicomte uttered a short laugh. "Easy to guess who *that* is for! the fair Violette d'Amour, of the Folies Frivoles—"

"I've heard her sing!" cried Fanny triumphantly. "So she is a friend of Bazin's!"

"Hm—if spending a half million francs a year on her can assure her friendship. Though they say of late she has been smiling on Irman Pasha as well. But I beg your pardon, mademoiselle, for speaking of such *canaille* in your presence," added de Chatellerault, with a look of respect. "So it is your scheme to carry the coat back and leave it for Bazin at the Ritz?"

The flying auto cleared the Arc de Triomphe and sped on its return way down the Champs Élysées. Fanny bit her lip.

"Yes—no!" she hesitated. "Do you not see, monsieur, the thing for us to do is to keep Bazin in play while you go to the embassy and copy the treaty? If I could put on the coat and keep him following me. But it's not a woman's coat."

She paused a moment, then the clear color blazed up suddenly into her round, pretty face. She turned to him excitedly. "Monsieur, I have it! You must put on the zibelline coat and trail Bazin, and I will go to the embassy!"

"What!" The young man stared at her astounded. "Your idea of the false letter is superb. I take off my hat to you. But to allow you to steal into the Turkish embassy—which, as you know, is not even French soil nor responsible to its laws—no! For a man, it means to take his life in his hands. But for a child, a beautiful child like you!"

Fanny gave him a look of compassion. "A child that has cut her wisdom teeth, as you may observe, Vicomte! But quick, we must decide. If you do your part well, what danger can there be for me? Go back to the Ritz now, wearing the coat. Saunter in the foyer, where Bazin can see you. At the very moment when he discovers the exchange, jump into your automobile! Then trail him over Paris, keeping always in public places where you will be protected by the crowd. All you have to do is to hold him, hold him on your track till half past four—yes, that should give me ample time. Then go back to the Ritz, leave the coat in the *vestiaire*."

"With the false letter in the pocket!"

"Precisely. At that hour he may obey it and take the train for Constantinople, or come to the embassy if he chooses. In any, case, I shall be gone."

The young Frenchman surveyed her with open admiration.

"Here are the letter and keys. Here is a revolver. It is lucky that I have two, for I am likely to need one myself in my little game of tag with Bazin! Listen; take writing materials with you. Do not carry off the treaty, or leave any signs that it has been disturbed. That would ruin everything. Copy it. You write quickly?"

Fanny nodded. "And when it is copied?"

"Take it back to the Ritz with you. This evening, if I am still alive, I will call for it, Mademoiselle Gordon, there at your hotel."

She nodded. "I shall expect you. But, monsieur, I must not go back with you now! Here we are in the Rue Royale. Stop the auto—let me get into a taximeter."

He obeyed her. She turned toward him quickly. "Monsieur, I left all my money at the hotel. If you will kindly lend me a trifle for my taxi—"

Hastily he pushed a hundred-franc note into her hand. She saw that he was very pale, but his only words were: "Au revoir!"

In the crowded Rue Royale, Fanny was left alone. "It's sink or swim for me now!" she said, and set her teeth.

III

AT THE MILLINERY counter of the Galeries Lafayette stood Fanny Gordon, trying on hats. One especially dashing affair, crowned in violets and with a sweeping *pleureuse* at the side, took her eye. She remembered the description she had heard of Bazin's fair friend, and smiled.

"So I'm Violet, too!" she said to herself whimsically. Then aloud: "*Combien, mademoiselle?*"

"Seventy-five francs, madame."

"I will wear it. And—here; kindly send the black velvet hat I was wearing to this address."

The address she gave, was naturally, a wrong one. For her object in changing headgear was to effect, as far as possible, a disguise.

Having already dismissed the taxi in which she had driven to the Galeries, she took her seat in a new one.

"Rue Faubourg Saint Honoré—number 301," she said resolutely, and fell to studying the letter that was to be her guide.

At the door of a large and beautiful mansion of gray stone, remarkable for the fact that all its shutters were tight closed, her taxi stopped.

"No, chauffeur; the side door, around the corner!"

At the side door she was received by the concierge, a stout Frenchman with a sleepy eye.

"From the modiste in the Rue de la Paix, for madame!" she said, using the phrase indicated in the letter as the "open sesame" of the outer door. There was an instant of horrid suspense, while the man's lazy eyes fastened themselves on her thick white lace veil.

"So you forgot something, mademoiselle!" he said sleepily. Fanny's heart had a cramp. Had she really bungled the password? In spite of his criticism, however, the concierge seemed to find her countersign sufficient, went back to his arm-chair, and relapsed into his somnolent calm.

Fanny entered the embassy.

From this side door an ancient staircase of bare gray stone wound upward. Complete silence reigned. An odor of garlic and of coffee penetrated to her nostrils as she sped up the stairs. At the first landing she beheld a negro servant in a yellow and black livery, standing motionless as a statue. Those fantastic words that had started from the page before the flame of the chafing-dish—was it possible he could recognize them? She murmured a jargon of Eastern syllables that she had learned by rote, and he bowed submissively.

Onward upstairs she flew, and down a long corridor. The first door at the right—here it was! And at the door sat another negro, huge and misshapen like a eunuch of the Arabian Nights, whose white turban made a gleaming spot in the semi-darkness.

For the first time Fanny realized the wild nature of the adventure into which she had so thoughtlessly plunged. Raoul's words came back to her: "Remember, in the embassy you are no longer on French soil, nor protected by its laws!" For a moment her voice almost quavered from her control as she uttered the magic phrase that was to open the door of the envoy's cabinet to her:

"There is but one God, and Allah is his prophet!"

The next moment she almost swooned in relief and joy. The negro, rising to his feet with a low bow, opened wide the door and ushered her in. Then the door closed behind her and she was left alone.

She cast a swift eye about her. Had she traveled two pairs of stairs, or two thousand miles? For the vast room was the Orient complete.

Red silk curtains shut out the daylight. A divan, covered with embroidered cushions, ran around the wall. Rugs of an unimaginable depth and richness covered the floor. In the middle a tiny fountain played. The air was heavy with myrrh and attar of roses, and spicy cigarettes recently smoked. The only touches that might recall the Western world without were a heap of smart luggage by the door, a splendid fire of logs, and a large carved writing-table of dark wood.

Dominating the overpowering impression made by her surroundings, Fanny tiptoed toward the table. For an instant she smiled in sudden relief as through the mysterious Oriental twilight there came to her straining ears a little homely sound: "Tick-tick-tick-tick." She turned the switch of the desk-lamp and glanced at the traveling-clock beside it. To her amazement, it marked half past seven. Another passing spasm of fear shook her until she saw that it had stopped. She snatched at her watch. Only three o'clock. Her time was ample, and everything was going splendidly.

One, two, three, four! The fourth drawer from the top on the left-hand side. The little key, inserted by her trembling hand, slid and skated on the polished brass plate before she pushed it home and turned it. The next instant the drawer flew open, and under her eyes lay a sight that made her forget the present terror that dogged her footsteps, the tragic uncertainty that lurked for her in the great Paris without. For there lay a black seal attaché case, whose polished padlock caught the light.

A hundred thousand francs! Fanny's hands shook as she arranged on the table the writing materials which, according to the Vicomte's instructions, she had bought at the Galeries and brought with her in her bag. Her ears strained themselves. She swallowed hard, laid down her sharpened pencil on the table, and inserted the second key in the padlock of the attaché case. Her terrors vanished; her eyes blazed as she saw that it contained a single paper—a long slim, oblong of pale blue, folded once and secured with a rubber band.

Her breath stopped as she crouched to pick it up. The next moment her face went white and her jaw dropped. The crackling sheets, as her hands passed over them, were completely blank. An odor of violets, oddly fresh and Occidental among the blend of Eastern perfumes, rose to her nostrils. But that was all.

Then her chest heaved in a little laugh that was a gasp of relief. Aha! Their tricks had not fooled her the first time, with the blank letter from Bazin's pocket up there at Amenonville! Was that a step? Her breath stopped, her ears strained.

No, the silence was unbroken. With the new-found document in her hand, she ran over to the hearth and held out the blue sheets of papers to the heat of the blazing logs.

She waited. Then she saw that, instead of transforming themselves into pages of manuscript under the action of the heat as the letter had done, they remained blank. She held them slanting to the light. Not a scratch, not the faintest marring of the paper was visible.

Slowly the dreadful truth penetrated her brain. Either Bazin had been there before her, or Irman Pasha had made a mistake and the treaty had never been placed there at all.

The tears started to her eyes. Desperately she rummaged the drawer, ran her hands about the lining of the attaché case. Nothing! Then, in fierce haste, she tried her key on the other drawers of the writing-table. One by one, they refused to yield to her touch. It was clear, the key in the Pasha's letter was adapted only to the drawer that she had already opened. And in that drawer what she sought was not.

With unsteady hands, she replaced the blank sheets of paper, locked the attaché case, locked the table drawer. The dark red curtains seemed to wave. For the first time fear seized her, together with a sickening sense of her own utter failure. Panic-stricken, empty-handed, she turned and fled from the room.

The tall negro rose to let her pass. Down the stairs she sped. The March wind was cold on her tear-filled eyes as she emerged on the sidewalk and gave the command to her waiting driver:

"To the Ritz."

IV

AT NINE O'CLOCK that evening, when Fanny had barely finished her frugal supper, a card was brought in to her:

"*Raoul de Chatellerault de Beaumont*"—with the Vicomte's crown above.

"Show him upstairs."

A few moments later the *valet de pied* knocked on the door of her salon, and the Vicomte de Chatellerault, with the most *dégagé* air in the world, entered the room.

He bowed. The door was shut. Fanny, her finger at her lips, tiptoed toward it, glanced up and down the corridor, then returned to her visitor. Suddenly from his smooth forehead the veins started out like snakes. He came toward her.

"You went to the embassy? You found *it* there?"

Fanny Gordon bent her pretty head low.

"No, Vicomte, the treaty was not there."

"God!" The exclamation was wrenched from the young man's lips like a groan. His face withered, his hand shot out behind him to clutch the air by which he stood. Then he murmured bitterly:

"I ought to have gone myself."

Fanny, who had opened her lips to speak, shut them with a snap at this reflection on her powers. Then she inquired shortly:

"What do you think you would have done?"

The Vicomte, regaining his self-control, surveyed her with reproachable superiority.

"Instead of wasting our time in useless discussion, mademoiselle, suppose we hear what was actually done—or not done!"

With dry brevity she recounted her adventure of the afternoon.

"And so, mademoiselle," cried de Chatellerault bitterly, "while I was trailing Bazin up and down Paris, risking my life every instant, you simply returned here to the Ritz?"

Fanny shot him a look out of her bright eyes. "Almost. But, you see, I was stopped!"

"Ah!" Her listener started violently. "The hounds! then they dared—"

"No, Vicomte, it was none of Bazin's crowd that stopped me. It was—yes, it was a pretty lady in a pale purple gown, holding a glass of champagne in her hand!"

In the haughty blue eyes bent upon her, reproach was changed to pitying contempt. "Mademoiselle, I will now leave you. I recommend you to go at once to bed—"

"No, Vicomte, my brain is not giving way. One moment, please! Have you not seen it on the street, the poster of the new *revue*—'Embrasse-Moi Vite!'

"Ah!" This time the Vicomte's tone was anything but contemptuous. Laying down his hat and stick again, he came toward Fanny with a new interest in his eyes.

"At the Folies Frivoles!—Violette d'Amour!"

Fanny nodded. "I recognized the name as soon as I saw it—you had said, Bazin's lady-love!"

"Yes!" returned her listener excitedly. "And, mademoiselle—then?"

"Then there came into my head, like a flash, one or two other little odd circumstances, which seemed like nothing at the time but which came back to me now with meaning. For instance, the concierge at the embassy, when I said the password to him, replied: 'So you have forgotten something, mademoiselle?' I thought he meant I had forgotten part of the phrase. Now I realized, all of a sudden, he meant something else. He meant: 'Is it to look for something you have forgotten that you come back?' What other woman wearing a violet hat, such as I was wearing myself, had entered that door of the Turkish embassy before I entered it myself this afternoon? That the first comer had possessed the necessary password was evident. Bazin possessed the password, or was about to. I knew there existed a woman, a brilliant adventuress, with whom Bazin was on intimate terms, and for whom he bought bottles of violette de Parme. And, Vicomte, those blank sheets of paper which I had found in the attaché case where the treaty ought to have been—they gave out a faint perfume. And that perfume was violette de Parme."

In a swift undertone, Fanny brought her long speech to a close. The Vicomte leaned toward her in tense excitement.

"Not bad! Your reasoning, at least, was not bad, mademoiselle. And then—"

"Then, monsieur, I said to my driver: 'I have changed my mind. I do not go to the Ritz, I go to the Théâtre des Folies Frivoles!'"

"But in the afternoon—"

"I know; but I meant to find out the address of the house of Mademoiselle d'Amour. When I arrived at the theater, however, I found that, luckily, there was a special matinée for the benefit of the Aged Actors' Retreat. So I went to the stage entrance, I announced myself as the sister of the star, and demanded to be taken to her dressing-room! Naturally, there were objections. Mademoiselle was on the stage; I must wait:

"'Wait,' I cried. 'For my own sister? Make me wait here one instant longer, and you shall see what Mademoiselle Violette will give you when she comes!'

"My impudence! However, it carried the day. They took me to the dressing-room—a little bijou place, all tufted in lilac satin, and a great silver bowl full of violets—the biggest I ever saw. But the perfume was stifling. And then, my fear when I thought, 'Suppose she comes!' So I told the maid I was faint, and gave her a louis to go and get me a glass of wine.

"She said: 'It is twenty minutes before madame leaves the scene. Madame will not tell madame her sister that I went out?'

"I promised not to tell. She went. I was left alone. And the next ten minutes, monsieur. I hunted—oh, how I hunted!"

"But, mademoiselle," cried the Vicomte incredulously. "Such a search was mere childishness! You risked your life, perhaps—for what? Not even a clue!"

"Vicomte, if as I thought, Mademoiselle d'Amour had been at the embassy before me, then she had had no time to go home before coming to play her matinee. She must have driven direct to the theater. The manuscript of the treaty was too bulky for her to conceal on her person when she went on the stage; ergo, the treaty must be there in that little dressing-room. I knew her intelligence; and, like the man in Poe's story, I based my search on the idea of that intelligence which I had to meet. There was a pile of loose music. I thumbed it through. Inside the huge silver puffbox. No!

The violet silk cushions—they held only down. The time was so short, the possible hiding-places so many! Suddenly my eye fell on the silver bowl of violets—something like the bowl of violets on my table yonder, Vicomte!

"Suddenly into my head popped the idea, 'How strange!' For, to judge by the perfume they gave out, it was plain that those violets were fresh to-day like mine. Yet their petals drooped as if they had been gathered days ago—or as if the silver bowl that held them were dry."

She paused abruptly, and, rising from her seat, went over to the little Louis XIV guéridon which held the violets in their large silver bowl. With a light finger she caressed the fading purple petals.

"Poor little flowers! Dear little flowers! To keep flowers without water, Vicomte, seems to me a cruelty, like keeping a baby without milk."

The color flared into de Chatellerault's face. He took one look down at the silver bowl; glanced back into Fanny's face; then threw himself upon the flowers with a wordless cry. Right and left on the pale carpet went the dark shower of violets. And, there, in the dry and shining bottom of the bowl, lay a folded document of pale blue paper, secured by a broad rubber strap.

There was silence. Then the young man's hand shot out—his quick eye ran over the typewritten sheets. As he turned over the last page, which held the signatures and seals, he slowly nodded his head. His face blazed crimson. In his eyes were something like tears. He paused a moment; then, dropping on both knees at Fanny's feet, he took her hand and kissed it as if it had been the hand of a queen.

"I doubted you," he said in a low tone; "I doubted you. Forgive me. You are sublime. And I—I am not worthy to kneel at your feet. But I kneel and pay you my homage to your intelligence, to your courage, and to you!"

"That's all right," returned Fanny briskly. "And now, please do get the thing hidden away again. B-r-r! It makes me shiver to have it out loose like that!"

The Vicomte, rising, glanced hurriedly about him.

"I'm off," he said quickly. "I must take this to the Bulgarian embassy before the theft is discovered in the rue Faubourg Saint Honoré. Mademoiselle, can you give me a large envelope to put it in—or, better still, a newspaper such as our friend Bazin used?"

On the floor by the door lay the evening paper, which, by its late occupant's command, was still left nightly at the suite. In response to Fanny's gesture, the Vicomte picked it up and hurriedly unfolded it.

"Name of a name!"

De Chatellerault stood like a statue, his eyes glued on the journal's front page. With a little gesture of feminine curiosity, Fanny Gordon came tiptoeing up behind him. In flaring headlines, this is what she read:

BOMB EXPLOSION AT TURKISH EMBASSY—
PASHA BLOWN TO ATOMS

"Irman Pasha—he's dead!" she heard the Vicomte's voice in her ear. Then, in an accent of sudden horror:

"Mademoiselle, at what hour did you leave the embassy?"

"Half past three," she answered faintly. The Vicomte searched the printed column before him.

"The explosion was at a quarter before four," he said solemnly, and there was silence.

"But Irman," he added suddenly—"what was he doing there? I noticed he had deserted Bazin! And the bomb? Who could have thrown it? The police are absolutely without a clue—"

"The bomb!" Fanny gasped. "I know now! That was what I heard, and I thought it was a clock. Ticking, ticking under the table. A time-fuse—that was what it was. And I thought it was a clock!"

Sick and giddy at the thought of the hideous death that had passed her by so nearly, she flung herself into an arm-chair. De Chatellerault stood looking down at her with eyes into which had leaped a new emotion.

"A quarter hour after you left! Mademoiselle, had you found the treaty there, as we hoped, and sat down to copy it according to our plans—" With a violent shudder, he desisted. Then he added:

"Whatever were her intentions, mademoiselle, it was Violette d'Amour that saved your life, and we may thank her—her and the *bon Dieu*—that you sit here alive to-night."

Fanny's face was still white, but she managed to smile. With a sudden start, de Chatellerault turned, folded the treaty inside the newspaper, thrust them into his pocket, and held out his hand.

"And now, with full speed to headquarters," he said. "Mademoiselle, I beg you not to forget to lock your doors well to-night! To-morrow, at half past eleven precisely, I return to the Ritz to report to you what I have done. And now—good night and *au revoir!*"

V

ON FANNY GORDON'S bed was heaped a snowy pile of embroidered blouses and ruffled lingerie. Outside, the clocks of Paris were pealing the hour of noon. The *blanchisseuse*, on the other side of the bed, placed one fat hand on her bulging hip, while with the other she extended her bill.

"Twenty-four francs fifty centimes, mademoiselle," she said.

Fanny turned faint; for the hour of the promised visit had already passed, and no word from Raoul de Chatellerault. Had she been a fool, after all, so lightly to trust a stranger with a treasure for which she had risked her life? Here before her, red-faced and imperious, stood bankruptcy incarnate; for in the whole world she possessed only six francs twenty-five centimes.

The next moment she had caught her breath—an instant's respite, at least!

"Give me your bill," she said indifferently. "I will initial it, to be paid downstairs at the *bureau*. I can't be troubled with these little accounts myself, you understand!"

The *blanchisseuse*, passing out through the door, bumped her fat form against a hurrying *valet de pied*. Deep respect was in his voice as he announced the exalted name:

"Mademoiselle, the Vicomte Raoul de Chatellerault!"

"Show him upstairs."

The awaited visitor entering the room, came with a changed aspect: a light suit of English tweeds and a morning face.

"Mademoiselle, a thousand excuses for my tardiness. I was detained at the foreign office. This affair of Irman Pasha! Have you seen the morning papers?"

"Yes. But it appears nothing is known."

"And nothing will be known. Trust the government for that! Nevertheless—I can trust your secrecy, mademoiselle, since your life depends on it as well as mine!"

"My word of honor, monsieur!"

"Then listen, mademoiselle! It appears it was not Bazin, as we thought, who provided Mademoiselle d'Amour with the keys and password and sent her early to the Turkish embassy—it was Irman Pasha himself! And when that bomb blew him to fragments yesterday, it was no more than Heaven's justice that was done. For the man was doubly a traitor. Having betrayed his uncle the envoy to Bazin, he proceeded to betray Bazin on his own account—all for a woman, but for a woman the most worthless, the most rapacious of Paris! Do you remember I told you yesterday Irman had been making advances to Violette d'Amour? It was for her that he took Bazin's money—and then, when her greed was still unsatisfied, afforded her the means to enter his uncle's strong box and steal the treaty, while he himself detained Bazin at the Ritz."

Fanny trembled at a sudden dreadful recollection.

"But the bomb—the bomb, monsieur!"

"I am coming to that! Bazin, having solid motives for wishing that the theft should remain a secret from the governments concerned, could be trusted merely to copy the treaty—as could you. But a greedy, illiterate woman, with neither the time nor the motives for a troublesome piece of copying—her intention which she carried out, was, of course, the plain one of stealing the priceless document itself. To hide this theft from Bazin who had paid him, as well as from his uncle who had trusted him, Irman evolved the neat and efficient scheme of a bomb with a time-fuse attached. So that while Bazin was copying the treaty—"

He stopped short, with a gesture of a dreadful significance. Fanny shuddered.

"Yes, *I* know! Did I not hear its ticking?" Then, with a sudden thought: "But, monsieur, if Irman knew the danger, why did he go back?"

"Because his plans had been thrown out, mademoiselle. By whom? By you and by me! For when Bazin, by the loss of his overcoat, was delayed in his visit to the Faubourg Saint Honoré, it is evident that the dear young Pasha became uneasy in his mind. So he slipped back to the embassy and crept up to his uncle's room. Who knows? Perhaps he wished to change the hands of his clock to a later hour. But, as we know, he arrived too late."

He stopped short, with the horror of the recent tragedy still on his face. Fanny demanded impatiently:

"But Bazin—what will he do?"

"Bazin, mademoiselle, has already followed the advice you gave him in lemon juice yesterday, and taken the Viennese express for Constantinople. He, of course, follows the Turkish envoy! While Violette d'Amour, who naturally considers him responsible for the theft of yesterday, has left Embrasse-Moi Vite! and flown after Bazin. So we may leave them to devour each other. At any rate, thanks to our happy idea, we are safe from them. And now—"

Rising, he thrust his hand into the inside pocket of his gray tweed coat. Then on the table between them he placed a bulky packet, corded and sealed. Fanny's breath came quickly.

"This morning, mademoiselle, I visited a certain personage of exalted station who represents the Balkan Allies here in Paris. I delivered the treaty to him. He in return, paid me the promised reward."

With quick fingers he tore apart the seals and parchment envelope, displaying a thick symmetrical pile of fresh pale-blue and lavender bank bills.

"Notes of the Bank of France," he said briefly, "for a thousand francs apiece. A hundred of them. Mademoiselle, you have acted, not as my assistant, but as my partner; and it is my profound hope that this is not the last time we may work together. Meanwhile—"

He fell to counting the crisp squares of delicately tinted paper. Then he pushed over an impressive pile to Fanny's side of the table.

"Your half—fifty thousand," he said. "Mademoiselle, will you verify my count?"

Fanny gasped. She had hoped for a percentage. Five thousand francs to pay her hotel bill and take her home to America had been her wildest dream.

"You know, I owe you a hundred francs," she stammered.

At her naïve honesty, her flushed and kindling prettiness, the young Vicomte smiled. "We will not quarrel over that! And now, mademoiselle, will you permit that I escort you at once to your bankers?"

THE QUEEN'S PEARL

I

The Vicomte de Chatellerault, sitting beside Fanny Gordon, spoke cautiously into her ear: "This time the affair is about a pearl." Fanny shifted her little black Pomeranian to the other arm, pulled down the skirt of her pink morning dress, and echoed softly:

"A pearl?"

The Vicomte nodded. "The great pearl of Swabia, presented long ago by the Doge of Venice to the famous Frederick of Swabia. And now Frederick's great-great-great-granddaughter, the present Queen Regent of Swabia, in her moment of weakness, entrusted the pearl to her handsome consort. And the Prince Consort, in a moment of weakness, entrusted the pearl to a beautiful lady, the Baroness Hélène von Wilmhutz—merely, he declares, in order to test which was whiter, the pearl or her neck: the most perfect neck, they say, in Europe. The Baroness, however, proceeded to pocket the pearl, and bolted here to Paris with it, leaving the Prince Consort, whose royal wife is the most jealous in Europe, in a condition that you can imagine. All the more that the christening of the heir apparent is next week, and the Queen must wear her full regalia. And when she discovers the loss, mademoiselle, it is an open secret that her rage will imperil not only the peace of the Prince Consort's mind, but that of Europe as well."

Fanny, letting her little dog slide to the flour, sprang alertly to her feet. She seemed to take on a new personality, hard almost to ruthlessness, with the dilated eyes and quivering pink tongue-lip of a hound that has caught the scent.

"And now," she said crisply, "the facts!"

The Vicomte's conciseness matched hers. "That the Baroness von Wilmhutz—as she calls herself—has brought the pearl with her to Paris is vouched for by the fact that she left behind her in Swabia no real friends to whom she could possibly have entrusted such a treasure. Besides, in the Prince's dread of coupling his name with hers, she knows that she finds her best safety. It is certain, therefore, that the jewel is in her own immediate possession."

"And the pearl itself?" asked Fanny.

"The most splendid, they say, in Europe!" replied the Vicomte. "A gem which, by its immense size, as by its white and fairy-like luster, might be identified on the beaches of Ceylon! The size of a walnut, slightly elongated, slightly flattened. The tint, in spite of its age, a perfect white, with a faint touch of pink and green iridescence at one end. Its value, apart from its historic associations, is estimated at not less than three million francs. So, you can imagine, the reward—"

Again Fanny nodded. "And now, tell me what has been done!"

"On the Baroness' arrival at Paris, her trunks were detained at Customs and searched. Since then her apartment at the Hotel Astoria has twice been thoroughly ransacked; once at night, when her maid—a person in our employ—had drugged her mistress' after-dinner coffee. The second time was yesterday, when her chauffeur, acting under our direction, punctured a tire of her automobile and kept her four hours at Fontainebleau. I can personally guarantee that, in the meantime, the search of her rooms was thorough! On her return to the hotel in the evening, a person in our employ contrived to rub against her, and immediately after raised the cry of robbery. On this person's charge, the Baroness was arrested and taken to Saint Lazare—a brutal measure, but necessary. At the prison she was thoroughly searched by those grim crones who make a thorough business, be sure, of searching a young and lovely woman. But, mademoiselle, they found nothing. At the hotel, the police found nothing. So I said to myself, match

Greek with Greek! Where ancient hags have failed, where men have failed, it is possible that another young and lovely woman may find the weak spot and penetrate the secret of the Baroness Hélène!"

Fanny turned a gleaming eye upon him.

"I think I understand now. If I need any more information, I'll send a note to your apartment. And now, please to run along. I've got to think. And when I've thought, you can see for yourself what a lot I shall have to do."

Then, as her visitor bent over her hand in adieu, she added dreamily:

"To penetrate from the outside, and without any help, into the intimate center of another person's life—it seems a task beyond the limits of civilized modern life, doesn't it? Still, I'm glad at least to hear that she takes singing lessons and keeps a little dog!"

II

TWO DAYS LATER, at a stylish modern hotel near the Étoile, arrived, with a quantity of luggage, a young American girl who registered as Miss Hazel Perkins, Detroit. When she entered the dining-hall she was half an hour late and alone, but for the company of a small dog which she led by a leash that might have restrained a bulldog. After calmly making the tour of the room, she finally chose a table between two others, occupied respectively by a handsome blonde woman in black charmeuse, with a little white dog by her side, and a couple of eager-looking old German ladies.

Five minutes after being seated, Miss Perkins had scraped acquaintance with the latter and was naïvely favoring them, in a loud American- French, with a stream of autobiography:

"Momma and I just arrived at Liverpool last Monday, on the *Lusitania*. Oh, I was so seasick! It's the first time I crossed, you know. Yes, I learned to speak French at the Berlitz, right at home in Detroit. Oh, thank you—I do speak pretty well, don't I? Well, nothing would suit momma but a trip to the English lakes. She'd read a paper about them at the Iris Club last year, you see. But I was just dying to get to Paris to begin my vocal. Yes, that's what I've come to Europe for. I'm going in for grand opera, you see, so naturally I didn't want to lose a day. So I let momma go on her old trip with some women we'd met crossing, and I just trolled over here to Paris alone. And right after lunch I'm going straight out to arrange for my voice lessons. Who'm I going to take of? Calderoni, of course. They tell me he's the only one in Paris—the most expensive, anyway. And I've a very sweet, high soprano of wonderful volume, so you can bet I don't want it ruined by any of these ordinary voice-teachers. Oh, yes, I think Paris is perfectly splendid—I'm just crazy about it. Towser, if you don't stop rubbering at that little white dog over there, I'll pull your tail!"

That afternoon, the greatest singing master of Paris was, by the sheer force of his visitor's exuberant vitality, persuaded not only to give a favorable judgment on her small, high soprano voice, but also to consent to the immediate learning of a duet to be sung with one of his other pupils—in order, as the new arrival explained, to dazzle "momma," when she arrived, into agreement with her daughter's operatic schemes.

Leaving the master's studio, by the strangest coincidence in the world she almost ran into the lady in black charmeuse whom she had already seen at the Astoria. For the next five minutes Miss Perkins stood outside the closed door, listening to a powerful mezzo voice uplifted in the dramatic strains of an "Ave Maria."

On her way home she stopped at a music store and ordered a piano for a month. By humming a strain of the "Ave Maria" that she had just heard, she was able to have the music identified, carried it home, and that very evening was picking it out on her new piano.

Four days later, by dint of hard study and tactful manipulation of her master, the new pupil was admitted to the glory of her first duet practice; the music chosen being that of Saint-Saëns' beautiful "Ave Maria," and the mezzo-soprano no other than a charming Swedish lady, the Baroness von Wilmhutz, who, it appeared, was already studying the music.

"You are at the same hotel? Excellent!" cried the master, when the two voices had tried the music and been found to blend with a fairly harmonious effect. "You must practice your duet together before the next lesson. But see, mademoiselle; be careful not to flat this F—"

The Baroness, who seemed to be pining with boredom, showed as active an interest in the new employment as did even the raw little American. And that afternoon they met for practice in the latter's room at the hotel.

The piano, however, proved to be sadly out of tune. As the tuner could not be had before the next day, the Baroness, after some hesitation, invited her fellow singer across the hall.

In the dainty little Louis XV salon, where innumerable bibelots and signed photographs relieved the hotel monotony, the young American girl stared about her.

"My, what a cute room! Do you mind if I just have a good look around?"

"But after our music!" smiled the Baroness winningly. After the duet practice, however, she remembered an appointment with her dressmaker, and the two went out together.

The next day they met again in the same place. The young American, as before, played the accompaniment—a task which she performed with no great brilliancy but with sufficient correctness. The piano, however, vexed her.

"Wants tuning!" she remarked bluntly. "Gee, it's worse than mine! Here, listen to this D in alt—it's all to the blink. Listen!"

She sounded it. It jangled. The Baroness laughed nervously.

"Is it? Then I'll speak to the tuner tomorrow. But come— I've sung enough. I'll ring for tea."

"No!" returned Miss Hazel Perkins stubbornly. "Cal said we ought to do that duet three times at least, and we haven't done it but once and a half."

"To-morrow!" cried the Baroness.

"Another three times to-morrow"' retorted the implacable American, with a grin. "Pooh! I'll bet I can mend that smashed note myself!" And, springing alertly to her feet, she began to clear the music from the little grand piano, preparatory to opening it.

Suddenly there was a piercing scream. Turning, she beheld the Baroness rising slowly to her feet with both hands pressed convulsively over her breast. Her face was contorted almost beyond recognition. The next moment, with a groan, she fell to the floor like a log.

The young girl, horror-stricken, rushed to the rescue.

"It's my heart!" gasped the Baroness. "It comes on every little while. What pain! The brandy, quick! There, I'm better. Will you go and put on your hat, *chèrie*, and take me to my doctor's?"

Miss Perkins, forgetting her late musical enthusiasm, ran to obey. After five minutes she returned, to find the Baroness feebly struggling into a long cloak of fur and satin.

Half an hour later she left the interesting invalid at her doctor's on the Boulevard Haussmann, and returned alone to the Astoria.

Slowly she walked down the corridor on her way back to her room, alone but for her little dog. Suddenly she was aware of a rather odd circumstance. The door of her opposite neighbor's room stood slightly ajar, and from within came the whining of a dog.

Her recent curiosity, baffled by the Baroness' fainting attack, returned, to possess the young girl's soul. She hesitated a moment; then, stooping, she slipped her pet's leash. The next instant he had bolted through the open door, and from within came the worrying sound of two little dogs at play.

"Towser, come here!" cried his mistress.

Then, as Towser vouchsafed no response, his mistress whistled once, strode to the open door, and knocked loudly. Then, pushing it wide, she advanced boldly into the room.

Singular! The white Pomeranian, usually indulged to the extreme, was seen chained to a leg of the center-table. And, singular again! In the brief interval while her visitor had departed to put on her hat, the Baroness had evidently conquered the extreme weakness induced by her heart attack. For the piano, the lid propped up by its wand, stood blatantly open, flamboyantly empty of all but its own silvery mechanism.

The American, surveying it, caught her breath. Then, suddenly stretching out her hand, she sounded the D in alt. In marked contrast to an hour before, the note rang perfectly true and clear.

The color rose in her face. She hesitated a moment, then, catching up her little dog, turned to the door. Coming down the corridor in a flutter of plumes and perfumes, whom should she meet but the tenant of the room. "Baroness! Now do excuse me. But the door was open and Towser bolted in—"

"Of course, *chèrie!* But, you see, I left everything in such confusion. But now the doctor has given me some splendid medicine and I'm quite well."

A glance passed between the two women—a single spark, questioning and enigmatic. Then Miss Perkins retired to her room and wrote a note:

> The Baroness has just been at the pains to set a neat trap, baited with her little dog, in order to show she has guessed why I am here; also to let me know the treasure has been removed from its hiding-place of an hour ago. At the same time, however, she has disclosed to me the fact that the treasure is here with her at the hotel.
>
> F. G.

And, carefully sealing the missive, Miss Hazel Perkins, *alias* Fanny Gordon, carried it with her own hands to the post.

III

ALMOST TWELVE O'CLOCK. A tap on Fanny Gordon's door, and in slid a pale woman in a pink crêpe dressing-gown, whose gestures were full of terror and whose eyes were full of tears.

"Please," she whispered brokenly, "do you mind if I come in for a little while? I'm frightened to death!"

For an instant Fanny stared, then forced her gently to an armchair by the bed.

"Poor dear! Of course you are miserable, after your attack of this afternoon. Won't you let me make you some nice hot tea?"

"You little darling! No, I'm quite well again—it's not that. It's just that I can't stand this life any more. For I'm hunted. No, I'm not raving. I'm hunted day and night like one of those Apaches on the outer boulevards, that they track down with dogs!"

Fanny caught her breath. No, the woman before her was not raving. Who should know it better than she, who was one of the dogs?

Suddenly her visitor caught her hands in an icy clasp.

"Listen! I tell you the truth. Of course, when your mother comes she won't let you have anything more to do with me. And quite right! For I'm not—I'm not what's called a good woman, my dear!"

She rose to her feet and paced rapidly up and down the room.

"There! it's out! But don't judge me too hardly. Sold in marriage to a wicked old man when I was still an innocent child like—like you. Then, later, giving heart and soul—all I had!—to a man that—"

Her beautiful face worked. She drew a long breath and, stopping short in her walk, bent over the bed.

"Listen, *chèrie*," she said excitedly. "You are an American, and every one knows that Americans pay their bills and keep their word. And your eyes—one sees in them you'd give your life rather than break your word. So, if you'll give it to me, I'll trust it like God's. Listen! Do you want to hear a secret? Do you want to accept a trust?"

Slowly Fanny nodded. "I give you my word," she whispered slowly.

"Then look!" her visitor whispered back.

She pulled up her pink chiffon petticoat, and from her left garter detached a small chamois bag. From the bag she took what appeared to be a wad of cotton wool and laid it on the bed. Fanny, clearing away the wool with trembling fingers, beheld the shimmer and whiteness and mystery of a gigantic pearl.

"The night that my prince hung it around my neck," whispered the Baroness dreamily, "he said, 'Thy skin is whiter still!'"

"Yes," murmured Fanny, her hypnotized eyes still on the great pearl. There, at one end, was the iridescent gleam of pink and green of which Raoul had spoken.

"And now," went on the passionate woman before her, "he blackens me! He declares that I stole the jewel from him—his gift, the one link that binds me with my life when it was a life! And, as I have refused to yield it except with my life, he abandons fair means and takes to foul. That's what I mean when I tell you I am hunted. For the secret police of Paris, whom he has set on me, are dogging me day and night. Till now I have managed to elude them. But they are crawling up on me. Even now I heard them behind my chimney-board, searching like rats—"

She stopped short, with an expression of nausea. Fanny, smitten with compassion and remorse, cried out:

"But you *are* ill!"

"No, no," returned the other; "it's only the thought of rats. They—they affect me as snakes do other people. One sees that my maid must have betrayed my weakness. For even my maid and chauffeur, you see, are in their pay. Oh, my dear, do I demand too much when I ask you to take this pearl and keep it for me till I am at liberty to ask for it back again?"

A soft kiss dropped on Fanny's forehead. A swish of silk, a gently closed door, and Fanny was left alone with three million francs' worth of concentrated sea-magic shimmering on the counterpane before her.

IV

NEXT MORNING, when the lesson was done, Fanny and her fellow pupil came down the stairs together.

"Baroness, listen! You must let me give you back your pearl. I can't—"

"Hush! We mustn't talk here. Meet me by the north shore of the lake in the Bois in half an hour."

By the little sheet of blue water, among the budding flowers of early spring, they met. The Baroness hushed Fanny's protestations:

"Ah, my dear. The one person in all Paris that I can trust! Then you mean I must not ask another favor of you? For I confess—"

With mingled feelings, Fanny interrupted her:

"You know, I'll do anything for you that I can!"

"Do you mean that?" returned the Baroness Hélène eagerly. "Then will you do an errand for me?"

Fanny nodded. The other continued quickly:

"It's his letters—his dear, dear letters! Those also he has been trying to rob me of, lest I blackmail him. Small danger, alas! So, as a box of letters is not hidden in one's garter like a pearl, I dared not bring them to the hotel. When I arrived in Paris fifteen days ago, I simply checked the valise containing them in the parcels room of the Gare du Nord. While they remain there they are safe. But now, before I leave Paris, I want them! Followed as I am—do you see that man on the bicycle yonder?—I dare not go for them. Will you do me a last favor? Will you go and get that valise for me?"

After all, why not? Fanny nodded. "Certainly!"

"Here is the check!" The Baroness opened her gold bag, opened the purse within it, and extracted a small slip of white paper. "See! I will put it here on the grass under this stone. In a moment you must stoop to tie your shoe, and pick it up."

An instant later, as Fanny stooped:

"And when I have taken the valise out, where do I carry it? To you at the Astoria?"

They walked away together. The Baroness replied:

"No, no! is it any safer there than it was two weeks ago? In a few days, now, I am leaving Paris for Italy, where—who knows?—perhaps I shall find peace. Carry the valise, therefore, to the Gare de Lyon; leave it there at the *consigne*, and bring back the check to me."

Fanny, returning to her taxicab, drove first to the Gare du Nord, where in exchange for her check she received a handsome valise of English leather. Then she was whirled the length of Paris to the far-off Gare de Lyon, where in exchange for her valise she received a numbered slip of white paper, two inches by three. Then back to the hotel, where she presented the check to the waiting Baroness.

As the evening had closed in chilly, she had ordered a fire, and already the cheerful flames crackled in the chimney. Standing by the hearth, she made up her mind.

"Hang it, I'll give her back her old pearl!" she declared to herself, "and then fight her for it fair and square! Poor Hélène! But, after all, my first duty is to Raoul."

Pulling out her hairpins, she released her shining dark hair from its compactly twisted knot. In spite of her strained and careful gestures, or perhaps because of them, she fumbled the pins. The hair slipped through her hand. And, to her horror, with a crash like that of a dropped billiard-ball, the great pearl fell to the stone hearth at her feet.

With a swift contraction of her muscles, Fanny pounced upon it. Then, as she slanted the marvelous gem toward the firelight, her heart seemed suddenly to become like the heart of the dead. With an inarticulate gulp of horror, she ran to the electric light.

Yes, it was true. Across that surface of flawless beauty, from the slightly iridescent tip to the swelling whiteness of the middle, ran an unmistakable and hideous crack.

V

At eleven o'clock the next morning, as Fanny was sipping her coffee after a sleepless night, she received a visit from her neighbor across the way.

"My dear child, you are pale! Here—I will throw away my cigarette."

"No, no, Baroness—I don't mind at all!" In spite of Fanny's effort at self-control, a heavy sigh escaped her. For a moment the two sat in silence, while the Baroness Hélène puffed at her cigarette and the two little dogs played together upon the floor. The Baroness' cigarette-case, an odd, Oriental-looking affair of fine woven grass studded with turquoises, dangled from her hand. Suddenly Fanny's little black Pomeranian, frisking near, seized the cigarette-case in his mouth and scampered off under the bed. The other, barking, followed him.

The next moment Fanny almost doubted her senses. A whirl of pink draperies; a hoarse, thick voice screaming French words of unbelievable vulgarity; and the Baroness, seizing the heavy iron poker from the hearth, hurled herself after the little gamboling dogs.

Mere instinct gave Fanny courage. She seized the infuriated woman by the arm, with words such as are used to calm the hysterical. Then, swiftly doubling her gloves in a ball, she tossed them into the air. In pursuit of this new prize, the little dogs immediately relinquished the old. Fanny picked up the cigarette-case and, with a bow, presented it to its owner. Swiftly the Baroness examined it inside and out, to satisfy herself as to its undamaged condition.

Shortly after, clutching her little white dog in one hand and her precious cigarette-case in the other, she took her leave.

Fanny, remembering her own troubles, fastened the pearl inside her blouse, called a taxicab, and drove to Cartier's.

At this foremost jewelry establishment of Paris, she asked for the chief expert on pearls. A few moments later she was ushered into the private room of a dapper, blond-bearded little man, who courteously demanded what he could do for her.

Fanny's voice, trembling with the emotion that her resolution could not dominate, propounded her momentous question:

"Is it possible, monsieur, to mend a cracked pearl?"

VI

THAT AFTERNOON, after two hours' painful and intense thinking in a darkened room, Fanny Gordon leaped from her sofa, snapping her fingers like one who has found an answer to a knotty problem. And, sitting at her desk, she swiftly wrote the following lines:

> We have been working on the wrong track. Please be in the hall of the Astoria to-night at half past six beside the desk of the clerk. I have information for you.
>
> F. G.

This missive she despatched by special messenger. Then, having stood for an instant deep in thought, she unlocked her trunk and took from it a stationery box of cardboard, about eight inches by six. The cover, when she removed it, disclosed the interior already packed neatly with tissue paper and white absorbent cotton. Taking a sheet of note-paper, she hurriedly wrote a couple of lines upon it, signing the name of Hazel Perkins. Laying this message on top of the tissue paper, she tied up the box with professional neatness and a large number of accurately made red seals. Taking up the pen again, she wrote the address:

Baroness Hélène V. Wilmhutz
Hotel Astoria

The package thus completed, she carried it downstairs to the clerk, and bade him put it at once into the safe; then at eight o'clock, when the Baroness came down to dinner, to deliver it personally into her hands.

This little affair concluded, she went off, deep in thought, to her singing lesson.

The lady who represented the object and intention of these lessons did not, however, appear. The lines on Fanny's white forehead deepened. But an hour later, when, with her little dog under her arm, she knocked at the door of the Baroness' room, nothing could have exceeded the care-free rosiness of her girlish beauty.

"Say, Baroness! I've got just the dandiest news ever—a letter from momma. She'll be here to-morrow night! Isn't that grand?"

"Then adieu to our charming intimacy, dear child!" The Baroness, a beautiful picture in her tea-gown of white satin and fur, moved languidly on her pink silk cushions and sighed.

"Now, madame, don't say that!" returned Fanny, with an embarrassed air, "I'm sure momma'll be every bit as crazy about you as I am myself! And, anyway, we have to practice our duets. Oh, say! why weren't you there this afternoon, at the lesson at Calderoni's?"

The Baroness sighed again delicately. "I don't know. I didn't really feel in the mood. And then, I've a bit of a sore throat—"

The young judge pointed severely at the elegant trifle of braided grass and turquoises, lying open on the tea-table beside her hostess.

"Too many of *those*," she said accusingly. "You're smoking them all the time. Of course, you've got no voice left!"

"Which being true," smiled the Baroness Hélène, "I might as well, profit by the fact to take another!" And, stretching out a creamy and jeweled hand, she helped herself to a gold-tipped cigarette.

Fanny, stooping, gave sugar to the little dogs. Her eyes were, however, on the cigarette-case.

"What a perfect stunner it is—so original and artistic," she observed. "I don't wonder you were ready to eat these two brats when they ran off with it this morning. May I look at it?" And with a sudden gesture she reached out her hand and picked up the cigarette-case from the wide arm of the Baroness' chaise-longue. A sharp sense of adventure possessed her, born of two circumstances: the Baroness' quick breath, which had in it something indescribably menacing and savage; and a flashing vision of the morning's strange scene, of the uplifted iron poker, and the foul words shrieked at the little dogs.

"It's so precious to me!" sighed Hélène sentimentally. "You know why, *chèrie*. Here—please give it back to me!"

With a sympathetic smile that veiled a sigh, Fanny laid the open case upon the table. After all, was it not possible that the Baroness spoke the truth?—since a minute examination of the cigarette-case had proved the absolute nonexistence of any reason, except the sentimental one alleged, for its amazing preciousness to its owner. Lining it had none, nor secret pocket; nor the slightest possibility of any contents except its normal and legitimate one of a row of gold-tipped Egyptian cigarettes.

With a greedy gesture, the Baroness stretched out her hand to snatch up her treasure. Then, catching Fanny's eye fixed upon her, she seemed by a great muscular effort to dominate her betraying eagerness, bestowed merely a light caress upon her beloved souvenir, and sank back again among her embroidered cushions. By some strange super-sense, rather than by the exercise of her actual sight, Fanny was aware that the gray eyes smiling so sweetly upon her were on guard like those of a lion-tamer.

"When momma comes, we must all go to the opera every evening," she began. Then suddenly her voice wavered, her color rose. She caught her breath.

"Towser, there, you quit biting my shoe!" she cried, with a poke of her foot at the tiny Pomeranian. Then, with the gayest air in the world, she continued to outline schemes of entertainment. But her head whirled, her spine was ice.

For only in that instant had her eyes taken in the fact that, of the half dozen cigarettes in the open case of the Baroness Hélène, one was fully a quarter of an inch longer than its mates, and tipped with dull instead of with burnished gold.

VII

HER LIPS CONTINUED to move, outlining the schemes of an automobile excursion with "momma" to Saint-Germain-en-Laye, the while her mind worked busily.

"In this woman before me it is evident that I am dealing with an intelligence of the very first order. Such intellects, we are told by foremost students of crime, hide their objects of value by not putting them in hiding-places at all. Circumstance, however, has forced Hélène to betray that her cigarette-case is the hiding-place of something exceedingly precious. And now the question is: who is going to win out, she or I?"

Meanwhile, with her eyes on the clock, her sudden thought ran:

"Twenty after six. No, she's a desperate woman. Best for me not to move alone. At half past six Raoul will be downstairs—"

So for ten minutes Fanny talked.

Ting!

The gilt clock on the chimney-piece chimed one. Half past six!

Fanny started. Then she swallowed hard, licked her dry lips into a smile, and leaned toward the other woman:

"Say, but I've pretty nearly talked you asleep, haven't I? And I've talked myself dry, I know that. Say, maybe you're right about cigarettes being good. If you'll let me, I'll try one!"

And, laughing, she stretched out her hand toward the case. In spite of her languid grace, the Baroness von Wilmhutz was quicker than her guest.

"Permit me, *chèrie!*"

And, selecting a cigarette with a burnished tip, she passed it smilingly to her guest. Then, striking a match from her little gold box, she performed the graceful service of lighting it.

On the table, like a little frontier province between two hungry powers, lay the case.

Whatever was Hélène's inward attitude, her outward calm was superb. "You make me quite envious. I must have a smoke too!" she said. The next moment it was with difficulty that Fanny restrained herself from shrieking aloud; for her hostess, carefully selecting the longest cigarette, placed its dull gold tip daintily between her rouged lips, and, striking a wax match, touched the yellow flame to the tip.

The tip glowed red. The white spiral of smoke went upward. Fanny trembled all over. As Hélène's large gray eyes met hers, it seemed to her that she saw in them a cold and contemptuous defiance.

"Bah! Mademoiselle, these French cigarettes are no better than poison. Fling yours away—like this!" And, suiting the action to the word, she pinched the smoldering tip of her cigarette and tossed it behind her.

There it lay on the rug. For an instant Fanny contemplated the use of violence. But not only was the blonde Baroness larger and more powerful than Fanny, but, if she acquired notoriety in the. police courts, Fanny would entirely ruin her future with the Secret Service of Paris. No; softly, softly—

She smiled winningly at her hostess. "I'm going back to my room to dress now," she announced. "And say, when are you going to let me give you back that pearl? Three million francs—" She stopped short. Into the back of her brain shot a recollection of certain words of the Baroness, that night she had come to the young girl's room with the pearl. She had been shaking with horror—of what? And was that horror real or feigned? At any rate, here was the only straw in sight, and Fanny grasped it.

"Three million francs," she whispered. "It's more than one person is meant to have the responsibility of, and I—*oh, Baroness, there at your foot! A rat! A big gray rat!*"

The room echoed to the Baroness' answering shriek. Gathering her white satin draperies about her, she sprang nimbly upon the table. And Fanny, hurling herself forward, snatched the coveted cigarette from the carpet, and fled toward the door. In the instant in which she fumbled with the knob, her backward glancing eyes beheld an infuriated woman with a knife upraised in her hand.

The door yielded. Fanny, slipping through, slammed it behind her. The thought in her mind was: "How lucky that I kept on my street clothes, while Hélène must wait for a cloak!"

Down the corridor she flashed. Luckily a lift was descending. She signaled it, and a moment later found herself downstairs in the hall of the hotel. Raoul, that good Raoul! Sure enough, there he was, standing by the desk. She walked up to him, smiled, and spoke in a swift undertone:

"Vicomte, quick! Give me your cigarette-case!"

For an instant he stared at her as if she were mad; then, with admirable sang-froid, drew from his pocket a case of plain burnished silver, which he opened and politely presented to the young girl. With a swift gesture she selected one of the gold-tipped cigarettes within, replaced it with the slightly burned cigarette she carried in her hand, snapped the case shut, and restored it to him.

"Into your inside pocket! Quick!"

"*Mon Dieu*, mademoiselle! But you Americans are born mad!"

Nevertheless, he obeyed her. The next instant the door of the lift opened, and a tall figure, wearing a long wrap of black satin and fur, emerged and almost ran down the hall. Fanny, with a slow step, as if her walk had been an uninterrupted one, strolled on toward the door. With furious haste, the Baroness von Wilmhutz swept up to the desk, where the clerk, sleek and prosperous, sat watching over the comfort of his guests.

"Monsieur, I demand that you detain that young American lady! Call the police! Search her—search her room! She has stolen from me a pearl worth three million francs!"

For an instant there was silence. Then the foyer hummed with excitement. While Fanny Gordon, the center of all the excitement, turned deliberately and walked back to the desk. The Vicomte de Chatellerault, standing dignifiedly aloof, groaned within himself.

"She's bungled it! That's what I get for trusting an American. She'll get us into the papers, and spoil all!"

"Search her!" demanded the Baroness fiercely. "Seize her! Telephone for the police!"

"Mademoiselle!" besought the horrified proprietor, "I am sure, if you will, you can explain this disagreeable circumstance—"

Fanny Gordon, with unruffled calm, turned to the clerk.

"Monsieur, will you kindly fetch the package that I gave you this afternoon?"

The fat little Frenchman turned to his superior. "Monsieur, it is in the safe. If you will have the goodness to help me open it—"

A moment later they reappeared, the clerk carrying Fanny's neatly sealed stationery box.

"Monsieur, one instant. At what hour did I give you that package?"

"At four o'clock this afternoon, mademoiselle!"

"And with what instructions?"

"That I should give it to the Baroness von Wilmhutz when she came down to dinner, mademoiselle."

"Very well. You may give it to her now."

The Baroness, taking the box with obvious reluctance, hesitated and turned away.

"I'll take it to my room," she said, with a coldly shrinking look at the crowd about her.

Fanny raised her hand. "No. Stop! Monsieur the proprietor, the Baroness von Wilmhutz has publicly brought against me a charge of the utmost gravity. I have the right to demand that my vindication be as public. Demand of madame that she open that box!"

Before the proprietor could open his mouth, the Baroness turned with a look of disdain. "There's no need of this theatrical display," she said. "If you insist, of course I will open the box here. Give me a knife!"

Awkwardly her soft hands cut the knots. In spite of his deliberately assumed indifference, Raoul de Chatellerault was among those who crowded up to see what the opening of the box would disclose. The next moment the blood rushed into his brain. For there, when the tissue-paper wrappings were withdrawn, his straining eyes descried for a moment the white and luminous outlines of an enormous pearl. Then the Baroness' beautiful gray eyes, raised for an instant, fixed themselves fiercely on the cigarette in Fanny Gordon's hand.

"Read the card, Baroness, and you'll understand what a mistake you've made!" said the latter sweetly.

The Baroness, covering the pearl, picked up a card that lay beside it. She started, flushing an angry red. Then, thrusting her recovered treasure under her arm, she forced herself to calmness.

"It was a mistake. Mademoiselle, I withdraw my charge. Good evening!" And, drawing her cloak about her, she swept up the hall toward the lift.

For once in his life, the Vicomte de Chatellerault came near to losing his self-command. He walked up to Fanny. His face was white, his eyes glittered like two pin-points of rage. He spoke under his breath:

"Mademoiselle, I trusted you! And yet, having obtained possession of—of it, you deliberately gave it back to that woman!"

Though Fanny's mien was one of careless and delicate coquetry, her reply was of a frantic force.

"Vicomte, obey me! We have not a second to lose! Take a taxicab, give the man a louis for extra speed, drive to the Gare de Lyon! Unroll that cigarette I gave you, present the slip of paper at the *consigne*. Take the article to which it entitles you. Then, on driving back, call for a member of the Secret Police—the Chief, if possible! Then to the Ritz—engage a private dining-room. I will join you there in an hour's time. If I am late, wait for my coming before opening the bag."

The Vicomte, listening to her coldly, shook his head.

"Pardon me, mademoiselle, but I have time for no wild-goose chases to the Gare de Lyon. Now that I have seen the pearl with my own eyes, it shall not slip through my hands as you let it slip through yours. No; now I have the certainty of its whereabouts, I telephone to my Chief from this very hotel. I remain here, and we take decisive measures to-night!"

"I take full responsibility for the Baroness. In a moment she will descend on her way to the Gare de Lyon. For the love of God, Vicomte, do as I say—go!"

By the very intensity of the will power that blazed from her dark eyes, by the icy force of her whispered command, she bent the unwilling young man to obedience. With the helpless gesture of one who despises himself for obeying, he repeated her directions, turned, and swiftly vanished through the hotel door.

Fanny Gordon, deep in thought, returned to her room. As she fumbled with her key, the door of the room opposite suddenly opened and the Baroness slid out. The next instant Fanny's wrist was seized and, with a dexterity that spoke of expert knowledge, Raoul's cigarette was extracted from it. The next instant the opposite door was closed and the corridor was as lonely as before. Fanny gasped. But for the vanished cigarette, she might have thought the incident a dream.

Then she grinned. "It begins to look as if my theories might have some basis of fact!" she said to herself. And, entering her room, she made a hasty toilet for dinner.

VIII

AT EIGHT O'CLOCK, with a discreet dinner dress of dark blue iridescent embroidery under her cloak, Fanny Gordon entered the Ritz.

"Please take me to the private dining-room of the Vicomte de Chatellerault!" she commanded briefly.

The next moment she was ushered into a small dining-room furnished with great elegance in the English style; while on either side of the prettily set table stood the Vicomte de Chatellerault and a short, stout man with fierce mustaches.

"Here is the young lady, Inspector!" said Raoul wearily, as, rosy and sparkling in her white cloak, Fanny Gordon entered the room. The waiter closed the door. Fanny uttered a little gasp of delight; for there on the table, amid the glistening whiteness of linen and crystal, she beheld the valise of English leather which she herself had carried from the Gare du Nord to the Gare de Lyon.

"Mademoiselle!" began the inspector, with unconcealed anger, "I hear that a very grave blunder has been made. The Swabian pearl, for which the reward has to-day been raised to half a million francs—I repeat, to half a million francs—has deliberately been given back into the hands of the thief, while Monsieur the Vicomte de Chatellerault and I are sent about like porters, carrying pieces of old luggage about Paris—"

Fanny Gordon raised her quivering hand. Her voice was shaky, her color was high.

"Please, monsieur," she begged, "won't you open the valise first? Afterward you can scold me as much as you like."

The inspector, grunting, drew a bunch of skeleton-keys from his pocket. In a few moments the valise, sprawling open, displayed a highly colored and confused assortment of such articles as ladies carry with them when they travel.

Swiftly the contents were hurled out to right and left over the dainty settings of the dinner-table: silk stockings, lingerie, yellow-backed novels, satin slippers, silver and crystal toilet boxes, a morocco jewelry case.

Upon this last the inspector flung himself. It contained a watch and chain, set in turquoises. With a muttered explosion, he flung it to the floor. Raoul meanwhile, with eager hands, was opening and testing the books. The inspector, with a grim face, began on the crystal pomade-boxes and the rolls of lingerie.

Fanny, very white, ran her hands about the lining of the valise. Nothing!

"Mademoiselle, I hope you are pleased with the result of your cleverness!" snarled the inspector, in a bitterness of disappointment that overcame his good manners.

Raoul said nothing; but his blue eyes, fixed in silence upon her, made her realize that she had lost his respect.

"And yet," she said, with tears in her eyes, "it is impossible that I should be mistaken in my reasoning—"

"Mademoiselle," returned the inspector brutally, "it is not your reasoning that we are seeking, but the pearl—"

Suddenly, with a little cry, Fanny flung herself on a pair of satin slippers, each on its tree, which had been flung into the heap of searched and rejected articles. With swift hands she jerked out the wooden forms from the slippers. The second tree, turned upside down, proved to be roughly hollowed out beneath and filled with cotton wool.

"Pardon me, mademoiselle!" The inspector had taken the tree from Fanny's trembling hands. With a fork from the dinner-table, he carefully pried out its closely packed contents. Then, with a swift touch, he unrolled the cotton wool.

"*Nom d'un nom d'un nom!*"

For there, upon its bed of white wool, shining with a white luster that held in it something of enchantment, lay an immense pearl.

IX

HALF AN HOUR LATER, in the crowded dining-room of the Ritz, Fanny Gordon and the Vicomte de Chatellerault sat facing each other at a little flower-trimmed table.

"But, mademoiselle, two pearls! I can not understand—"

Fanny laughed. "One pearl, Vicomte," she corrected, "and one exquisite piece of imitation!"

The Vicomte drew a long breath. "Then that was the pearl which the inspector took off with him just now? And the imitation which you restored to the Baroness von Wilmhutz?"

Fanny nodded. Her bright eyes danced with triumph. Her youth, the consciousness of success, made of her an entrancing vision.

The Vicomte flung out his hands in token of surrender. "And I—I thought you were a fool!"

"But you didn't know all the facts!" returned Fanny eagerly. "You see, the other day, after the adventure of the piano, the Baroness divined that I was after the pearl. So she muzzled me in a manner that was a compliment to my character—by presenting me with the pearl itself, to keep for her. So there I was, bound in honor, bound hand and foot! Then, by accident, I dropped the pearl. It cracked. My despair!"

"But the very fact of the crack," cried Raoul, "proved that it wasn't a pearl at all!"

"So I learned when I carried it to Cartier's to be mended. And I learned, moreover, that they themselves had obtained that magnificent piece of spoof for a lady, a client of theirs, only the other day. So I said to myself: 'What is her motive in placing this false pearl in my possession? And where is the real one, the great pearl of Swabia? Not in her possession.' So much your elaborate search had proved. Then all of a sudden I remembered that valise! the valise which she herself was afraid to approach, and had employed me to carry for her from the Gare du Nord to the *consigne* at the Gare de Lyon—the *consignes* of Paris, monsieur, where thieves hide their booty, even murderers their dead!"

The Vicomte nodded quickly. "Yes, even last week—! But go on."

"So this morning my opinion was confirmed. By accident, an odd little adventure with my dog caused her to betray the immense value she attached to her cigarette-case—which could not possibly contain the pearl itself, and therefore must contain the key to its possession!"

Softly the Vicomte clapped his hands. "Well reasoned, mademoiselle! Go on!"

"What else is there to tell? When I wrote you this afternoon to ask you to be at the hotel at half past six, it was to tell you that our search must now be directed, not toward seeking the Queen's pearl, but a claim-check on the *consigne* at the Gare de Lyon; a slip of white paper three inches by two. Had the Baroness Hélène, in rolling it into a cigarette, clipped a quarter inch from its length and gilded its tip with gold leaf instead of ordinary gilt paint, she would probably never have lost it. However, she neglected these little precautions. While I, on my side, had luckily taken my precautions against the purpose with which I was sure she had put the false pearl in my keeping; that is, if necessity arose, to charge me with its theft. As you saw, I had already placed it in the hands of the clerk, with a little message inside: 'Ask Cartier to buy another one for you, and send the bill to me!' So, seeing I knew of her fraud, she swallowed her defeat in silence."

The Vicomte leaned across the table. "I suppose you heard," he said in a low voice, "that the Prince Consort, grown desperate, wired to-day that the reward had been increased to half a million francs. You, mademoiselle, deserve it all! But, unluckily, it must first pass through the hands of the police. But, I vouch for it, your share shall be no less than a hundred and thirty thousand francs."

The color deepened in Fanny's face. Never had she looked more disarmingly youthful, more fragilely feminine. "Not bad, for a week's work!" she mused. Then she raised her glass, with a little triumphant smile.

"Come, Vicomte, let us drink to the two much coddled little pets that we have saved from disaster—the Swabian Heir Apparent and the Peace of Europe!"

THE THREE KNOCKS

I

"HELLO! Mademoiselle Gordon?"

"Here!"

"This is de Chatellerault who speaks. Tell me, mademoiselle, do you turn sick at the sight of blood?"

"What!"

"Blood in quantities, I mean. Does it make you faint?"

"No!"

"Good! Then meet me at half past twelve at the restaurant of the Quai d'Orsay. I'll give you luncheon, if you'll accept it, and an explanation."

Three quarters of an hour later, Fanny Gordon, chic and charming in her new summer suit of corbeau satin, entered the smoky dining-room of the great station—as unobserved a place for a rendezvous, perhaps, as exists in Paris. Raoul de Chatellerault hurried to meet her.

"Mademoiselle! I thank you. Here—this corner table. Give me your parasol. Here—let me help you to caviar. And now—mademoiselle, we want your help!"

"*We?*"

"The Secret Service. In the affair of the Queen of Swabia's pearl, my chief was immensely impressed with your wit and courage. Your name was mentioned in his official report. And now, mademoiselle, the Chief of Police sends me to ask your services in this mysterious affair of the Vaucaire murder."

Fanny started as he named this celebrated case which had since yesterday morning rung through Paris. The Vicomte went on quickly:

"A fine old boy, the Duc de Vaucaire, who at sixty-three preserved the life and spirit of twenty! Nevertheless, like many others of the ancient nobility of France, his traditions were all of the past. *Mon roi* was his religion. From his beautiful old palace in the Faubourg Saint-Germain all modern life was excluded—newspapers, books, even electric light, because electricity is supplied by the republican city government. It is even said that in the year '70, when the Republic was proclaimed, he imitated the example of a certain famous ancestor of his in the Hundred Years' War—sold all the family domains and securities, and stored away the cold, lifeless millions in gold coin in some secret corner, rather than permit the government that he detested to profit by any of his investments. As he wished his line to die out, he never married. And when, this past month, the mysterious knockings began in his house, he refused to call in the police of the detested Republic—but, instead, he invited all his friends to a great fancy-dress ball to help him defy the ghostly death sign of his race. I myself, mademoiselle, was present at that ball, only night before last; and I heard them with my own ears, those three mysterious knocks!"

He paused a moment; then, leaning across the little table:

"Mademoiselle," he asked abruptly, "are you one of those who believe the boundaries of another world sometimes overlie and overlap those of ours so that we see what mortal eyes are not meant to see and hear what mortal ears are not meant to hear?"

His voice had sunk very low. The restaurant, lit only by what light came through the huge glass roof of the station, was half in shadow, and the acrid smoke of the arriving and departing trains filled the air. Fanny shivered.

"It all depends on whether you ask me that question at noonday, in a crowded place like this, or if you come to me at midnight, in the silence—"

"It was at midnight that I heard them, mademoiselle—those three knocks which since a thousand years have been accepted in the Vaucaire family as the hand of the Great Intruder himself, knocking for admittance to their house—and which they say have invariably been followed by catastrophe. Twelve years ago, before the Duke's sister died—again in the year '69, before the sudden death of his father—those three mysterious knocks heralded the event. So in this past month, when again they began to sound through the partly closed up palace night after night, sometimes loud, sometimes soft, but recurring often more than a dozen times in a night—"

"And you heard it, Vicomte?"

"The night of the ball, when we had all gone downstairs to supper. The picture gallery, where we had danced, was empty. I had gone back to fetch my partner's fan, so I can vouch for that fact! We sat at supper. The atmosphere was tense—we all knew why we had been invited. We talked and laughed and ate—and listened! Suddenly we heard it. From the deserted ball-room above us, the sound of a strong hand knocking, imperatively and slow—once! twice! thrice! Mademoiselle, laugh at me if you will; but I hear them still—those three knocks!"

Angrily Fanny Gordon flung off the influence that his words produced upon her.

"Yes," she cried; "and you were all so taken up with your own wonderful sensations of artistic horror that I suppose no one had the time to go and hunt in the picture gallery!"

"You wrong us, mademoiselle! As a matter of fact, the echo of the last knock had hardly died away before some of us were already in the deserted picture gallery—the English nephew of the host, Sir Ffyles, I myself, one or two others that were young and ran upstairs fleetly. We found nothing! The endless rooms of the palace were empty. The gardens—empty. The concierge at the gate had opened to no one.

"*Mon Dieu!* How I hated to leave him, dear old Vaucaire! But he held his head high. He even insisted on sending his nephew to the Ritz to sleep that night, because he said the poor boy was worn out with lack of sleep, from the recurrence of the mysterious sign for the past few weeks. So we left him alone—alone with the servants and his other nephew, the Abbé Fornarini. And the next morning the Duc de Vaucaire was found dead in his bed, behind doors that were bolted from the inside and windows that were barred, with not a chink or a cranny by which the assassin could have entered or escaped—alone there in his bed, hacked to death with a knife!"

II

THE TAXICAB STOPPED before an immense pile of gray stone, square-roofed in the Renaissance style, and surrounded by a ten-foot wall garnished with iron spikes. A silent concierge admitted them through a great stone gate surmounted with armorial bearings in faded gold.

In a vast library where the daylight filtered through stained glass, the visitors were received by Sir Geoffrey Ffyles, the young English nephew of the dead Duke. Though his handsome face still bore traces of a recent horror, he greeted them with cordiality.

"Upon my word, de Chatellerault, this is good of you!" he exclaimed earnestly. "And Miss Gordon, too! Miss Gordon, I've heard from de Chatellerault, here, you're the keenest in Paris; so I wouldn't rest till he called you in. These Parisian police Johnnies—you know what they are! Take an idea into their heads, pull facts this way and that to suit their theory till they have the crime 'reconstructed'—then cop their man, with their dashed reconstruction as proof! And I say, Vicomte, who do you suppose the beggars are after now?"

"This morning, when I saw the Chief," returned Raoul, "he told me they had not yet—"

"Oh, but now they have! And who do you suppose? The Abbé Fornarini! You know him, of course—he's lived here with my poor uncle for the past ten years. A sort of nephew on the other side of the house. The most decent sort of chap, Miss Gordon! But just because he's a Jesuit, these dashed republicans are after him as keen as mustard. You see, he was missionary to the Assawabis, on the West Coast, for years after he left Rome; and he's got rather a jolly collection of native weapons and that sort of thing. And now, by Jove, these dashed beggars are claiming it came from the Abbé

Fornarini's collection, the knife with which my poor Uncle Vaucaire was—was—"

He broke off, and, crossing to a side table, poured himself a stiff drink of whisky.

"Have some, Vicomte? No? Excuse me, Miss Gordon, but I'm a bit on the ragged edge, with all these horrors piling up one on top of the other. And I was frightfully fond of my Uncle Vaucaire—by George, I was fond o him—"

"Pardon me, Sir Geoffrey. But you yourself—have you any information, any theories?"

The other shook his head in dreamy bewilderment. "Me? What theories could I have? I only know the padre didn't do it, poor old scout! And, by Jove, I'll tell you one thing—I'm glad now, for the first time in my life, that I'm not my uncle's heir. You know he has willed everything to the King of Spain? And certainly they can't say Alfonso did it! I say, I'm dashed glad, too, I didn't sleep here that night myself, or it's a sportin' chance these beggars'd be spinnin' their dashed 'reconstruction' about *me!*"

"Ah, yes—your uncle insisted on your going to the Ritz to sleep that night. Why?"

"Because he knew I hadn't had a decent night's sleep for a fortnight, by Jove! with all those infernal spirit rappin's, and warnin's, and what not! So, to please him, I went. And next mornin', when my man came with my things, he told me that my poor uncle—"

He shuddered, passed a shaking hand over his face, and reached out again for the whisky.

"Those mysterious knocks," said Fanny Gordon thoughtfully, "they were last heard—"

"In the picture gallery, as I told you!" interposed Raoul de Chatellerault. "At first, the Duke himself told me, they were heard in various parts of the palace. As you see, it is immense, with many parts closed up. Lately, however, they seemed always to come from the picture gallery—on the last night, that of the ball, certainly so."

Five minutes later, Fanny and her guide, having mounted the wide stairway, came to a pause before an open doorway, watched by a silent policeman.

In marked contrast to the rest of the house, darkened in token of mourning, this room was brilliantly alight in the afternoon sunlight, streaming in through the two wide-open windows. By one of the windows stood a uniformed official, writing in a little book. Fanny's eye was, however, held by the chief article of the room's furnishing: a huge, old-fashioned bed with beautifully gilded woodwork and a high, tent-like canopy and curtains of dark red silk. In the bright sunlight, she beheld the dark red tint hideously repeated in an immense stain like a pool, darkening the snowy surface of the embroidered sheets.

Deliberately she dragged away her eyes, and nodded in grave acknowledgment of her presentation to the Chief of the Secret Service.

That official bowed. His eyes showed that while as a man he approved, as a minister of the law he expected little from the vision of girlish prettiness before him.

"You are English, mademoiselle?"

"I am American, monsieur!"

"Hum! Ever handle a murder case before?"

Fanny assumed an air of extreme meekness. "No, monsieur! The Vicomte de Chatellerault will tell you I have only helped—"

"Well, well! I may as well tell you, mademoiselle, the police believe that they have found an indication, which we are at present following up. However, we should be glad to have you take your own independent line—if your woman's intuition suggests you one!" His patronizing air said, plainer than speech: "Play about all you please, little girl!"

Fanny's dark eyes blazed, but she held them resolutely down.

"Monsieur, if you will be so good, I should like the facts!"

Addressing himself to the Vicomte rather than to the young American, the official began the brief narrative of the crime.

"On Thursday night, as you know, Monsieur le Vicomte, the Duc de Vaucaire received his friends at a fancy-dress ball. Dancing was continued till three o'clock. At half past three the Duke retired. I must explain that the Duc de Vaucaire was a gentleman of most methodical habits. Every night, after his valet had made him ready for bed, he was accustomed to dismiss the man, lock and bolt the door on the inside, and go immediately to sleep. In the morning, when he woke, he rang his bell. The valet was not allowed to wake him, but waited for this signal that his master was ready for his coffee. After ringing, the Duke invariably rose for an instant and unbolted his door, so that the man, arriving with the coffee-tray, could carry it in to his master's bed without a moment's delay. Monsieur le Vicomte—mademoiselle! here is the most baffling feature, perhaps, of this whole mysterious case. On the morning of the murder—nay, at the very instant, perhaps, of the murder—that bell was rung!"

"There is no possibility it was another bell that rang?"

"None whatever, Monsieur le Vicomte. For Philippe, the valet, had, it seems, this custom: toward eight o'clock in the morning he would seat himself in the corridor where the row of bells hang—old-fashioned bronze bells with wire-pulls, you understand, since the Duke's prejudices allowed no electricity in the house. With his eye on the bells, the valet could see the first quiver of No. 18, that of his master's bedroom. And on Friday morning, he swears that the bell swung and jingled with precisely its customary motion and tinkle. The usual morning ring, neither more nor less. So Philippe dashed to the kitchen,—his master was always very angry if the coffee were cold,—seized the silver tray from the cook, ran full speed up the stairs, tried the handle of the Duke's door, and for the first time in twenty-three years found it locked. He knocked. Then suddenly, to his horror,—he seems to be a slow-witted fellow,—he heard a low moaning sound within. At his knock, the cries became articulate. He recognized his master's voice: 'Help! Assassins! Help!' Should you care to interview this fellow Philippe, Monsieur le Vicomte?"

"Later, later! What did he do then? Break down the door?"

"He tried it, and found it beyond his strength. He seems, in short, to have lost his head, as did also the other servants. They describe the cries as heartrending. So, while half a dozen of them fumbled at the door,—it is a massive one, as you see,—the others ran out into the street and summoned the police—the police of the

Republic, that poor Monsieur le Duc detested so! However, it was a policeman who finally managed to break down the door.

"Through the burst panels, the policeman entered first of all. He found the Duke already dead, transfixed by a huge knife that had been thrust into his body at the left thigh—thrust in with such violence that it had completely severed the femoral artery and buried its point for two centimeters in the bone. The superhuman violence of the blow, as well as the fact that it had been dealt from the side, renders the idea of suicide physically impossible, even had we been tempted to entertain it. Yet the doors were bolted. The windows, impossibly high from the ground, were barred. The room was empty. The murdered man was alone!"

"The witnesses?" asked the Vicomte quickly.

"The Duke's servants. Also the young policeman, André Chabanne, who himself stood guard at the broken-down door till I arrived. Together we made a scientific search of the room, which yesterday afternoon was completed by two of my experts. No sliding panel or any other dissimulated entrance exists. The walls, ceiling, and floor are as solid as a fortress. That the assassin, having done his foul work, should have escaped before that door was battered down is a physical impossibility. The concierge at the gate saw no one pass. Yet, by what superhuman means we have yet to divine, the murderer did escape!"

III

Fanny Gordon spoke: "Monsieur, you have twice used a certain word: *superhuman*. Do you mean—"

"Mademoiselle, I beg you, do not offer the famous knockings as a clue! We are not here to arrest the family ghost!—that figment of an overwrought imagination, of an exaggerated pride of race. The supernatural? Bah!"

"Monsieur, not supernatural. I used your own word—*superhuman!* The prodigious violence of the death-blow, the incomprehensible means of the assassin's escape—do you mean, then, to hint that the knife was perhaps driven home by another agency than that of a human hand?"

"By the hand of a gorilla, perhaps, as in a certain famous romance? Mademoiselle, abandon these fancies. It is a human murderer that we seek; neither wild beast nor ghost. Indeed, I may say that already, in our reconstruction of the crime, we have admitted the idea of a certain person."

"And the motive of the crime—that is included in your reconstruction?"

"The motive—we have already established at least that it was deeper than mere robbery! The wardrobe and escritoire before you, where the Duke was accustomed to keep not only a large sum of money but also certain valuable family jewels, have been found to contain all their treasures intact. The desire to profit by his death may also be excluded, as it appears that the Duke, a fanatical Royalist as you know, has left all his property by will to the last reigning Bourbon, King Alfonso of Spain. There remain the motives of revenge, of homicidal mania—"

"But the treasure?" asked Fanny slowly—"the gold of tradition, hidden by the Duke's ancestor at the time of the Hundred Years' War—to say nothing of the mass of wealth in cash added by the Duke himself, you said, Vicomte, when he sold his estates on the proclamation of the Republic? Did I not understand, it is all secreted somewhere in this ancient house?"

"Possibly! Though this family treasure, after all, exists perhaps nowhere but in tradition. But, in any case, nowhere in the Duke's room or in the whole house was there the slightest sign of a rifled hiding-place. Besides, remember this: the mere escape of our criminal unencumbered amounts, in this case, to a miracle! How much more impossible, then, the idea of his flight, whether at the moment of the crime or later, weighed down by the bulk and immense weight of a treasure in gold coin!"

Fanny walked up and down the room. "You have made a thorough search of the palace?"

"Surely, mademoiselle! The rooms, a hundred and two in all, have been thoroughly examined—even the luggage and persons of their inmates."

"Those inmates—in what did it consist, the household of the Duke?"

"A bachelor establishment—the Abbé Fornarini, his kinsman; the young English lord, his nephew; twenty-eight servants, excluding the concierge and stableman, who sleep outside; six maid-servants, the housekeeper, and the butler—"

"And, besides the valet Philippe, there were other servants that had admission to the Duke's bedroom?"

"The chambermaid, Armande Lainois, who took care of the room."

"Ah! And may one examine these two servants?"

"The valet Philippe Duval, yes. As to the woman, it appears that she was impertinent to the housekeeper on the night of the ball, received her eight days' notice, and disappeared immediately. She is being searched for; in a few day's we hope to lay our hands on her."

"Ah!"

Fanny paused. Then, in a changed voice and with a slight gesture toward the bed: "And, Monsieur, he—*it?*"

"The Duc de Vaucaire, mademoiselle, lies downstairs in the chapel of the palace."

"You have, of course, before removing the body, taken the usual measurements and diagrams?" asked de Chatellerault.

"Traced here upon the sheet in black crayon you will find the exact outline of the body as it was discovered on the breaking down of the door. The large black cross, made afterward, indicates the exact position of the wound. Here are also the photographs, made from nine different views. As you see, the wound is in the left thigh, between the hip and the knee—a part, of course, not usually considered vital, but rendered so by the piercing of the great femoral artery, which emptied the blood-vessels of the body before the door could be broken open and aid supplied."

Fanny's eyes lit up as she took the photographs offered her. In silence she bent over them.

"Singular," she murmured. "The wound is at the side of the leg, passing out toward the back."

"As I told you, mademoiselle! A fact which we explain by the position of Monsieur le Duc. As you see by this photograph, he lay half rolled over on the mattress, with extended arm—presumably to grasp the bell-rope for the summons which brought the servant Philippe upstairs—too late."

"Then you take it for granted, monsieur," returned Fanny thoughtfully, "that it was the hand of the Duke himself that rang the bell?—that singular summons, neither violent, as if he had already perceived the horrible vision of the assassin—nor feeble, as if the death-blow had already fallen!"

"Mademoiselle, there were two persons in this room. It is perfectly obvious that the murderer rang no summons to the household at the very instant of his crime. Ergo—that bell was rung by Monsieur le Duc himself!"

"Two persons in the room—" murmured Fanny dreamily. "You say two persons in the room."

And the impatient official, following the direction of her bright, dark eyes, saw them travel from the large red silk tassel which lay upon the pillow, up the heavy red silk cord of the bell-pull to the brass triangle which, by the old-fashioned system, connected it with the wire beyond. So long she stood motionless, with her eyes fixed upon that commonplace instrument, that the chief became slightly ironic.

"Romances again, mademoiselle? No; the murder was not committed by a trained snake who crawled down the bell-rope and returned later to the loop of her master's whip. The aperture through which the wire passes has been examined, and would admit the passage of not so much as a trained earthworm."

"What is that long loop of gray twine up there, dangling from the lower apex of the triangle?" asked Fanny suddenly. The official started, then resumed his ironical calm.

"The loop of the whip perhaps, mademoiselle? Or else, a hundred years ago workmen were perhaps as careless as they are today, and as likely to leave traces of their packing material behind on the finished work! And now, mademoiselle, it happens that the serious aspects of this case call me—"

"Monsieur, one thing more! I should like, if I may, to see the knife."

The chief turned, unlocked a flat black valise, and took from it a long slim paper parcel. In a moment he had produced a savage-looking knife, whose polished blade was obscured near the point with dark and sinister stains. The Vicomte de Chatellerault bent over it.

"A brutal weapon—from one of the Congo tribes, as Sir Geoffrey said," he remarked in a hushed voice. "They use them as javelins, to hurl at the enemy. Do you observe the tiny handle of elk-horn, perforated for ornament? And the disproportionate size of the blade, with the extra weight so skilfully introduced toward the tip—precisely as our own early ancestors, monsieur, tipped their arrows with stone!"

With a gesture of contained horror, Fanny took the repulsive-looking weapon into her hands.

"But your explanation, Vicomte, does us no good—because, to hurl the knife, one must be in the room just as much as to stab with it! And, for a savage, the problem of escape later would be just as difficult as for a civilized man!" Then, bending again toward the ugly blade in her hands:

"What is this little piece of black and scarlet floss, knotted through one of the perforations of the handle?"

"Probably a memento of the last war dance in which it figured before it was brought to Europe, mademoiselle," returned the Vicomte. "All savages, as you know, decorate their weapons, as they do their persons—"

He was interrupted by the Chief, who sat in a brown study. "The Abbé Fornarini was missionary among the West Coast tribes for ten years before he came here to Paris," he observed in a low tone.

De Chatellerault knit his brows. "Circumstantial evidence. Where is his motive?"

The official hesitated. When he spoke, his voice, though almost inaudible, yet crackled with the hatred born of modern and republican prejudice:

"Understand me, Monsieur le Vicomte! I make no charge, as yet. But the abbé is a Jesuit. As you know, the Society of Jesus is all-powerful in Spain."

Fanny rose to her feet.

"Monsieur, I will detain you no longer. To the courtesy you have already shown me I will ask you to add three favors more."

"Name them, mademoiselle!"

"First, I want this house guarded. Understand me! I do not speak of half a dozen policemen—I want the whole place thoroughly sentineled, night and day. A policeman for every two or three rooms, in day and night shifts, who will patrol constantly. And in the picture gallery, monsieur, I should like to have always two men!"

The Chief surveyed this rosy-faced young vision in dark blue satin, issuing her orders so decidedly. The excess of her presumption seemed almost to please him, like the impertinence of a pretty child.

"Indeed, mademoiselle, your requests are not small ones! And yet, the Apaches are quiet for the moment; our men have little to do—perhaps forty or fifty men could be spared. For eight days, no longer. And, mind, at the end of those eight days I shall expect results!"

"Perhaps even sooner, monsieur! And now for favor number two—a step-ladder!"

"Ah! I should have expected you to ask for the Eiffel Tower! A ladder you shall have. And then?"

"The freedom of the house for the week, monsieur!"

"You shall have it. And now—by the way, I am informed that the legatee has offered, through the Spanish Ambassador here, a reward of fifteen thousand francs for evidence leading to the capture of the assassin. Had you heard that? *Au revoir!*"

IV

"I SAY, MISS GORDON! Do you mind if I trot around after you a bit?"

"It's a pleasure, Sir Geoffrey!"

"Thanks. You know, I'm just back from my poor uncle's funeral. This house—it gives me the creeps. I'm all in."

With a violent shudder, Sir Geoffrey Ffyles sank into one of the high, carved chairs of the little private chapel where, for the instant, Fanny's researches had led her. His handsome face was haggard.

"I say, I didn't sleep a wink last night. This house—ugh! It's haunted."

"But the knockings haven't been heard since—since the night the Duke died, have they?"

"No—don't you see, that makes it all the worse? It all goes to show there was somethin' uncanny in the business! Hang it—bein' a historic family—it's poor sport. I remember, there at Ffyles Court, before my poor father died, our family banshee whoopin' and screechin' about the tree-tops all winter long. And he died. Then my poor mother came over here to her brother, my Uncle Vaucaire. And the knockin's began, for her. And she died. Then, now, after twelve years, the knocks begin again for my poor uncle. And *he's* dead, the Lord knows how."

"Sir Geoffrey, it will do you good to take your mind off these horrors! If you don't mind, I'd like to ask you a very frivolous question."

"Fire away!"

"That pretty gray camel's-hair wrapper of the abbé's that I saw the housekeeper sewing on this morning—I'd so like to get one like it, to send home for a present to my uncle! Did you ever see it, Sir Geoffrey?"

"The abbé's wrapper? The—no; I never saw it in my life! Haven't an idea what the poor old scout gets into when he slips out of his blacks, I'm sure!"

"Too bad! I hoped you could tell me where he bought it."

"Hush! Speak of angels—"

At the upper end of the little chapel, from behind the altar, suddenly appeared a tall figure in a black cassock. At sight of the baronet and his companion, the newcomer paused. Then, with bent head, he advanced slowly down the aisle.

"*Bon jour*, mademoiselle. *Bon jour*, cousin. Any news?"

Fanny's pretty rosy face drooped into lines of unwonted discouragement as she answered:

"None at all, Monsieur l'Abbé. I know the police are all at sea. And as for a girl—what can she hope to do, against such a criminal as this?"

Her visible shudder thrilled like electricity through her two listeners. The priest's pale aquiline face was, however, immovable as he answered sternly:

"Against an enemy such as this a young girl, provided her heart be pure, can do more than the entire police of this republic of Anti-Christ."

"Then you think, Monsieur l'Abbé," asked Fanny, in a hushed voice, "that the murder had a supernatural origin?"

"What you call supernatural, mademoiselle," answered the Abbé Fornarini, in his cold voice, "may perhaps be, for God, the most natural thing in the world."

"Who knows?" murmured Fanny. "Those mysterious knocks of warning—tell me, abbé, when were the last knocks heard?"

"Four nights ago, in the picture gallery—the night before the Duke died."

"And not since then?"

"No, mademoiselle. Their warning has been fulfilled."

Was this to be the abbé's defense of himself before the court? Fanny gazed at him with eyes of fascinated speculation. His sardonic eyes pierced her thought.

"And in your search through this ancient house you have, then, found evidence which leads you to doubt it, this theory of mine?"

"Alas, no. Though I have come on strange things—traces of a far-away past that you, doubtless, can interpret better than I. For instance, look at that window there behind you—there to the right—"

Simultaneously the two men turned, the young Englishman more quickly than the other. The abbé, jostled by his cousin's shoulder, half fell against the window. There was a smart crash, a vision of the priest recoiling with a bleeding forehead, a tinkle of broken glass on the stone courtyard below.

"I say—was that my fault?" cried the bewildered baronet. "By George, I'm frightfully sorry, old scout! See here, shall I—"

"It is nothing!" interrupted the abbé coldly—"a scratch that will be healed to-morrow!" And, with his handkerchief pressed to his temple, he turned back to the young girl. "Mademoiselle, you had something you wished to show to us!"

His penetrating eyes were met by the young American's, as clear and steady as his own. "Monsieur l'Abbé. I regret that I have no longer anything to show you. The pane of glass where the ancient writing was is gone; it lies in fragments on the stone flags below us."

"Writin'?" cried Sir Geoffrey Ffyles, with interest. "I say, weren't they jolly proud of their diamonds, in those old days? Queen Bess, and Raleigh, and all of 'em goin' around spoilin' all the windows—"

"Not so badly as it is spoiled now, that window," returned Fanny, dryly. "I am sorry, because perhaps you could have told me the meaning of those doggerel lines in old French that were scratched there. However, now they are gone forever. And, if you will excuse me, I must go, too. The Chief of the Secret Service is waiting for me. *Au revoir!*"

V

SURE ENOUGH, in the library she found the Chief waiting for her, with Raoul de Chatellerault.

"Well, mademoiselle, any results?"

Breathlessly she related the incident that had just passed. The official, who invariably scoffed at Fanny's methods as "dreams," nevertheless gave to this unsuccessful attempt a sudden and exaggerated importance.

"My God, mademoiselle! So this is American intelligence! To show your discovery to the Italian priest, of all men in Paris! You do not show it to me, or to Monsieur le Vicomte here; you do not even take a copy—"

"Pardon, monsieur!" Fanny opened her hand-bag. "Here is a tracing of the writing on the window. Here are two photographs that I made myself yesterday. Here is a translation into modern French, made by Professor Bôchet at the Sorbonne. Here—"

The Chief snatched the papers. With eager eyes the Vicomte leaned over him. They read:

Curieux qui frappez
Là sur la place
Ou vous m'entendrez
Cherchez avec audace
Hòtel de Vaucaire
Et son trésor si cher.

De Chatellerault sprang to his feet. "The family hoard!"

For once, the Chief did not scout this idea as fantastic.

"One sees now why the Abbé Fornarini did not wish you to read these lines!" he commented briefly, then returned to the doggerel rhymes: "'You, inquisitive one, who knock there on the place where you shall hear me, seek with boldness the Duke's palace and its treasure so dear!'"

He paused.

"'*Me!* when you shall hear *me!*' Evidently the writer of these lines directs us to go about, pounding on the walls of the palace, and when we hear him answer from underneath, to hunt boldly and we'll find the treasure.

"Bah! The Vaucaire who first hid his money doubtless had his own bones buried with it, and planned to watch over it and answer when the right person came to hunt. Quite a reasonable scheme, for those days! And probably it seems very reasonable to the priest, who is the inheritor of all their superstitions. In fact, it would not surprise me to know that these recent mysterious tappings were the work of the abbé knocking on the wall to get an answer from the ghostly sentinel within. Bah! I have two minds to arrest him before he goes to eat his luncheon."

Fanny shook her head. "No, no! we have nothing to gain by haste. But look, Chief! Look again at these lines. Do you not see it is written there who it is that the knocker shall hear answer from within, when he has found the spot?"

"Written here? A name written here?" The Chief returned to his reading, first with bewilderment and then with anger. "'There where you hear *me* answer, hunt boldly—' Mademoiselle, if you say that it is written here who this me is that we should hear beneath the wall when we knock, then I tell you that you are simply mocking me! And I command you, in the name of the law, if you have found a clue to the whereabouts of this hiding-place, to lead me to it at once."

"I regret, monsieur, that is what I am unable to do. If you, however, will kindly give me your aid, I hope to do better."

"What?"

"I hope to make the murderer himself lead us to it!"

De Chatellerault, to whom experience had given a considerable respect for Fanny Gordon's powers, leaped to his feet. The older man, however, preserved his skeptical calm.

"Pardon me, mademoiselle. You will excuse me if I wait to be startled till you shall have made your words good. As for my aid, I will not refuse it to you—"

"You will even begin now, by answering one or two questions for me, monsieur?"

"Certainly!"

"Tell me, that pretty gray camel's-hair dressing-gown of the Abbé Fornarini's, that the housekeeper was sewing on yesterday—have you seen it?"

With a puzzled expression, the Chief shook his head. Fanny leaned forward.

"You haven't? I asked the same question of Sir Geoffrey Ffyles, and he never saw it, either! In fact, no one has seen it, that gray wrapper of the abbé's, except just the housekeeper and me."

"*Bloodstains?*"

"Not a stain, I assure you! And the pockets were empty. I draw your attention to this incident of the wrapper merely to emphasize the fact that even his own cousin denies having ever seen it! And now—the woman Armande Lainois: has she been found yet?"

With the annoyed expression of one who confesses a failure, the Chief shook his head.

"The description of her—will you please let me see it? Thanks! Hum—large dark eyes; nose, small Roman; stature, medium; tinted red hair, which continues to grow in a narrow downy ridge along the nape of her neck and disappears under her collar. That's not very common! Moles, left arm above elbow. That's enough. Chief, have you ever thought in what a very singular place it was, that death-wound of the Duke?"

"I have, indeed!" returned that official stiffly.

"Though the Duke, in the act of lifting his left arm toward the bell, left his heart completely exposed, still the murderer drove home his knife in a part which, had aid arrived promptly, would not even have proved vital. Singular clumsiness! Inexplicable circumstance—that this atrocious criminal, whose fiendish skill enabled him to slip in and out of a closed room like a spirit, yet bungled his work so awkwardly at the crucial moment that it was only by accident that it was successful!"

"Evidently," returned the Chief stiffly, "he lost his head when his intended victim managed to ring the bell and give the alarm!"

"Probably. And yet, the startlingly haphazard nature of the death-blow—I commend it to your attention, monsieur. And now, will you kindly accompany me upstairs to the bedroom of the late Duke?"

Five minutes later the three stood together in the grim chamber of sudden death, unchanged except that the red stains of the bedclothes had become nearly black. Fanny Gordon's eyes were full of a dancing fire. Her color was high.

"Chief," she said in an excited voice, "I just had an idea. I have come here to prove it. On it hangs my theory. Listen. Your sentinel there at the door will give you his word, corroborated by that of the night watchman, that I have not entered this room, except in your presence, since the day I was introduced into this house."

The Chief bowed in silence. The Vicomte fixed keen eyes on his protégée. Fanny walked over to the bed; then recoiled.

"Messieurs, I will own my weakness—I can not touch that bed. Will you be so kind, Chief, as to look under the mattresses—here, on the left side of the bed—and see if there is anything bulky between the mattress and the springs?"

At the unoccupied side of the bed indicated by Fanny, the stout official stooped. He puffed as he tugged at the sheet and heaved up the edge of the mattress. Then:

"Name of a toad! Look, Monsieur le Vicomte!"

There, beneath the deep woolen mattress, carefully arranged on the covered springs, were rows and rows of cushions—white pillows, satin cushions, little embroidered head-rests, all neatly flattened together to form a smooth, symmetrical slope. The Vicomte drew his breath sharply.

"Mademoiselle! What does this mean?"

"You have as much reason to know, Vicomte, as I! And now—I beg you, Chief, do me the kindness of looking beneath the mattress on this other side—here beneath the spot where the poor Duke was lying."

Nervously Fanny's slim hands clasped and unclasped, while the Chief, strangely obedient now, carried out her directions. Then he announced:

"On this side, mademoiselle, there are no cushions."

"Ah!" Fanny's breath exhaled itself in a long gasp. She stood for a long time in thought, staring at the bed; then spoke beneath her breath:

"No. There can be no more doubt now, any more."

"But, mademoiselle, explain—"

"No, Chief. Later! Now the time is short; we must act quickly. Listen—will you carry out my directions?"

"That depends—"

"It must not depend! You have asked me for results. I have done all that I can, and the rest depends on you. I want you to make immediate public announcement, through the telephone to the evening papers, that to-day the municipal guards are removed from the Duke's palace. This afternoon I want you to remove all your men, conspicuously, openly—all your men, without one exception. You will then give charge of the house over to the late Duke's solicitors, to be handed over to-morrow to the legatee, the King of Spain. And to-night—"

"To-night, mademoiselle?"

She lowered her voice. "To-night, messieurs, I will ask you to meet me at eleven o'clock at the Quai d'Orsay. You, Chief, must bring two of your best men. All must be armed. We will drive to the corner of the Rue Langlois. There we will descend, and proceed on foot to the servants' gate of this house. The housekeeper, with whom I have made friends, and who was passionately devoted to the late Duke, will be waiting for us there at half past eleven o'clock. We will enter the house by the servants' stair, in complete darkness. And then, if those conditions have been faithfully observed, I think I can hope to show you some results."

In the young girl's voice ran a vivid intensity like the crackling of an electric current. The official tried to shrug his shoulders, but failed, and contented himself with saying:

"Melodramatic to the last! Ah, well, be it as you will, mademoiselle."

"In melodrama we should have suitable weapons!" returned Fanny suavely, as she unfolded the satin jacket that she carried on her arm. "Should you care to carry this instead of your revolver, Chief?"

She handed him a hammer whose head was carefully sewed up in black cloth. The two men pounced upon it.

"Where did you find that?"

"I found it where I looked for it—in the picture gallery!" said Fanny Gordon.

VI

To wait in the dark for the coming of a murderous criminal is a far from pleasant business, even when one's fear is merely that he may come. The unpleasantness, however, becomes far more pronounced when one's fear is that he may stay away! Such was the terror of Fanny Gordon in the long watches of that stifling summer night, as she lay crouched in the picture gallery behind a carved oak chest, and waited.

Half past one had already struck. In hardly more than an hour it would come now, the early June dawn. Suppose it broke, and this wearisome watch, planned by her, had been all in vain! In spite of the heat, Fanny shivered and the cold sweat broke out over her body.

"Two and two make four!" she argued fiercely to herself for the thousandth time. "And, just as surely, he must come here tonight. He can't fail—he *can't!*"

Suddenly her muscles stiffened, her breath stopped. Surely, at the end of the long gallery, a door had opened cautiously.

Silence. Then, through the dark, came the unmistakable padding sound of soft-shod feet.

Silence again. Then the spurt of a match flame. A faint blue flare. A moment's pause. Then, suddenly, on the wall near her hiding-place a hand knocked.

For the first time, Fanny realized how terrifying it was in its stark and naked simplicity, that traditional death sign of the house of Vaucaire. Fear, instinctive unreasoning fear, numbed her muscles and made her stomach quiver. A second knock. Her qualm had passed; the intellect and the will resumed their sway. For from within the depths of the wall, rendered dim by intervening bricks and plaster, echoed the thin answering tinkle of a bell.

Boldly now, with no shelter but that of the darkness, Fanny lifted her head. Not twenty feet from her, she beheld a tall figure in a dark dressing-gown, holding a candle in one hand and running the other down the faded gilt frame of a large antique portrait. The next moment the whole portrait swung out like a door. A pause. A gasp.

"Rose! Where are you?"

The tender whisper thrilled with the secret quality of the voice that speaks for one ear alone. Then suddenly the veil of mystery and silence was stabbed by a dreadful cry:

"*Dead! Dead! Rose, you are dead!*"

The sudden glare of electric torches, the leaping out of men's faces, the cocking of revolvers, the rush of feet. Fanny, heedless of possible danger, was the first to arrive at the dark aperture in the wall. The next instant she had recoiled. There at her feet, staring up in the faint light with fixed, wide-open eyes, was the beautiful white face of a woman.

"*Nom d'un nom d'un nom!*"

It was the Chief's voice. The dark figure, huddled over the motionless body of the woman, lifted its head and showed the face, blanched and distorted, of Sir Geoffrey Ffyles.

"Get a doctor!" he screamed. "Don't you see she's dead? But perhaps she's not dead, after all. If you're quick, perhaps she can be saved. Run for a doctor—quick!"

So intense was his emotion, he seemed not even conscious of the interruption of armed intruders. His face, distorted like a mask by the intensity of his passion, was bent over the woman, who lay motionless in her black and white servant's uniform, with the candle-light shining on her red-brown hair and on the piled-up heaps of golden louis that surrounded her on every side.

Stooping, the Chief picked up one waxen hand and laid it over his electric torch. Between the fingers shone faint lines of yellowish gray. He turned back the lids from the staring dark eyes, lifted the beautiful heavy head. There on the back of the limp white neck, following the line of the spine, the hair continued in a thin dark line of down.

"Rose d'Artigny!" exclaimed one of the detectives below his breath. The Chief nodded solemnly, while the crouching creature in the brocade dressing-gown, stripped of all his lordly nonchalance, watched him as a wolfhound glares at the intruder who handles her pups.

The Chief said:

"This time, however, she has paid for her devilish trick with her life. She has been dead two days, at the least."

Again Sir Geoffrey, in an abandonment explained not only by his grief but by the fumes of whisky that rose from him, flung himself upon the body.

"Rose! Sweetheart! Sweetheart! Why did you steal a march on me? Didn't you know it was for you I did it? And now it's no use any more. You are dead, my little Rose! Dead!"

From his wild lamentations Fanny's keen ear picked out one phrase: "*It was for you I did it.*"

Summoning the whole force of her will power, she stooped and transfixed the wretched man's eyes with her own.

"Listen to me, Sir Geoffrey Ffyles," she said sternly. "It was you, with the aid of this woman, who murdered your uncle the Duc de Vaucaire—then tried to fasten the crime on the Abbé Fornarini. The whole chain of proof is in my hands. Look into my eyes and deny it if you can—deny it if you dare!"

The detectives crowded around. With a visible effort, Sir Geoffrey raised his bloodshot blue eyes. With a ghastly imitation of his usual manner, he addressed her in English:

"By George, I don't know what you come rottin' me like this for! And; anyway, if my uncle went cuttin' off his own flesh and blood to leave everythin' to that snob of an Alfonso, what the doose did he expect? And as for Rose—"

His eyes wavered. He collapsed upon the floor.

"I don't know how you found it all out, but, after all, what difference does it make? Take me away—to the guillotine, if you like! If I wanted money, it was only for her. And now she's gone, why shouldn't I go too? Rose! Rose! Rose!"

VII

Next morning, Fanny Gordon, paler than usual, sat in her little salon, facing the Vicomte de Chatellerault and the Chief of the Secret Service.

"After all," she observed, almost apologetically, "it was only a question of getting the right idea at the beginning—woman's intuition, as you very justly say, Chief! As, for instance, those lines of ancient doggerel that I copied from the window—it's merely an acrostic. Read downward, Vicomte, the first letter of each line!"

"C-l-o-c-h-e," read the Vicomte; then, in a burst of admiration, "Bravo!"

"*Cloche*—bell!" repeated the Chief slowly. "Hum—very simple, as you say. For it was a bell that we heard beneath the wall, was it not, when Sir Geoffrey knocked there in the picture gallery last night!"

Fanny nodded. "But how many nights had he and his accomplice knocked, in other parts of the house, before they heard that answering tinkle from beneath the wall to assure them that the hiding-place of tradition was found? Ah! it was not a dull idea, to utilize the ancient legend of the three death knocks, not only in order to sound the walls but also to lend a supernatural air to the murder which later would be necessary to clear the house and make the removal of the treasure possible."

"The murder!" said the Chief excitedly. "Now, young lady, since your wit has fathomed a secret which, for the first time in twenty-two years, has left me baffled, I await your explanation. If not by supernatural means, then how did the murderer escape from the sealed chamber after dealing the death-blow to the Duc de Vaucaire?"

"He did not escape, monsieur!"

"But you are mad—that room was empty!"

"Because, messieurs, the Duc de Vaucaire was alone when he died."

The two men sprang to their feet. "But it has already been demonstrated that suicide was impossible!"

"The Duc de Vaucaire did not die a suicide."

"Mademoiselle, explain—explain!"

"Messieurs," returned Fanny solemnly, "I will ask you now to combine in your minds several detached circumstances of which the significance, it seemed, was revealed to me and not to you. Those knockings, which, if we accepted them as an attempt to profit by the secret of the ancient rhyme, showed so intimate a knowledge of family secrets, so close a knowledge also of the Duke's character, who, in his devout attachment to tradition, might well be expected to conceal his treasure nowhere else but in the hereditary hiding-place of his race. Then, also, there was the question of the opportunity to knock on the walls. All of which circumstances narrowed down an inquiry to members of the Duke's immediate household. Of the two who might be supposed to possess sufficient intelligence for such an attempt, secret inquiry proved one nephew to possess the spotless character of a model priest; the other—"

"But Sir Geoffrey possessed an excellent character!" cried the Chief, aggrieved. "His bills, his club dues, his gambling debts, all were promptly paid. His reputation—"

"Was above suspicion, Chief, in his relations with other men! But, American though I am, something told me that when a man embarks on a secret and perilous enterprise, not only the springs of his action but the confidante of his crime must be sought rather in a member of my own sex. My inquiries, therefore, were limited to Sir Geoffrey Ffyles' relations with women; and I found that for the past three years he had been the lover of the notorious Rose d'Artigny—famed as a sort of female Apache, who by her beauty and fierce rapacity for money had driven countless men to crime.

"At the same time, I found that the woman who had obtained admittance to the household as chambermaid, and who had contrived to get herself discharged on the very night of the crime, answered to the same physical description as Mademoiselle d'Artigny—to the very fact of the downy strip on the back of the neck, a bizarre distinction of which Rose, it appeared, was inordinately vain and would not have removed even to escape possible detection. Besides, what detection did she have to fear? Taking, no doubt, alternate nights, they thumped the walls of the old house at their leisure, till at last in the picture gallery their perseverance was rewarded by the answering bell that they had hoped to hear."

"But, mademoiselle the murder, the murder!"

"The simplest business in the world! You noticed that little shred of black and scarlet floss attached to the handle of the knife? Yes, but I think you did not notice the gray camel's-hair dressing-gown, presented by Sir Geoffrey Ffyles to the Abbé Fornarini on the very night of the ball, so the housekeeper informed me—though, as I told you, Sir Geoffrey himself denied ever having seen such a garment. That wrapper, messieurs, was secured about the waist by a cord of black and scarlet silk—which the housekeeper, when I saw her, was changing for black. I carried off a tassel. Even under the microscope, that red and black floss proved to be precisely identical with the scrap that remained upon the knife."

"Yes! but, even so—"

"Even so, we might deduce merely a detail of the dastardly attempt to fasten the crime on the abbé—like jostling him so that it should be he, and not Sir Geoffrey, whose head broke the window and destroyed the legendary verse; like stealing the very knife from the collection of the returned missionary—that strange savage weapon, half knife and half javelin, weighted at its tip to assure greater accuracy of aim."

"Mademoiselle, I begin to see—"

"Which you will do entirely when I tell you that my searches with the ladder revealed to me the presence of that same silk in yet a third place." She paused a moment, lifting her hand in an impressive gesture. "In the iron crossbar of that old-fashioned bed canopy, immediately above the place marked X to indicate the wound, there clung a shred of black and scarlet floss. Do you see now?"

"Almost! Ah, *mon Dieu!* But—"

"Do you remember, messieurs, that loop of gray twine—not ancient, as we thought, but ordinary string of modern commerce—that hung attached to the old-fashioned bell-pull where it entered the wall? That loop of twine, when tested, proved *exactly of the length to reach the point in the bed's canopy where the betraying floss still clung*—that frail silk loop which held the sword of Damocles suspended all night above the sleeping Duke. Then, when he awoke in the morning and pulled the bell-cord, the brass triangle of its mechanism flew around, the twine was jerked suddenly taut and snapped the loop of flimsy floss to which it was attached. The silk broke, down came the knife not in the heart or throat as an assassin would choose, but in that singular part of the body of which we have already spoken, but which, alas, proved to be deadly enough."

Solemnly the Chief rose and extended his hand.

"Mademoiselle, I compliment you—you and America! You have done excellently. And though the reward offered is, doubtless, a mere bagatelle for a lady like you, I will see that the fifteen thousand francs are paid to you without delay. And now, one or two small remaining points. Why did the Duke not see it when he went to bed, that horrible blade suspended there above his head?"

"You forget, monsieur, his prejudices! From his home electric light was excluded. And by candle-light, especially when one goes to bed wearied by a ball, one sees little."

"And the woman, Rose d'Artigny—how did it happen—"

"Monsieur, what more natural than, having betrayed her master, she should betray also her lover? On the night of the ball, knowing that, by the obstinate kindliness of his uncle, Sir Geoffrey was forced to sleep out, she thought to accomplish a fine stroke of business by rifling the Vaucaire hoard alone. The final knocks with which she resought the exact spot were doubtless those you heard when you sat at supper, Vicomte! And it was probably at the very moment that you dashed upstairs to the picture gallery that the wretched woman, in her alarm, swung the secret door to upon herself. Ignorant of the fact that the police prevented her lover from coming, she waited. He came at last, as we know—too late!"

"Mademoiselle," said the Vicomte suddenly, "one last point! Those cushions beneath the mattress—how did you know they were there?"

"I took it for granted that, having set their trap, they would not risk the chance that their predestined victim might lie on the wrong side of the bed! And, by a system of carefully graded cushions, it was easy to insure that, even in his sleep, his body should slip to the point where they desired it to be, beneath the knife. Cleverly designed, was it not? And now, if you won't think me too frivolous, I'm going to shake off these gruesome horrors that I've been living among—and, if you'll excuse me, I'm going straight down to the summer sale of the Galeries Lafayette. They announce bargains in peignoirs and in trimmed hats!"

THE ORCHID OF SUDDEN DEATH

I

"For a woman to lie to her husband is only normal; and the more she loves him the oftener, of course, she will lie. But when she begins to deceive her brother, it's a bad sign."

The Vicomte de Chatellerault, who, after refusing an invitation to dinner, had run in for coffee afterward, seemed strangely absent-minded and nervous. He gnawed his lips, glanced at the straight back of Fanny's new English chaperone, then spoke beneath his breath:

"I am troubled, mademoiselle, about my sister Blanche-Marie."

Fanny glanced up with quick compassion. "The Duchess d'Ubzac? She is ill?"

He shook his head. "No! But, mademoiselle, it has an ugly look when a woman, married to a millionaire who adores her, yet comes three times in two months to borrow fifty thousand francs from her brother who is not a millionaire at all. Her money gambled away at bridge, a pressing account from Doucet—that was the story. But, mademoiselle, what am I to think when, with the idea of relieving her from anxiety, I seek the dressmaker, inquire about this pressing overdue account, and am told that ever since her marriage the account of the Duchess d'Ubzac has been promptly settled at the end of each month?"

"Perhaps another dressmaker?"

"She explicitly stated Doucet. Mademoiselle, having heard this, I went at once to my sister's house. Blanche-Marie was not at home. It is now nearly nine o'clock, and she has not yet returned!"

Fanny lapsed into deep thought. "Vicomte, did you find whether the Duchess had received any letters this morning?"

He nodded. "Old Nanette showed them to us. She herself carries the morning post to her mistress, so she could vouch that they were, all there. The singular thing, however, was, they were all unopened!"

"Ah!" Into Fanny's dark eyes flashed the dancing brightness that lit them when her passion for investigation was aroused. "Does madame your sister read the newspapers?"

He nodded. "The *Grand Journal* was there on the night table, folded beside her letters."

"Folded as it comes from the press?"

He hesitated. "N-no. I remember noticing that an inner sheet with marked reports was folded on the outside."

Fanny rang her bell. Her little maid appeared. "Clémentine, here is a sou. Please go to the little shop on the Avenue Kléber and buy me a *Grand Journal* of this morning."

"Yes, mademoiselle!"

Raoul sat with a troubled face, like one who has loosed forces that he is minded to check.

"Who knows? Perhaps you are right. She may have been speculating on her own account, and met with disaster—poor child! And, in any case, it is very likely that by this time she has returned home. Mademoiselle, may I use your telephone?"

Five minutes later, as de Chatellerault turned with an agitated frown from the telephone, the breathless Clémentine entered the salon with the desired newspaper.

"Blanche-Marie has not yet returned, mademoiselle." Chatellerault's high-featured face was slightly pale. "Ah, the *Grand Journal*. We will look at the stocks that have fallen badly these last few days—"

"Your idea is an excellent one, Vicomte, but before looking at the Bourse reports on page 5 we will look first on page 4, which folds open at the same time and contains a column far more important to our purpose."

Fanny Gordon paused a moment and glanced anxiously at the Vicomte. "When I read the personal column," she murmured, "I always feel as if I were looking into other people's letters."

Raoul caught his breath. "The personal column! Why didn't I think of that?" Snatching the newspaper from Fanny Gordon's hand, he ran his eye fiercely down the page. Fanny leaned over his shoulder. Then their fingers touched as, at the same instant, they indicated a paragraph:

> Boul'd H'n. 25,000 francs—not a sou less. This evening. Otherwise immediate consequences. Avoué. Rue Longlois 18.

The Vicomte jumped to his feet. "Twenty-five thousand! The very sum she asked me for yesterday! If it should be she!"

"The clue is at least worth trying, as it is the only one we have," responded Fanny. Then, crossing the room:

"Mrs. Walden, excuse me for breaking up our party, but I am called out immediately upon the most urgent business. Do not sit up for me. I will take my key."

The English lady nodded in shocked resignation.

"And now, Vicomte, wait till I put on a hat and cloak, and have Clémentine call a taxi."

"But, mademoiselle, surely it is my place to go, rather than yours!"

"Yes; and if the Duchess is really there, directly she hears your voice she will suspect pursuit—"

"True! But, mademoiselle, it is night and for a young girl like you—"

"Nonsense! I will take my revolver."

Five minutes later, with her little dog, Towser, on her arm, she stepped into the taxicab.

"It is now nine o'clock. At half past ten, Vicomte, telephone to Mrs. Walden. If I am not yet at home, come to the Rue Longlois. *Au revoir!*"

II

In a quiet, dimly lighted street, Fanny Gordon alighted from her taxicab. No. 18 showed a façade typically old-fashioned, respectable, and austere. Just inside the door sat a neatly dressed concierge bending over her sewing in the dim light.

"Monsieur l'avoué?"

"Third story to the left!"

Up the ancient stone staircase Fanny mounted, until, at the door indicated, she pressed the electric button. Though she could hear the shrill ringing of the gong within, she was forced to repeat the summons twice before the door was finally opened. The maid, clad in an unexpected chic costume of black and white, was a small, pretty creature whose face was rendered striking by her high-bridged nose and by the dark eyebrows which touched fiercely in the middle over a pair of immense black eyes. These eyes met those of the newcomer rather wildly, not to say defiantly.

"Monsieur l'avoué?"

The servant answered breathlessly, as if she had been running:

"Monsieur l'avoué is—is out!"

Fanny noticed the uncertain quality of her tone, as well as the streak of light that shone from a door that stood ajar half way down the unlit hallway. With a sudden resolution of daring, she clutched her dog, pushed the maid aside, and walked rapidly to the lighted doorway. She knocked on the door; then, receiving no response, pushed it open and boldly entered the room. It was empty.

"I will wait for monsieur l'avoué!" she said firmly. The maid-servant immediately vanished.

Fanny, reassured by the elegance and calm of the room that she had thus forcibly entered, looked about at the well filled library shelves, the antique furniture of dark, carved wood, the rich Persian rugs upon the floor. Fanny's Pomeranian, however, whimpered a little and thrust his head under his mistress' arm.

"Little idiot! Is it the flowers you don't like?"

More than once, indeed, Fanny had had occasion to notice her pet's antipathy to the scent of flowers; and here, in addition to the other marks of refined luxury, a large box of magnificent yellow orchids lay open on the immense carved writing-table. Fanny, who loved flowers, strolled across to inspect them. With a strange cry that was almost like a child's, Towser leaped from her arms and ran back to the hall door. Unable to scratch it open with his little paws, he remained with his tiny body pressed against the crack, his eyes rolling, his fluffy black fur rampantly erect.

At the same time there came to Fanny's slower human nostrils a smell that explained the dog's paroxysm of disgust. What an odor they exhaled, those beautiful flowers! From the heap of magnificent flesh-colored blossoms, with their strange spots of orange and brown, Fanny leaped back as from a reptile. The breath of a rotting tropical swamp, the miasma of pestilence and of death no less, it seemed, assaulted her nostrils in the acrid perfume of those strange, brilliant flowers. Her head swam, and she ran to the nearest window. For an instant her hand fumbled; then she discovered that it was closed, by way of weather-strips, with a heavy, sausage-like roll covered with red cloth and filled with sand.

Fanny jerked this aside and opened the window, thrusting out her head into the air of the little court. The air restored her self-possession. As she turned back to the room, her mind worked quickly. She thought: "When the avoué comes, I'll tell him that I am an orchid-fancier, too!"

By the door, the small dog continued to whimper. Fanny went over and stooped to comfort him. But, as she raised her eyes, suddenly her heart stood still. What was that white object on the rug, at the very edge of the light made by the lamp? A few steps forward, a searching glance, and she beheld a man's hand, palm upward, on the rug.

For an instant she stood like one paralyzed. There, in the shadow of the table, and half hidden by a tall carved arm-chair, lay the body of a small middle-aged man.

The sprawling disorder of his limbs, which offered a strange contrast to the sober elegance of his black attire, left no room for doubt. From that upturned marble mask a cold air seemed to rise; while a livid bruise on the bald temple spoke, as it were, through the still air with the dumb cry of "murder!"

Blind and reeling, possessed by the single thought of escape, Fanny rushed to the door. It was locked!

For the first time, Fanny Gordon lost her head from terror. Frantically she ran to the window. The silent court echoed to her shouts, and to the shrill barkings of her little dog.

"Help! Murder! Police! Help!"

The dark court burst into light and life. From various windows heads were thrust. After ten shuddering minutes, which seemed to the imprisoned girl to last as many years, the doorbell suddenly rang.

"Open, in the name of the law!"

A moment's silence—a repeated summons; then the crash of rending planks, voices, tramping steps, confusion.

The next moment the key clicked in the library door, and two officers flung themselves into the room.

"Mademoiselle! You are hurt?"

Fanny, whom horror had momentarily deprived of her voice, pointed mutely to the motionless figure beside the table.

"Murder?"

An instant later one of the policemen had departed to telephone for a doctor and for the Chief of Police, while the other mounted guard at the door of the apartment. From without sounded a babel of footsteps and voices. Within was the silence of death. Fanny tiptoed toward the policeman at the door.

"Please search the apartment!" she whispered, in horror of what might be. "I came here to search for a lady—"

"When my comrade returns," replied the man stolidly.

Within half an hour the apartment was full of people. Fanny Gordon, bewildered by the ugly nightmare into which her casual footsteps had led her, found herself detained as a witness. Her evidence, which was swiftly taken and written down, centered, of course, on the vanished servant-girl—the white-faced, staring creature who had turned the key on the unfortunate visitor and the dead man together, and slid out into the night. Fanny's description of her was brief but precise. In hot pursuit of this single clue, the Chief of Police sent downstairs for the concierge. She positively identified the dead man as the avoué Cheruel, the owner of the apartment.

"Did you notice a woman leaving the house this evening?" she was asked.

"Yes, monsieur. Just as I was about to close the great door, at ten o'clock, the new maid of monsieur l'avoué—she only arrived in the place this morning—came running downstairs. She wore a dark ulster over her apron. She demanded a cab. The taxicab in which this young lady arrived still waited at the curb, and the maid leaped into it and whirled off."

"The address?"

"I tried to hear it, but she spoke too low."

Fanny jumped to her feet. "Monsieur, that taxi was taken from the stand at the Trocadéro. Its number is 1964. The driver's name is André Cagliotti. Send for him!"

"Bravo, mademoiselle!"

An instant later a man had departed in the official auto. The Chief, with sudden sympathy, turned back to Fanny.

"Mademoiselle, you are faint. Here—some cognac!"

"Many thanks, monsieur. And now, for the love of heaven, search the apartment!"

"Mademoiselle, it has already been searched. No sign of any other human being, dead or alive, is to be found."

"Thank heaven!"

Thus relieved of her unnamed fears for the safety of the Duchess d'Ubzac, Fanny breathed more freely. The swallow of brandy from the Chief's flask braced her nerves. Her hunting instincts awoke. The little dried-up lawyer lying dead there on the floor was nothing to her; but the purple mark on his temple told of monstrous human passions which but recently had galloped through this room, and she was filled with eagerness to find the murderer.

She turned back to the concierge, who was being examined further by the Chief.

"Tell me, madame, who else has entered this apartment to-day?"

"Just his ordinary clientele, monsieur—the people that come here always for their little affairs. The last one came about five o'clock. Since then, nobody."

The Chief sat pondering. "And, though he has been dead for some time,—too long, for instance, for us to suspect mademoiselle, who, as you say, arrived at a quarter to ten only,—yet it is plain he has not been dead so long as five hours. Hem! The maid came back from her errands at eight—two hours—yes, he may have been dead two hours."

Fanny spoke:

"And the occupants of the other apartments, madame—for instance, this Madame Lebrun, whose name I saw on the door on the other side of the landing from the avoué Cheruel?"

"Ah, mademoiselle! Small fear that the Widow Lebrun was mixed up with this annoying affair. She was occupied this evening with a visitor."

"A visitor—what sort of visitor?"

"A monsieur chic, all wrapped up in a blue cloak like a workingman, even the hood drawn up over his head, though it was not raining—and he came in a cab, about seven o'clock."

"Ah! And it is certain it was the apartment of the Widow Lebrun that he visited?"

"Yes, monsieur—because I asked her maid, and she owned that madame had had a visitor, a handsome young man in a cloak. I asked her, you see, because, though I was sitting there sewing in the doorway all the time, I never noticed him pass by on his way out—though at nine o'clock I suddenly looked up and the cab was driving away. How he had passed by me and I never heard him—"

"Enough, enough! We are not here to consider the gossip of the neighborhood. Listen to me! You saw this maid of the avoué Cheruel—you can swear to her face if you see her again?"

"Among a thousand, monsieur!"

"Good! And now, let us search the room, though it is evident we are not the first to reach it. Look! Though everything is in perfect order, one sees that this portfolio has had the padlock cut away; these table drawers have been ransacked and hastily shut again. Ah! look here! This tin box, evidently forced open, but left with its contents intact—several thousand francs in gold louis. *Parbleu!* We begin to see that, though the assassin's motive was robbery, it was not money that she sought!" He reflected for a moment. "A fact which renders his correspondence of special interest. Here—let us look through these letters."

Fanny's sharp eyes ran over them. "Look, monsieur! Here is the same handwriting as that on the box of flowers—two letters."

"In which the writer begs the avoué to accept twenty thousand francs instead of thirty. Ha! unsigned, perfumed. Yes, it is evident he was blackmailing her. Then why did she send him flowers? Mystery! Unless she chose them specially for their bad odor. Faugh! How revolting! Those flowers smell of death."

Fanny, controlling a shudder, stooped toward the motionless figure on the floor.

"What is that, monsieur, in his hand?"

"A black silk tassel, mademoiselle. Look! Note with how firm a grip his fingers are twined in the silk. One sees it was in the very extremity of self-defense that he tore it from the person of his assailant. Another proof, if we need it, of the sex of the assassin. When we find the woman, let us search for a scarf or a boa with a tassel missing."

Fanny nodded. Then, as the Chief, disentangling the betraying tassel from the rigid fingers, laid it on the table beneath the lamp, she stooped toward it. A black silk tassel about seven inches in length, limp and pendant—nothing could have been more completely impersonal and insignificant.

Fanny began to roam about unnoticed, while the Chief aided his men in their examination of the room. For a long time she paused before a carved Dagobert chair covered with a crimson taffeta cushion, which stood beneath an odd little stained-glass window placed high in the wall. After a minute examination of the cushion, she tiptoed to the other side of the room, fetched the short library ladder designed for reaching the upper rows of books, climbed up to the high, stained-glass window, and made a prolonged survey with her electric pocket-lamp.

"Mademoiselle! What are you doing there?"

"I am looking for the weapon, monsieur!"

"Oh! Do you find anything?"

"I find a most significant trace of it."

"Good! Let me see."

The young girl came down, and the eager little official scrambled up. He uttered an exclamation of angry disappointment.

"You make a fool of me, mademoiselle. There is nothing here!"

Fanny smiled. "That is a significant trace, monsieur."

The bell rang, and Raoul de Chatellerault was ushered into the room. With his usual care for appearances, he gave no sign that he had come here to meet the young girl. A moment later the Chief of Police had related to this distinguished member of the Secret Service the facts of the crime before which they stood. They were still in deep conversation when again the bell rang, and immediately after appeared the messenger who had been despatched to seek Fanny's recent chauffeur.

"Monsieur! I found the man Cagliotti. He says that he carried a woman from 18 Rue Longlois to 184 Boulevard Haussmann. His description of her tallies with that of mademoiselle. If necessary, he can identify her."

The Vicomte's voice, abrupt almost to ferocity, cut in on the man's tale:

"Mademoiselle has already given you a description of the missing maid-servant? Let me see it!"

With surprise, Fanny noted that the young man's hand trembled as he held it out to the Chief. Briefly his eye ran over the paper whereon, according to Fanny Gordon's evidence, were enumerated the points of the runaway servant's appearance:

"Stature, small; eyes, large and dark; nose, small Roman; eyebrows meeting in the middle, running in a straight line beneath the forehead and giving a striking aspect to the face—"

"Monsieur le Vicomte, you are ill. It is the odor of these horrible yellow flowers. Here—come to the window."

"Nonsense!"

Nevertheless the young man followed the Chief's suggestion. Fanny, filled with friendly anxiety, moved toward him. With amazement she perceived that the look he bent on her was one of rage and despair. He spoke in an undertone:

"Mademoiselle! Now that you have set the bloodhounds on the track, who is to turn them?"

Fanny's head whirled. "What do you mean?"

"I mean that 184 Boulevard Haussmann is no other than the mansion d'Ubzac; and that the description you have furnished to the police is, point for point, that of my sister Blanche-Marie!"

III

THE TIME WAS the next morning, the place the library of the late avoué, where, though the murdered corpse of its owner had been removed, there still lingered the shadow of its presence.

With a grave gesture, the Chief of the Secret Service turned to a beautiful little fairy of a woman seated beside the Vicomte de Chatellerault. From beneath level black brows meeting in the middle over a little high-bridged nose like the Vicomte's, her immense black eyes met the Chief's with a somber yet pathetic defiance.

"Madame la Duchesse, in spite of your positive identification by the chauffeur Cagliotti and the concierge of 18 Rue Longlois, you reaffirm that it was not you who came here last night in the dress of a servant?"

The Duchess' reply was low but resolute: "I do affirm it."

"And the handwriting of the unsigned letters on the box of orchids?"

"Forgeries!"

"And the orchids?"

"I know nothing of them!"

"Nor of the variety they represent?"

"Nor of the variety they represent!"

Incredible stupidity! Suicidal folly! Fanny, though she had declared that the darkness of the corridor the night before prevented her from testifying with certainty as to the identity of the maid, yet could feel no moral doubt that her eyes again rested on the same woman. Why, then, this wholesale denial on the Duchess' part? If only she had admitted the fact of the disguise, for which a dozen motives might be offered besides that of crime!

The Chief of the Secret Service, opening a box beside him on the table, took out a strange flesh-covered blossom, marked with brownish spots.

"Open the window, Inspector! Madame la Duchesse, I have it, on the word of no less a person than a member of the Academy of Sciences, that this orchid is the rare, almost unknown *Orchis mortis repentinae*—the 'Orchid of Sudden Death,' whose discoverer paid for it with his life; though, it is affirmed, the deadly properties of its effluvia have long been known to certain Oriental races. For a delicate or elderly person, like the avoué, the sudden opening of a sealed box of these flowers in a hermetically closed room such as was this—have you observed the weather-strips on the window-sills? —might very possibly result in death.

"I learned, moreover, that the sole examples of this terrible flower to be found in France are in the Jardin des Plantes at Marseilles and in the famous conservatories of the Duchess d'Ubzac! Madame la Duchesse, will you not be warned? Will you not be wise in time? Will you not speak openly?"

The Vicomte de Chatellerault started to his feet.

"Monsieur, let us understand each other. You are accusing my sister, the Duchess d'Ubzac, of being instrumental in causing the death of the avoué Cheruel, by sending him these poisonous flowers? But the avoué Cheruel died from the effects of a blow on the temple—a blow with a heavy blunt instrument, such as the Duchess, a small and fragile woman, would have been totally incapable of inflicting!"

"You are right, Monsieur le Vicomte. But no such weapon is to be found. I call your attention to the reconstruction of the case by the police, wherein the avoué, overcome by the deadly fumes of the flowers, fell to the floor, and in falling struck his temple against the corner of the writing-table. As a matter of fact, it was beside the table that his dead body was found."

After a brief pause the Chief continued:

"Madame la Duchesse, with such evidence as we possess, the natural course would be to place you in immediate confinement. Owing, however, to the influence which monsieur your brother has exerted in high places, a delay of ten days has been obtained. During these days you will remain under the surveillance of officers of the law, who will enter your household disguised as servants."

The Duchess jumped to her feet. Her delicate self-possession was shattered.

"Police in my house? Then my husband will know?"

"Madame la Duchesse, let us hope that before the end of the stipulated time you may be able to prove to us that the whole affair is a terrible mistake. In that case, your husband need know nothing about it, and the whole affair will be as though it had never been."

Ten minutes later, at the special request of Raoul, Fanny accompanied the half fainting Duchess downstairs to her limousine.

"Mademoiselle, my brother says you have the keenest head in Paris. Tell me what to do!"

Like a broken flame, the Duchess collapsed in a corner of her limousine. Fanny bent toward her.

"Duchess, that was you, last night?"

Two large tears rolled down the lovely little white face of Blanche-Marie.

"Of course! Mademoiselle, to a clever person like you, what a poor, stupid little wretch I must appear! But listen. When they came this morning, and Raoul so stern, they caught me unawares! So of course I denied everything. And, having denied it, how can I take back my word without appearing guilty of everything they charge me with? And I'm not—oh, I'm not!"

"Tell me, Duchess!" interrupted Fanny quickly, "have you no aid to give us? No clue, no suspicion even, as to the identity of the assassin?"

"None whatever," returned the Duchess d'Ubzac, with sudden solemnity. "The avoué Cheruel was a total stranger to me except"—she swallowed and spoke with difficulty—"except for certain blackmailing transactions with which he had approached me. I own, I had already paid him thousands for—for some private affairs of my own which concern no one. And if he was as unscrupulous, as merciless, with the other poor wretches in his power as he was with me, then it is no marvel that one of them rose up at last with the resolution to crush him like a viper. But I swear to you, mademoiselle, that he was already dead when I came back in disguise to this dreadful house last night!"

Fanny, leaving her in the limousine, went upstairs again. The Duchess' words commanded belief. From the peak of one supposition to another, Fanny's active mind leaped. As she reentered the stillness of the murdered man's apartment, she stooped suddenly to a pair of very smart varnished boots that stood beside the door—boots which, with their pale gray suede tops, made an odd note of carelessness in the primly ordered library. The Chief's sharp eye caught her.

"Yes, I confess they puzzle me. They bear the mark of the Trott Company, one of the most chic American shoe shops on the Boulevard des Italiens, while the shoes on the avoué's feet, and the four pairs in his armoire, are old-fashioned black boots with elastic sides, made by a little shoemaker in the Rue Longlois. However, mademoiselle, may it not be that the avoué wore plain shoes on week-days and had a fancy pair for Sundays?"

"But yesterday," returned Fanny, "was not Sunday! And we know from the concierge that in the afternoon the avoué did not leave the house at all. A singular circumstance, that he should have left out his best boots in the middle of his library floor! And look! the avoué's black shoes are size 38. These varnished shoes by the door are marked size 9D, in The American fashion, which probably explains why you have overlooked the fact that they are two centimeters and a half larger than the plain ones."

The Chief, in obvious mortification, bent over the shoes she handed him. "Yes—those American numbers! And yet—let us be reasonable, mademoiselle. A man who comes and goes, even with the purpose of murder, does not leave his boots behind him!"

"A thousand pardons, Chief!" Fanny Gordon, in the excitement of a new idea, dropped the boots with a thump to the floor. "Chief—that tassel in the dead man's hand—in searching the wardrobe of the Duchess have you found its mate?"

He hesitated. "Hm—in the armoire of her elderly maid, from whom she evidently had borrowed her disguise, we found a black silk collarette trimmed with tassels, of which one is missing—tassels almost exactly identical with the one we found last night!"

"Almost!" returned Fanny dreamily. "That 'almost.' But—the orchids?"

"There, mademoiselle, there is no 'almost'! In spite of her foolish denials,—poor little Duchess!—we found the facts even as the professor had told us. In one corner of the conservatories of the mansion d'Ubzac there is a set of pots, in rank, luxuriant bloom, of the *Orchis mortis repentinae*—a corner filled, mademoiselle, with so nauseating and deadly an odor that it is tended by special gardeners, who approach it, in rotation, on different days!"

"Ah! Yet the Duchess, you think, approached it,—she so fragile, so small!—breathed the venomous pollen, plucked the flowers, arranged them, packed them in their box—the box which later the avoué Cheruel, elderly but by no means decrepit, died from merely opening! Hm!—the theory that he died from mere inhalation of fumes, however poisonous—does it not seem to you just a bit fantastic?"

Again the flame of a swift thought passed over Fanny's bright face. With a quick step, she approached the high little stained-glass window that had drawn her eyes the night before.

"Look!" she cried with intensity, as she stooped to the Dagobert chair that stood below it. "Some one has climbed up to the window—so much is plain! I beg you, examine this crimson taffeta cushion on the stool. What do you find?"

He stooped.

"Nothing, mademoiselle! Not so much as a betraying atom of dust!"

"Really?" cried Fanny, in glee. "No doubt? Then I did not deceive myself! Now, monsieur, come here to the spot beside the table where the corpse lay last night. Take your glass, examine the rug carefully. Any dust? Do you find any—any dust there?"

With heaving breast and closed eyes, Fanny stood waiting, as if she herself dared not look. The Chief, stooping, scraped the rich red surface of the rug with an inquiring finger.

"Dust? No. But here—yes, a black, no, a tiny trail—Dust? No; it is sand—white sea sand!"

Fanny's usual calmness deserted her. "Sand? Sea sand? Ah, *mon Dieu!* I dared not hope it, though I knew it must be so!"

Then, while the Chief stared, she took a few steps forward and spoke with a vehement solemnity:

"The third presence that passed through this room last night—Chief, do you not perceive it in the traces he left behind—the shoes at the door, the tassel in the dead man's hand, the dustless footprints on the red silk cushion, the rare orchids, the sea sand on the floor? Monsieur, it is plain that the dark crime committed in this house last night was not a single but a double one! One victim lies in yonder bedroom, dead; and the other victim, unless we save her, is already destined to tragedy and shames that are worse than death."

"Revenge? All very fine," returned the official, with indulgent superiority. "But the department does not want romance, mademoiselle—it wants proofs!"

"Which I will give. A woman so tiny and so slight of stature as the Duchess—could she, even by standing on the stool beneath, have spanned the distance to the high stained-glass window, and taken down the weapon whose traces still show freshly in the dust of the sill? Could she have struggled with the avoué—who, as the tassel in his hand shows, did not die without fighting desperately for his life? Or, even admitting these facts, could her fragile arm have dealt that death-blow?"

"The bruise on his temple," cried the Chief, with some peevishness, "was caused by falling against the table—"

"Or with this!" and Fanny, walking to the window which she had flung open the night before, picked up the sausage-shaped weather-strip with which it had been sealed, and which still lay on the wide sill.

"Monsieur, look! All the other windows in the apartment are closed against the entrance of air by the same strip, covered with the same crimson wool damask. And in the little high window above the Dagobert chair the dust shows the fresh traces of a similar weather-strip recently removed. Ah, monsieur, take it! In the hands of a muscular and bloody-minded man, could a more effective weapon be found?"

The sausage-shaped roll sagged heavily from the Chief's hand as he took it. He exclaimed sharply:

"A sand-bag!"

Fanny nodded. "Which ripped from the force of the blow, and, as you saw, leaked a portion of its contents on the floor; so, evidently, the assassin picked it up and carried it away with him—at least, it has vanished from the apartment."

"A sand-bag!" mused the Chief. "An interesting theory, if we accept romance instead of facts! And the facts indicate that the avoué Cheruel was smitten, not by a blow, but by the deadly fumes of the orchids—those rare and terrible exotics which, in all Paris, are well known to exist only in the conservatories of the Duchess d'Ubzac—"

"Precisely! So well known that, in order to fabricate circumstantial evidence against the Duchess, one would only have to procure a boxful of those same orchids and a sample of her handwriting—both difficult feats, but, for such a criminal as we are supposing, by no means impossible. This much accomplished, there only remained that in the house of the doomed man the Duchess' presence should coincide with the arrival of the fatal box—an arrangement easily made, in this case, by a paragraph in the *Grand Journal* summoning the Duchess to the Rue Longlois."

The Chief, dropping his superior manner, jumped to his feet.

"Paragraph in the *Grand Journal?* Mademoiselle, it becomes plain to me that you know more about this case than you admit. In the name of the law, I command you to tell me what you know of the assassin of the avoué Cheruel!"

Fanny picked up her gloves and hand-bag. "Monsieur, I advise you to search for a young man, tall, muscular, elegantly dressed, a smoker of strong cigars, a foreigner—yes, plainly he was not a Frenchman! and a devout man—unless all signs fail, an exceptionally religious man!"

"A religious man?" returned the Chief, in sudden horror. "You mean—a ritualistic murder, here in Paris? No, mademoiselle! In spite of your great services in the case of the Vaucaire murder, it is plain that your fantasy outstrips your reason. Tell me: can you produce the person that you describe?"

"Alas, no, monsieur!"

"Mademoiselle, produce him within ten days, and your theories will have won. Otherwise, the case is too black against the Duchess. And, in spite of her beauty, her money, and her rank, in spite of her brother's influence, the department will do its duty."

IV

FANNY GORDON stood confronting the Vicomte de Chatellerault, who for ten minutes had been pacing up and down the drawing-room in perplexity and a sort of raging despair. Three days had passed, and as yet no defense of Blanche-Marie had been formulated.

"Vicomte, it is useless to ask questions of the Duchess, so I have come to you to ask where madame your sister obtained her specimens of the celebrated Orchid of Sudden Death."

The Vicomte frowned. "The first year after her marriage, mademoiselle—I remember it particularly, because I was with her when the box arrived—anonymously. By great good fortune, she gave it to a footman to open. Young and strong as he was, he was ill for a fortnight after. Blanche-Marie, the most capricious of women, insisted on placing the horrible things in her conservatory; and, though she declared that the sender, whose intentions against her life were obvious, was absolutely unknown to her, still, year after year since then—five times in all—the box of orchids has arrived with unfailing regularity in the month of September. As she never showed any inclination to have me take up the matter, naturally I never attempted any inquiry. And, to tell the truth, I don't think she has ever mentioned the affair to my brother-in-law at all!"

"Vicomte, forgive me if I ask you a delicate question. Madame your sister—has she to your knowledge, or to your suspicion, ever had a love affair—with other than her husband, that is—either before or after her marriage? I implore of you a truthful answer to my question, so far as you are able to give it!"

"No, mademoiselle. Blanche-Marie as a girl was very headstrong, very romantic, but cold as ice to all who presented themselves as claimants for her hand. She was already twenty-five years old when Armand d'Ubzac came. Ah, poor Blanche-Marie! If she had been ice till then, it was like ice she melted. Another man? To one who knows Blanche-Marie the mere idea is a burlesque. Never was there such a love as hers for Armand—which perhaps is the very reason why she treated him so atrociously.'

"Atrociously—how?"

"Ah, mademoiselle, you who are a woman, you shall judge of the truth of my theory. Know, then, the wedding-day was fixed. Then came the catastrophe—Armand, who was then a cavalry officer, was promoted to be first lieutenant in the 75th Chasseurs d'Afrique. As his father was then Minister of War, he might easily have obtained a transfer. But, as the 75th was just setting out for Morocco, Armand considered that his honor forbade him to seek a change of regiment, and, without consulting Blanche-Marie, accepted the post in the Chasseurs.

"Ah, mademoiselle! It was a bad business. Though I do not attempt to defend my sister for what she did, still I think Armand should have gone through the form of asking her if she would live in Africa. Never have I seen a woman so wounded, so enraged. And when Armand stubbornly refused to withdraw his acceptance, she abruptly broke off the engagement. She declared that she would marry the first man that asked her, no matter what he was; and, bending my father by the force of her determination, compelled him to carry her off for a voyage around the world."

With parted lips and glistening eyes, Fanny listened.

"But she married him, after all!" she remarked tentatively.

"Of course! Before two months were up, she received a telegram from Armand offering to resign his commission, to do anything she liked, if only she would come back! So, as luckily she had traveled no farther than—"

"Vicomte, wait! With your permission, I am going to write for you the name of the city where your sister was when she received the message."

She wrote, folded the paper, and passed it to de Chatellerault. He opened it, and exploded in astonishment:

"Mademoiselle! You have heard this story before! My sister has told you—"

"Never, on my sacred honor, Vicomte. I shot an arrow into the air, that was all—and it seems to have hit the mark! Vicomte, Unless my calculations fail, I hope before the ten days are up to introduce to you the assassin of the avoué Cheruel."

V

NINE DAYS AFTER the murder in the Rue Longlois, the Vicomte de Chatellerault conducted his sister to the Élysées Palace Hôtel, to the apartment of the celebrated orchid collector, Mrs. Mountington V. Shaife. The Duchess, haggard and desperate in anticipation of the terrible to-morrow, had at first utterly refused the expedition. Her attention, however, was drawn to the flaring advertisements in the *Grand Journal* and the *Matin*, where the American millionaire, already famous through interviews and photographs, offered the price of a round half million francs for an authentic specimen of the rare, almost unknown *Orchis mortis repentinae*—the only species, it appeared, that her magnificent collection lacked.

"Do not forget, Blanche-Marie," said her brother gravely, "that we have a battle before us; and the more money of your own you can command, the better it will be!"

The Duchess nodded quickly, controlled a shudder, and rang for her head gardener. Upon giving orders for the culling and proper packing of a specimen orchid, she learned, to her surprise and dismay, that the Duke had just given the same command. In these terrible days she shunned her husband's company, fearing self-betrayal. However, in this case it could not be avoided, and all three set out together in the limousine.

"Poor little angel!" said the Duke tenderly. "She looks pale. It will do her good to come out and see this orchid-hunter, who, to judge by her picture in the *Illustration* this week, must be a droll type of old lady."

The droll type was, unfortunately, confined to her bed when they arrived at the hotel on the Champs Élysées. However, they were invited to go upstairs, where her secretary would receive them.

The lift whirled to the top floor. It was a strange room that they entered—a medley of gorgeous blossoms, a glistening room of bell-glasses, a vapor of strange scents, a moving babel of visitors of various nationalities. And, at one end of the long room, a young girl with flushed cheeks and dancing dark eyes, pouring tea for a tall, handsome, languid young man in elegant English clothes and a Turkish fez. The Vicomte, leaving his sister at the door, approached the young secretary. He started in amazement.

"Mademoiselle! What—"

"I am Miss O'Hara, Mrs. Shaife's secretary. You bring orchids?"

"No, but I—I accompany a lady who does. She is waiting—"

"Ah! Will you have the goodness to take her into the little salon adjoining, and I will send her some tea, while I clear this room of people. So many orchids, and as yet not one real specimen of the kind we are looking for. Poor Mrs. Shaife will be quite heart-broken!"

Summoning a servant, she began to pour the promised tea to send to the Duchess. A hasty movement, the crash of a china cup, and a large silver urn of hot water tipped sideways to the floor, falling over the foot of the young Ottoman by the girl's side. From his attitude of courteous waiting, he hopped into the air with a subdued shout:

"*Bismillah! Nom d'un—*"

In obedience to the young secretary's swift commands, the room was cleared of the swarming orchid venders, and the Duchess and her husband were conducted to the little salon that opened off one end of the reception-room. In the meantime, the young Turk, with polite protests, allowed the boot to be unbuttoned and removed by the fair author of the mischief.

"Oh, Monsieur Harboosch Bey! Have I killed you?"

"It is nothing, mademoiselle! If you will examine my orchids—"

And he began to untie a long, slim roll of white cardboard that he carried in his hand. The young American held up his boot.

"I see you buy your shoes at Trott's on the Boulevard des Italiens. Number 9—let me see, that's thirty centimeters long, isn't it?"

She handed the boot to a footman, and ordered him to dry it and replace it upon the young Turk's foot. Raoul de Chatellerault, having left his sister and her husband in the little salon, approached

Mrs. Shaife's young secretary and her visitor with a barely veiled perplexity. He was in time to hear the young girl exclaim:

"Yes, but first tell me about fezzes! Is it really true, what one reads, that the tassel must fall to within just one and a half centimeters of the edge, no more and no less—and that no good Mohammedan, even the Sultan, can have more than one fez at a time? Rather inconvenient, if something happened to that one!"

"Certainly," returned the young Bey, with a haughty stare. "And now, my orchid—"

"Just a minute! First, tell me, Bey, what happened to your fez? The tassel is all jagged at the end, and the silk frazzled out. Tell me, did you lose the old one, and buy a new one that was too long, so that you had to cut it off to the proper length with scissors?"

The Vicomte, taking pity on the young Turk's obvious annoyance, exclaimed:

"Pardon, mademoiselle, but my sister is waiting!"

But the young girl, turning her back on the speaker, leaned toward the Bey. In a harsh and vibrating whisper, she demanded:

"The original tassel of your fez—where did you leave it? By any chance, did you leave it—in a dead man's hand?"

A hissed exclamation—the crash of an overturned tea-table—the tramp of heavy feet, the impact of strained breathing and of laboring muscles. Then out of the confusion emerged the tableau of the young Bey standing erect by the door, his face purple, his convulsed limbs held by two livened servants. The young secretary's voice rang out:

"Monsieur the Chief of the Secret Service!"

The Chief appeared.

"Chief! arrest Monsieur Harboosch Bey for the murder of the avoué Cheruel in the Rue Longlois!"

It was like the explosion of a bomb. There was an instant of quivering silence; then the Chief demanded:

"But first, Mademoiselle Gordon, your proofs!"

"If this attempt at violent escape does not convict the Bey of conscious guilt, Chief, then look at the hacked-off tassel of his fez, which proves it a substitute for the original. Return to the Rue

Longlois and examine the tassel found in the hand of the avoué. If you will hold it to your nose you will find it bitter with the scent of the strongest black cigars—the same odor, Chief, as at this very instant you may perceive in the clothes of the Bey!"

"Very good, as far as it goes," returned the Chief, hesitating, "but hardly sufficient for arresting this man."

"Chief, I have only begun!"

From the long center table, amid the gorgeous confusion of flowers, Fanny picked up a parcel which, swiftly unwrapped, disclosed a sausage-like roll covered with red wool damask, whose dead weight sagged from her hand. This time, the Chief started.

"Mademoiselle—where was that found?"

"In the kitchen of the Bey's apartment in the Rue Mogador, this very morning!"

"Ah! by whom?"

"Myself, in a simple disguise—the same disguise in which, last week, I assured myself, from the maid of the Widow Lebrun, that while on the evening of the murder her mistress had indeed received a visit from a handsome young man with the hood of his cloak drawn up over his head, he had remained only five minutes, and gone away—the two women thought, away from the house! We know that he only crossed the hall to the apartment opposite. His departure, however, was not so well managed."

"On the contrary, mademoiselle, when he managed to step past the lynx ears of a Paris concierge unobserved!"

"The very fact, Chief, which, when one had started on the right track, served as an additional confirmation of his race and his religion!"

The Bey started violently. The Chief exclaimed:

"Religion! You speak always of his religion!"

"Yes, Chief! If, as a boy, you were a reader of the Arabian Nights, surely you know that there is a religion—one of the most widely spread and dominant in this world—which imposes on its followers the duty, when they enter a room, of leaving their shoes at the door? A rule no doubt remitted to the faithful Mohammedan when he comes here to the land of the infidel. But is it unreasonable to suppose that, by a common psychological phenomenon, the prowling assassin reverted, in that moment of terrible excitement, to the religious training of his race, and removed his shoes upon entering the appointed scene of his crime?

"Then, as the two shoeless footprints on the crimson silk cushion showed, he mounted in his stocking feet on the Dagobert chair, to take down from the high stained-glass window the convenient weapon that his quick eye had detected. Then, having battered down one victim, and having arranged orchids and letters so as to fasten guilt upon the other, he fled red-handed and in panic from the scene of his crime—without stopping to reclaim the tassel of his fez, or even to put on the shoes he had left at the door!"

The Ottoman, who till now had listened to his accuser with the cynical phlegm characteristic of his race, now burst out in a sudden rage.

"My other victim? What do you mean by my other victim?" he cried in excellent French, glaring at Fanny Gordon. "If you know anything at all about the murder in the Rue Longlois, you know that the assassin was not I, but Blanche-Marie de Chatellerault!"

This name, shouted aloud in furious tones, brought steps running from the little inner salon. The Duke d'Ubzac, tall, fair, his eyes blazing with indignation, precipitated himself into the room. Behind him appeared the white face of the little Duchess. As her eyes fell on Harboosch Bey, she stopped upon the threshold like one shot.

"My wife's name! Who dares pronounce my wife's name in such a voice?"

The Bey, however, took no notice of him. His eyes were fixed like those of a sleep-walker upon the pate, lovely image in the doorway.

"Blanche-Marie!"

His voice was like a prayer—or like a curse. The Duke's face turned white.

"Blanche-Marie, do you know this man?"

Her colorless ups moved, but were unable to produce any sound. Her terrified eyes were on the Turk; while he, obviously prey to an agitation even more profound, twisted in his hand the spotted, flesh-colored orchid which in the struggle with the police had come unwrapped from its coverings. Its evil smell filled the silent room. Then in an explosive voice he spoke.

"Yes," he said, "she knows me! You, monsieur, are her husband? Then you will be interested to know that she was in the Rue Longlois, in the disguise of a servant, on the night of the murder. Why did she come there? To meet me! I was her lover five years ago in Constantinople, before she deserted me, the very week before our wedding-day, to fly back to Europe and marry a Frenchman! But she was mine first, as these letters prove"—with fierce hands he sought for his pocket-book—"these letters, which she came to buy back from me in the Rue Longlois. Will you read them, monsieur?"

And, opening his pocket-book, he took from it a packet of half a dozen pale blue envelopes addressed in faded ink, which he held out, with a terrible smile, to the Duke d'Ubzac. The Duchess, immovable in the doorway, made a little moan like a sick child. With a slow gesture, while the waiting group about them held its breath, the Duke held out his hand and took the letters.

"Give me a match, Raoul!"

Silently his brother-in-law complied. The next moment between the fingers of Armand spurted a quick blue flame. The letters, as he held them out, blazed like a torch.

"It is not my habit to read other people's letters, Bey! And as for the scurrilous accusations that you dare to bring against the Duchess d'Ubzac, that is what I give for them!" And, with contempt, he flicked from his fingers the last fragment of gray ash.

There was in this proceeding something of the Frenchman's love of dramatically splendid action, but not a little of native nobility and of high-minded, generous love.

"Armand!"

And the next instant the Duchess, disregarding the rest of the company, dashed forward into the room and flung herself into her husband's arms.

"Oh, my darling, I thank you! And I swear to you that, before or after our marriage, I have never wronged you! These foolish letters—wrote them to that man five years ago, when, in rage and spite, I had deserted you and France—and engaged myself to Harboosch Bey in Constantinople. Would I ever have married him? I do not know, for, thank God, your telegram came in time! Those strange orchids that came to me—I thought they might be from him, but could I *know?* Then, two months ago, the avoué Cheruel approached me with certain letters which he said had been stolen from the body of a Turkish officer after the siege of Adrianople—my mad, foolish letters that I had written when I was engaged to Harboosch Bey. I couldn't bear to have you know what a wicked little fool I had been. I sold my jewels, I begged money from poor Raoul. At last came the night when, in response to a paragraph in the *Grand Journal*, I borrowed Nanette's clothes and went to the Rue Longlois to make the final payment. The blackmailer was there waiting for me—on the floor, dead."

She clung to her husband. He soothed her with tenderest caresses.

"*Ma chèrie*, you thought I would take the word of a blackmailer against your truth and purity? You thought I would believe any word in the world against yours?"

A strange sound drew the eyes of the company back to the Turk. Between the two livened servants, now revealed as officers of the police, he stood erect. His eyes were on the pair before him. From his knotted and discolored face blazed those awful flames of hate and jealousy which the human soul can on occasion throw out, and which in the highly colored Oriental character can so terribly exceed the fiercest fires of the European.

"In his arms!" he muttered. "Blanche-Marie in his arms! No, I can't bear that! *Bismillab!* When I killed the avoué Cheruel that night, why didn't I wait and kill her too? I can live no more! Allah, Allah, hear me—"

His voice failed; his handsome face turned gray. With a cry, Fanny Gordon sprang forward.

"The orchid in his hand! It's gone! *He's eaten it!*"

At the corners of his twitching blue lips, the marks of yellow pollen showed the truth of her words. Between the two inspectors, their prisoner sagged limply. The Orchid of Sudden Death had done its work.

"Get him away!" cried the Duke. "Take him out of here!"

He was obeyed. Half an hour later, when Fanny and the little Duchess had to some degree recovered from the shock of the suicide, Raoul de Chatellerault came to the young American.

"And now tell us, mademoiselle, how did you find him?"

"By advertising for him, Vicomte! Having once made up my mind that the mysterious third presence that had passed through that room was a Mohammedan,—having satisfied myself that the scene of the crime was no more than a stage, prepared to make the Duchess d'Ubzac appear guilty of murder,—I had nothing left but to seek for the unknown enemy. From you I learned that the Duchess had never had any romantic adventure except that which terminated in her marriage. I learned, however, that, at a period of peculiar emotional disturbance, she had been in a city which, in view of the traces left in the Rue Longlois, was precisely the one I should have guessed—which I *did* guess, as you remember, Vicomte! Thus encouraged in my hypothesis, I ventured a wire to Constantinople. I learned that the name of Mademoiselle de Chatellerault, during her brief stay there, had been connected with that of a wealthy young Turkish officer.

"Fierce Oriental passion, mysterious Oriental revenge—was this the clue for which we were seeking? Suppose that Turkish officer were now in Paris! I recalled what I heard from you, Vicomte—that ever since her abrupt return from Turkey the Duchess had periodically received boxes of those strange orchids, which, we are told, are a favorite poison among Orientals. Why were they sent? To poison her? Or was it rather that her name might become connected with them, so that in the fullness of time they might be used as a piece of circumstantial evidence against her? So, baiting my trap with the offered reward, I played the farce you know of the orchid-hunter, Mrs. Shaife. Poor Mrs. Walden! How she has suffered this week, even with permission to keep her room and leave her devoted secretary to receive the reporters and water the orchids!

"From the Turkish Embassy I obtained a list of wealthy Ottomans now in Paris, and sent them copies of the newspapers with my advertisement in it—superfluous pains, after all, as the offer of half a million francs reward is a winged messenger that carries one's quest to the ends of the earth!

"Last evening, among a thousand letters that offered me specimens, I received one signed Harboosch Bey. Was I on the track? I obtained his address; and this morning, disguised as a milk boy, I managed to visit his apartment in the Rue Mogador. A gilt brooch and a couple of kisses to his cook—and she allowed me to rummage in the box where the waste of the week was thrown. It was there I found the sand-bag covered with red damask. The rest you saw for yourselves! Duchess, to-morrow the ten days will be up—but, thank God, we can all sleep in peace to-night."

The little Duchess, with her lovely face tilted upward like that of a child, walked over to Fanny. With both gloved hands upraised, she unfastened from her throat the magnificent string of gleaming Ceylon pearls that encircled it.

"Mademoiselle, will you accept this keepsake, and wear it always for my sake? And will you give me something in return?"

"If she hasn't done enough for you—!" began her brother.

With a graceful gesture, the Duchess clasped the pearls about Fanny Gordon's throat.

"But, Duchess, this is too much! And in return—what have I to give you?"

"Your friendship!" returned Blanche-Marie sweetly. And, drawing the lovely girl's wistful face down to hers, she kissed it twice, once on either round pink cheek.

THE RADIUM ROBBERS

I

THE CURTAINS PARTED, and Fanny Gordon, in trailing chiffon, slipped into the box. In spite of Tannhäuser's solo, rising from the great stage beneath, the Duchesse d'Ubzac and her brother sprang to their feet to greet the newcomer.

"Mademoiselle, what news?"

Fanny, seating herself, waved her fan slowly as she smiled at her friends and surveyed the house. Then, in an almost imperceptible whisper, she said:

"First, look away from me—look down there at the stage. That is right. We must not appear to be talking secrets."

And, still more softly, she breathed: "I have found the six grams!"

The ruddy face of the Vicomte de Chatellerault became quite pale. He turned to his sister and whispered:

"Blanche-Marie, you hear what this child has done? She has solved the problem that for the last month has baffled the police of Paris. She has found the six hundred thousand dollars' worth of radium that Arsène Lupin himself stole from the Radium Institute a month ago—six grams of radium salts, at one hundred thousand dollars a gram! Mademoiselle, you have secured it—and *him?*"

"*Him*—no! But *it*—the little leaden box that contains it is safely packed in my suit-case, and the suit-case itself lies snugly in the safe-deposit vault of—of a curtain provincial city whose name I will tell you, Vicomte, when I am making my report at the headquarters of the Secret Service."

"Ah, then you have not yet reported to the Chief?"

"I telephoned from the station when I arrived in Paris two hours ago. But he, it appears, is at Lille,—chasing a false scent, poor man!—and will not be back till tomorrow morning at nine, when I am to make a full report of the whole affair, and—" With an odd little shudder that spoke of strained nerves, she broke off short and glanced behind her. "But here—talking is dangerous! Please, if you are my friend, give me leave to enjoy the music for a little while. I am very tired."

A knock on the door of the box. "Madame la Princesse de Lippenhohe begs that Madame la Duchesse d'Ubzac will do her the honor to come for an instant to her box!"

The Duchess hesitated and glanced at her newly arrived guest. She was visibly perplexed.

Fanny Gordon smiled.

"You are not hesitating on my account, Duchess? When I assure you that I want only to rest and listen to the music!"

But the weary girl's desire was not to be satisfied. Two minutes after the little Duchess's departure on the arm of her brother, came another *rat-tat-tat* on the door of the box, and there entered a breathless, important official in the uniform of the Secret Service.

"Mademoiselle, Monsieur the Chief, by taking a racing automobile, has just arrived from Lille. He begs the favor of your immediate presence at the Sûreté."

There is no anodyne for weariness like the opportunity to reap the reward of one's work. Fanny sprang to her feet.

"But Madame la Duchesse?"

"I have sent my companion to inform Madame la Duchesse, also Monsieur le Vicomte. However, it is Mademoiselle that Monsieur the Chief desires so urgently to see. Mademoiselle is ready? The limousine is at the side door."

Four minutes later Fanny Gordon, snugly shut into the luxurious limousine attached to the Secret Service, gave herself up to those happy dreams that are the portion of the successful. And what a success—how spectacular, how stupendous—was hers! To be sure, the thought of her powerful and subtle opponent, still at large, was disconcerting. But the sight of the two broad uniformed backs, seen through the glass in the front of the limousine, could not fail to reassure her.

In spite of her exhilaration, her eyelids slowly fell. She was drifting into a momentary doze when suddenly she pulled herself together with a start. What did it mean, the prodigious speed at which the machine was traveling? Hardly had she had time to ask herself the question than she perceived a change in the swift panorama that streamed past on the other side of the glass. The flashing lights, the shining windows, the myriad eyes of the boulevards—where were they? For, on either side of the road, her straining eyes descried only the dark and infinite monotony of trees.

The Bois de Boulogne! Since when had the road from the Opéra to the Secret Service led through the Bois de Boulogne?

Then, in a sickening revulsion which, like a fall from a great height, seemed to reverse all the processes of life, Fanny Gordon understood. She had relied too complacently on her own astounding cleverness, which had so easily made her the superior of her famous opponent, and she had congratulated herself too soon. How easily Lupin had caught her, and in how simple a ruse!

Too late she realized that the message from the "Princess," which had left her alone in the box, had been of his concoction. And now here she was in his power!

On the driver's seat before her, the two broad uniformed backs still sat immovable. Suddenly, as if perceiving her movement, one of the men turned. It was he who had come to the box at the Opéra. His glance, meeting hers, was as respectful as ever; but in his lifted hand Fanny's quick eyes caught for one instant the dark gleam of a revolver—and the mouth was pointed toward her.

As an anodyne for nervous restlessness the open mouth of a revolver beats all the drowsy syrups of the East. Still as a mouse Fanny Gordon sat, while for hour after hour the great car thundered on through the dim French countryside; and finally the pallid autumn dawn crept up like a ghost out of the dark.

II

Tennis racket in hand, Fanny Gordon hit her ball up against the high stone rampart of an old château. Her ambition was to hit it back a thousand times without stopping. In the ten days since she had been shut up here, a prisoner, her leisure for practice had been ample. And, for any prospect that she could see of release or of escape, it seemed likely that she would have time to arrive at the coveted thousand mark.

On the first morning after Fanny's arrival here, when she had opened her eyes from the deep sleep in which exhaustion had plunged her, she had jauntily slipped on the pretty sports costume that she found beside her bed, and gone out to escape as to an easy matter.

Alas! Her first day had not half expired before she found that her sole attendants were the discreet, impenetrable, perfectly respectful man who had taken her from the Duchess's box at the Opéra, a deaf old lady, and a young servant-maid who spoke an unintelligible patois. Nothing to be done here! As to the wall of the château, it was not only twelve feet high, but crowned with a vicious fringe of broken glass that would render even a ladder impracticable—and she had no ladder. The hope remained of a rescue from attracting the attention of some passers-by. To this hope, however, a quick ending was given when a stroll to the great gate of the château revealed the discreet brass plate attached to one of the pillars:

Maison de Santé du Docteur Pierre

A private lunatic asylum! With a thrill of mingled horror and admiration, Fanny recognized the masterly simplicity of her enemy's methods. And she realized that the struggle over the prize six grams, which she in her vanity had thought ended, had in reality only begun.

For, in spite of her present helplessness, one weapon remained in her hand with which to fight the redoubtable monarch of French crime: Silence.

And so, for the past ten days, she had fought him.

Any time that she chose to open her mouth and disclose the hiding-place of the precious radium of which her recent brief triumph had robbed the robbers, she knew that she might walk out of those iron gates a free woman. But no—never would she yield her secret! Never, never would she tell!

In the meantime, if only she could get word of her plight to her ally, Raoul de Chatellerault! But where was he? Where, behind the mystery of the horizon, was Paris? And where, in all the wide land of France, was she herself? For, in that wild night ride that had brought her here, all sense of direction had been lost; and neither in the landscape about her nor in the speech of her jailers was there anything to tell her whether this remote corner of France was that of the Bretons, of the Basques, or of the Provençals.

She banged her seven hundred and tenth stroke. "I'll never give up, never!" she vowed to herself. "I'll never tell him where that radium is—not if I die here!"

Clap-clap—clap-clap—clap-clap.

What was that dry, unreverberating clatter that suddenly filled the misty stillness about her? In this castle of silence, a sound?

Throwing down her racket, Fanny shaded her eyes with her hand and looked eagerly down the slopes that fell away from the wide terrace where she stood. The walled park of the château—empty! The far-off winding road beyond the wall—empty!

"Hello!" cried a voice almost in her ears.

Fanny flung up her head. Swooping down over the dark battlements of the château, she beheld the astounding spectacle of a descending monoplane.

Her heart leaped into her throat. In the mist above her head, the machine hovered and wheeled. Then, in a daring volplane, it coasted downward. Lightly striking the smooth stone of the terrace, it bounded once or twice into the air, ran forward a minute or two on its tiny wheels, then, at the far end of the terrace, came to a full stop. The excited girl dashed forward. The scarlet-clad airman, springing from his seat, jumped to the ground and staggered down the terrace to meet her.

"Oh, oh!" cried Fanny Gordon, running to meet him. Her pink cheeks, and her dark hair spangled with rain-drops, made of her a brilliant picture.

"Pardon, mademoiselle,"—the bewilderment in the newcomer's eyes gave place to a startled admiration—"but will you please tell me where I am?"

Fanny noted the extraordinarily brilliant eyes, and the fresh odor of a violet shaving-soap. Breathlessly she replied to his question with another:

"Why?"

"*Mon Dieu!*" returned the flying-man impatiently. "Do you not know, then, what it is—the air? Before dawn this morning, mademoiselle, I left Vienna for Paris—the Kisseldoeffer Cup Race; of course you have heard of it? I rose at once to two thousand feet, and left all competitors behind. But when I came to the French frontier—*tonnerre de Dieu!* A blast came out of the east, and I ran into a hole in the atmosphere, through which the air poured in sluices. For an hour I fought with death in those vast uncharted spaces where the airman rides. Beneath me the clouds were like a floor. Into what part of France that easterly gale carried me, how could I tell? And, until I know where I am, my compass is useless. Mademoiselle, for the love of heaven, tell me in what department of France we stand! And Paris—is it to the north, the south, the east, or the West? Mademoiselle, tell me—quickly!"

In the pale, high-featured face of the speaker the color rose. He took a step toward the young girl. The drizzling cloud, settling down over them, shut them off together in a world of their own—a world whose whereabouts, by a strange coincidence, remained to them both as mysterious as the back of the moon.

"What!" gasped Fanny Gordon. "Then you don't know, either, where we are?"

"*What?*" echoed the flying-man.

There was an instant of blank silence, and in his eyes Fanny saw the flicker of a sudden doubt.

"No!" cried Fanny vehemently. "I'm not mad—any more than you are yourself. I was brought here—Listen!" And in swift words she recounted her story, omitting, for the sake of prudence, the special motives that had animated her abductors.

Into the brilliant light eyes of the listener regarding her sprang that fierce sparkle that warms the heart of woman: the anger of the stronger aroused by her wrongs and in her defense.

"They've ill-treated you? They've dared—"

"No, no!—other than in holding me here. Oh, monsieur, take me away!—Take me with you to Paris."

"If I could! But, alas, mine is a racing-machine, capable of lifting one person and no more. *Mon Dieu!*" He bit the finger of his fur-lined glove. "The wall! I might lift you over it, but just now as I planed downward I saw beneath me the sparkle of broken glass. Remains the gate. If I could force the concierge—"

"If you are armed, monsieur."

He shook his head. "If I had known! But, in a race, one avoids all extra weight. Listen! I will go directly to these rascals at the château—"

"Without a revolver, it would be useless."

She shook her head despairingly. The mortification of Perseus, in surveying this charming Andromeda whose rescue lay beyond his powers, was apparent.

Fanny knit her brows. That horrible brass plate at the gateway! The mere thought of it precluded the idea of beseeching the stranger to raise the alarm for her outside the walls. No; rescue must come from Paris.

"Mademoiselle, I'll come back for you. I'll give the alarm to the police. I will post a letter to your friends—"

"Ah, a letter!" returned Fanny, with relief.

"But please, mademoiselle, make haste. This race—my whole career depends on it!"

Five minutes later she was in her room in the château, dashing off a letter to Raoul de Chatellerault, in which she bade him go at once to her apartment in the Rue Léo Delibes, to demand of Mrs. Walden and of Clémentine the green volume of "Cyrano" on her writing-table and the bunch of kitchen keys. In "Cyrano" he would find the receipt of the Crédit Lyonnais of Toulouse for a valise left in deposit in their vaults. On the key-ring he would find a tiny brass key with the number 1678—the key of the vault in Toulouse where the valise lay. And, in the valise, the treasure that the police of France were seeking.

Then a scrawl to Mrs. Walden, begging her to hand over to Raoul the keys and the book that he should demand. Next a line to the Toulouse bankers, presenting the Vicomte de Chatellerault as her messenger. And last, a note to the Duchesse d'Ubzac, describing her plight.

Quiet as a mouse, she hurried down the stone staircase. She carried a pale yellow tea-rose, culled from the little winter garden in the upstairs hall. Five minutes later, on the misty terrace, she consigned her letters to the modern carrier-pigeon who was to take the news of her plight to the outside world.

"Thank you, mademoiselle, for your trust in me!" He paused. "My name is Paul de Czerny—a name well known, I may say, at the Aëro Club and in Paris!"

"And my name," she returned, all in a breath, "is Fanny Gordon."

Three minutes later, with her letters buttoned into his tunic and her rose fastened to his hood, de Czerny shouted to her to cast off the ropes. Breathless in the strong wind of his propellers, she obeyed. The delicate winged mechanism flew forward, bounded lightly from the terrace, then, rising, shot upward with increasing speed. A moment later it had vanished in the mist.

Fanny, drenched and shivering, turned slowly back to the grim, silent château. As if in confirmation of the new hope that warmed her heart, the pale drizzle about her was suddenly pierced by a yellow glow. Before she had reached the door of her prison, the drifting clouds were parted; and above her she beheld a rift of clear blue, wherein a single black dot cleft its path toward the sun.

III

TWO DAYS LATER, into a small French railway station dashed Fanny Gordon, with muddy shoes and a face glowing from the warmth of exercise. Three-quarters of an hour before, she had found the gate-keeper of the château asleep, with his insensible head resting on the table before him, beside a bottle of cognac. By the simple expedient of filching the key from his pocket and unlocking the great gate, she had in two minutes regained her liberty. And now, by dint of inquiries and a hot foot, here she was at the village station.

Timidly she presented herself at the ticket-seller's window.

"Monsieur, a ticket for Paris, third class. And, please, as I have only four francs sixty centimes, could you possibly accept this gold purse? It cost two hundred!"

With a painful blush, she waited for his answer. The red ticket was punched and tossed to her.

"One franc eighty centimes!"

Somewhat unsteadily Fanny walked out upon the platform. There, above the station door, was an immense blue sign answering the question which till now she had not dared put: "Bar-sur-Seine."

Only an hour from Paris!

The name, from frequent motor excursions, was familiar to her. So this was her remote corner of Provence! And the wild night ride that had brought her here had been a mere endless circling of the dark countryside, to land her at last on the very outskirts of Paris! And Paul de Czerny, deceived by wind and cloud as she by the art of her enemies, had risen into the air two days before, to find his goal almost won and to post her letter to Raoul de Chatellerault that very evening.

An hour later she arrived in Paris.

At her little apartment in the Rue Léo Delibes, she received the wild welcome of Towser, her little Pomeranian, and of Clémentine, her maid, as well as the near-sighted peck on the cheek of Mrs. Walden, her stately English chaperon.

"Has the Vicomte de Chatellerault called at the apartment, with a letter?"

"Yes; two nights ago—just at dusk, when Clémentine was absent on her evening errand; so that I myself, Miss Gordon, was obliged to light the electricity and open the door and hunt up the papers mentioned in your letter."

"Ah, yes; the papers in the volume of 'Cyrano'—you found them, Mrs. Walden?"

"Certainly; I gave them to the Vicomte, as you desired me to do, and the bunch of kitchen keys as well. That is, I managed to, in spite of the very ill-bred growlings and barkings of Towser. Really, I must own that that dog becomes more of a bore every day he lives."

Fanny politely cut short these complaints on a long-standing grievance, and sent Clémentine for the household keys, where, true to the principle of hiding a precious object by not hiding it at all, Fanny had hung the key of the bank vault at Toulouse where the radium lay hidden. Good! The little brass key had vanished. Without doubt, her errand was already done.

An hour later, after a bath, change, and dinner, she called up the headquarters of the Sûreté on the telephone, demanded a guard for the night, and asked for news. To her surprise, she learned that nothing had been heard from the Vicomte de Chatellerault. What! Having received such a summons as hers, had he neglected to obey it?

Her face became grave. She picked up the telephone receiver again, and called up the apartment of the Vicomte de Chatellerault. From Marcel, his man, she learned that, while Monsieur le Vicomte was out for the evening, it was the first time for three days that he had left the house, having been confined to his rooms by an attack of influenza.

Ineffable stupidity! Incredible faint-heartedness! Fanny spent ten minutes more at the telephone, trying to find Raoul at his sister's or at his club. Then, tossing down the telephone, she went off to her room; from which, an hour later, when the promised guard arrived from the Sûreté, she emerged in a tweed traveling costume and with a dressing-bag in her hand.

"Clémentine! Take my bag. Go and call a taxi-cab. Not the first that offers—turn that away. Also the second. Take the third, even if you go to the Étoile to find it!"

Half an hour later, with the silent plainclothes man by her side, Fanny Gordon stepped from the cab into the station of the Quai d'Orsay. They were just in time for the express leaving Paris for the south at a quarter before eleven o'clock.

Next morning, in the quaint old half ruined city of Toulouse, the doors of the Crédit Lyonnais were, as usual, opened to the public at ten o'clock. The first one to enter the bank was a slim young woman in English tweeds, whose fresh beauty showed no traces of a wearisome night.

"The safe-deposit vaults, if you please! I have left a valise here in deposit."

The keeper of the vaults, recognizing her, greeted her with equal joy and surprise. She smiled at him winningly.

"Monsieur, I was obliged to leave Paris without the key. But you recognize me—you will open the vault for me with your duplicate key, won't you?"

"*Parbleu*, mademoiselle! As it happens, Monsieur le Vicomte de Chatellerault left the key with us yesterday, when he came from Paris with your letter!"

Fanny's head whirled. "But the Vicomte de Chatellerault has not left Paris!"

"Pardon, mademoiselle!" returned the bank officer positively. "Monsieur Vicomte was here yesterday morning with the key of the vault, and a letter, signed by you, directing us to deliver the valise to him to carry back to Paris."

That imbecile of a Marcel! Tears of vexation sprang to Fanny Gordon's eyes.

The bank officer was saying:

"But Monsieur le Vicomte said it was possible that you might be here before he saw you, mademoiselle. So he left a letter of explanation, with an object of value, in the vault itself. If you will accompany me to the vaults, mademoiselle, I will give them to you."

The air of the vault-room struck cold on her cheek. The key grated in the lock. The bank officer smiled the knowing and sympathetic smile of a Frenchman in the presence of romance as he opened the box and extracted from it a thick white envelope.

"Monsieur le Vicomte especially charged me that this letter is most important!"

Fanny did not hear him. She had torn open the envelope, and was gazing at a sheet of paper embossed with the large gold crest of the Aëro Club, out of which dropped a withered yellow tea-rose.

The letter ran:

> Mademoiselle, forgive me if, in pledge of my hope of renewing your charming acquaintance, I leave for you the most precious object that I possess—your rose!
>
> Faithfully,
>
> Arsène Lupin.

The rose petals fluttered from Fanny's nerveless fingers. She knew now who he was, the gallant, scarlet-clad airman to whom, on the terrace of Bar-sur-Seine, she had blindly entrusted her letter and her rose. She knew who it was—the "Vicomte de Chatellerault" that, two evenings before, had visited her apartment at dusk, when sharp-eyed Clémentine was absent on her before-dinner errands, and poor old near-sighted Mrs. Walden, blinking in the newly lit electricity, had failed to heed the little dog's warning and failed to penetrate the disguise.

And, worst of all, Fanny knew who it was that yesterday, armed with her letter of introduction and her keys, had presented himself here at the bank, had opened the vault, possessed himself of the radium, and left only this mocking letter behind.

The bank officer escorted her to the door, then gazed after her drooping figure in a chivalrous rage.

"Name of a dog! is that Vicomte, then, a man, to treat that beautiful little one in such a manner?"

And, sighing, the honest man went back to his ledgers. Fanny Gordon, without waiting for any breakfast, returned to the station and took the first train back to Paris.

IV

Up the dainty spiral staircase that leads to the private offices of the Aëro Club of France, Fanny Gordon mounted with the Vicomte de Chatellerault. A moment later the president had bade them be seated.

"De Czerny? The Baron Paul de Czerny?" Their host wrinkled his forehead, turned to a card-catalogue, then answered decidedly:

"No, Vicomte. We have no such name among our members, active or honorary."

"But the Kisseldoeffer Cup Race?" faltered Fanny.

"Here is the list of competitors. The name you mention is not among them."

Fanny Gordon colored deeply. It was mortifying that her blunder be thus exposed before Raoul de Chatellerault. With an effort, she winked away the tears of mortification that rose to her eyes, and drew from her brown morocco bag the mocking letter which Lupin had left behind for her in the vault of Toulouse.

"Marquis, the crest and address of this paper—they are genuine?"

Carefully the president of the Aëro Club inspected the missive handed to him, compared it with a sheet of paper which he drew from his desk, and finally pronounced:

"Though our rule stringently forbids any but members from using our stationery, there can be no doubt: this paper is that of the Aëro Club."

But the morning sunlight, falling across the paper, had called out to Fanny's quick eye a difference which to the far-sighted young aeronaut was not apparent. With a "Pardon, Marquis," she took the letter and the blank sheet of paper, and held them up between her and the sunlight.

"The watermark?" cried Raoul, with quickened interest.

Fanny nodded. "This sheet of club paper which the Marquis took from his desk is of English manufacture. The letter, on the other hand, bears the watermark of a French house—"

"Then it is a forgery!" cried the Marquis excitedly. "For the Club uses nothing but English paper, bought in London and stamped here in Paris. So now, if you will have the goodness to wait for a short time, I will immediately call our manager, and have the engraver summoned and examined."

An hour later, as Fanny and the Vicomte waited in the ladies' salon of the Club, a card was handed them from the president:

> The engraver has confessed that the paper in question was supplied by him a week ago to Monsieur Ernest Distram, Hotel Athène. My thanks and that of the Club to Mademoiselle Gordon, whose keen eyes detected the fraud!

De Chatellerault 's eyes brightened. "Good! And now, mademoiselle, if you will leave the affair in my hands, I will undertake to give you news this very afternoon of our friend Monsieur Distram!"

Fanny colored deeply. After the ignominious bungle that she had made of the business, it was no wonder that Raoul was taking the affair into his own hands. She inquired meekly: "You will go at once to the Hotel Athène?"

"At once? No; I have an appointment at this instant with the Chief of the Secret Service. Immediately after I will begin my investigations."

Five minutes later, de Chatellerault had handed the crestfallen girl into a taxi-cab and given the address of her apartment to the chauffeur.

The automobile, whirling out into the Champs Élysées, took its way uptown. In one corner sat the miserable Fanny Gordon, chewing the cud of utter defeat.

Suddenly her face stiffened and new fire leaped into her eyes. Leaning forward, she called resolutely to the driver:

"Turn about—take me to the Hôtel Athène!"

Her breath came quickly. If she bungled things again, in the face of a direct prohibition, she knew that she would lose not only Raoul's respect but his friendship forever

Five minutes later she entered a smart modern hotel just off the Boulevard Haussmann.

"Monsieur Distram?"

The clerk at the desk shook his head. "I am sorry to say, mademoiselle, that Monsieur Distram left the hotel not a half hour ago, with his luggage!"

Sharp disappointment ran through Fanny's heart.

"Ah! His destination?"

"London!"

"Many thanks, monsieur!"

With a quick step Fanny turned. The boat-train for Calais left, as she knew, from the Gare du Nord at eleven-five. It was now twenty minutes before eleven. With a keen chauffeur, she might make it.

A sudden thought arrested her steps. If the mysterious Monsieur Distram were really the man she sought, then she might take it for granted that his destination was any in the world rather than the one he had announced. She hesitated, made a quick decision, and turned back to the desk. Her lip quivered; her bright, dark eyes sparkled with sudden tears.

"Monsieur! For the love of the *bon Dieu!* This is probably a false address. He—he—has left me! It is all a horrible mistake. If I could only see him once, and explain—"

With a Frenchman's quick interest in romance, the chivalrous manager flung aside all other business to aid the abandoned damsel before him. The porter who had carried down the late guest's luggage, being summoned, accompanied them to the stand of taxicabs attached to the service of the hotel. At that very instant there rolled into the courtyard an automobile whose chauffeur the porter recognized as the one to whom he had given the gentleman's luggage.

"What! Already back from the Gare du Nord?"

The chauffeur touched his cap. "No, m'sieu'. The monsieur changed his mind, and made me take him to the Gare de l'Est!"

"Ah! What destination?"

"I heard him tell the porter who took his luggage, the express for Vienna!"

Fanny's heart throbbed and the brightness came back into her eyes. She rewarded the two men with ten-franc pieces, the manager with her most ravishing smile. Then, having ascertained that the Vienna express left at a quarter before twelve, she jumped into the cab before her and gave the address:

"To Morgan, Harjes, Boulevard Haussmann!"

At the bank she drew five thousand francs. A stern chase lay before her, and funds were necessary. Then:

"To the Gare de l'Est!"

Fifteen minutes later she had bought her ticket for Vienna and boarded the waiting train. By great good luck she found a first-class compartment quite empty. Leaning back in her dark corner, she allowed her thoughts to fly.

"Vienna! Yes, it all hangs together. In Austria are the famous pitch-blende mines, the world's chief supply of radium. In all the capitals of the world, it is in Vienna alone that radium in large quantities might be offered for sale without exciting suspicion—"

"Mademoiselle, pardon."

With a start, she glanced up. In the half-light of the station she saw before her a railway official in a smart uniform and gold-braided cap.

"A thousand pardons, mademoiselle. I regret, but this compartment has been reserved for the use of her Serene Highness the Duchesse of Ixe. If mademoiselle will have the goodness to follow me, I have reserved another place for her."

It was vexatious, but there was no help for it. Reluctantly Fanny rose and followed the guard along the corridor of the train, from one crowded coach to another, till at last, before the door of another first-class compartment, he paused.

"Here is the place that I have taken for mademoiselle. There—the seat in the corner, by the widow."

Fanny handed him the gloves with which he had marked her place, bowed her thanks, and sank into her new seat. The comfortable luggage, cushions, and wraps of her fellow travelers made her realize the bareness of her own outfit for a twenty-two hour trip such as lay before her. A brown velvet suit with a Russian blouse and a slashed skirt, a fox muff and boa, and a brown morocco hand-bag for her sole luggage. If the weather should be cold! With an anxious hand she touched the steam-pipe that ran up beside the window. Aïe! It contained boiling water, no less. But, at least, it allayed her fears for a cold journey.

In a train de luxe of twenty coaches, how was she to discover the man she was seeking?—if, indeed, she were not flying off on a wrong scent and leaving the redoubtable Arsène Lupin behind her in Paris! However, such thoughts were now too late. The train had already started, and had left the shadows of the station for the bright sunlight of the French countryside.

V

As is usual in such a case, the occupants of the compartment took their first good look at each other. Fanny saw a stout, elegantly dressed woman of middle age, whose multiplicity of small luggage, silver appointments, and traveling rugs were all embossed with the initials "B. de W." and a countess' coronet. Her other fellow travelers were a fat German professor with spectacles and a huge graybeard, and a pale, ascetic-looking French priest who read industriously in his breviary.

In the two hours that passed before *déjeuner* was announced, Fanny's youthful hunger had time to grow to a ravenous point. As soon as the garçon passed with the welcome announcement, she rose and flew to the dining-car. Five minutes later she found herself facing the lady from her own compartment; who, after a few remarks of commonplace courtesy, applied herself to the excellent menu.

Fanny ate little. In her veins ran the icy tang of fear—not of violence, but rather the cold dread of failure which an actor sometimes feels before he steps on the stage.

She had made up her mind, as soon as the train had passed the French frontier, to declare to the conductor the theft of a diamond-studded watch, and to demand a search of the whole train before it arrived at Strassburg. Suppose this inspection of the passengers revealed to her the presence of Arsène Lupin—what then?

Suddenly the great train slowed down—then, for the first time since leaving Paris, came to a full stop in a swarming white-tiled station. Fanny's searching eyes perceived the huge blue sign, "Lunéville." Already the German frontier!

Suddenly, with an exclamation of intense amazement, the Countess on the other side of the little table jumped to her feet and fluttered her handkerchief. With an instinctive gesture of curiosity, Fanny's head flew around to follow the direction of the other's staring eyes down to the platform outside the window.

A crowd of French officers, of peasant women with huge black bows on their heads—nothing remarkable! Her disappointed gaze came back to the table. There, as if by accident, a slight but curious phenomenon caught her keen eye.

In one of the glasses that stood at her place, the pale yellow wine leaped and quivered, then, undulating slowly from side to side, came to rest. But for five minutes the train had been standing as still as a house! And the liquids in the other glasses showed their curving rims shining and unbroken. Yet, that glass of white wine before her table companion—was not the undulation of her own faintly repeated within it?

With a carefully controlled gesture, Fanny raised her glass to her lips. When she had drunk from it before, a slight nick in the rim had inconvenienced her lip. Now, though she cautiously twirled the stem in her hands no such nick encountered her searching tongue. Stay—was that a faint odor that rose from the amber depths of the wine? A cold shudder ran through her, and she replaced the glass upon the table without drinking.

There could be no doubt about it. In the instant when the exclamation of the Countess had caused her to turn her head, the two glasses had been exchanged. Why had this glass of drugged wine been given her, if not for the object of preventing her arrival at Vienna? Already, so easily, had her redoubtable enemy fallen upon her tracks?

In that instant Fanny Gordon knew the sensation of the hound that, in full cry after the fox, turns his head suddenly to find the whole pack snarling at his heels. From the pursuer, she knew that she had become the pursued. Her skin burned, and her breath came quick.

Suddenly, on the floor beside the table, Fanny's searching eye perceived the embroidered handkerchief which the Countess had fluttered at the window. Quick as a flash, Fanny let drop her napkin over it. "Garçon, my serviette!" The waiter restored to her the napkin, with the handkerchief within it. A moment later, as the train slipped through the dark of the city's tunnels, Fanny swiftly seized a tiny dish of a certain condiment from the table, emptied it into the handkerchief that she had appropriated, folded the handkerchief, and slipped it into her bag. Since the press of circumstances had forced her to leave Paris without her revolver, it was well to provide herself with such weapons as chance tossed in her way.

An hour later, back in the compartment, Fanny Gordon watched her late table companion like a hawk. On toward Strassburg the great train thundered. If she was to put into execution her plan of an alarm of "Thief!" then she must act quickly. And yet—how bungling, how coarse were such tactics as these against the delicate artifices which her enemy had already initiated against her. For that the conductor who had moved her to this compartment had been in the pay of the all-powerful Lupin she could not doubt. And, now that she was here, since the knockout drops had failed, by what means was she to be prevented from arriving at Vienna?

Fanny Gordon, though possessed of a physical courage above the ordinary, was conscious of a sudden suffocation. What wild foolhardiness had been hers, after the warning she had received, to return to this compartment with that terrible woman! For an instant she was conscious of a rising faintness, and struggled desperately with the window-fastening. Then, panting, she turned to the German professor, who sat nursing his pile of Baedekers upon his knee:

"Pardon, monsieur. Please open the window!"

He stared. She repeated her request in German. He grunted, carefully placed his books on the seat, and interposed his bulky form between her and the window. As he did so an odor struck her nostrils—the scent of a widely used American brand of violet shaving soap.

Her first thought, "How funny, that a man with a big beard should smell of shaving soap!" was immediately superseded by another: "But, just a little while ago, where was it that I smelled this same violet soap?"

She started. More powerfully than the fresh air, her sudden thought brought the blood tingling through her veins. The last time she had smelled that fresh odor of the violet shaving soap was on the terrace of Bar-sur-Seine.

Slowly she inhaled the outdoor air, clenched her hands in her muff, and let her gaze wander idly over the compartment. In spite of the gray beard, the padding, and the spectacles, why had she not recognized him before—the brilliant young aeronaut whose intense and ardent individuality had burned so deep a scar upon her consciousness? Not so much by feature and line as by the odd nervous excitement set up by his nearness, she knew the heavy gray man before her for the dashing and perverted genius that ruled over French crime.

Her rash step in taking this train being thus justified, what should be her next move? First of all, surely, to protect her own safety by letting him know she had penetrated his disguise!

For a moment she hesitated. Then, with a sudden impulsive gesture, she opened her bag, reached down into the open letter that she had carried to the Aëro Club that morning, and drew from it a crumpled and faded yellow rose. Leaning toward the impassive professor, she dropped the withered blossom into his hand.

"I think, monsieur, this belongs to you!" she whispered, with a snap of her dark eyes.

Her disguised enemy did not move a muscle of his face. Instead, he rose to his feet and, reaching up his arm, suddenly jerked the brass handle which, in all Continental trains, hangs from the ceiling of each compartment.

The signal of alarm!

The clang of an electric gong—a hoarse scream from the engine—the whistling and grinding of brakes suddenly applied—shouts, footsteps, screams. For the first time in her life, Fanny beheld the thrilling spectacle of a great express train arrested in mid-flight by the imperative warning of *danger*.

But why? Fanny's first thought was that the professor, finding himself discovered, meant to jump from the train. He sat, however, absolutely placid, with his pile of Baedekers on his lap, while footsteps and shouting voices stampeded through the train, sweeping down on the compartment where they sat. The penalty for an abuse of the alarm bell was, as Fanny knew, severe. She did not doubt that in a few minutes she would see her enemy placed under arrest. In that case, how should she best profit by his stupidity?

The door of the compartment burst open and two uniformed officials precipitated themselves forward.

"The alarm—what is it?"

The professor, jerking his thumb toward.

Fanny, answered in guttural German: "That fräulein—she rang it. Ask her!"

Fanny's head whirled.

"What?" she gasped. "It is a lie! He rang it himself!"

"Who rang the alarm bell?" demanded the guard sternly of the other passengers.

"That young lady!" returned the Countess coldly.

And the priest, raising his pale eyes from his breviary, leveled an accusing finger at the bewildered girl.

"It was mademoiselle who pulled the alarm signal. Why I do not know!" he declared in calm tones; then, dropping his finger, returned to his book.

Too late, Fanny perceived the nature of the trap which Lupin and his confederates had set for their pursuer, and which she by her own rash action had sprung. She saw the folly of protest in face of the testimony against her, and remained silent while the enraged guard took the names and addresses of the three witnesses, and sternly informed her that she was under arrest and would be removed from the train by the police at the next station.

Again, and in a single move, Arsène Lupin had checkmated her. The tears scalded her eyes as she hung her head and reflected what Raoul would think of her if he could see her now.

The train by this time had left the flat plain of the Rhône valley and entered a region of mountains. Suddenly, for the first time since they had left Lunéville, they plunged into the thunderous darkness of a tunnel. Crouched there in the blackness, locked in with a criminal band whose strongest interest was to suppress her, Fanny knew for an instant the full horrors of physical fear.

The tunnel was long. In a moment, by fierce use of her reasoning powers, Fanny shook off her momentary spasm of terror. Since her enemies had already, by so neat and safe a trick, rid themselves of her pursuit, why fear the incautiousness of violence? She forced herself to draw a long breath, open her eyes, and look about her in the dark.

In the blackness that surrounded her, she suddenly *saw* something.

VI

HER BLOOD THRILLED. Every nerve in her body awoke and stirred to that double intensity of life which intense need can kindle in human flesh. A moment later, daylight! As the train roared out from the tunnel, she snatched up her time-table and studied it. At half past five o'clock they would be in Strassburg. An hour remained to her—only one hour!

In that moment, Fanny Gordon's life was of less value to her than the glove on which her hot cheek rested, unless she could win back the lost radium and vindicate her damaged reputation in her own eyes and in those of Raoul de Chatellerault.

Her mind worked with desperate swiftness. The train—yes, the fact that it was laboring up a steep incline at a much diminished speed—the very train was favoring her! Ahead, across a bend in the curving track, her quick eye caught a glimpse of a knoll with three huge dark pines upon it.

Opening her bag, she hastily took out a pair of motor-glasses and put them on; then clutched with desperate quickness at the folded handkerchief which she had placed in her pocket at the lunch-table. Then, leaning her head through the open window, she uttered a sudden little artless cry:

"Oh, the aëroplane race!"

Moved by a common irresistible impulse, the faces of her three impassive companions crowded toward the window. Like a cat lashing out in her own defense, Fanny dashed into the three faces the contents of the handkerchief. Then, across the shout of pain that rose from their temporarily blinded faces, she shot out her arm and snatched a camera in a japanned traveling-case from the luggage-rack above the professor's head.

For an instant her keen eyes glared from the window. The knoll with the three dark pines—was that a stagnant pool beneath it? The next moment, splash! The camera was hurled from the window and disappeared beneath the green scum of the water. A telegraph-pole flashed by—Fanny's quick eye caught the number 946. The next instant the automobile-glasses had followed the camera out of the window, and Fanny Gordon, with her hands in her eyes, was shouting, sobbing, and sneezing even more loudly than her three infuriated companions.

"Ker-choo!" screamed the Countess. "Pull the signal. Ker-choo!"

"Ker-choo!" sneezed Fanny. Then, in a low, intense voice: "Too late now! Do you think they will stop the train a second time for the alarm-bell rung from this compartment?"

For a moment, from a corner of one half opened eye, Fanny saw the gray-bearded man put up his groping hands to the rack above his head and marked the distortion of rage that passed over his face.

The next instant the door was flung open, and the guard, followed by the pushing faces of inquisitive passengers, entered the compartment.

"What does this noise mean?" he demanded sternly; but was cut short by a sudden sneeze, echoed by the inquisitive swarm behind him. "Ker-choo! Ker-choo!"

"She flung pepper in our eyes!" screamed the Countess.

"Pepper in our eyes—ker-choo!" groaned the priest.

The official, strangling his agony, demanded fiercely: "Who? This same young lady?"

Fanny, coughing and choking, held up her hand to demand a hearing.

"Monsieur, it is, then, in a compartment of lunatics that I find myself! The first time I had no proof to offer of the falseness of their accusation. But this time my proof is ready. It was not I, but that lady, who flung the pepper—with what purpose I can not say!"

"And the proof?" growled the gray-bearded man gruffly.

"There, under your feet—that handkerchief, monsieur!" Then, as the conductor stooped to pick it up, Fanny leaned eagerly toward him.

"See—it is still stained with the pepper that remains in it. And the embroidery in the corner—look, 'B. de W.,' and a countess' crown!"

The guard stooped first to examine the pepper-stained handkerchief; then, following her gesture, turned his gaze toward the elegant hand-luggage in the rack above the stout lady's head, which bore the same device: the initials "B. de W." and a nine-pronged crown.

"My own handkerchief, if you would care to see it," went on Fanny sweetly, "here, monsieur. My purse—my gold vanity-case all, as you see, with 'F. G.' engraved on them—"

"*Genug!*" growled the guard. "I see for myself. *Donnerwetter!* This compartment is nothing but a box of monkeys! Fräulein, do you wish to give the lady in charge for assault?"

Fanny's mind worked rapidly. Having achieved so much of her purpose, her object now must be to shake off her foe and his confederates from her track. She herself, being under arrest, was to descend perforce in less than an hour's time—a necessity which accorded perfectly with her desires. Her present object must be to prevent Arsène Lupin from alighting as well. How to cause him to remain on the train—at least as far as Munich, the next stopping-place after Strassburg.

The conductor, threatening the unruly crowd with awful penalties if they offended again, finally withdrew. The four passengers, left alone, glared at one another with reddened eyes. Fanny, feeling her enemy's cold glance upon her, realized her own peril and the necessity for immediate action. At once, and with gestures of the most conspicuous caution, she began to rip open the satin lining of her muff.

The professor, leaning back in his corner, seemed to sleep. Those gleaming eyes that had flashed into hers on the terrace of

Bar-sur-Seine—even reduced to a hidden pinpoint, she was conscious of their superhuman acuteness. With cautious gestures, on the side between herself and the window, she forced her gold vanity-case inside the opening she had made in the muff's lining. Then, with her hands still inside her muff, she unbuttoned her right-hand glove, and with a resolute gesture held her naked wrist against the hot steam-pipe which ran up from the floor beside the window.

As the railroad was generous in the matter of heating, the pain was severe. But, like the immortal Spartan boy with the fox in his sleeve, Fanny Gordon sat immobile with her delicate wrist pressed against the boiling hot steam-pipe. The tears started to her eyes, but she did not wince. Then, after a few moments, with gestures of infinite caution, she turned around so as to face the compartment, and thrust both arms deep into her muff.

So she was sitting an hour later, when the train slid into the vast station of the capital of Alsace. As the locked door of the compartment held them all prisoners, Fanny continued to sit in the same position for fifteen minutes more; when, accompanied by a brusque and imposing police officer, the guard of the train returned.

"Here—this young lady, for pulling the alarm-bell without just cause. I have already taken the depositions of the witnesses. And now, if the fräulein wishes to give the other lady in charge for pepper-throwing—*mein Gott*, what a gompartment!"

"No, no!" returned Fanny hastily. Her only wish for her fellow passengers was to see them safely out of Strassburg. Then, turning to the police officer, she remarked plaintively:

"But I do hope, monsieur, you're not intending to put any handcuffs on me! Because my wrist—it's all burned! Just this last hour or so—I don't know whatever has happened to it!" And, plucking her hand from the depths of her muff, she extended it toward the official. Sure enough, plain for every one to see, the delicate white skin was disfigured by the angry red welt of a new burn.

"No handcuffs—come, the train departs, fräulein!" returned the policeman gruffly.

For a moment Fanny heard the hissing intake of her enemy's breath. When he spoke, his voice was like a knife:

"Officer, one moment! The fräulein is about to leave wearing the furs of the other lady. I noticed particularly, the young lady wore those pale sable furs when she boarded the train at Paris!"

The Countess, taking up the cue, made a clamorous demand for restitution. Fanny, with her heart dancing in triumph, relinquished her beautiful black foxes with an apology. Then, with the showy imitation sables wrapped about her, she stepped from the train. A moment later, as the train pulled out of the station, she caught a glimpse of her late fellow passengers through the window of the compartment. And now her business was to get quickly out of Strassburg before her enemy should discover her hoax and return upon her tracks.

By that magic talisman, ready cash, she was able to compound her offenses against the peace of the German Empire. A fine of two thousand francs was imposed and paid—she sighed as the French notes were paid out into the thick-fingered German hands. Two minutes later, however, she stood in the streets, free! And Arsène Lupin was thundering on to Munich!

Two hours later, when the great express from Vienna to Paris made its customary evening stop at Strassburg, a dark-haired young girl stepped aboard. She was dressed in a brown velvet Russian blouse and skirt, a hat with a pale yellow osprey, and sable furs of striking design and doubtful authenticity. From a brown morocco hand-bag, discreetly ornamented with the gold monogram "F. G.," she produced a return ticket to Paris. A telegram, as she explained to the conductor, had prevented her from continuing her voyage to Vienna, as she was entitled to do.

Half an hour later, in another part of the station, another young woman stepped aboard a third-class compartment of a local accommodation train. The highly sunburned state of her face, and especially of her nose, was explained by the vizorless cap of green knitted wool which she wore dragged down over her hair. A faded green knitted jacket to match and a full skirt of large plaid completed a costume which—she explained to her sleepy fellow passengers in a loud, cheerful voice—was intended for a tramp in Switzerland with her husband. The knapsack strapped to her shoulders, the alpenstock, and the huge hobnailed shoes were well in character with her intention. All wished her *bon voyage* when, in the early morning hours, she alighted at the tiny mountain station where she was to take her train for Berne.

But, as soon as the shabby little train had puffed out of the quiet station, the sturdy young pedestrian seemed to change her intention. With the solitary cabman waiting beside the little station in the icy dawn, she made a rapid bargain for the immediate purchase of his strained horse and shabby carry-all. Then, waiting only for some hot coffee at the station, she shook the whip over her newly acquired steed and set out over the hills.

VII

INTO THE WRITING-ROOM of the Vicomte de Chatellerault was ushered a visitor whose insistence had passed good breeding. With an annoyed frown, the busy Vicomte looked up from his work—a disappointing report on the radium theft which he was making to the Chief of the Secret Service.

"*Eh bien, Madame?*"

Marcel, coughing discreetly, left the room.

The visitor stood awkwardly in her hobnailed shoes, which, with her knitted cap and jacket of faded green, made a costume more suited to a rainy mountain-top than to the classic French elegance that surrounded her. Then, as the man shut the door behind him, she suddenly sprang forward.

"Vicomte, have you a slab of zinc?"

"Mademoiselle Fanny?" gasped the astonished young man.

But the girl, without pausing even to greet him, unbuckled the knapsack from her shoulders and slung it upon the table. From the knapsack her swift hands extracted a camera whose metal case had not protected it from slime and rust. Placing this lamentable object upon the table, she turned swiftly back to the Vicomte.

"Vicomte! I have not dared to open it till I could do so with proper precautions, so that—so that, in case there is anything inside, not a grain should be lost. Have you a slab?"

Into the young man's troubled face sudden understanding flashed. "Here—this mirror. Glass serves our purpose as well as zinc, and when we lay the mirror flat on the table—"

His hands shook as he picked up the shabby camera. Fanny Gordon, whirling suddenly about, walked over to the window. The Vicomte stared after her grotesque figure in astonishment.

"Mademoiselle, you don't want to open it?"

"Open it—open it!" she cried feverishly, with her back still turned. "But, please, I don't want to see. Suppose there is nothing inside, after all! Open it—open it!"

For a few moments there was no noise in the room except the crack of rending wood and the click of metal. Then a moment of complete silence. Fanny, standing by the window, pulled off her knitted cap and wiped her forehead. Then a cry.

She whirled about. Raoul de Chatellerault stood contemplating a small metal box which he held open in his hand. Fanny, tiptoeing toward him, bent over the little open box. It was filled to the brim with grayish-looking salts. She drew a long breath, then, raising her eyes to de Chatellerault's face, saw that it had vanished suddenly in a mist.

"It's—*it?*" she breathed.

"Six hundred thousand dollars' worth of radium—those dirty-looking salts!" he murmured below his breath. Then, dashing to the telephone, he called up the headquarters of the Secret Service.

"Yes—the Chief himself—with his limousine, with a chemist and four of his best men, all armed—urgent. At once!"

An hour later, when the precious salts, weighed and verified by the expert, had been duly sealed into the Chief's strong box, her two colleagues turned to Fanny:

"And now, mademoiselle, we are waiting to hear all about it!"

With the faintest flicker of a triumphant glance toward Raoul, Fanny began the story of her adventures. The ringing of the alarm-bell by Lupin—her own arrest—her terror as the train plunged into the long black tunnel.

"And in the tunnel—he dared? What happened?"

"My breath stopped—for I saw something!"

"But you said it was completely dark!"

"That is the point, Vicomte! When one *sees* something in the black darkness, one's breath is likely to stop for a moment! What I saw was a luminous moth floating in the dark a little above me—a stray moth with phosphorescent wings. So strange, so pretty, with the little shooting lights that sparkled and played upon its back. I snatched at it in the dark, and caught nothing! Then, all of a sudden, the train roared out into the sunlight, and I saw that the air before me was empty. My eyes, straining straight before me, mechanically altered their focus, and I perceived that my line of vision was on the luggage-rack above the professor's head—on one piece of his luggage, in fact, out of all the others. So I thought hard—hard! I said to myself: 'This intense anxiety to prevent me from arriving at Vienna, which causes him even to have me brought to his own compartment, this elaborate trickery—what can it mean except that he is carrying his treasure to Austria, and does not intend to have me there interfering with him while he disposes of it. Very well, then; it is certain that he is carrying *it* with him. But where? Hardly in his trunk! Nor yet on his person, for fear of the terrible Becquerel burn—that hideous scarlet welt which radium eats into human flesh as surely as a coal of fire!' Where, then, had he hidden it? From the excessive care with which he held those Baedekers on his knee, he evidently wished to give the impression that they contained something precious; so I might take it for granted the radium was not there! But that small piece of luggage which showed a luminous spot in the dark—that little camera in its japanned metal case, tossed so carelessly in the rack above his head—"

"Ah!" The Vicomte started to his feet "I begin to understand! Of course, when he had packed the stolen radium in the camera, a tiny fleck had sifted out upon the case—"

"Precisely my reasoning, Vicomte! A single tiny grain, invisible in the daytime, but flaring out like a betraying beacon in the darkness! So, by a simple trick, I deprived Lupin and his band of the use of their eyes for a few minutes, while I snatched down the camera from the luggage-rack—and took immediate means to place it in a safe place where later I could come back and claim it. The hiding-place that I chose, though a bit damp, left the radium salts unharmed, as you see. Having succeeded so far, my next step was to induce Lupin to go on with the train, while I alighted at Strassburg. So, by ripping my muff and slipping into it my vanity-case, which was about the same size as the radium-box, and by producing on my hand a very fair imitation of the Becquerel burn, I managed to convince him that I had slipped the radium from the camera and hidden it in my muff. Having possessed himself of my muff, he was delighted to go on to Munich. *Bon voyage, petit Arsène!*"

"But, when he found out, you were not afraid of his pursuit?"

"Of course I was! And so my first step, at Strassburg, was to look up a young woman of my height and complexion who wanted to go to Paris—luckily, I found her in the restaurant where I dined! So I changed clothes with her, gave her my ticket to Paris, a thousand francs, and a warning of the precautions she must take—and she was off on the limited that very night, as happy as a lark! And I in her clothes, as you now see me—went off for a little mountain-climbing and a bit of fishing. The result of my fishing you see for yourselves. Tell me, Chief, is it all there? The six hundred thousand dollars' worth of radium—it is there intact, Chief?"

The Chief nodded, then extended his hand.

"Every last grain of it! Before the end of the week I shall see to it that a check for the amount of the reward is sent to you—two hundred thousand francs. And, more than that, all Paris shall know that, for the first time in history, Arsène Lupin has been defeated."

CLARA PRYOR

Carolyn Wells

Carolyn Wells was well known for her many mystery novels, but this is a (dare I say) cute story with a fun twist on the traditional Sherlock-style detective accompanied by a narrating Watson. It was published in *Lippincott's Monthly Magazine* in 1906.

THE MYSTERY OF THE JADE BUDDHA

FROM THE MOMENT I laid my two honest gray eyes on Clara Pryor I just adored her.

Excuse my speaking of my eyes like that, but you see everybody described them that way, and, though I knew my eyes were no more honest than those of the average young American girl, yet I rather liked the phrase and did my best to live up to it.

It was at college that I first met Clara, and through the whole four years we were chums. And now a year had passed since we were graduated, and, though I hadn't seen her in all that time, we were about to meet again at a house party down at her uncle's country home in Winchester. I had no idea what other guests were to be there, but I was so crazy to see Clara again that I didn't care.

Still, there would probably be someone worth dressing for; so I packed my pink mull and my flower sunbonnet, but all the time my thoughts were with Clara, rather than the possibility of masculine admirers.

Well, the first day or two after I reached Winchester, Clara and I both talked to each other at once and we both talked all the time. There was so much to say that it seemed as if we would never get talked out. We roomed together, and of course we talked all night. Then by day we took long walks or drives, and it wasn't until Guy Hilton came that either of us cared to associate with any one but our two selves. And then a lot of people came, and of course we had to be smiling and sociable with them all, and I was glad I had brought my pink mull and my flower sunbonnet.

But really Clara is the one I'm going to tell you about, so I must stick to my subject.

Clara is a girl who always has some definite purpose. These are so various, and come and go so rapidly, that in anyone else they would be called fads. But Clara isn't that sort. With her they are serious matters, and the funny part is that every new one she takes up she is sure it's to be her life-work. I should think she'd learn after awhile, but she doesn't.

At this particular time, down in Winchester, she told me that she had concluded to be a detective.

This almost shocked me, for I like to read detective stories myself, and have always thought I'd like to meet a real detective,—a refined, gentlemanly one, I mean,—but I'm very sure I'd rather see than be one.

But Clara felt different about it. She said that she was convinced that she had wonderful detective talent; and she thought, too, that a woman was better fitted for the work than a man. She said a woman's perceptions are more delicate and her sense of deduction more acute.

Then she went on to talk about vital and incidental evidence, and the apparently supernatural powers of trained observation, until, as she was glibly gabbling of the mistake of theorizing from insufficient data, I turned my honest gray eyes full upon her and said:

"Clara Pryor, what have you been reading?"

She looked a little crestfallen at first, and then she smiled, and owned up that for the past two weeks she had just crammed Sherlock Holmes, Anna Katherine Green's stories, Poe's tales, "The Moonstone," and a lot of Gaboriau's and Boisgobey's books in paper covers.

Not that the paper covers made any difference, but it showed to what lengths the fastidious Clara had gone in the enthusiasm of her latest definite purpose.

"Have you ever detected anything really?" I demanded.

"No," said Clara, "but then, you see, it's only about two weeks that I've known I had these peculiar powers, and there's been no occasion. But my opportunity will come."

She spoke in a tone of confidence, and her straight nose somehow had an air of Sherlockian inscrutability,—if you know what I mean,—and so I was greatly impressed.

"I'm sure it will," I responded heartily; for so great is my admiration for Clara that I can't help believing everything that she believes. "I'm positive you will be a celebrated detective, and I know exactly what I shall be. I'll be your Dr. Watson and write your memoirs."

"Do," cried Clara; "and you must always go with me on my secret missions, and I'll tell you how I deduce my inferences."

I wasn't quite sure that last phrase of hers was technically correct as to diction, but that was Clara's part of the affair, not mine. I was more than satisfied to play the part of the admiring though often snubbed Watson. Not that Clara had ever snubbed me, but I could see at once that as a successful detective she would be obliged to do so, and, indeed, was quite ready to begin.

When Clara had a definite purpose, she always acted the principal part with a fine attention to detail.

It may seem strange that an opportunity for detective work occurred the very next day, but if it hadn't this story wouldn't have been written, so you see it wasn't so much of a coincidence after all. It would only have been another story about another episode, for murders or burglaries are bound to occur, if a detective with a definite purpose waits long enough.

Well, that very evening we were all in the library after dinner. Guy Hilton had asked me to walk on the veranda with him, and I had said I would; but Mr. Nicholson—that's Clara's uncle and our host—was showing off some of his curios, and common politeness forced Guy and me to wait until he had finished haranguing about them.

I had no interest in the carved ivories, and tear-bottles, and scarabs, and neither had Mr. Hilton; but Clara loved them. She knew their histories almost as well as her Uncle Albert did, and was never tired of learning about them, looking at them, and even fingering the rusty-looking old things.

Coffee was served in the library, and I remember it was just as I took my cup, that Parsons offered me, that Mr. Nicholson held up the Buddha and began to tell about it.

It seems that that particular Buddha was a very old bit of wonderfully carved jade and its value was enormous.

Well, from what I listened to of what Mr. Nicholson said, I gathered that it was really one of the most remarkable curios in existence, and about as valuable as if it had been made of solid diamond.

I never shall be able to explain the strange sensation that suddenly came to me as the owner of the jade Buddha was discoursing on its marvels.

I wasn't looking at the speaker or the curios; indeed, I was so impatient for the talk to be over that both my attention and my honest gray eyes were wandering all over the room.

And all at once I became aware that every blessed soul in that room was intensely interested in that jade thing.

I mean especially so.

Clara, of course, was devouring it with her eyes. But so were Mr. and Mrs. Upham, a staid, elderly couple who had arrived at the house the day before. So also was Janet Lee, a lovely girl who was trying to cut me out with Mr. Hilton, but who, so far, had not succeeded.

Two or three other young men were present, and the gaze of each was riveted on the idol.

Even Miss Barrington, who scorned anything that was not made in America, seemed hypnotized.

But I concluded all this must have been my imagination, for that night, after Clara and I had gone to our room, I asked her if her detective instincts were aroused by the scene. And she said no, it hadn't occurred to her,—but she wished to goodness somebody would steal the Buddha, so she could detect the thief.

I thought quite seriously of stealing it myself, so as to give Clara the chance she wanted. But I decided that such a course would interfere with my role of Dr. Watson, so I gave up the idea.

Well, if I've told my story properly, you won't be much surprised to learn that, when Clara and I came down to breakfast the next morning, Mr. Nicholson informed us that the Buddha was gone. He didn't say it was stolen; he just said it was missing from his cabinet, and he didn't know where it was.

My honest gray eyes sought Clara's, and her's were just dancing with delight.

Her opportunity had come!

Right after breakfast we walked down by the brook to talk it over.

"I shan't tell Uncle what I'm doing," said Clara, "for I know he'd only laugh at me. So I shall let him take whatever steps he chooses to recover the Buddha, and meantime I shall go systematically to work and find out who took it."

She looked so capable and determined that I adored her more than ever. I felt so proud to be a Watson to her.

In order to play my part exactly right, I had read up in Sir Conan Doyle's works myself. And I knew that now was my time to sit still and listen to Clara's plans, which, of course, she would only hint vaguely to me; and perhaps occasionally I must throw in a word of appreciation.

"First, I must consider the characters of the guests," Clara began. "Janet Lee, now, is sweet and pretty in her effects, but I know that her real self is sly and deceitful."

"Good gracious!" I exclaimed, quite forgetting my part; "you don't think some of Mr. Nicholson's guests stole his Buddha!"

"I don't think it; I know it," said Clara, and her correct coldness of tone brought me back to a realizing sense of my position. "I have possessed myself of the facts, and I find that the library windows were all fastened on the inside, and the house securely locked. No one could have entered from outside."

"But the servants," I ventured, again forgetting that I was not supposed to suggest.

"They are all old and trusted ones," said Clara, "except Parsons. He is new, but he was well recommended, and Uncle has no reason to suspect him."

"Now, it seems to me," I went on, eagerly, "Parsons is just the one to suspect. He is such an all-round man. He is butler, house-servant, valet, and soft-footed. Oh, Clara, he's just the one to suspect. Do let's suspect him! At first, anyway."

Clara gave me a pitying glance and then resumed her far-away look.

It was efficacious, and I said no more about Parsons, but I couldn't help thinking he was ideal for a criminal.

"Miss Barrington," Clara went on, "seems like an honest lady; and yet she is fond of valuable trinkets and may have been overwhelmingly attracted."

"Miss Barrington!" I exclaimed. "She wouldn't accept as a gift anything of foreign manufacture."

"That may be merely a clever pose; and besides, jade Buddhas are not manufactured."

I was getting used to being snubbed, and took it with a fine imitation of Watsonian meekness.

"The Uphams," Clara proceeded, "are staid old people,—apparently,—but you never can tell. Mr. Hilton—"

At this I flared up.

"If you're going to suspect Mr. Hilton," I said, "you can get somebody else to write your memoirs. I won't!"

"Mr. Hilton," Clara went on, as if I had not spoken, "looks so frank and honest that I seem to deduce a mask of candor, hiding—"

"You're an idiot, instead of a detective!" I interrupted, and then I walked away to find out for myself what Mr. Hilton's candid mask hid.

A few hours later I found Clara alone on the veranda, and I asked her how she was progressing.

Her ill-natured remark about Mr. Hilton had ceased to annoy me, for I had discovered for myself that that gentleman's mask of candor hid a frank, ingenuous nature.

"I haven't yet formed a definite conclusion," she said, in a low tone. "But I have proved Sherlock Holmes's statement that no one can go into a room and come out again without leaving evidence of having been there. I have examined the library thoroughly, and I found Miss Barrington's handkerchief, Mrs. Upham's gloves, Mr. Hilton's magazine, and several men's cigar-ashes."

"Go on," I said, breathlessly, for I fully expected she would deduce from these the wretch who had stolen the Buddha.

"That's all," she responded. "As I say, I haven't exactly discovered the thief, but these things may be valuable clues."

I was disappointed in Clara then, and I dare say I showed it.

"They were probably left there yesterday afternoon," I said, "before the idol disappeared at all. Couldn't you find anything more vital as evidence?"

Then Clara forgot her impassiveness, and exclaimed, almost angrily, "Perhaps you'd better go and search the library yourself."

"All right, I will," I answered, for I really thought I could find something better than handkerchiefs and gloves.

But there wasn't a thing that could be called a clue. I hunted everywhere. One of the maids had set the room in order; dusted it, and arranged the furniture and ornaments in their proper places.

Somehow I couldn't help wishing I could find something, if only to please Clara.

I stood looking at the dark rich colors of the Persian rug, when a stray sunbeam came in at the window and made something glitter right at my feet.

I picked it up, hoping it might be a diamond. But it wasn't. It was a tiny flake of glass, round and marked with little concentric curves, like a miniature clam-shell. How shall I express its size? Well, it was about as big as the iris of a person's eye,—not a dilated iris, but a normal one.

Wrapping the bit of glass carefully in my handkerchief, I flew back to Clara and whispered to her to come with me up to our own room. There, behind a locked door, I triumphantly showed her the clue I had found, and waited for her expressions of delight.

But she only said, "What is it?" and looked rather blank.

"Why, Clara," I cried, "don't you see what it is? It's a chip from somebody's eye-glasses! And, of course, whoever stole the Buddha last night dropped his glasses and this bit broke off."

"Of course," exclaimed Clara. "That's what I have already thought out. I just wanted to see if it also occurred to you. Give me the chip, Ethel."

I gave it to her, glad to be of that much assistance to her in her great work.

"Now," she said, "we've only to discover who is wearing a chipped eye-glass to know who is the criminal."

"Yes," said I, "unless they have bought a new pair or owned other glasses."

"Of course I meant unless that," said Clara calmly.

Well, if you'll believe me, Mr. Upham came to luncheon wearing a pair of eye-glasses with a little place chipped out at one side! They were rimless glasses, and the defect, being on the edge, didn't at all interfere with their usefulness. I almost fainted, for I remembered what Clara had said about the staid old gentleman.

He did indeed seem to have an honest face, but I felt sure I detected criminal signs in the wrinkles round his nose.

After luncheon Clara went bravely up to him and asked him to walk round the sundial with herself and me. The walk around the sundial was a favorite constitutional with everybody. Mr. Upham looked a little surprised, but he politely said yes, and we started off.

Clara was polite too; she always is. But I could see she meant to show no mercy. And, indeed, why should she?

Well, she began a little abruptly, I thought, by saying:

"Mr. Upham, if you will return the jade Buddha to my uncle, I will promise not to tell him who took it."

"Bless my soul, child! What do you mean?" exclaimed the old man, stopping right where he was and turning red in the face.

"I mean," went on Clara firmly, "that I know you took my uncle's jade idol, and I'm telling you that if you'll return it I won't have you arrested, for I don't want any publicity or excitement about it."

Instead of looking alarmed, Mr. Upham seemed amused, and he said, with a funny little smile:

"Thank you very much for your kind consideration, but suppose I deny that I took the jade image?"

"Then," and here came Clara's moment of triumph, "I should tell you that I have positive proof of your guilt."

It may have been the tragic tone of Clara's declaration, or it may have been the throes of a guilty conscience, but anyhow Mr. Upham turned fairly white, as he said:

"Indeed, miss, and what is your positive proof?"

In the stillest silence I ever heard, Clara unfolded a little pink paper and showed the tiny scale of glass.

"That," she said, impressively, "was picked up from the library floor. It precisely matches the flaw in the edge of your eye-glass. Is further proof needed?"

Of course, not being a born detective, I may have misunderstood the expression on Mr. Upham's face, but it seemed to me he had all he could do to keep from bursting into laughter. "Does it match?" he asked. "Let us try."

But after he had taken off his glasses to make the test, he couldn't see at all.

Just then Mr. Nicholson came walking toward us.

"Hallo, Albert," said Mr. Upham; "lend me your glasses a minute, will you?"

Mr. Nicholson did so, and Mr. Upham put them on and gravely examined his own pair, matching Clara's bit of glass to the flaw in the edge.

"Fits exactly!" he declared. "Now put on your own glasses, Albert, and look at this."

Mr. Nicholson did as requested, and agreed that the chip must have been broken from that very place.

"Now," said Mr. Upham, "I say nothing in my own defence, but, for the further assistance of this young lady in her laudable work, I wish to state that I lent these particular glasses to our host, Mr. Nicholson, last evening, he having mislaid his own. When I retired, I left Mr. Nicholson still in the library, reading, with these particular glasses on his nose."

This gave a new turn to affairs, which, if logically followed up, would seem to prove Mr. Nicholson the thief of his own Buddha.

But Clara had no notion of accusing her own uncle or of letting him know of her efforts in his behalf; so, as Mr. Upham walked away (and I am sure he did so to hide his laughter), she merely asked Mr. Nicholson if he were the last one in the library the night before.

"How do I know?" he exclaimed. He was an irascible sort of man. "I sat there, reading, until about eleven. Yes, I had Upham's glasses on. I had left mine upstairs, and we wear the same number. About eleven, I think it was, I went up to my room. I met Parsons in the hall, and I gave him the glasses to take to Mr. Upham.

I presume he did so, for I saw that gentleman had them on at breakfast this morning."

"Were they chipped when you were reading with them, Uncle?" asked Clara.

"No, they were not. And I didn't break them, either. Probably Parsons let them fall on the floor or stairs, as he took them to Mr. Upham."

Without waiting to make further explanations, Clara grasped my arm and fairly dragged me toward the house.

"I told you so!" she said; "I knew it was Parsons all the time. He crept into the library and stole the thing after uncle gave him the glasses and before he took them to Mr. Upham. In the library he was probably startled by some noise, and dropped them on the hardwood floor or the hearth, and the little chip of glass flew over on the rug."

I remembered distinctly that it was I who insisted on suspecting Parsons, but I wouldn't have said so to Clara for anything.

Together we went in search of Parsons, and found that household treasure in the butler's pantry.

"Parsons," said Clara, in a gentle tone, "if you will give me the little stone idol, I will see to it that you are leniently dealt with."

"Miss?" said Parsons, looking at us both with a sort of deferential wonder.

"I say, repeated Clara, "if you will give me the little stone idol,—the jade Buddha—"

"Why, it's been stole, miss. Haven't you heard about it?"

"Parsons," exclaimed Clara, thoroughly exasperated at his imbecile expression, "don't attempt to deceive me! You were in the library last night after my uncle retired."

"No, miss. Excuse me, miss, but Mr. Nicholson put out the library lights himself. He came upstairs just as I was passing through the hall, and he gave me a pair of eye-glasses, miss, which he said I was to take to Mr. Upham's room."

"Parsons," and Clara's gaze would have forced the truth from Ananias, "did you go at once to Mr. Upham's room with those glasses?"

"Why, no, miss. You see, it was this way. I met young Mr. Hilton a minute after, and he asked me to get him some hot water. He was in a hurry, and he said if I'd go for it at once he'd hand the glasses to Mr. Upham for me. So I gave the glasses to Mr. Hilton, miss, and I went to the kitchen for the hot water."

"That will do, Parsons," said Clara. "It is just as I thought." And with an air of entire success, she stalked away, and I meekly followed.

"You see," she declared, turning on me tragically, when we reached our own room, "it was your Mr. Hilton, after all!"

"Nothing of the sort!" I exclaimed angrily. "And for pity's sake don't go and tell him he's a thief. Let me cross-examine him."

I was so afraid Clara would be rude to my friend that I forgot my inconspicuous role, and forged ahead.

Leaving Clara, I flew down to the veranda, where I knew Guy Hilton sat, smoking, and said to him, without apology or preamble:

"Mr. Hilton, as a personal favor, will you tell me to whom you gave Mr. Upham's eye-glasses, last night, after you took them from Parsons?"

"Certainly," he said, just as casually as if I had asked him to tell me the time of day. "I saw one of the house-maids just outside Mr. Upham's door, and I asked her to hand the glasses to Mr. Upham."

"Thank you," I said, and I smiled at him and ran away.

I told Clara that her suspicions had to be moved again, and she said that quite fitted into her theory. Indeed, she had deduced it already.

Well, then we suspected Norah, of course, and we went for her.

It was getting to be an exciting game now. Suspicion shifted so rapidly that it kept us on the jump.

As Clara said she had surmised, Norah informed us that she handed the glasses, herself, to Mrs. Upham directly after Mr. Hilton had asked her to do so.

I felt a little diffident about accusing Mrs. Upham of being a thief and a robber, but Clara was inexorable.

She marched straight to the lady, and I thought she was going to tell her that if she'd give up the stolen goods we wouldn't arrest her.

But Clara didn't do that this time; she said, "Mrs. Upham, pardon me if I am indiscreet, but will you tell me what you did with the eye-glasses that Norah brought to your room last night?"

Mrs. Upham smiled pleasantly,—you know Clara is very pretty,—and said:

"Certainly, my dear. I laid them on the chiffonnier in my husband's dressing-room."

"Were they chipped or broken at that time?"

"No, I know they were not, for, as they seemed a trifle cloudy, I cleaned them myself, as I often do. They were in perfect condition. Why do you ask?"

"Oh, nothing," said Clara, and she seized my arm and hurried me away.

"It was Mr. Upham, after all!" she whispered, and her face grew pale with excitement. "Late at night he put on his glasses, went down to the library, and stole the Buddha. In the dim room his glasses fell off, or were somehow knocked off, and the chip flew on the floor."

Well, the strange part is, that's the exact truth. Mr. Upham, it seems, was a monomaniac on the subject of jade, and he did go down to the library, just as Clara said, and take the Buddha. He owned up to it finally, but he told Mr. Nicholson he didn't intend to keep it. He said he wanted to study it by himself. But, if that was so, why didn't he borrow it openly?

So, you see, Clara was a real detective, after all, and that tiny piece of glass was the clue to a strange adventure, which I am proud to be the one to record.

THE "GUM-SHOE"

PHILIP CURTISS

This story (riffing on the appearance of well-polished "gentleman detectives") by Philip Curtiss was published in 1921 by *Scribner's Magazine*.

THE "GUM-SHOE"

THERE ARE CERTAIN professions which have an innate fascination for even the least illusioned of us, which probably explains why I always went out of my way to talk to Frank Casey, the house detective of the Hotel St. Romulus. At any rate it could not have been Casey's personal charm, for he was a fat, red-faced man with puffy lips, while a mind more strictly literal than his I have never encountered. As for the poetry of his particular office, it consisted largely of looking intently and fiercely at certain well-dressed persons who seemed to think that the lobby of the St. Romulus was maintained solely as a free social and recreation room for their benefit, while occasionally he was called into service by a head-waiter or clerk to explain to some Latin that the customs of this country and his own were not always the same. As a romantic figure he was distinctly a disappointment, and once I almost told him so.

"Frank," I said one night, "sometime before I get too old to enjoy it, I would like to meet a detective who really looks like a detective."

Frank considered the matter coldly.

"What's the matter?" he asked. "Don't I look like a detective?"

"Yes," I replied, "you do look like a detective. That's just the trouble. I meant a detective who looked like a detective in a book. That's the kind I'd like to meet."

"So would I," replied Frank fervently.

The conversation seemed at an end, but standing alone in a hotel lobby had given Frank a vast power of soliloquy, and I waited patiently while he rocked back and forth on his heels, his eyes following the figure of a young man in a brown derby who was wandering toward the newsstand. The young man bought a copy of "The Signboard," and Frank lost interest but his eyes still roved.

"You write books," he said at last. "But you don't have long hair or a sissy necktie do you?"

The question seemed superfluous, but burly Frank Casey had a disconcerting way of thrusting his nose in your face, and demanding answers to even superfluous questions.

"Do you?" he insisted.

"I hope not," I hastened to reply.

"Well, then."

My quest did not seem to meet with much encouragement. It passed from my mind and I thought that it did from Frank's too, but I reckoned without his elephantine memory, for one night, a full year later, he hailed me at the foot of the elevator.

"Say," he said, with a ponderous jerk of his head which made the elevator-boys look at me sharply, "come here, I want to talk to you."

He led me a few steps away, and then with rough confidence he vouchsafed in a low tone:

"Remember you said detectives never looked like detectives? Well, there's a fellow here I want you to meet."

Standing at the point where Frank usually stood was a tall, striking-looking man of forty in evening clothes. A silk hat was pushed back easily on his head, a yellow cane hung over his arm, and a pair of gloves were crumpled in his hand. From the languid, humorous way in which he stood watching the crowd in the lobby he might have been a typical man-about-town, but his lean, rather gaunt face, with its blond mustache, had a tanned, weather-beaten look which made him notable in that pallid company. It was the type of face which one usually attributes to a British officer.

"Mr. Blake, shake hands with Mr. Munson," said Frank, and as we obeyed he added: "You boys ought to know each other. You'll have things to talk about."

Blake and I smiled as we studied each other, and my scrutiny, at least, was one of interest, for Blake did look like the kind of man who would have things to say. In my business clothes he made me feel dingy, and his air of cool self-possession rather awed me. I waited for him to make the advances but he waited too, and Frank had to start the thing moving.

"Would either of you like a sandwich or something?" he began hopefully.

The tall man smiled.

"I would like *something*," he said.

He seemed to express the will of the party, but hardly were we seated at a dark oak table in the cafe when a bell-boy whispered in Frank's ear, and our host stood up.

"I'm sorry, gentlemen, I've got to run off, but stick around. I'll be back. If you want anything sign my name."

With his hundreds of friends among traveling men, actors, reporters, and other casuals who flowed in and out of the St. Romulus lobby, it was seldom that worldly-wise Frank was as lordly as that. The note in his voice increased my respect for this stranger who commanded such deference, but our conversation, as soon as he left us, concerned Frank himself.

"A great character—Casey," remarked Blake as the huge, waddling back disappeared through the door.

"A fine fellow," I agreed, but a certain whimsical twinkle in the eyes of my new companion told me that our conversation need not be limited to platitudes and I struck out boldly on the line which had failed with Frank.

"I can never see Casey," I suggested, "without thinking how different are most of the detectives you meet in real life from—well from what you imagine detectives would be."

A deep pair of parenthesis lines formed around my companion's mouth. He looked down at the wooden table-top and slid the glass in his hand idly about in small circles as if to see how hard he could do it without spilling its contents. I gathered that my remark was not wholly novel.

"Well," he replied in a not unkindly way, "in real life, you know, a detective is usually nothing but a high-grade roughneck, a sort of glorified policeman."

He kept his eyes on the glass in his hand and put on the brake just as the contents swirled up to the edge. Then, as if he had found out all that he wanted to know, he suddenly shoved it aside and continued:

"And, when you come down to it, that is just about the way that it should be, for detective work, like any other business, is largely a matter of acquaintance. The best man to sell bonds is the man who knows the most investors. The best man to catch crooks is the man who knows the most crooks."

He made it sound disappointing but I still clung to my cherished romance.

"Then you think the detective stories we read are impossible?"

My companion laughed.

"I wondered if that was what you had in mind."

As if he could not concentrate without doing it, he began circling his glass again.

"No," he continued, rather hesitatingly, "I wouldn't say that the stories are impossible. I wouldn't say that anything was impossible."

By the long time that he sat in silence gazing at the table-top he seemed to be giving my question a flattering amount of thought.

"The difference between a detective in a story and a detective in real life," he began at last, "is that the detective in the story goes on the principle that things are seldom what they seem, while the real detective goes on the principle that things are almost always just what they seem."

"It sounds simple," I said rather vaguely.

"If it weren't," replied Blake, "few crooks would ever be caught."

Then, suddenly, as if he had been playing a part, as if he had been holding himself in restraint, he leaned back and laughed.

"I don't want to spoil your romance," he said. "Perhaps I can show you what I mean by a little instance."

I summoned all my attention and also summoned the waiter.

"I'll have the same," said Blake, nodding, then lighting a cigarette, he asked: "Do you happen to know the motto of the Enterprise Agency?"

I shook my head.

"Well," explained Blake, "the motto of the Enterprise people is, 'Evidence where evidence exists.' That covers about the whole of detective work right there, but the more you think of it the more it means. First off it means not to go chasing half over the world looking for things that exist right under your nose; but it means something else that you don't realize at first.

"When you spoke about old Frank there," he continued, "I couldn't help thinking about a man I once knew who had all the ideas you find in the storybooks—the international intrigue, the gentleman sleuth stuff. So every time I am tempted to laugh at the books I think of this case and have to believe them after all.

"You see, most detectives are honest chaps who have graduated from patrolmen, or have made investigations for lawyers, or have been private watchmen, or express-messengers. Then there are lots of foreigners, especially Italians. You have to have them at any price because they speak the language. But this boy was unusual. He went into the business deliberately, just out of pure romance. He went into it to keep life from being dull, like our old friend Sherlock. He was a college man, had traveled abroad, had done some writing for the newspapers—"

"And his name was—?" I interrupted.

Blake flushed but smiled in spite of himself.

"Well, call his name Smith, because that is easy to remember and you won't trip me up on it. Anyway Smith—how's that?—Smith, with his college clothes and his happy smile walked into the Enterprise office one morning and asked the chief for a job. Can you get it? Young Hopeful breezing into that place with a fraternity pin and a little cane and calmly saying, 'I want to be a detectuv!'

"I—well I might as well say that I was there. Anyway, you can imagine what happened. Even the stenographers got it and began tittering until the poor kid got all red and flustered, and ended up by wishing that he'd never been such a romantic ass. But he stuck to it, and after looking him over a minute and trying to keep his face straight the chief asked him into his private office and said: 'So you want to be an operative, do you?'

"Of course—what did I call him? Smith had never heard that word before, but he nodded and then the chief began to do some quick thinking, for, although he didn't let the kid know it, he was a gift on a blank Christmas. He was exactly the kind of man the chief wanted for a case he had in hand, and exactly the kind hc thought he could never get, for that office, like every other office, was filled up with Frank Caseys, only they weren't all so fat. The youngster looked to the chief too good to be true. He was almost afraid of a 'plant,' but he asked him some questions, got some references, and the next day he took him on, after which he began to teach him Lesson Number One.

"'Now, er Smith,' he said, 'this may not be your idea of the gay and happy life of a gum-shoe, but you know that all our work does not consist in tracking murderers to their lairs or putting the Prince of Moravia back on his throne. The job I'm going to give you is like a lot of work you'll get in this business, and you can take it or leave it.'

"Then he told him about the job, which really is of a sort that you get all the time in some agencies. The client was a nice old gentleman. You'd know him in a minute if I told you. He was not a multimillionaire but one of those solid old boys who has dinner at four o'clock on Sunday afternoons, serves on all sorts of committees, subscribes to the opera and the horse show alike, and never gives a hang whether the market goes up or down. And the old gentleman had a daughter. And the daughter had a young man who wanted to marry her, and gave signs that he was going to do it, too."

Blake lit a fresh cigarette from his old one, and the parentheses around his mouth deepened again at the memory of that case.

"So there you are," he said between puffs. "Doesn't that sound like Chapter One?"

I agreed that it did and Blake went on:

"To make it better this suitor was a foreigner. At least, he was an Englishman. He was almost a stage Englishman. He was one of those young fellows that you used to see in droves in the hotel tearooms before the war—tall, languid, long nose, little mustache, handkerchief up his sleeve, and all the rest of it, a great ladies' man, a regular parlor-snake."

"Is this what Smith told you?" I interrupted suddenly.

Blake grinned.

"Presumably so," he answered. "Anyway that's what Smith told the chief. Of course that was the job, to go out and shadow this Englishman, for although everything about him was beautifully plausible, the old gentleman began to suspect what was in the air. He wanted to get rid of him, and he wanted to get rid of him before things had gone so far there would be a muss. Plenty of people in New York knew the Englishman but they didn't know anything about him. He had drifted into New York the way that lots of others had done—letters to somebody who gave him letters to somebody else until he was there and nobody remembered exactly where the original letters had come from. He claimed to have been an army officer and a younger son of some one important at home, but after a while people had begun to talk and the father was getting scared.

"So that was the case as the chief laid it before young Smith. He gave the names and the general facts, told him that the Englishman was visiting the family at their country-place down on Long Island, and then he put it to him straight:

"'Now, boy,' he said, 'you may have to do some things in this business that you think no gentleman would do, and if you feel that way about it you've got to remember that this is no gentleman's game. First you're to meet old Mr. So-and-So at his club on Forty-fourth Street and get acquainted. Then you're to go down there and visit. You're a guest from—well what place do you know besides New York?'

"'I was brought up in Akron,' answered the kid. 'And I went to school in Ann Arbor.'

"'Right,' said the chief. 'You can take your choice, only let me know which you choose in case some friend from your home town should have reason to call you up on urgent business. You're to fix up some reason for visiting there. Get a simple one and one that will come easy to the old gentleman, for remember that you're going to carry the work, not he. Then, when you get there, I want to give you one rule. I want you to forget that you are a detective or have ever been one, which you only have for fifteen minutes. If you think of it you will show it and somebody else will guess it. You won't have to wear any false whiskers or do any hiding behind doors. You're to fool yourself into believing that you are just what you pretend to be, a guest of the family from Akron or that other place. Act natural, eat natural, sleep natural, and make yourself agreeable without slopping over. Don't shadow this Englishman, just remember that he's there, that's all, and make up your mind about him as you would about any new fellow you meet. Without seeming to watch him think him over and get his number. Every time he mentions a name or a place or a date let it sink in and, when you get a chance, write it down. Don't try to draw him out. Let him hang himself if he's going to. As you get more names and places and dates, check them over and see if they agree, and then bring them in to me.'

"'Is that all?' asks the kid.

"'No, it's not,' said the chief, looking suddenly pretty hard. 'There's one thing more and the most important of all. I told you to forget that you are a detective, but I don't want you to forget that you are working for me and that I am working for my client. My client is paying me to spot this bird, and I am paying you to do it. He may be as pleasant as a day in June and may put you under obligation to him, but no matter how noble a lord he may seem to you, don't forget that you are working for me, not him. You get that, don't you?'

"This sort of talk and the sneery way the chief said it made the kid feel kind of uncertain, and wonder whether he wanted to be a detective after all, but he thought he was in for it now, so he went away, made his appointment with the old gentleman, and two days later, when he came back, he was feeling a whole lot better. So was the chief.

"'Well,' he said, 'how do you like the work? Or are you sorry you ever learned the trade?'

"'To tell the truth,' the kid had to confess, 'so far I like it fine, only I can't make it seem like work. I haven't done anything but play golf and ride horseback and live off the fat of the land.'

"The chief grinned.

"'That was what I told you to do, wasn't it? But how about this bird you're watching?'

"At that young Smith got sort of embarrassed, but he had at least one thing to report: 'Anyway, I've found out that he really has been in the army.'

"'How do you know that?' asked the chief.

"'Well,' said the kid, 'he was telling a story at dinner last night about a soldier in his company. It was a long, long story, and the soldier talked all the time, but not once did he use the word "you" to the officer. He always addressed the man he was talking to in the third person. "The leftenant this," and "the leftenant that." Nobody who has never been in the army can keep that up without slipping.'

"'That's a new one on me,' said the chief. 'Still he might have been the soldier himself and not the officer. That's fine as far as it goes but what more of him? What kind of a fellow is he?'

"At that the kid got red again and finally he burst out: 'To tell the truth, I think he's a dandy.'

"The chief couldn't help smiling a little but he gave a grunt. 'I told you he was a smooth article. He wouldn't be there if he wasn't. He's working you, boy, just as he's working the rest of the family.'

"'I don't know whether he's working me or not,' said the kid. 'But that's the way he looks to me so far.'

"'Awright,' said the chief. 'Stick to it and do a little snooping around now.'

"A couple of days later Smith reported again, and this time he had a long list of names and places in England, but the story was about the same. He couldn't find an edge in the Englishman anywhere and the chief was getting impatient.

"'You know it is costing our client good money to keep you out there, don't you?' he asked. 'From all I can make out the bird is getting ready to stay there for life, and that's what you're to keep from happening.'

"'Yes, sir,' said the kid, looking and feeling pretty rough about it. 'But to tell the truth, sir, I can't get a single thing on him from anything that has happened.'

"At that the chief looked at him hard and half shut his eyes.

"'Happened?' he said; 'can't you make something happen? Suppose things were made easy for him? Put in his way? How about a little card-game with you playing the easy-mark, or a little trip and a couple of bottles of fizz? Places do occasionally get raided, you know, if the right people have the tip. Do you get me now?'

"The kid's face must have been a study. For a long time he thought he was going to balk, but he also was awfully uncertain about himself, for he wanted to be game.

"'Yes, sir, I get you,' he said at last, but he didn't say it with much heart.

"'Very well, then,' said the chief. 'Now get back there and give us some action.'

"For three days Smith never showed up at all, and when he did come in he had made up his mind about the detective business, bag and baggage. He went up to the chief as if the chief were a waiter.

"'I think, sir,' he said, very lordly himself now, 'that my career as—as an *operative* is over.'

"The chief looked him over from head to foot

"'You think what?' he howled.

"'I think,' repeated the kid, 'that my career as an *operative* is over. I not only think it but I know it.'

"This time the chief got the situation and he became quieter.

"'Before you go into that,' he said, 'you might give me your final report on this chap that you were sent out to lose.'

"At that the kid burst. 'My report,' he said, 'is that he is one of the cleanest, finest fellows I ever met in my life.' He was looking at the chief now just as hard as the chief was looking at him, and something was going to crack. 'He told me his whole story last night. The facts are there on that paper. You may not believe it but I believe every word of it. My report is that if your client could get that man for a son-in-law he would be lucky. I came here to be a detective, not a blackmailer. That's my report, sir. Now is there any reason why I should not resign?'

"'None whatever,' answered the chief, 'except that we want to keep you.'"

Blake lighted another of his interminable cigarettes which he had been smoking all during his story. He watched the first puffs of smoke reminiscently and then he went on:

"For a long time both of them sat there without saying a word but at last the chief asked:

"'Young man, did you ever see the motto of this agency?'

"Of course Smith had, for it was on all the letter-heads, but the chief told him just the same:

"'The motto of this agency is "evidence where evidence exists," and among other things that means only where evidence exists. Pleasant or unpleasant, it is our business to dig up the facts, but we have never yet had to go into the business of manufacturing them.'

"The chief," explained Blake, "was not exactly a man for the heart-to-heart business and he did a good deal of hemming and hawing, but he was trying to be square.

"'Young man,' he said to Smith, 'I want you to stay with us because I think that you are the man I have been looking for ever since I have been in the game. I have given you rather a raw deal but I had to do it. Every agency in the country needs a man of your education and standing, but there's not one in five that has got him. There are plenty of so-called gentlemen who will take money from us, but a man of education who goes into this business in nine cases out of ten is merely a parasite, a failure at everything else. All he wants is a soft living and easy money. He is not a detective, he is a sneak. He will lie about his friends if we pay him to do it, and a man who will lie about anything is no use to us. You have got to learn the tricks of the trade. We can teach those to any scoundrel, but if a man hasn't got a love of truth in him we can't teach it to him. I gave you plenty of chance to fake, but I have checked you up from day to day and if you had faked one fact you would have been through before now.'

"The kid looked at him with his mouth wide open, and the chief let him look just to give it a chance to sink in.

"'As to this particular case,' he said finally, 'you've told me just what I thought from the start, and I may as well tell you now that it wasn't necessary to send you clear out to Long Island to get what I wanted. I got all the dope on our British friend the day after I wired to London for it.'

"'But—but,' asked the kid, 'what is the dope about him?'

"'Exactly what you said it was,' said the chief. 'He's straight as a die. And I'll tell you this. There are people in England who are more worried about his marrying our client's daughter than our client is about her marrying him.'

"'As for that,' said Smith, 'I don't think she meant to marry him, anyway.'

"The chief gave him a look. 'What makes you think that?' he asked.

"'Oh,' stammered the kid, 'just things she said from time to time.'

"'To you?' roared the chief.

"'Yes, to me,' confessed the kid, and at that the chief lay back and threw up his hands.

"'Smith,' he said, 'I wouldn't have missed you for money. It's all right once, but don't think it's part of your work to have a love-affair every time I send you out on a dress-suit party.'"

Blake emptied his glass and looked at me smiling.

"So that," he said, "is my one real detective story."

"But," I said, puzzled, "you haven't finished it. Did Smith himself marry the girl, or did the Englishman, or what?"

Blake laughed.

"If I could tell you that, I wouldn't have to call him Smith."

I was disappointed but I could hardly pursue it.

"Well, anyway," I insisted, "how did the chief get his own line on the Englishman? How was he able to check Smith up from day to day?"

"Oh, that," replied Blake. "That was routine. Of course when he sent out Smith, the chief planted one of his roughnecks, one of your glorified policemen, to watch him."

As if the words were a signal, at that moment the fat, red face and immense shoulders of old Frank Casey came towering into the room, but I had to hurry.

"You might as well tell me," I begged. "You were Smith, weren't you?"

Blake laughed at my persistence and then relented.

"No," he replied, "I wasn't Smith. I was the glorified policeman."

Also Available

CoachwhipBooks.com

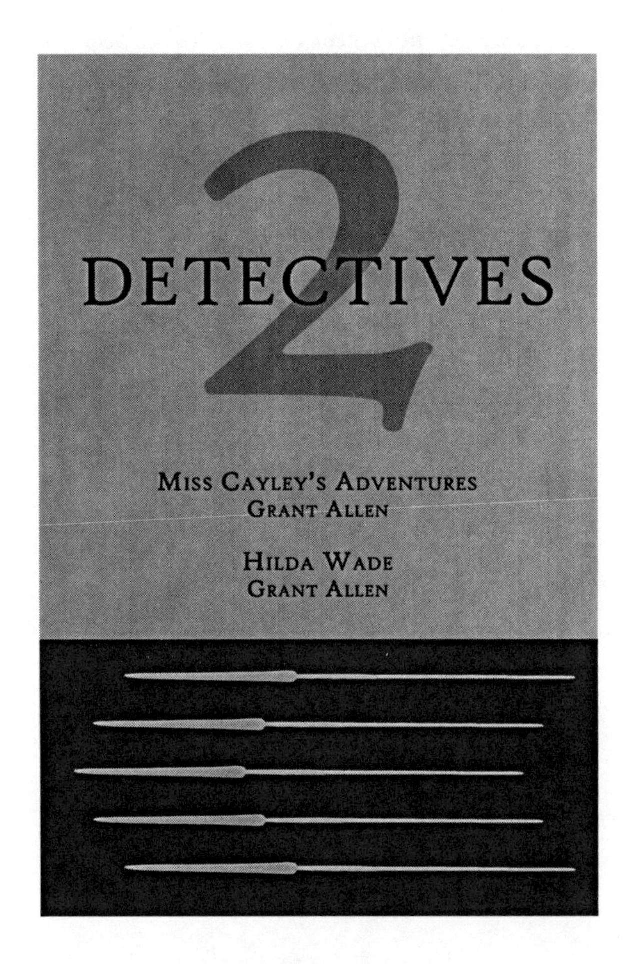

2 Detectives:
Miss Cayley's Adventures /
Hilda Wade

ISBN 1-61646-125-X

ALSO AVAILABLE

COACHWHIPBOOKS.COM

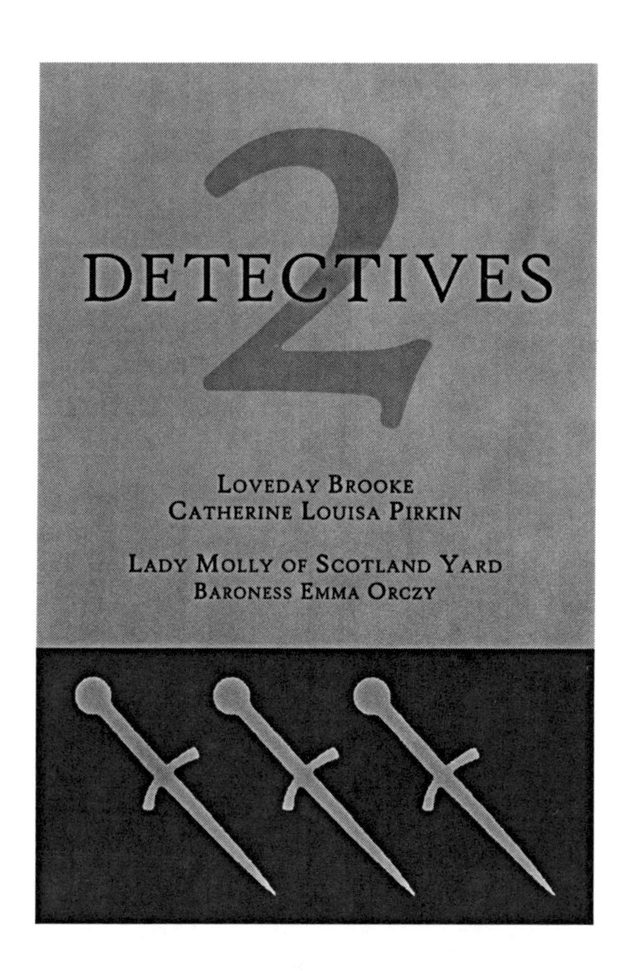

2 DETECTIVES:
LOVEDAY BROOKE /
LADY MOLLY OF SCOTLAND YARD

ISBN 1-61646-112-8

Coachwhip Publications
CoachwhipBooks.com

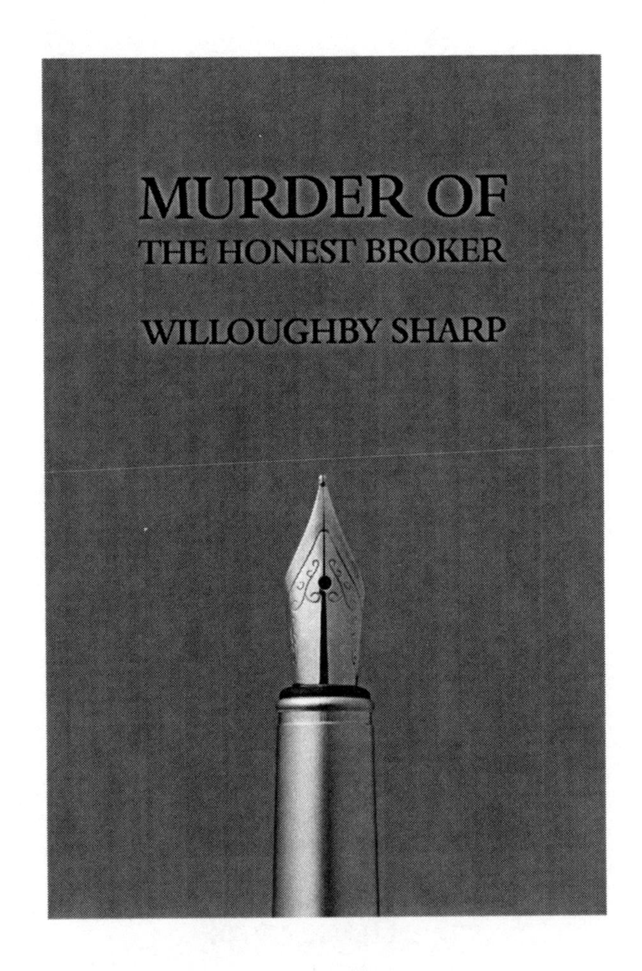

ISBN 978-1-61646-211-6

Coachwhip Publications

Also Available

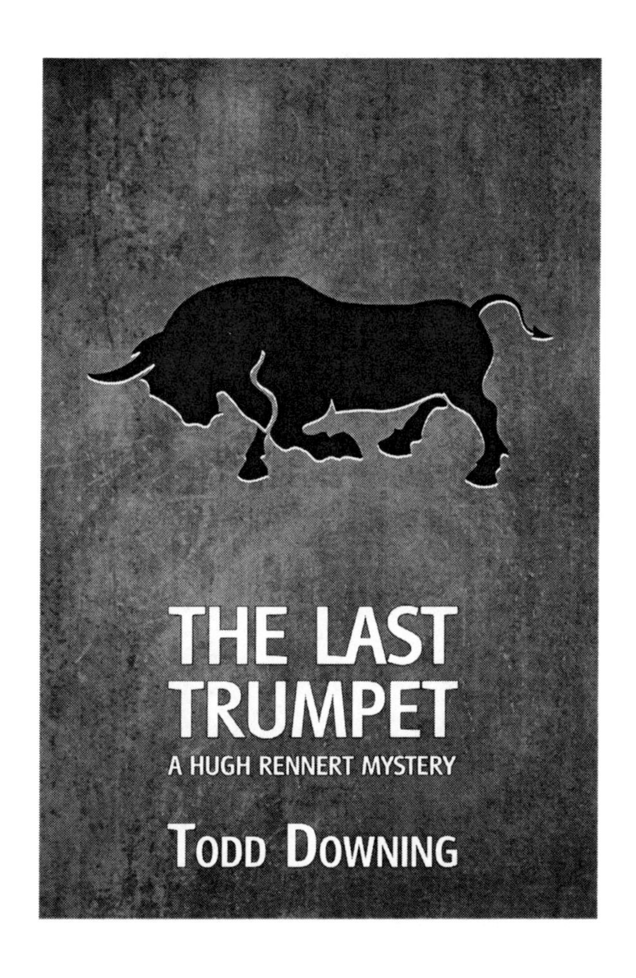

ISBN 978-1-61646-152-2

COACHWHIP PUBLICATIONS

COACHWHIPBOOKS.COM

ISBN 978-1-61646-222-2

Coachwhip Publications

Also Available

ISBN 978-1-61646-223-9

CPSIA information can be obtained at www.ICGtesting.com
Printed in the USA
BVOW05s2026270514

354625BV00001B/36/P

9 781616 462260